William Honeycutt

MURDER OF GRACE

WILLIAM HONEYCUTT

Murder of Grace

Copyright 2014: William Honeycutt

All rights reserved

This book is a book of fiction. All characters places and events mentioned in the book either are the product of the author's imagination or are used fictiously.

William Honeycutt

PROLOGUE

I just got home from work. It had been a long day. I went straight to my bedroom and lay down on the bed to relax for a few minutes.

I was drifting away. I had closed my eyes. I was losing it. Before I realized it, I was asleep.

I saw a beautiful blonde headed woman about twenty-five years old. She seemed to be the happiest person in the world. It was as though nothing had ever been wrong in her life. She seemed that everything was going just the way that she wanted it to go.

A strange looking figure appeared in the room with her. It was something that did not need to be there. I was dreaming. Oh, my God. I was having another one of those dreams. I could not wake up I hated to have to have these kinds of dreams in my life. But they seemed to be a major part of my life any more.

The dark deep figure came towards her. She recognized that she was not alone in her house anymore. She did not know what she was going to do about it. She ran to the other side of the room hoping she could get through the door and out of the room before he could get to her.

It was looking more and more like a person than anything else. He was getting closer to her and she ran to the living room. He had a long blade in his hand and she was getting scared She feared his being in her house with a blade in his hand. She wondered why he had a blade in his hand. She got behind the couch and grabbed the heavy ashtray sitting on the table and threw it at him and he dodged it. It barely missed him.

By now she was trembling. She was scared out of her mind. She wondered what was going to happen to her if she could not get away from him. She grabbed another ashtray on the other table. She threw it at him and it hit him on the side of the arm just below the shoulder. It hurt. He hollered. He was pissed at her, so he ran closer to her.

She ran from behind the couch to the other side of the room and grabbed the small lamp from the table jerking the cord from the outlet box and throwing it at him hoping that she would hit him with it. She hit him on the right side of the head with it. It startled him. He was in a daze for a few seconds. And then he regained his posture. He was really pissed off by now and he really did want to get her and take care of what he had come there to do.

She was in an awkward position in her house now. She seemed to have nowhere to go to get away from him. He had her pinned in the corner of the room near where she had thrown the lamp from. He reached out and grabbed her by the arm and jerked her real hard toward him. When he did she fell on the floor in front of him.

He was really excited that he had gotten her to the point that she was in his control now. He could do what he wanted to. He laughed at her. She was scared to death. She was shaking all over.

She started begging him to please not hurt her. He kept looking at her and laughing at her. She did not know what to do. She started to try to get up and he knocked her back down on the floor again. She fell on her left side on her elbow. It hurt but she endured that pain and tried to get up again and he jerked her up and grabbed her around the neck.

She was sacred now and she did not know how she was going to get out of this. She tried moving but found it almost impossible to move any part of her body. She was drifting away, and she did not like this at all. She did not know what to do now. She finally could kick backwards with her foot and she hit him on the shin. He almost did not feel the pain from it. She was not able to do it again. She was drifting away. She knew he was going to kill her. She was convinced of it. He had come to kill her, and she knew that for sure now.

He put her in a sleeper hold. Her mind was thinking what is he going to do to me before he kills me? But she could not do anything. She was still conscious right now and she could still think. Think slowly. But think. She was almost gone.

It seemed all I could do was just be there and let him do whatever he wanted to do. I was unable to do anything about it. I had gone almost completely out. My life was over. I knew it. She finally collapsed. She was gone. She could not move anymore. It was over.

He took her back into her bedroom and laid her on the bed. He was looking at her. He had dreamed about her all his life. He had always wanted to be with her, but she never would pay him any attention. He finally has his chance to be with her but just not the way he wanted it to be.

He had made up his mind that if he could not have her that nobody else would have her either. He would take care of that tonight. He decided that he would undress her before he killed her. She was completely gone now. She did not realize that anything was happening any more. He took her clothes off and had her completely nude.

He took her hair in his hands and he run his hands through it and caressed her shoulders and wished that he could have done that when she was awake. He pulled the long strands of her hair from under her back up and made it flow over her front side

He took her hands and he placed them over her stomach and he rubbed her breast and thought what it would have been like to have had her while she was awake. He had taken just about all that he could stand now. He took the blade in his hands and the run it through his fingers and licked his lips and looked at her for the last time before he killed her.

He cut her throat from one side to the other without even thinking about it. He made sure that he got the jugular vein so that she would definitely die. She was gone like a light. It was over. Her life had ended.

He mutilated her body. He cut her fingers off. He was having so much fun. Then he cut her hands off. He put them in the plastic bags he had gone in the closet and got. He decapitated her and cut her feet and legs off.

He had them all bagged up and ready to take to the river and dump them when he heard a noise and it scared him. He ran to the closet and hid so no one could see him. But no one came in the room where all this was taking place.

I woke up from the dream and I feared what had just happened to me. I had to do something about it. I knew that the incident had not happened yet but that it was going to happen. I had to find somebody to talk to about it and get it out of my system. I had to hear a human voice.

William Honeycutt

CHAPTER ONE

I had to make a phone call although it was 1:00 AM. I needed to talk with somebody. I will call my best friend Catherine. She knew about my dreams. She emphasized with me concerning them. She knew that when I had them and told her about them that they always came true. I also knew that she would not get mad at me for calling her in the middle of the night.

I called her, and she answered on the first ring.

"Hello." Very sleepily.

"Hello Catherine."

"Jason. What is wrong? You have had another one of those dreams, haven't you?"

"Yes."

"Was it like the others Jason?"

"No, it was much worse."

"What kind was it Jason?"

"I dreamed of an awful murder. It was so detailed."

"I am so sorry to hear that Jason."

"I do not want to go into any details about it right now, but can we meet tomorrow sometimes and I will tell you about it."

"Sure, that will be OK. Where would you like to meet Jason?"

"We can meet at Charlie's, they have great T-bone steaks."

"That will be a good place. I love T-bone steak. What time?"

"Whatever time is good for you Catherine is OK with me."

"1:00 PM is good for me Jason."

"OK. That sounds good. I will let you go back to sleep. And I am so sorry I bothered you now of night."

"You can call me anytime you need to. Don't worry about it. I will see you tomorrow at 1:00 then."

"Bye see you tomorrow."

I lay back down on the bed. I closed my eyes and I went to sleep. My alarm went off at 5:00 AM. I got up and pulled on my jogging shorts. It was time to run my five miles that I run every morning.

I made it back to the house and went in and took me a shower and shaved. I went to the kitchen and fixed a pot of coffee and grabbed me a cinnamon roll and went in the living room and turned the TV on to watch the morning news for a minute.

When I had finished, I got my things and headed out toward the office. I had some paper work that I had to get done this morning before I left to meet Catherine today at 1:00 PM. I got to the office and I got my folders down and buried my head in my paper work hoping that it would keep my mind off the dream until it was time to meet Catherine.

The morning had gone by fast and it was time to leave to meet Catherine. We made it to Charlie's at about the same time.

"Hello Catherine."

"We look like twins today Jason. How are you?"

"Great minds think alike Catherine. I am doing fine. And, how are you?"

"I am fine and thank you."

She was dressed in blue jeans with a red t-shirt and tennis shoes with red socks. She always looked really nice. I had on my blue jeans with tennis shoes and a red western shirt. I had not seen her in about two weeks. I just did not like the circumstances that we were meeting under this time.

We walked inside the restaurant and found us a table in the back corner. There was not anyone around near the table we choose. We kind of wanted to be lost in the place so that we could talk confidentially. I did not want the world to know that I had these dreams. It was bad enough that I had them.

The waitress came to the table to take our order. She was all smiles and very pleasant. She greeted us with a fantastic hello and offered to leave us the menu

"I do not need a menu. I will have the T-bone steak with a baked potato and a green salad." Jason told her.

"I will take the same thing." Catherine told the waitress.

The waitress took our order and went and turned it in.

"What have you been doing Jason? It has been about two weeks since I have seen you."

"I have been busy working on some new cases lately. What are you up to Catherine?"

"I have been in court a lot. They have me swamped with an overload of new cases."

She was an attorney. She worked in criminology. That was what she enjoyed the most. She works for McCarthy and McCarthy Attorneys at Law. She had been working for them for about five years now.

I was a private investigator. I own my own business. Caffrey's Investigations. I have been in business for about three years now and enjoy what I do.

"How much time do you have today Catherine to spend together?"

"I have all afternoon Jason. I am finally getting to take an afternoon off."

"That is nice Catherine. I do not have anything pressing me either."

The waitress brought the food to the table and set it down for us. Boy did those T-bone's look good today. They always are anyway.

We ate our lunch and while we were eating we just talked about old times.

"Catherine, do you remember grade school days?"

"How could I forget them Jason. We had a lot of fun."

"You remember the time that Johnny Stabler came up behind me and shoved me down."

"Yes, I remember that."

"When he did, you kicked him in the stomach and he doubled over with pain."

"Yes, I remember that really well. He was a bully Jason. I hate bullies."

"You were a fireball back then."

"I still am." She said laughingly.

"We had a lot of fun when we were growing up."

"Yes, we did."

Now it was time to get down to business. I told her that I had to tell her this one in detail because I knew that it was going to happen. I knew that there was something that we would have to do. We needed to try to stop it if there was any way.

So, I explained to her that the dream had started with my seeing this beautiful woman. Of course, that got a good laugh from her.

"What else should you dream about" she said.

"I wish it were just that simple" I said.

William Honeycutt

"I understand that Jason."

"She saw this strange figure and then realized that it was a man in her house."

"Could you tell anything about the man Jason? How much did you see of her to recognize her?"

"I only had an image of a man. She was getting scared Catherine."

"I imagine she was."

"She ran to the other side of the room and threw ashtrays and a lamp at him."

"At least she is a fighter. She was trying to get away from him."

"He had a blade in his hands and was rubbing it in his hands and licking his lips Catherine. It was awful."

"I can imagine."

"He got close enough to her that he was able to get a hold of her arm and jerk her to the floor in front of him. He had the advantage of her now. He put her in a sleeper hold and she finally collapsed."

"What did he do then Jason?"

"He drugged her to the bedroom and laid her on the bed and he undressed her Catherine."

"Did he have sex with her Jason?"

"No. All he had on his mind was killing her at the time."

"What did he do then?"

"He mutilated her body and hid in the closet because he thought he heard something. Then I woke up."

"That is the worst of the dreams you have ever told me about Jason."

"That is the worst one I have ever had Catherine."

She was more than willing to do anything that she could do to help. I knew that she would. She had a lot of friends in law enforcement. Everybody liked her. She was always so nice and so pleasant to deal with. I knew if anybody in the world could help me this time that it would be Catherine.

I explained to her that I was going to see Jeff tomorrow morning. I had already arranged an appointment with him. That is the Sheriff of Sylacauga, Alabama. Jeff and my brother Kerry were good friends in school. He came over to the house a lot and we all played together. He always loved picking on me and always paid me a lot of attention. He was like a big brother.

"The afternoon is slipping by Jason. I guess I need to go."

"OK. I have a few things I need to do myself. I will talk with you later."

I took the tickets and paid for our lunches. We left the nice waitress a handsome tip.

I needed to go and do some grocery shopping. So, I went to the Winn-Dixie that was the closest to where I lived. While I was in the grocery store I saw Jim Sax. He is one of my best friends also. Jim is a big man very muscular about six feet tall. He has dimples with a long face and square jaw. He has blue eyes. He has dark black hair with bushy eyebrows. We were next door neighbors when we were growing up. I always enjoyed spending time together.

"Hello Jim."

"Hello Jason. How are you?"

"I am good Jim. What are you doing in the grocery store?"

"Jane ask me to come and pick up a few items for her because she did not have time to get them and needed them she told me."

"I have to do this every now and then and I hate to have to come here."

"Yea. I know what you mean. What have you been doing lately Jason? I have not seen you lately. Of course, I am gone most of the time anyway."

"I have just been working mostly and trying to keep my life afloat."

We talked for a little bit about what we had been doing and the things going on in our lives. I have never told Jim about my dreams. I always wondered how he would take it if I told him about them. Little things he had told me over the years always made me hesitate to tell him. I was scared that he would think I was crazy or something. Jim was a great guy. He was a pipe fitter. A lot of times he would be gone out of town for several days and sometimes weeks at a times before he would get to come home. But he made excellent money and he was very happy.

"I guess I need to get this shopping done and get home Jason. I will talk with you later."

"Yea me to Jim. It was nice to see you. See you later."

I finished up my shopping at the store. It was getting late and I needed to go home and get a few things done before it got dark on me. I left the store and went down Broadway Avenue towards home. I lived in a big two-story house on Broadway near the city limits. I was near the house when it started to rain. Well that was all I needed some rain. I knew that was not what I wanted to see right now. Rain! Why? I guess we needed it because it was doing it.

I arrived at my house and turned into the drive way and was wondering why a 1957 solid red two-tone Chevrolet had been following me all this way. They slowed down, but I could not tell who was driving the car. They had a Coosa County tag on their car. That was unusual. I wondered what that was all about and who it might be. I did not get enough of the tag number to run it. They went on down the road and I went on into my drive still wondering what was going on.

I got out of my car and got the few groceries that I had bought to take them into the house. I got in the house and before I could set them down the phone rang. I set the groceries down.

"Hello. Jason Caffrey speaking."

"Hello Jason. I saw that red 1957 Chevrolet following you and wondered why. Do you know them?"

"I saw them following me and wondered who it was and why."

"I was a little concerned."

"Thanks Catherine for watching out for me."

"I did want to talk with you about a sketch artist Jason that I know."

"A sketch artist?"

"Yes. You told me that you could describe the woman. I was thinking that maybe we could get a sketch of her and maybe someone would recognize her."

"That sounds like a good idea Catherine."

"If you would like for me to, I can talk with her and get some arrangements set up for you to meet with her."

"That sounds like a good way to go Catherine. Maybe that would be a good way to find out who she is."

"Ok I will talk with her and get it set up then. Is there any particular time that would be best for you?"

"Anytime will be OK."

"I will let you know when it will be after I get it arranged."

"Thank you very much Catherine."

"I will let you go for now. Talk with you later."

"OK. Bye. Talk with you soon."

After we had finished our conversation and hung up the phone, I put the few groceries I had bought up and decided that it was time to eat me a small bite for supper. I boiled me a couple of eggs and made me a chef's salad. It was delicious.

I went and turned on the TV to watch a little news to see what was happening in my community. Just as I sat down in my big comfortable recliner to relax for a while the phone rang again.

"Hello. Jason Caffrey speaking."

"Hello Jason. How are you? This is Susan."

"I am great Susan. What are you doing?"

"I have not heard from you in a few and I wanted to touch base with you and see how you are doing."

She worked for the FBI. She had been working for them for about eight years now. She was the head investigator for the special crime unit. She and I had been friends for at least ten years now. I always call her when I am working on a very sensitive case that I need to have someone who can get me in the know and to the right people that I need to talk with when I need to know something. Susan is the one I always depend on. She is very good at her job and knows everybody.

She was familiar with paranormal experiences. I had told her a little about mine but had never told her much detail about it.

"I had one of those awful dreams again. It was about murder this time."

"I still think you should go to a psychiatrist and let them help you to overcome those dreams Jason."

"That is something I must think about Susan."

"Have you been working hard Jason?"

"I have been staying pretty busy lately."

"Maybe we will get to work on another case together soon."

"That would be nice Susan. I would enjoy that."

"I guess it is time for me to get off this phone. It was nice talking with you Jason."

"The same here Susan. You take care and I look forward to hearing from you again soon."

Susan was one of my old girlfriends. We dated for a while. She is a very sweet person. She has long blonde hair and is tall and slender. She has baby blue eyes and has a fabulous personality. She was one of my old girlfriends from high school. We dated a couple of years.

I sat back in my recliner and was hoping that the phone would not ring anymore tonight. I just wanted to relax and take it easy. I had a bad night last night and a long day today and all I wanted to do was take it easy.

I was sitting there in my great big comfortable recliner. It was about 8:00 that evening. The doorbell rang. Well the phone did not ring but the doorbell rang. I was still not going to get to just relax. I got up and went to the door. I opened the door and there stood Dexter Ward. Dexter was the Sylacauga Police Chief. He is a tall and slender very handsome man. He is six foot four inches tall with blonde hair and deep blue eyes. He is very muscular. He has a long face with a square jaw. He is always very solemn. Dexter was good friends with my brother Frederick. He used to come around a lot and spend time at our house. He always picked at me and paid me a lot of attention. He was like an older brother

"Hello Jason. May I come in?"

"You can come in anytime Dexter. How are you?"

"I am fine and what are you doing?"

"I am just relaxing a little. What are you doing out this time of the night?"

"I had to do a little shopping for my wife and I saw your lights on and thought I would stop in and say hello and see how you been doing."

Dexter knew that I had those dreams and that they always came true. He always wondered how that I could always be right about them. I told him that I supposed someone needed to know that something was fixing to happen, and I guess that is why that I had the dreams. Maybe it would lead to someone being able to do something about it.

"Can you keep a secret Dexter?"

"I am the police chief Jason. I have to keep secrets."

"I had another one of those dreams Dexter."

"I still think you need to go to a psychiatrist and let them help you Jason."

"I have had them all my life Dexter and you know that. They cannot do anything about it."

"You will never know if you do not go and try."

"I do not see the need to waste the money when they can't help me."

"You are stubborn Jason."

"I take after my mom Dexter."

"Yea. I know. And I love your mom. She is great."

"She is great Dexter."

"We have had more crime in the city lately Jason than we been having."

"I have noticed that Dexter."

"Wonder why it is more now."

"It might be that we have had an influx of people coming through lately."

"That will usually spur it up some. But I did not expect it to this much."

"You never know Dexter."

"Well I just wanted to stop by for a little bit and be sure you are Ok. I will go for now. Talk with later."

"See you later Dexter. Have a great night."

When he went out the door I locked it and turned out all the lights in the house and went up to my bedroom. I pulled my clothes off and lay down on the bed to get a good night's sleep. I was lying

Murder of Grace

on my back when my eyes got really heavy and I floated away into the distance. I was sound asleep.

CHAPTER TWO

Suddenly I heard a strange noise in my bed room and I jumped. Then I realized that it was my alarm clock. It was 5:00 AM. Time to get up and take my morning exercise. I got up and slipped on my jogging shorts. I always looked forward to Monday, Wednesday, and Friday because my next-door neighbor ran with me.

I went out and Jane Weatherford was waiting on the sidewalk for me to come out.

"Hello Jason."

"Hi Jane. It is time for another big one."

"Big what Jason?"

"Run for the day." Jason said laughingly

We started on our way. Jane was about five feet seven inches tall. She had gray eyes and short brown hair. She had it cut in a blow and go. She had a perfect figure. She had a great smile and a great personality. She was always fun to be with.

"How thing been going lately Jason?"

"Working mostly. What about you Jane."

"Studying a lot. Some of these classes are about to drive me crazy."

She was taking nursing. She was going to be an RN she told me at least to start out.

"I know what you mean. I have been there."

We made it back to the house and it was time to get ready to go to work.

"See you Monday Jane."

"Yea. For sure Jason. It is always nice to see you."

I went in the house to get ready to go to work. I put on my blue jeans and a western shirt, short sleeve. I wore my blue tennis shoes. I went to the kitchen and fixed me some cornflakes with a banana in them for my breakfast. I finished eating and went in the living room and turned on the TV to see a little of the morning news.

The doorbell rang. I went to the door and opened the door.

"Hello Jason."

"Hello Alice. How are you this morning?"

"I am doing very well Jason. How about you?"

"I am doing good Alice."

Alice is my maid. She comes two times every week on Tuesdays and Fridays. Alice is 47 years old. She is about five foot six inches tall. She has long black hair and she wears it in a bun on top of her head. She had light blue eyes and is medium build. She is always smiling and is always very pleasant.

"Is there anything special that you need me to do today Jason?"

"No. Nothing special Alice just your normal work."

I had about 15 minutes to get to Jeff's office before our appointment. Of course, he would not be upset if I were a little late, but I did not intend to be late. Jeff was a very easy-going person. He was relaxed most of the time. He tried to not let things get to him and upset him.

I got to Jeff's office just in time for our meeting. Surprisingly he was not busy and our meeting got started on time just like we had planned.

"Good morning Jeff. How are you?"

"I am fine Jason. How are you this morning?"

"Great man. I ran my five miles this morning and I feel better already."

"That is good Jason. I run in the morning but I don't run five miles."

"It is good for me Jeff. It keeps me alert."

"Anything to keep the mind working Jason is good for you."

"I needed to talk with you about the dream that I just had."

"You had another one of those dreams Jason?"

"Yes. But this one is different from the rest."

"How do you mean different Jason?"

"It was an awful murder scene Jeff. It was the worst one I have ever had."

I told Jeff about the dream and the details of what had happened. He was amazed at how detailed the dream had been.

"Jason how can you remember it so vividly?"

"How can someone who has ever had a dream like that forget it? I will never forget this one. It is too awful."

"I am sure I would never forget it either Jason if I had a dream like that."

"I have a couple of people I need to talk with and ask them some questions. I will be back with you when I finish."

"OK. I will out here Jeff. Maybe we can think of something we can do to stop this one before it happens."

He finished with his interviews and took a couple of phone calls and finished a couple of details he had to get done and then he was ready to go.

"Jason I would like for you to ride with me this morning for a while if you have time to."

"I have plenty of time Jeff."

He told me had some things that he wanted to talk with me about and that would give us plenty of time to talk about them. He said he would like to get my opinion on them. Why he wanted my opinion I do not know. I am just a private investigator.

"These are some buildings that we have been having some break-ins lately."

"These old warehouses. We have never had a problem with them before." I told him.

"They seem to think that is some teenagers doing it but they are just guessing."

"Why would they just guess at it Jeff. This is not a guessing game."

"They want to believe that is all it is and that is why they are saying that. I believe there is a lot more to it than that myself."

"There probably is. I do not see why a bunch of teen agers would want to mess with these old buildings in the first place."

"Jason what I really wanted to talk with you about is personal."

"Personal?"

"Yes. I needed somebody to talk with and you are the only person I trust."

"OK. What did you want to talk about Jeff?"

"We are having trouble in our marriage Jason."

"What? Nobody would ever know that Jeff."

"I have not told anybody but I needed to talk to somebody."

"OK."

"She told me that if I did not get out of law enforcement that she would have to divorce me."

"Wow. I am sorry to hear that Jeff."

"We have two children Jason. I do not want a divorce and I love what I do. She told me that she did not know if she could live with never knowing if I would come home that day or not for the rest of her life."

"This is not good Jeff."

"I do not want to quit my job and I do not want a divorce either."

"Has she made it final Jeff?"

"No. She told me that she was going to think about it and that she would let me know what she decided."

"That is good. Maybe she will decide that she really loves you more than she can stand and that she could not stand leaving you either."

"I hope she does Jason. It is about to drive me crazy thinking about it."

"You hold it in good Jeff. Nobody would ever guess it for sure."

"On those warehouses, Jason, I have been thinking about getting someone to do a little surveillance on them to see what is going on. If I decide to do that could you do it for me?"

"Sure, I would be glad to."

"OK. I will let you know what I decide."

The morning was slipping by. We went back to the office.

"See you later Jeff. I have to go and get some paper work done now."

"Talk to you soon Jason. I will let you know what happens on all accounts Jason."

I went to my office. While I was looking over some paperwork that I needed to get organized the phone rang.

"Good morning, Caffrey Investigations. May I help you?"

"Good morning Jason."

"Hello Catherine. What are you doing this morning?"

"I was calling you to let you know that I have the arrangements made for you to meet the sketch Artist."

"That is nice Catherine. When it is?"

"She said the best time would be Tuesday at 3:00 PM. Is that OK with you Jason?"

"Yes, that is fine. I will be there. What is her name and where is she?

"Her name is Sharon Jeffery. She is in the mall on Jackson Street next to the Mexican Restaurant."

"Thanks for all your work Catherine."

"Don't mention it Jason. It is the least I can do. I will let you go for now Jason. Talk to you later."

"OK. Catherine. Talk with you later.

I worked on my paper work and got it all organized. I was leaving early Saturday Morning to go to Manassas, Virginia. I had a friend there I had met about three years ago, and we intended to spend some time together. Something we had not got to do in a long time.

It was getting late and I had to meet Jarrod at the park to play some tennis with him. I pulled up and parked at the park and got out of my car.

"Hello Uncle Jason."

"Hello Jarrod. I am here to beat you in some tennis this afternoon." I told him laughing while I was saying it.

"In your dreams uncle Jason. You only wish you could beat me."

"We will see when it is over. I feel good today."

"Come on. Give it your best. I will beat you." He said with a big grin on his face.

We played a couple of games and had a lot of fun. He beat me of which he does most of the time anyway.

"What are you going to do now Uncle Jason?"

"I am going to the house and eat me something. Alice was there today and she always cooks me a meal."

"That is nice Uncle Jason."

"Would you like to come and eat with me? I am going to the gym after I eat and you can go with me if you would like to."

"Sure, that all sounds like fun. I like to work out. It does my muscles a lot of good."

William Honeycutt

I told him to leave his car at the park and we would pick it up when we finished tonight. We went to the house and I looked in the refrigerator and Alice had cooked enough chicken for two meals easy. I took it out and heated it up with the mashed potatoes and butter beans.

We sat down at the table to eat.

"Uncle Jason this is a meal fit for a king."

"We are kings Jarrod." Jason said jokingly.

"Yea. I like that Uncle Jason."

We finished our meal and left the house and headed to the gym.

We walked in the door and Roxy saw us and called me and told me to come over there. We walked over to where she was.

"Who is this good-looking young man you got with you today Jason?"

"This is my oldest nephew Jarrod, Roxy."

"Hello Jarrod."

"Hello Roxy.

Roxy is twenty-one years old. She has medium length brown hair. She has almost a perfect figure. She has deep blue eyes and long face with a pointed chin. She has a sexy mile and is always winking at the young men when they come in to make them feel good.

We walked over to the weights to press a few and Roxy came with us. She loves to lift weights.

We worked out in the gym for a couple of hours and we left and went back by the park for Jarrod to pick up his car.

"I might go there more often Uncle Jason. Does Roxy go there very much?"

"She works there Jarrod."

"That is nice. I could make sure she was working the days I go. I like her Uncle Jason."

"I don't blame you for liking her Jarrod. She is beautiful and is a very nice person. She has a great personality.

"I will see you later Uncle Jason."

"See you Friday for sure. Take care and bye."

I got to the house and went in and got me a barq's root beer. I sat down in my recliner and about the time I got set down good the phone rang.

"Hello. Jason Caffrey speaking."

"Hello Jason. What are you doing?"

"I just got home good Jeff."

"I just wanted to call and make sure you are OK."

"I am fine and thank you for caring. Catherine set up an appointment for me to meet with a sketch artist for Tuesday afternoon. Maybe that will lead us to who the woman is."

"That is good Jason. I will not keep you long. You take care OK."

"Bye Jeff. Talk to you later."

I went to the bedroom and packed my little suitcase and took it down stairs with me and set it beside the door so I would not forget it.

I sat back down in my recliner to watch a little evening news and the phone rang again.

"Hello. Jason Caffrey speaking."

"Hello Jason. This is Rita."

"Hi Rita. What are you doing?"

"Are you still coming this weekend? I have not heard from you and just was making sure."

"Of course, I am still coming." I said.

She had been looking forward to my coming. It had been awhile as I have said before. We were both looking forward to the visit.

"OK. Just checking. See you tomorrow."

"I will be there." I said.

It was late. I made sure all my doors were locked and turned out all the lights and went upstairs to my bedroom. I pulled my clothes off and lay down on the bed. I was staring up at the ceiling thinking about how much fun it would be to see

William Honeycutt

Rita again. I really like her a lot. It was not long, and I was out light a light. I was sound asleep.

CHAPTER THREE

When the alarm went off I jumped. I always jump when it goes off. I looked at the clock. It was 4:00 AM. It was early. I jumped up and grabbed my new blue jeans and bright red shirt that my mom had bought me. I put on my grey sneakers which were also new. I went to the kitchen and got me a glass of orange juice and a cinnamon roll.

When I finished eating I got my suit case and headed out the door. I was on my way to Birmingham to catch my 6:15 AM flight out of Birmingham to Dulles. I was to be there at 9:23 AM. I was going to see a friend that I had not seen in a long time now.

We had met when she was sent to Birmingham to work on a murder case. I was asked to come and help work on it because they thought the murderer came from my area. Will Jenkins, the special crimes unit head knew me from our school days.

I had got to Birmingham and was working on the case with Will. We were looking over some files when this beautiful woman with short brown curly hair stuck her head in the door and said I am here Will. She had stunning deep blue eyes. She had a figure like a coke bottle turned upside down. She was gorgeous.

Will introduced Rita to me. Rita Barnett was from the special crimes unit of the FBI from Quantico. She trained in Quantico and she works there now. She was sent on this case to hopefully get it settled quickly.

I got to Birmingham, Alabama in reasonable time. The traffic for a change was not too bad. I had no delays. I parked my vehicle and got my things and hurried to the lobby. I usually am always early with everything but this morning I had not given myself the allotted time needed. I was kind of rushing things to make it on time.

I made it to the ticket counter and bought my ticket. I brought my small suitcase that I could take on board with me so that I did not have to check any baggage. I had just a little time left before time to check luggage. I went to the bath room. When I came out they were calling my flight for boarding.

This was exciting. I was looking forward to seeing Rita. I boarded the big jet and was ready for them to get it in the air. It left the airfield on time. We were in the air. That was nice. I could hardly wait till we got there.

The jet had a movie screen in it and they put on a movie for us to watch. That helped to pass the time away. In a little while we were in Dulles. It was nice to be there. I could not wait to get off the big jet and see Rita.

I stepped off the big jet and looked out to see if I could see her anywhere. I saw her in the lobby waiting on me to get there. She was waving and telling me to hurry.

I got to where she was, and she grabbed me around the neck and gave me a big kiss. I picked her up with my right arm and pulled her close to me.

"What have you been doing Rita?"

"Waiting for you to get here Jason."

"Well I am here now." He said laughingly.

"I see you are and boy do you look good." She said with a big grin on her face.

I put her down and she asked me was I ready to go. I told her I did not have any baggage to pick up that all we had to do was flee this joint. We left and found her car and headed out.

"Would you like something to eat Jason?"

"It is not quite lunch time yet. Let's wait a while before we eat"

"OK. We can just go to the house for a while and go out and eat later."

"Sounds good to me."

We got to her house. It is a brick home. It has a large front porch with a swing on it.

"I see you like swings."

"Yes, Jason, I like my swing. I use it a lot."

She unlocked the door and we went in and it was beautiful. We walked in the living room and it was decorated very nice. She had a beautiful leather, medium brown, three piece living room set. It was beautiful. A very nice solid wood, decorative coffee table and two end tables to match it. Two beautiful lamps with roses on the pedestal of the lamps, with big beautiful frilly shades sitting on the end tables.

She had a beautiful painting over the couch. It was one of the most beautiful scenery landscapes I had seen in a long time. Well, of course that is my opinion. The walls were lightly decorated but beautiful.

She had a beautiful recliner sitting in the corner close to the couch. Well I saw that and I knew that that was where I wanted to sit. I plopped down in the recliner. WOW. It was comfortable. She had it all. Everything that you needed to make a home comfortable.

She told me that her parents had bought it for her when she went to Quantico. They were very well off. They did not like the idea of her not having a place to live so they just bought her a home. It was a nice three bedroom, living room, den, dining room, kitchen and two bath home.

"I am going to get me something to drink. Would you like something?"

"Sure. Do you have a barq's root beer?"

She remembered that was what I like, and she had bought some.

"Yes Jason. I bought some."

She brought the drinks back in the living room and set down on the couch.

"What have you been doing Jason?"

"Working mostly."

"You had another one of those dreams didn't you Jason."

That was unexpected.

"Yes, I did. It was an awful one. I guess you want me to tell you about it."

"Actually, I would like for you to but if you do not want to I understand."

I told her about the dream.

She was amazed at how detailed the dream had been.

"Maybe there will be some way that you can find out who the woman is Jason and can stop this one before it happens."

"That is what we are hoping for Rita. That would be nice if we could."

"It is getting about lunch time Jason. Are you ready to eat?"

"Yes, I could use something about now."

"You like good steak don't you Jason?"

"I love a good T-bone steak."

"I know just the place to go."

We left the house and headed out to get some lunch. She knew where a great steak restaurant was. She pulled into a place called Steak and Ale. I was familiar with Steak and Ale. They had good food and fabulous steaks. We got out and went in and found us a table in the far side next to the window. The restaurant was not crowded and that was nice.

The waitress came, and I ordered me a thick juicy well done T-bone steak. My usual when I eat steak. Rita likes Sirloin tips.

"It is so nice to have you here this weekend Jason."

"I have been looking forward to it Rita. We can enjoy these two days."

"What do you want to do Jason other than going to the club tonight and dancing some?"

"Just spending my time with you will be enough. I have been looking forward for it."

The waitress brought our food to the table. I was ready to eat something by now. It looked fabulous. We ate our meals and I took the tickets and paid them and we left the restaurant.

We enjoyed sitting and just talking while we were waiting on our meals.

Our meal came, and we were both ready for it by then for sure. We ate our fabulous lunch and enjoyed it very much. It was delicious.

I took the tickets and went and paid them. We left the waitress a very handsome tip. We went back to the house just to enjoy the afternoon together.

We sit down in the swing when we got to the house.

"This is very nice Rita."

"How long do you plan on living here?"

"I do not know Jason. I might decide to get out of the FBI and do something different one day."

"I love private investigation myself. I own my own business and I do not have to listen to any one else telling me what to do."

"That is something I have thought about Jason. I do not want to get out of law enforcement."

"Do you think you will leave this area?"

"I don't know Jason. I might meet some body one day and have to leave if I want to marry them."

"Marry? Are you thinking about that?"

"Not right now but you never know."

"Well maybe it will happen for you. I hope it does."

"Maybe it will happen for you to Jason. Geeze it could be us you know."

"I do not have marriage on my mind right now Rita. That is for sure."

"That could change Jason. You know that."

"Yes. It could. Well one day I am hoping you can come to Sylacauga and visit a few days. That would be nice."

"I would love to Jason. I enjoy seeing other places."

"I think you would like it Rita. It is a small city and fairly quiet most of the time."

We got up from the swing and went in the house. I sat down in the recliner. Boy was it nice and comfortable. She went in the kitchen and got us something to drink and came back and sat down on the couch.

"Do you plan on working in private investigations for your career Jason?"

"Yes. That is what I enjoy."

"That is good. What does your family think about it?"

"They worry about me. I get in some dangerous situations sometimes and they do not like it. They are always trying to get me to do something different."

"Yea. I know what you mean. Mom and dad support me. They wish I would not work in the field like I do. They worry about me."

I got up and went over to the couch and sat down beside her and put my arm around her should and told her that I worried about her to.

"Oh, Jason you do not need to worry about me."

"I would not want anything to happen to you Rita."

"There is nothing going to happen to me Jason."

"You never know Rita. Anything could happen."

"I will be ok."

I gave her a big kiss on the lips and told her that I would always worry about her and that was just the way it would be.

"I really like you a lot Rita."

"I like you a lot to Jason."

"You never know where life might take you that is for sure." Jason said with a big grin on his face.

The afternoon was slipping by fast. We had decided that we wanted to go out to the club and have a drink or two and do a little dancing. We both enjoyed dancing.

"Do you want to eat something before we go dancing after a while?"

"Yea. I think we need to." Jason said.

"What would you like Jason?"

"Anything will be OK with me Rita."

"Do you like pizza?"

"I love supreme pizza. It is delicious."

"I can order it and have it delivered and we will not have to go anywhere to eat."

"That will be good."

She called Pizza hut and ordered one pepperoni and one supreme pizza. At about 7:00 PM the doorbell rang. She went to the door and the pizza boy was there with our pizzas. She paid him for them and brought them in the kitchen.

We found the pizza cutter and sliced the pizzas. We got some paper plates to put them on and sat at the bar to eat them. They were delicious. We finished our pizzas and went in the living room.

William Honeycutt

It was about time to start getting ready to go to the club. We wanted to get there before it got too crowded, so we could enjoy dancing without a big crowd on the dance floor if that was possible.

She wore her blue jeans and red button up top. Looked good on her. I think anything would have looked good on her. She was beautiful anyway. She put on her red Nike sneakers. I put on my new blue jeans and a bright red shirt that my mom had bought me for this trip. I slipped on my brown Nike sneakers and we were ready to go. We looked sharp.

We went to the club called The Night Life near her home.

We got there at 8:30 pm. It was not too crowded yet and we liked that part. The dance floor was not be too crowded right now. We ordered a Singapore sling.

We took in a few dances and had four Singapore's that night. We had danced a lot and we definitely were not drunk or very high from the alcohol. We had danced it off. It was getting late and was time to go home. We left the club and stopped at McDonald's to eat. I got me a fish sandwich meal and she got a big mac meal. It was fun. We had nothing but time anyway.

Well, it was about 1:00 am. It was time to go home and get some rest. We left and headed for home. We got there about 1:20 am. We were just having a good time getting to spend some time together of which we got to do very little of because of the distance between us.

We got to her house and went in. Rita showed me the bedroom I could sleep in. I took my things in the room and got ready for bed. She had gone in her bedroom and gone to bed. I lay down on the bed and I heard a voice.

"Jason." She said it just loud enough I could hear her.

"Yes. What you want Rita?"

"Come in here for a minute."

I had my pajamas with me. I got up and walked to the door.

"Yes." I said wonderingly.

"Come over here."

I walked over to the bed and sat down on the side of the bed.

"I am here." Laughing and a little embarrassed when I said it.

"You can lay down here with me for a little while if you want to."

"OK. I guess I can do that."

I lay down on the bed beside her and put my arms around her and she snuggled up close to me and said I like this. She gave me a big kiss.

I woke up the next morning and looked at my watch and it was 8:00 AM. I was lying on the bed with just my briefs on. What in the world had happened? I got up and went to the bathroom and could smell something good in the kitchen.

I finished in the bathroom and went to the kitchen and she was cooking bacon when I walked in. The coffee smelled good. I found me a cup and poured me a cup of coffee. She told me to just sit down and that breakfast would be ready soon. She had on that low-cut silk gown that she had slept in. She did not have on a bra under it and it was obvious.

I sat down at the bar. She finished breakfast with grits and eggs and bacon and pancakes and on the side. It was nice and smelled delicious. She was a good cook. That much I could tell from this breakfast.

We ate our breakfast and went into the living room and sat down.

"The morning is going by fast Rita and I do not like that."

"I know it is. I dread to see the day end."

"I would like to stay longer. I do not have anything pressing me for tomorrow. Maybe I can reschedule my flight and go back sometime Monday."

"I can take the time off and get you to the airport if you can work it out."

"I think that is what I am going to do. Do you mind if I call the airport and see what they have?'

"Sure call them and see what you can come up with."

I called the airport and they had something. I chose the 4:25 PM flight back to Birmingham. It would arrive at 5:31 PM in Birmingham. That was enough time for me to get home and have plenty of time to rest.

"I am leaving tomorrow at 4:25 PM."

"Good. I can take the day off. That is nice."

We got in her nice Ford Taurus and headed out. We were not in a hurry to get anywhere in particular We decided to take a ride just for fun and go somewhere and do something and just enjoy the day. It had been a long time since I had been to the area, so we decided to go to Washington D.C.

We got into Washington DC and decided to ride a little and just look around. We drove over to the Capital building and decided that we did not want to go inside. We just mostly wanted to ride and talk. She decided that we had plenty of time to dive down to Quantico where she worked and let me see the quarters that she worked from.

So, we headed towards Quantico and just took our time taking in the views that I had never seen before. It was a beautiful part of the country. I was really enjoying it. We finally made it to Quantico and she took me through the area and let me see what it looked like. Quantico, Va. Is a small town with 11 streets and nicely laid out. Now I do not have to wonder anymore what it looks like where

Murder of Grace

Rita is from and where she works. I saw it all first hand.

It was getting late in the afternoon. We decided that we needed to head back toward Manassas so that we would have time to get ready to go to our fancy dinner we had reservations for. We were both looking forward to this one.

We made it to her house at about 5:30 pm. We had one and one-half hours get ready before we had to be there. We went in and changed our clothes and got ready to go.

At 6:40 pm we left the house and headed for Malones of Manassas to make our reservations. As we drove up I was amazed at how beautiful the building was. It was gorgeous. We got inside and the hostess led us to a booth near the window and handed us our menus to order from. It was nice. We ordered our meals and the food was exquisite. It would melt in your mouth. We finished our meal and left the restaurant and went back to Rita's house.

It was already 9:00 pm. We got us something to drink and sat down in the living room just to relax and talk a little.

"What are we going to do tomorrow Jason?"

"We can just stay around the house and enjoy our time together."

"We can do our own cooking. I enjoy that when I have time to." Rita said.

"That sounds like fun to me."

"What are you going to do when I leave Rita?"

"Go back to my boring life of doing nothing much except work and play the piano."

"You play the piano?" Jason asked surprisingly.

"Yes. I have a nice Steinway in the den. You have not seen the den yet."

"No. I haven't and I sure had no idea you could play the piano."

"I have been playing since I was about four years old. I have taken a lot of lessons over the years."

"I bet you are good."

"I can play fairly well. I am not that good though. I just enjoy it. It relaxes me especially when I am tense over something."

"Maybe I will get to hear you play before I leave."

"We can do that tomorrow. I will play for you."

"That will be nice." Jason said with a big grin on his face.

It was getting late. It was time to get a little sleep. We went to the bedroom and lay down on her bed. We snuggled up close and put our arms around each other. I gave her a big kiss on the lips and she squeezed hard and she told me to keep on.

The first thing I knew it was morning and she was not in the bed with me. I looked at my watch and it was 8:30 AM. I could not believe that time had slipped by that fast.

I went to the kitchen to see if she was there and she was cooking breakfast again. I went in to help her and she just would not let me help her cook breakfast.

I poured me a cup of coffee and sat down at the bar. She finished cooking and set the food on the table and we sat down and ate another fabulous breakfast.

"What do you want to do for lunch Jason?"

"We will cook us something. I hope you heard me Rita. I said WE will cook us something."

"OK. OK. Jason we can both do it. That will be fun."

"If you do not have any cubed steak, we can go to the store and get some. I will cook steak and gravy smothered in onions. It is delicious. And you can cook the vegetables."

She told me to follow her. I followed her, and she took me to the den. She sat down at her big beautiful Steinway piano. She told me to sit beside her. I did.

She put her fingers on the keyboard and started playing. It was a Bach Melody. I recognized it. She had told me she could not play that good but she kind of told a fib. She played it beautifully.

We sat at the piano for a while as she played some beautiful music.

"Jason, I don't have any cubed steak. We need to go to the store."

"OK. We can buy us a pie of some kind to eat for our desert." I told her.

We got up from the piano and went to the closet grocery store to her which was about a half mile. We bought our cubed steak and got an apple pie to fix for our desert. We went back to the house just to enjoy the rest of the day together. It would be a little while before we got to spend any more time together.

The morning was just about gone.

"Do you want to start getting lunch ready Jason."

"Sure, may as well. It will take a little while to get it ready."

We went in the kitchen and I got the cubed steak and cut it up and got it ready to fry. I put my spices on it and fried it and got it ready. I fixed the onions and then made the gravy and put the meat in the onions and gravy to let it cook for a while. Rita got the vegetables ready. She made cream potatoes and baked beans to go with it. We put the apple pie in the oven and cooked it. Our lunch was almost ready.

Everything was ready, and we put it on the table and sat down to eat. It was delicious. We finished our lunch and got up and went in the living room. We sat down on the couch together. I did not want to go home. I wanted to stay but knew that I could not.

I went upstairs to the bedroom and got my things ready to go. I brought them back downstairs with me. I was almost time to leave and go to the airport.

"It is almost time to have to go to the airport." I told her.

"I know. I am not looking forward to it."

It was 3:00 PM. My flight left at 4:25. Rita took me to the airport. We got out of the car and was standing there looking at each other.

"I will be back again just as soon as I can make arrangements to come."

"I hope I get to come to Sylacauga soon to visit you Jason."

"That will be nice Rita."

I put my arms around her waist and she put hers around my neck. I kissed her and told her bye. I turned around and walked away going towards the front entrance. She waved at me and told me she would see me soon. I got inside and looked back and she had gotten in her car and was leaving. I watched her till she was out of sight.

I went over to the ticket counter and bought my ticket. I went over and waited for them to call the flight. In a few minutes they called the flight. I boarded the big jet and was ready to go home now. In a few minutes it was in the air and headed towards Birmingham.

We landed in Birmingham on time. The flight was on schedule. That is unusual. The only thing I wanted to do now was go home. I found my car and put my things in it and headed out for Sylacauga. It was only about a forty-five-minute drive.

I made it to Sylacauga. The only place I wanted to go was home. I got there and parked my car in the garage and went in the house. I took my things and put them up and made me a pot of coffee

Murder of Grace

and poured me a cup and took it to the living room and sat down in my recliner.

I did not get set down good until the phone rang. I believe that everybody watches my house and knows when I come and go so that they know exactly when to call me or stop by.

CHAPTER FOUR

"Hello. Jason Caffrey speaking."
"What are you doing and where have you been?"
"I have been visiting a friend of mine in Manassas, Va. I spent the weekend with her."
"You must have enjoyed it." She said.
"Of course, I did." I said.
"Well Jason I was just calling to remind you that your appointment was tomorrow at 3:00 pm." She told me.
"I know. I will be there." I said.
"I will get off this phone and let you rest. I am sure you are tired from a busy weekend."
"I am but it was fun."
"OK. I will talk with you later. Bye."
"Bye Catherine and thanks for calling and reminding me."
After we hung up the phone. I went upstairs to my bedroom to just lay down on the bed and relax for a few minutes. I left all the lights on. I did not plan to go to sleep. It was only about 8:00 PM.
Just as I lay down on the bed and turned the TV on my doorbell rang. I got up and went to the front door and peeped out and Jeff was standing there. I opened the door.
"May I come in?' he said.
"Sure Jeff you know you can come in any time." He walked in and went over to the couch and sat down and then asked me what I had been up to.

I told him I had spent the weekend with Rita the young lady I had met in Birmingham when we were working a case together.

"So, you just had a lot of fun then, no doubt. When did you get back home?" He asked.

"Today. Well actually late this afternoon. Actually I have only been home a couple of hours."

"I know you must be tired from a busy weekend."

"I am but it was fun."

"Maybe you got rid of some of the stress from that dream."

"I have been kind of lazy with my work since I had that dream." I told him.

"You deserved a little time away from it all hopefully to get it organized in your mind and some relaxation." He told me.

"I feel better for sure. I had a great three days. We really enjoyed it."

"I just wanted to stop by and see how you are doing. You remember I told you that I might put an investigator on them old warehouses to see what was going on out there."

"Yes, I remember."

"I have decided that that is what I want to do. I would like for you to do it for me if you could."

"I told you I would, remember."

"Well, I am asking you to do it. When could you start watching them for me?"

"I would need to do that at night I am sure."

"Yes, that would probably be the best time."

"I can start that tomorrow night."

"Good. When you find out something just let me know. Just keep an eye out to see what is going on. Do not try to be a hero. Just get the information and then we can get the force out to take care of it if we need to."

"I am a hero Jeff." I said stroking my cheek and looking up at the ceiling laughing.

"OK. Enough with your funny stuff Jason." Laughing while he was saying it.

"I will let you know if I see anything at all. I am sure we are going to find out something fairly quick once we get out there."

"I hope so. I do not want this thing to drag out."

"That would be a good place for a drug ring to hide their drugs Jeff."

"Yes. And that is what I am thinking is probably going on out there. We just have to find out and catch them in the act if that is what is happening."

"If they are there we will get them. I am a good snoop."

"That is why I ask you to be my snoop Jason."

"I have been trying to get some things together on a case coming up that I have been working on for Catherine. I have to do that tomorrow. It is the one where a teenager had been accused of robbing a store and we both felt that he had not done it after we had talked with him. He has an air tight alibi. He has the right witnesses to speak in court for him. They are convinced that he did not do it. I believe it will work out for the best.

"You are talking about that young seventeen-year-old Kevin Jackson?" Jeff asked.

"Yes, that is who I am talking about." I said. "I don't believe he did it and I think I know who it was, but I just do not have any proof and cannot do anything about it." Jeff said.

"What do you have going on tomorrow Jeff, if I may ask?"

"They want me to come to talk with the district attorney but have not told me what yet. You know how that is. They always catch you unprepared and want to know everything about things you are not sure about yet.

"Yes, I know. That is how they do me to. I guess they think it is funny or something of the kind."

"Well Jason it is getting late. I guess I need to get out of here and let you rest."

"I will talk with you tomorrow I am sure."

"Talk with you later Jason."

When Jeff left I locked the doors and turned out all the lights. I went and got me a barq's root beer and went to my bedroom. It was time for me to go and try to get some rest now.

I lay down on the bed and drank my root beer while I was watching the evening news. I finished my drink and turned the TV off and was laying there staring up at the ceiling. In a few minutes my eyes got heavy and I went to sleep. I was dead to the world.

I heard that strange noise in my room again and I jumped and then realized that it was just my alarm clock. It always scares me for some reason.

I got up and grabbed my jogging shorts. It was 5:00 and time for me to get on the road jogging. I went out the door and headed out. When I had run my five miles and made it back to the house I made me a pot of coffee.

I went to the shower and took me a good hot shower and shaved and went and put me on some blue jeans and a western shirt, short sleeve. I went and got me a cup of coffee and cinnamon roll and went and sat down in my recliner to watch the news.

When I finished eating and drinking my first cup of coffee the doorbell rang. I got up and went to the door and opened it.

"Good morning Jason."

"Good morning Alice. How are you this morning?"

"I am doing great Jason. I am excited today."

"What are you so excited about Alice?"

"One of my great grandbabies is coming to spend a few days with me. Is it Ok if they come to work with me Friday?"

"Of course it is ok Alice."

"Is there is anything special you need me to do today Jason?"

"No Alice. Just your normal work is all."

"OK Jason I will get started."

"Alice your check is where I normally leave it and the check for the boys that clean the yard are with yours."

"OK Jason, I will make sure they get theirs."

"Tell them I will be by sometimes after a while to talk with them for a minute."

"OK. I will."

"There is also a check there signed for you to go and pick up your cleaning supplies with Alice."

"Thank you, Jason. I guess I better get started to work."

"I am gone Alice. I will talk with you later."

"Bye Jason."

I left the house and headed towards my office. I had a few minutes and decided that I would stop by The Grill and Eggs Breakfast Bar. I got there and walked in the door and saw Dexter. I went over and sat down with him.

"Hello Jason. How are you today?"

"I am doing very well and, how are you?"

The waitress came, and I ordered a cup of coffee and Dexter ordered his breakfast.

"What you got going on today Dexter?"

"I have a court case I have to go to this morning."

"Is that the ones dealing with those car thieves?"

"Yes, that is the one. We have it pretty well settled. They will be convicted. There is no doubt about it. They were caught red handed."

"I know you will be glad when that is over."

"You got that right. I have a lot to do and not much time to get it done in."

"I know how that is."

"Mayor Barker is fussing again. He is fussing about everything that needs to be done and he wants it all done right now, and he knows that it cannot happen that way."

"That is all he knows how to do Dexter. He is always fussing. I bet his wife has to tell him to shut up." I said laughingly but was serious.

"We have a lot going on Jason. Crime has picked up and we are catching it from both ends. Everybody wants everything right now."

"I understand what you mean. That is how it usually goes."

"Yes, it is."

"I have to go Dexter. I have to get to the office and get some things done this morning. I have that meeting with Sharon this afternoon. I will talk with you later."

"Ok. See you later Jason."

I left and went to the office and before I got settled in good the phone rang.

"Caffrey's Investigations. May I help you?"

"How are you feeling today after all that long trip yesterday?"

"I am fine and dandy. I just have to go to work now."

"Would you like to come and help me this morning?"

"If I were close enough Jason I would."

"You are so sweet."

"Aww thank you Jason. So are you."

"Sweet? I don't think so."

"OK Jason, I have a very busy day ahead of me. I just wanted to call and say hello this morning. I miss you."

"I miss you to."

"I will talk to you soon. Bye."

"OK. Bye.

I opened the file that I needed to work on. It was the one where the husband had been very abusive to his wife. He had been beating around on her and she finally got tired of it and decided to go to an attorney and talk with them. She went to Catherine and discussed it with her. Catherine told her she had a good law suit if she wanted to file it. She decided to push it and make him stop and go ahead and get a divorce and file for child custody and get everything she could.

Catherine had asked me to work on it and see what I could find out. I did, and I learned a lot about her husband. His name was Jim Beard and her name is Alice. I learned that he was an alcoholic who spent most of his time running around on her and most of his money on his whiskey. I had talked with several people that knew them both. They said he was nothing more than the scum of the earth. Everybody I talked with said that Alice was a very sweet person and they all liked her a lot. They have three small children and they do not have much to talk about. The children do without because of the daddy and his alcohol.

I just had to get my reports written up concerning the case. I just needed to get them to her in time for her to study them and be ready to present her case to the court. She was very confident that the man would end up spending some time in jail over his recklessness with the children, and for his beating up on his wife. The sad thing was the only thing the lady was going to get out of him was a divorce and the children. They did not have anything anyway.

She would be able to get some assistance that she had not been able to get before for help with the children once all this was settled in court. It was going to take me most of the morning and early afternoon to get all that worked out. I had to have it finished before I went to see Sharon and have it to Catherine, so she would have time to look it over.

I started to work on my project. It was fairly easy to get it written up for her. I had all the notes. I just had to organize them. I was finished by 1:00. I left and went to Catherine's office and the secretary showed me straight into her office.

"Hello Jason. Are you ready to go and see Sharon today?"

"Hello Catherine and yes I am ready. I am just a little nervous about it is all."

"You will be fine Jason."

"I know. I just kind of dread having to do it but it is something that needs to be done. Maybe we can find out who she is this way." I told her.

"That would help Jason if we could."

"I need to go. I have got to run by the house and see the yard boys and talk with them for a minute before I go to Sharon's."

"Talk with you later Jason. Let me know how it goes."

I sneaked up in the back yard and scared Jim. He jumped when I said hello Jim.

"Mr. Caffrey. I was not expecting you right now."

"Where is Austin?"

"He went in the house to get us something to drink."

"Can you guys paint?"

"Yes, and we are good at it to."

"My privacy fence needs to be painted. Do you think you boys could do that for me?"

"Yes Mr. Caffrey we would sure be glad to. When would you like for us to do it?"

"I would like for you to do it Friday if you have time to."

"Sure, we can do it Friday."

"OK. I will have everything here for you Friday then."

"Thanks Mr. Caffrey for letting us do it and we will do you an excellent job."

"I have to go. I will talk with you Friday."

"See you Mr. Caffrey."

I got to Sharon's office at about 2:55 pm.

"Hello Mr. Caffrey, I assume."

"Yes. You may call me Jason."

"OK. Just call me Sharon and we will get along fine."

"Sounds good to me."

"Are you ready to get this over with Jason?"

"Yes I am. I am a little nervous about it but I will be fine."

She took me in the room where she had her easel set up for her sketching. She motioned for me to have a seat just to the left of the easel beside her. I sat down. She looked at me and ask me how much detail I had of the woman for her to get a good sketch. I told her I could describe her right down to the color of her fingernails.

She told me that all I had to do was start describing her and that she would draw. So, here we go. I told Sharon the woman was about five feet seven inches tall, slim lady. She had long blonde hair. Pure blonde. Her face was kind of long and slender and her chin just a little pointed, not much. She had bangs, short. Her eyes were sky blue. She had on a pair of black nylon pants with a purple button up blouse. She was wearing a watch and had on some diamond earrings, hoops. She had an engagement ring with about a Carat diamond in it. She had long arms and long fingers. Her fingers were painted bright red. She was trim and fit and beautiful. She had medium light skin. And looked like she wore about a size eight in a shoe.

"How am I doing Sharon?"

"You are doing fine Jason."

"There is one other thing. She was smiling and had a very big grin."

"That is good Jason."

"Is there anything else you can think of?"

"No that is pretty much it."

When she finished with it and turned it so I could see it really good, I could not believe what I was seeing. It was a woman that I had seen around town but just did not know who she was. I had no doubt about it. Well I was hoping now that we could get some copies of it so that we could post them around town and see if anyone recognized her or that if she was in the area she would see it and contact us.

Sharon said that would not be a problem and that she would see to it that we had plenty of copies to post around. I told her that would be nice. That we needed to find her if there would be any way possible. She told me they would be ready tomorrow by lunch time. I told her I would come by and pick them up myself and get them to the people that needed to have them, so they could be posted around town.

"Thank you very much Sharon for your time."

"You are very welcome Jason."

"I will see you tomorrow."

"Bye Jason."

I left and went home. It was time to see what Alice had cooked for me today. I opened the refrigerator and found a lasagna that she had cooked. I took it out of the refrigerator and got me some on a plate and heated it up in the micro wave. It looked delicious.

I finished eating and put everything up and cleaned up the kitchen and made me a pot of coffee. When it was made I poured me a cup and went in the living room and sat down in my recliner and turned the TV on to watch the news.

I was sitting in my recliner drinking my coffee when the phone rang.

"Hello. Jason Caffrey speaking."

"Hello Jason. How did your meeting go with Sharon?"

"She was very nice and made me very comfortable. It was not hard to work with her."

"That is good Jason."

"I have seen the woman around town Catherine. I could not believe that I recognized her now and could not notice that after I had the dream."

"You were very upset then Jason. That is probably why you did not recognize her as someone you had seen."

"Maybe so."

"Maybe we can find her now."

"I sure hope so."

I asked her did she get a chance to go over the information that I had given her. She told me she had had plenty of time to look it over and that everything was going to work out for her fine. I told her to let me know how it came out and if she needed me to call. She told me that she did not think she was going to need anything else or anybody to get the case settled. It looked pretty much like it was in the hat.

I told her I was picking the posters up tomorrow at noon from Sharon. I guess I will take some to Dexter and some to Jeff, so they can be posted around town. I do not know if we will need to put anything on them or not. I did not ask Sharon if she could add phone numbers for the police to the sketch or not. Maybe she will think of it and just do it knowing what we want them for. She seems to be a very intelligent lady any way.

"I guess I need to go and get off the phone Jason and let you get some rest. I will talk with you sometime tomorrow." Catherine told me.

"Yes, please do call me and let me know how the case goes tomorrow. I know it is going to be fine but just let me know that it did. I hope he gets what he deserves." I told her.

"Good night. Talk to you later." Catherine said.

"The same to you. And have a great one. Tomorrow. OK." I told her.

It was about time for me to go over to the old warehouses and see what I can find out. I put on my old ragged clothes that I use for this type of surveillance. I went and got my old jalopy out of the garage that I keep locked up. I rode out close to the old warehouses and found me a place to park my car kind of out of view.

I walked up to the old warehouses and found me a place to hide and still be able to see everything without being noticed. I had my high-powered binoculars with me. I sat there for about an hour and three men looked to be about twenty-five years old. They had some bags in their hands and was standing there talking. About two minutes later three more walked up with bags in their hands.

They were all looking around. It looked like they were making sure that nobody was watching them. In just a minute one of them took some things from his pocket. He walked up to the old door and worked for a minute and he opened the door and they all went inside.

I sat and watched and waited for them to come out. They were in the building for about two hours before they came out. In a few minutes one of them walked outside and looked around and turned towards the door and said something and the others walked out. They all had bags in their hands carrying something in them. I did not know what it was, but I knew it had to be something that they did not want anybody to know about.

They left and got in their cars left the area. I went to the house and wrote a report about what I had seen tonight.

William Honeycutt

I decided that I would turn out the lights and go lay down on the bed. I was tired. I locked the doors and went upstairs to my bedroom. It was only 9:00. I pulled my clothes off and turned the cover back and lay down on the bed. I turned the TV on just for some noise.

In a few minutes I closed my eyes and was laying there thinking and was getting sleepy. Suddenly there she was in my dream. The lady with the blonde hair. I was upset. I did not want this. I did not need it. I could not get her out of my mind. She was there and there was nothing I could do about it. I was finally able to get my eyes open.

I got up and went to the bathroom and splashed cold water on my face hoping that would help. I went back and lay back down on the bed.

I turned over on my side and closed my eyes again. I did not see anything that time. That was nice. I kept them closed and slowly drifted off into a deep slumber. I did not know that the world was even there. I was gone. I slept hard and boy did I need it.

The alarm clock went off at 5:00 as it normally did. I woke up but I did not want to get up. It was Wednesday. Wednesday already. The week was going by fast it seemed like. All this started about a week ago with the dream of the woman being murdered. So far everything was good. Nothing had happened. We were in the process of getting posters out with hope that we could locate her, so nothing would happen to her. I was getting nervous because when I had these dreams things usually happened. I was doing everything I knew to do this time to hopefully stop it before it did.

I got up put on my jogging shorts for my five-mile run.

I walked out the door.

"Good morning Jason."

"Hello Jane. How are you this morning?"

"I am fine, and I sure missed you Monday. Where were you?"

"I was in Virginia visiting a friend."

We took off and ran our five miles and made it back to the house.

"I will see you Friday Jason."

"I will be here. Have a great day Jane."

I went in the house and took me a long hot shower and shaved. I decided to eat me a bowl of cornflakes with a banana in them. I finished my breakfast and went and put me on some clothes for work. I left the house and went toward the office at about 7:45. That would give me just enough time to be there by 8:00. I needed to get a little paper work done and start working a new lead that Catherine had given me that she needed me to check out for her.

I was the snoop guy. It was fun sometimes but at times it did get a little dangerous and sometimes downright dangerous.

CHAPTER FIVE

I got to the office at 8:00. I made a pot of coffee and made a few phone calls.

Catherine had given me some paperwork on a new case that she wanted me to do some surveillance. I was reading over the report to see who it was what I am supposed to be snooping on. I saw that Sarah Long and a supposedly friend of hers, Fred Johnson, were seeing each other at the city park down town. At least the report states they meet at the park. They are both married and her husband Henry Long wants to know what is going on. He does not believe that they are just meeting on a friendly notion. He feels certain there are other things going on. He is going to file for divorce if he finds that there is more to it than just meeting a friend to say hello. He is tired of it and he would like for it all to be settled now.

Today is Wednesday and I must pick up the posters from Sharon about noon. I don't have time today to start any surveillance on anybody. So, I picked up another file from Fred Jackson who needed me to help him out with some activity going on in his hardware store. Fred thought he had some hoodlums coming in his store and stealing things, but he just could not catch them. He wanted me to come and see if I could help him catch them. They were doing this mostly in the mid-morning. That would give me something to do today.

Murder of Grace

I went over to my clothes room to find me something to wear for this surveillance job. I found me a pair of my old faded blue jeans with a pull over shirt and my Sylacauga High School baseball cap. I got my worn out, well almost worn out anyway, blue sneakers and put them on. I was dressed and ready to go on my way.

I parked in the back of the store, so no one would notice that I was there and unless they were looking close they would not recognize me with my rags on. I went in the store and found Fred and talked with him about what kinds of things were going missing I asked him how long had this been going on. He told me only about a couple of weeks that he was sure of and that he had not lost much yet. But that he sure would like to know where his things are going.

He said mostly in the electrical tools is where he found things missing. So that is where I would take my stand in the store to see if I could catch anybody stealing from him. I went over to the power tools section in the store to familiarize myself with the department.

I counted the tools of each kind to see how many there were of each and each brand and made me a mental note of them. That way I would be able to keep up with what went missing when people would be in the store looking around.

While I was standing around looking at everything a couple of young boys about seventeen or eighteen years old came in the store and came straight over to the isle where all the power tools were. I kind of went on over to the hammers and saws and tools of that nature. I could keep an eye on them from there. They were dressed in some ragged jeans with holes in them and sloppy t-shirts that looked a mile too big for them. They looked like the type that would steal anything they could get their hands on.

William Honeycutt

Well they meandered around picking up the tools and looking at them. Looking as though they were trying to see what all the tools had on it for their use of whatever they wanted to do. And then they would set it back down. In a little bit the oldest looking of the two boys picked up a skill saw and told the other boy that was the one that they needed to do the job with. They took the saw and went to the cashier with it and paid for it and left. Well that ruled these two young men out. They only looked like the type that might would do that but they did not steal anything, instead they bought something. As the old saying goes, you cannot judge a book by it cover.

The morning was getting away from me fairly quick. I told Fred that I needed to go back to the office and change clothes and go over to see Sharon and pick up some posters. I told him I would be back hopefully tomorrow and maybe we can catch them. He thanked me for my time and I left and went on and changed back into my normal work clothes.

I left the office and rode over to Sharon's office to pick up the posters. She had the posters ready. She even thought of putting the phone numbers of the police department and the sheriff's office on them for contact if anyone knew her. I thanked Sharon for all her hard work and time. She showed me where they were. I got them and loaded them in the car and left.

I went over to see Jeff on my way out. He had just pulled into the parking lot when I drove up. We said our hellos and I told him what I was there for and showed him what the posters looked like. He was like me, he thought he had seen her around town but just did not know who she was. The face was awfully familiar though. He took part of them and told me that he would get them posted around the area today.

We chit chatted for a few minutes and I l left and went on over to see Dexter the chief of police. I took the posters in with me. He said the same thing that Jeff and I had said. He felt confident that he had seen her around and would recognize her face if he saw her. He did not know who she was but he knew that he had seen her in the area.

He told me that he would get the posters up and around the area. Maybe we can find her before anything happens to her. I sure hope that we can. I hoped that this was the dream that did not come true. I hoped that we were able to get ahead of the game this time. We both knew that we had to get it done soon because time was slipping away from us.

I took a few of them with me because I surely wanted to have done my part. And maybe being out and around with the posters I would see her and would be able to get to her before anything happens. I went on and started putting some posters up in the park nearest the police station. And then I just went around all over the city and put up all the ones that I had with me. I had all mine posted and it was about time for some dinner.

I had not eaten a sub sandwich in a while. It was time to go over to Ellen's Subway. Her shop is near the Sylacauga shopping center. I rode over and got me a sub way and sat down to eat it. Just as I sat down to eat my sandwich Catherine came walking in the door. She saw me and came over and ask me if she could sit down. I do not know why they always ask me if they can sit. They should know I am going to say yes. Common courtesy I guess. Was it nice to see her? I am always happy to see Catherine. She had just finished the court case with the divorce she told me. She told me that she got her divorce and that he was going to have to spend some time in jail but that the sentence had not been set yet. She went and ordered her dinner and came back to the table.

"Did you see the posters up around town?"

"Yes, I did. I don't know for sure, but she looks familiar. I think I may have seen her somewhere."

"That is a good sign that she must live around here somewhere close.'

"Yes, it is Jason. Or either that she comes to the area fairly often."

"I sure hope we find her soon. Like now would be nice." I said to her.

"Yes, I do to." She said.

"It would be nice if she just walked in that door right now. We could just talk with here right here and now." I told her.

"Yes, Jason that would be nice if that happened."

Maybe she will show up somewhere. I don't want another dream to come true. It is not any fun having these dreams and can't do anything about them."

"I understand Jason. I hope that someone does recognize her and knows her and knows where she lives. That would be nice."

"Maybe it will happen Catherine soon. I sure hope so."

"You never know Jason."

We had finished our lunch and it was time to go.

"I will talk with you later Catherine."

"OK. See you Jason."

I left and wanted to go by and see Dexter for a few minutes. I rode over to his house. He lives on Avondale Avenue near Pine Street. He was buying his home there. He had been there about five years now. I pulled up in the drive way and he was sitting on the porch taking it easy.

I walked up on the porch and we shook hands and I sat down.

"What are you up to Dexter?" I said.

"Just sitting here and relaxing for right now. I am a little tired from the hectic day today. Has been a busy one for a Wednesday. Since things have been picking up lately with more people coming through than normal I guess it just causes more little crime festivals taking place than normal."

"It is summer time now of course and all the kids are out of school and they are all out looking for something to do." I told him.

"Of course, and that does put more traffic on the road with all these teenagers having their little drag races that we have to go and chase them down. All the part of being a cop."

"We have all the posters up now." I said to him.

"Yes, maybe this will reap us some results. I had one phone call today at my office saying that they knew the lady by her face and all but just did not know her name." He told me.

"That seems to be the consensus around town." I told him.

"A lot of people saw the posters when we put them up and ask us what she had done. I explained that she had not done anything. That we were just trying to find out who she is because we could keep her out of trouble. They looked at us strangely but we did not need to tell them what the trouble was." He said to me.

"What are you going to do the rest of this evening Dexter?" I asked him.

"I am just going to sit around and take it easy and spend a little time with my wife and two children. I hope I do not have any calls tonight that I have to deal with. That would be nice for a change." He said to me.

"I wish you a lot of luck on that one. Being the Chief, you get disturbed a lot of times with things, when you are right in the middle of something, you surely do not wish to be bothered with." I told him.

William Honeycutt

"Yes, and I just wish they would leave me alone but of course that is not going to happen."

"I will go on and let you alone for now, so you can spend the rest of the evening with your beautiful family." I told him.

We shook hands and I left. I went back down to Fort Williams Street and headed toward Broadway Ave. to go home. I was not so tired today as I had been before. I needed to just go and relax a little though and think things over.

I got to the house pulled in my drive way. I looked back just in time to see the tail end of that 1957 red Chevrolet going down the highway. I still could not see the tag number. I think they are following me for some reason. It may be someone who knows I am watching them. That is what I do. I am a snoop. One day I am going to find out who that person in that 1957 red Chevrolet is.

I went on my porch and just sat down in my swing for a few minutes to watch the birds. That was always fun when I thought about doing it. While I was sitting there on the porch Jeff came up in my drive. He got out and came on the porch and sat with me watching the birds. They were always so beautiful.

"What are you doing Jason?" He asked me.

"I am taking it easy for right now. I have not even been in the house yet. I just wanted to sit on my porch a little bit because I have not done that in over a week now." I told him.

"We got all the posters out today Jason. Maybe somebody will know who she is and where she lives."

"I hope we find out who she is."

"I was passing by and wanted to stop and see if you were OK since I saw your car home."

"Thanks for caring Jeff."

"Maybe by tomorrow we will get some calls on her and can find her."

Murder of Grace

"I am hoping that we do but I wonder if we will ever hear anything or not."

"I am not going to stay long Jason. I will see you later."

"OK. See you later Jeff. Be careful."

It was time to go in the house now and turn the TV on and watch some evening new and see what was going on in our world around us and what the nation had up its sleeve. I got in the house and got the TV turned on and made me a pot of coffee. When it was finished making I fixed me a cup and went and sat down in my recliner to rest for a while. Guess what! The phone rang. I think everybody knows when I am sitting down in my recliner to relax. That is when they always call.

"Hello, Jason Caffrey speaking."

"What are you doing and where have you been?" My mom asked me.

"I have been very busy mom."

"I have not heard from you in over a week now and I was wondering what was going on." She said.

"I am drinking a cup of coffee and watching a little news to see what this world is coming to. And it is so nice to hear your voice mom. I had another one of those awful dreams and I had to get some things done and get them worked out hoping that we can do something about this one. I am sorry that I have not called you. Please forgive me." I told her.

"Well, you know you are forgiven even if I am a little peeved at you." She said.

"Thank you very much." I told her.

"When are you coming over to see me?"

"I will come by sometime tomorrow and see you if you are going to be home."

They lived in a big beautiful eight-bedroom home about ¾ of a mile off the Talladega Highway just as you get outside the city but not the city limits. It was a huge home. 5,000 square feet. It has a humongous kitchen with all the updated new furnishing that they had just replaced. All stainless-steel appliances. Dad had all the countertops replaced with granite counter tops. Mom had been tickled pink over her new kitchen. The formal dining room was massive. Then mom had her breakfast nook with a small table that she and dad used most of the time. The house had a front porch all the way across the front. It was twelve feet deep. It was large enough that mom had a swing put on both ends. She loves her swing. It has six full bathrooms. This is the home I was raised up in. We had plenty of room.

"OK dear. I wanted to call you and see how you were doing. Sorry to hear about you having another one of those dreams. I hope you never have another one." She said to me.

"I hope I never have another one to, but I probably will. You know I have had them all my life." I said.

"I know. I will let you go for now and you be sure to come by tomorrow. I need to talk with you about some things and I would rather not do it on the phone. OK."

"OK I will come by for sure mom sometime tomorrow. I do not know what time but I will be there." I told her.

"Well, I will be here all day as it seems. If I have to do anything I will let you know that I have to go and when I will be back."

"OK that will work for me mom. I will see you tomorrow. Bye."

"OK. Bye." She said and hung up the phone. Now I had made a promise and I had to keep this one. I needed to see her anyway.

I went to the kitchen to get me a cup of coffee and hopefully sit back down and enjoy the rest of the evening without interruption. Just as I sat down good the doorbell rang. I got up and went to the door and looked out the peep hole to see who it was. Well it was not someone that I knew. I opened the door.

"May I help you?"

"Are you Jason Caffrey?"

"Yes, that would be me. Why do you want to know?"

"You are a private investigator, aren't you?" he asked.

"Yes, I am but who are you?" I asked him.

"I am Jeremy Whitcomb. May I talk with you a few minutes?" he asked me

"Sure." I told him.

I walked out on the porch and sat down on my swing and he sat down in the chair close to the swing. I asked Jeremy what he needed. He told me that there was someone following him and that he did not know what to do expect stop at my house. I ask him did he know why they were following him. He told me that he did not know

"Mr. Caffrey, I thought this was your house and I stopped here because I thought I was at the right house. My aunt Alice works for you and she had told me about you."

"It is getting late Jeremy. Do you have a way to get home?"

"No. I will have to walk."

"Do you have anyone that you can call to come and get you?"

"No. We don't have a phone."

"I will take you home."

I locked the house and we got in my car.

"Where do you live Jeremy?"

"Weogufka near Weogufka High School."

As we were getting close to the school he told me to slow down that we were close to his house. In just a little bit he told me to turn into that drive way coming up.

William Honeycutt

"Thank you, Mr. Caffrey, for bringing me home. I was scared."

"You are welcome. Just do not be out like this by yourself with no way to get anywhere. It is very dangerous."

"I understand Mr. Caffrey."

I left his house and went back home. I went in the house and turned out all the lights and locked the doors and went to my bedroom and pulled my clothes off and lay down on the bed.

CHAPTER SIX

I turned over on the bed to close my eyes again and hope that I could go to sleep. I did. I was more tired than I realized. I went out like a light. I slept hard and long that night. It was nice to get another good night of sleep. I needed it. The clock went off at 5:00. I wanted to hit the snooze button but I knew better than to do that.

I got up and put on my jogging shorts and left the house. It was Thursday. Another week almost gone. I ran my five miles and got back to the house. I went and took me a good long hot shower and shaved and got dressed. I put on my new jeans and bright red western snap up shirt and new sneakers that I had just bought. I wanted to feel good today.

I went in the kitchen and made me a pot of coffee and drank me a couple of cups and watched the morning news for a few minutes. It was about time to go and find me something to eat this morning. I just did not feel eating at home.

I left my house and went to The Grill and Eggs Breakfast Bar. I walked in the door and saw Jeff sitting over by the widow at a booth. I went over and ask him if I could sit down. Of course he said yes.

"How are you doing, old buddy?" he said.
"Old?" I said and laughed.
"Why you call me old?" I asked him.
"What are you so dressed up for today Jason?"

"I just wanted to look good, so I would feel good today. Today is going to be a great day, I just know it is." I told him.

The waitress came and ask me did I want something to do. I ask her did I look like I needed something to do and let her know I was just kidding with her. I gave her by order for two eggs over easy, with ham and grits on the side with toast.

"What are you going to do today Jason?"

"I am probably going to do some surveillance for Catherine today about lunch time."

"What are you going to snoop on Jason?"

"A woman that is running around on her husband supposedly."

"I am hoping that we hear something today Jason."

"Me too Jeff. It would be nice."

In a few minutes the waitress brought my breakfast to the table.

"I am finished eating buddy. I have to get on the road. I will talk with you later."

"OK Jeff. Have a good day."

I finished my breakfast and paid my ticket and left the waitress a nice tip. I went to the office. I made a pot of coffee and called Catherine.

"Hello McCarthy and McCarthy Attorneys at Law. May I help you?"

"You guys need to shorten that name." I said laughingly.

"Yes, it is a mouthful Jason."

"What are you up to today Catherine other than the case with the young boy accused of robbery that he did not do?"

"That is about it Jason other than just catching up on some paperwork I need to do."

"Would you like to eat lunch with me today Catherine?"

"Sure Jason. Where you want to meet at?"

"Charlie's will be good if that is OK with you."

Murder of Grace

"That will be good Jason. Is 1:00 OK?"

"Sure, that will be fine."

"I will see you then Jason. I have to get going to the court house."

"See you at 1:00 Catherine and be careful."

I decided that today was a good day to go to the park and sit around and see if I could catch Sarah Long and Fred Johnson where they had been meeting. I needed to get started on this one.

I went to my dressing room and found me some old ragged pants with holes in the legs of them and a baseball cap and I put it on backwards. It felt good. I got my ragged blue sneakers with one sole on it flopping and the old blue shirt with the arm almost torn off it.

I wanted to look like somebody that had nothing and did not know where the next meal would come from. I left my office and went to the park and parked my car on the far end of the park and walked over to the center of the park and sat down on a park bench. As far as I knew neither one of them knew me and that was good. I surely did not know either one of them.

In a little while a blue Camaro pulled up and a lady got out of the car and went over and set down on a bench. In a couple of minutes after she sat down a Lincoln Continental two tone blue drove up and parked right behind the Camaro. He got out and went over and sat down beside her and kissed her on the cheek. They sat and talked for about five minutes and they got up and both of them got in his car to leave together.

That was proof enough that they were definitely seeing each other. I just watched them go toward Childersburg. Now that I knew about what to expect from them, I would follow them the next time to see where they went. I was sure they were going to a motel somewhere.

William Honeycutt

I left the park and went to the office and changed back into my work clothes. It was time to leave and go to Charlie's to meet Catherine.

I got to Charlie's and found us a place to sit. The waitress came to take my order. I told her I was waiting on someone. She told me she would come back.

I had been there about five minutes when Catherine walked in the door. I waved for her to see where I was. She came over and sat down.

"Hello kid." I said.

"Well, hi Mr. Sharp you look really nice today. What did you do? Try to get sexy on us."

"Yes. Why? I have been through the wringer lately, so I thought I would try to make myself feel really good. You should have seen me a little while ago you would have laughed at me." I told her.

"You think I would have." She said and laughed.

The waitress came to the table to see if we were ready to order. We both knew what we wanted. We wanted that big juicy T-bone steak and a baked potato and a chef salad to go with it. I had not had one lately and I was definitely ready for one. She took our order and left the table.

Catherine ask me had we had any calls or anything on the girl yet. I told her if they had had any calls on the girl I had not heard anything. We were sitting there minding our business chit chatting when I looked up towards the door and saw a tall slender blonde walk in the door. She is a lovely lady. Very pretty. I told Catherine to look at her. She did and was astounded at what she saw. We could not believe our eyes.

She came over to a table for two and sat down close to us. I knew that face. I knew that was her. It could not be anyone else. It was the woman that we were looking for and was hoping to find her somewhere. Well, she just walked into the restaurant and sat down.

I got up and walked over to the table where she was and introduced myself to her.

"I am Jason Caffrey."

"My name is Charlotte Taylor. And it is a pleasure to meet you." She said.

"Are you alone or is someone coming to meet you?" I asked her.

"I am alone."

"Would you like to join me and my friend and have lunch with us?' I asked her.

"I do not want to disturb you guys."

"We would love to have you join us if you will."

We really needed her to join us so that we could talk with her. She finally gave in and came over to sit with us.

"Catherine, this is Charlotte Taylor."

"It is a pleasure to meet you Charlotte."

"It is a pleasure to meet you Catherine. And thank you guys for inviting me to sit with you. I hope I do not disturb you."

"You are very welcome, and you will not disturb us."

I told Catherine I needed to make a phone call and told them I would be right back. I went over to a pay phone in the corner of the restaurant and called Dexter and told him that we had just found the young lady I had seen in my dream. We are at Charlie's. He was elated. That meant maybe we could stop what was fixing to happen.

I asked him if he would call Jeff and let him know that we had found her and where we were. He said he would be glad to. So, I left that up to him and went on back to the table. It was time to find out where she is from and see now what we can do to stop her from being murdered.

I went back to the table and sat back down in my chair and was a little tense because I was not sure where and how to start with anything. While I was gone making the phone call to Dexter the waitress took her order. I wanted to be relaxed for a little while before I started explaining to her what my reason for asking her to sit with us was in the first place.

This really made me nervous.

I was not looking forward to this part of the deal.

I would rather someone else deal with it.

But she was here.

And it had to be done.

So, I ask her where she was from. She told me that she was from Tuscaloosa, Alabama but that she had moved here and had been here about four months now.

"Are you married?" I asked her.

"No. I am not."

"What brought you to Sylacauga?"

"I needed to leave Tuscaloosa to get away from my boyfriend and I heard that this would be a nice little city to come to. So I came here to see if I would like it or not and so far I like it."

"We do have a nice little city here and we all enjoy it a lot." Catherine commented.

"Do you work anywhere?" I ask her.

"Yes, I got me a job at the mill here. I work the night shift."

"Does your boyfriend know where you are you think?" Catherine ask her.

"I hope not." she said. "Maybe he will not find me here."

"Is he a violent man?" I asked her

"He can be." She told me.

It was time to tell her why I was asking her all these questions that were so personal to her. I was not wanting to have to do that but I knew that I

Murder of Grace

needed to. It would probably scare her out of her mind when I told her. But I had to do it.

The waitress came with the food and set our food down and ask us did we need anything else right then. We told her no. She left. I told Charlotte that I had an ultimate reason for asking her to sit with us today when we saw her.

She inquired as to what that reason was. I told her I hoped she had plenty of time after we ate because I really needed to discuss something with her. I know by now she was very confused. I had never seen her before. That would make anybody wonder why you wanted to discuss something with them. She may have even wondered what she had done. Have I done anything?

I would be wanting to know why you wanted to talk with me and why that it seemed so serious if I had been in her place. She told me that she had plenty of time. I told Catherine I hoped that she had plenty of time and that she could stay with us while I discussed this with Charlotte. Catherine said that she would take all the time we needed.

We ate our lunch. I asked Catherine could we go to one of our offices where it would be more private to discuss this. She said we could come to her office because there would be more room there. She would just have all her calls screened while we were busy.

We would not let Charlotte pay for her meal. We took care of it for her. We met at Catherine's office and now it was time to share with Charlotte the reason that I needed to talk with her today.

"Charlotte this is not going to be easy. So, if you will just listen to me especially in the beginning. I know this is going to blow your mind and you are not going to be prepared for it, but I have to explain it to you." I said.

"OK. I will do my best to listen carefully." She told me.

William Honeycutt

I began to tell her of what I had seen. I told her that I had had a dream and that she was very vivid in my dream. She was shocked. I asked her did she see the posters posted around town. She said she did see them and decided that she must have a twin that there would be no way that that could be her unless her boyfriends was looking for her. She said that he would not go to that much trouble though.

I went on to describe to her the murder scene that took place. I explained to her that I knew that it was her that the dream was about and that I had done everything I could to stop it from happening. Everybody in law enforcement and Catherine here was trying to help me in any way possible.

I am glad we know who you are now, and we are going to try to protect you from anything happening to you if there is any way possible.

"You have just scared the life out of me." She told me.

"I am sorry. But I had to tell you about it and I hope you will let us protect you."

"I do not know what I am going to do now. I am scared." She said.

"Catherine may I use your phone for a minute. I need to call my mom. It is getting late."

"Sure, you can use it. Make yourself at home. Do you need some privacy?"

"No, I can do it right here."

I picked up the phone and called my mom.

"Hello." She said.

"Hey mom."

"I knew you would not come today for some reason." She said.

"I can still come it will just be later than I intended for it to be." I told her.

"I do not care what time it is when you get here. Just come as soon as you have the time to. It will be fine. I would just love to see you today."

I explained to her that we were having to have an unexpected meeting with a young lady and as soon as we finished with it that I would be over there. She told me that would fine.

I ask Charlotte could we have her phone number, and could we stay in touch with her. She seemed to not mind that at all. She gave us her phone number and we gave her our office and home phone numbers and told her to call us if she suspected anything at all. She told us she had to work tonight but that she would be off tomorrow night and if we wanted to, we could meet again sometime tomorrow.

We told her that would be fine. That we would be more than happy to meet with her tomorrow. That will be a great thing to do. We planned to meet at Charlie's Steak and Grill at about 1:00 pm. That would be a good time for the three of us.

I left the restaurant and went on towards the west end of town towards my mom and dad's home.

Mom must have been looking out the window watching for me. When I turned in the drive and started toward the house and got kind of close she walked out on the porch. She was definitely waiting on me to get there. She knew I was coming now. She saw me.

I parked in the drive and got out of the care. She came down the steps to meet me and hugged me and gave me a big kiss on the checks and told me she still loved me.

"Of course, you still love me I still am the baby you know." I told her.

"Yes, you still are the baby."

We were both excited that I was able to make it because it had been almost two weeks now since I had seen her.

We walked upon the porch and sat down, and chit chatted about life and everything in general.

"Have you eaten anything yet?"

"Yes, I ate at about 1:30."

"Would you like a little snack?" she said.

"Of course, mom if you already have something made I will eat a snack with you."

We left the porch and went into the kitchen to find something to snack on. She had some tuna fish salad. She made us a sandwich and got some regular potato chips to eat with it. We sit down at the table in the breakfast nook. She was ready to talk now. She told me that she had some things on her mind that she wanted to discuss with me.

I ask her was it important that we discuss it today or could I come over sometime Saturday and us discuss it. She said that would be fine if I would just come over Saturday because that would bel easier for her than Sunday.

She was usually a very busy person on Sunday. Everybody wanted mom on Sunday for some reason or other it seemed. I told her I would make it a date and I would be there. I asked her what time she wanted me to come. She told me about 10:00 Saturday morning would be a good time. As far as she knew there was nothing going on at that time.

I made that a date with my mom to meet her Saturday.

We just sit around and talked about the family and what they all were doing. She informed me of all the birthdays coming up soon and even what they were all asking for. I told her I probably would not remember all that. She told me I needed to learn how to keep up with it. She said for me to get me a book and she would write it all down for me. I told her if she wanted me to have it that bad to buy me a book and put it in it and give it to me for Christmas or something. She said that sounded like a good idea and that she just might do that. We both laughed.

I told her that if she did not mind that I needed to go today and rest if it would be possible. I have been so busy the last 8 days of my life. It was getting hard to keep up with what was going on most of the time.

That dream and all the things that we have been doing to try to keep it from happening. We found the girl today. That is the young lady that I was telling you we had an unexpected meeting with.

We were in the restaurant and she walked in the door and came and sit at a table near us.

We had to talk with her. Now we are going to have to try to protect her if there be any way that we can do it. She is aware of it and of course now she is scared to death.

I would be to if I were in her place.

I am scared for her.

And am not sure what to do right now.

So, you see mom I have had a very busy day today and a very busy week. I hope that it will get better soon. I went and spent the weekend with Rita last weekend. We had a good time and really enjoyed it. "Are you getting married?" Mom asked. "Married? What in the world ever made you ask me if Rita and I are getting married mom? She is a great friend." I told her. "You are twenty-five years old now. I was just wondering." She told me. "I will get married one day just not right now. Are Rita and I getting married? Not that we know of."

CHAPTER SEVEN

I left mom and dads and headed for home on the south end of town. I can't believe she had the nerve to ask me if Rita and I were getting married. I was not quite ready for that yet. I got home about 6:00 pm that evening. I pulled up in the garage and got out of my car. I went over to the porch and sat down to just enjoy myself and relax some before I ever opened the door to go inside.

I was sitting there on my porch and Jeff rolled up in my yard

"Well now tell me where you been you old goat." He said.

"Do I look like an old goat?" I replied.

"Well! YES." And he laughed.

I told him that I had been over to my mom and dad's visiting my mom. She wanted to see me today she said. I was late getting there so we just spent some good time together and made an appointment for Saturday.

"Well I heard you seen the young lady and talked with her today." He said.

"I did and hopefully she is going to meet me and Catherine tomorrow at Charlie's. Hopefully we will be able to make some arrangements to help her be safe."

"Maybe that will work out Jason. We do not need this thing to blow up on us." Jeff said.

"Well I am hoping for the same thing." I told him.

Murder of Grace

"What are you going to do tomorrow being it is Friday?" He asked.

"I have a couple of cases I need to look into tomorrow. I plan to start early in the morning and get it going so that I will have time to cover them both before 12:00. I suppose you just going to take it easy tomorrow huh?" I said. "

"I plan to if there is any way possible. Maybe it will be quite tomorrow. That would be nice."

"You never know what the day will be like till the day is over. Anything can happen."

"That is true. Something unexpected always comes up."

"I went over to the warehouses and I found six men breaking into the middle one. I watched them until they left. They had some bags of things with them when they left. They were small bags. It looked like drugs to me. I am going back over the first of next week and see what I can by getting a little closer with time."

"Maybe we need to go with you Jason. That could be dangerous."

"Naw. Let me go alone right now. I will be safe. Maybe I can get more information and have a better idea what they are there for. I think I can get in the old building from the back side anyway and hide until they leave."

"OK. Just be careful."

"I will. Don't worry about me. I am a snoop you know. I am good at it."

"Well Jason I will get out of your hair and let you rest and take it easy for the rest of this evening."

"You do not have to be in a hurry Jeff I have plenty of time." I told him.

"Well I need to go and take care of a few things on the way home. See you later man."

Just as I got the key in the door a car pulled up. It was my oldest sister's daughter.

"Hello Uncle Jason." Jenny said and got out of the car.

"Hi Uncle Jason" Karla, my oldest brother's daughter said.

"Hello girls. What are you up to?"

Jenny reached in the backseat of the car and got something.

"We brought you a carrot cake Uncle Jason." Jenny said.

"A carrot cakes? That is too much girls. Why did you bring me a carrot cake?"

"Mom baked it and asked us if we would bring it to you on our way to Walmart." Jenny said.

"We told her we would love to." Karla said.

"Thank you for bringing it girls."

"What have you been doing Uncle Jason?"

'Working mostly."

"Well we need to go Uncle Jason. I hope you enjoy your cake." Jenny said.

"I will, and you girls have fun."

"We will Uncle Jason." Karla said.

I went in the house and cut me a piece of the carrot cake and got my Barq's root beer. I took them and went and sat down in my recliner and turned the TV on. Maybe I could find something good that would be interesting to watch.

Wow the phone did not ring by the time I sat down in the recliner. That is unusual. It normally rings. I am glad it did not because I needed to call Rita anyway. I reached over and got the phone and dialed her number and it rang one time.

"Hello Jason, what are you doing?"

"Just sitting here right now taking it easy. I have had a very busy week." I told her.

"We ran into the woman in my dream. We have another meeting with her tomorrow. Maybe we will be able to help her before she gets killed."

"That is good Jason. That is a very positive start."

"My mom asks me when you and I are getting married."

"What? I can't believe that."

"Well she did. And then she told me I was twenty-five years old and she was just wondering."

"That is too funny Jason."

I might could get interested in her more than just a friend, but I am just not ready for that right now.

"Do you have a busy day for tomorrow?" I asked her.

"Yes, but that is just about always the case. I always look forward to the weekend but sometimes even they are busy for us." She told me.

"Yea I know how that is."

"Are you going to have a busy one tomorrow Jason?"

"Yes, I am afraid so."

"I have to call my mom tonight Jason. I need to get off the phone for right now. I will talk with you soon."

"Ok. You take care and I will see you soon."

We said our good byes and hung up the phone.

I leaned back in my recliner to just close my eyes for a minute and think about life a little bit.

I wandered what my life was coming to.

I was starting to get a little worried about it. I was getting a little old now.

I guess I needed to settle down a little more. Although about the only thing I did was work.

I went in the kitchen and made me a pot of coffee. When it finished making I poured me a cup and sat down at the table to glance through the paper tonight. That is something I did not do much of. I did not find anything in it that I was not already familiar with. I closed it up and got up and refilled my cup with some fresh coffee and went to the living room and set down in my recliner and leaned back.

About the time I leaned back the phone rang. I answered it and this strange voice said hello. I said hello. And then they told me that they had dialed the wrong number. I did not believe for a second that they had dialed the wrong number. In about two minutes it rang again. I picked it up. The voice sounded a little muffled. I just hung it up. I did not want to hear this. I was getting a little pissed. I did not like that at all.

I sat back again, and the phone rang again. I answered it and they said I am sorry, but I still have the wrong number. Their voice still sounded a little muffled. I hung it up.

In about five minutes the phone rang again. I was mad by now. I snatched it up and yelled at them and told them to quit calling me. I hung it up. The phone rang again almost immediately. I answered it nicely. My mom says what were you so mad about? I told her about the phone calls and apologized for yelling at her. I had no idea that it was her.

She told me she just wanted to call me and tell me that she loved me and to please do not forget our 10:00 am date for Saturday. I told her I would not forget it. She told me bye and that she would see me Saturday.

It was about 9:00 pm. I decided it was time for me to get a little sleep. I turned out all the lights and went to the bedroom and pulled my clothes off and lay down on the bed. I was looking up at the ceiling thinking about what tomorrow was going to be like.

I finally went to sleep.

My clock went off at 5:00. I wanted to hit the snooze button, but I knew better. I would oversleep if I did that. I got up and pulled on my jogging shorts. It was Friday morning.

I went out the door. I did not see Jane anywhere. I waited a minute and she came out her

Murder of Grace

door. She was always out before me. That was unusual.

"Hello Jane. How are you this morning?"

"I am ready to go Jason. And how about you?"

"Let's do it and enjoy it this morning."

I always enjoyed running with her. She is such a nice person.

We finished our run and made it back to the house.

"How are your studies going Jane?"

"They are going very well lately."

"That I good."

"I have one more year left Jason and I will be finished."

"I know you will be glad when it is over Jane."

"You better believe it."

"I need to get in the house. I will see you Monday."

"See you Monday for sure."

I went in the kitchen and made me a pot of coffee and took a shower and shaved. I put on some work clothes and was ready to go. I went back in the kitchen and poured me a cup of coffee. I went in the living room and turned the TV on the morning news. It seemed like that the little spurts of crime had increased in our little city. The doorbell rang. I went to the door and opened it. I knew that it was Alice. She is always on time.

"Hello Alice. It is good to see you this morning."

"Hello Jason. And how are you doing?"

"Great Alice. Who is this young man you have with you this morning?"

"This is my great grandson, Jeffrey."

"Hello Jeffrey."

"Hi." He said.

"Anything special today Jason."

"No. just your normal things Alice."

"I will get to work."

"The boys are coming today to paint the privacy fence for me. I have left their check with yours Alice."

"I will give it to them Jason."

"Thank you, Alice."

I got in my old 1968 Ford LTD and left to go to the office. It was ragged. Looked as though whoever owned it needed to buy them a new one.

I went to The Grill and Eggs Breakfast Bar to eat me some breakfast. I went in and sat down, and the waitress came to the table. Her name is Sally Worthington. She is my usual waitress. She asked me could she help me, and I told her I would take my usual.

"Oh my god Jason. What are you doing? You do not look like yourself this morning."

"I am just taking the day off and going to have a little fun today messing around."

That was a lie for sure.

"What are you doing all dressed like a hippy?"

"I just thought it would be fun today."

She knew what my usual was. She took my order and left. When she brought my food to the table I ate and left the restaurant.

I went the office I needed to catch up on my paper work this morning before I went over to Fred's store to do a little surveillance for him.

It felt good that it was Friday finally. I was so glad that the weekend was coming up. I was ready for a break from everything. I was going to see my mom tomorrow and enjoy some time with her. I was looking forward to that.

I got my folders down and started going over my reports to see what all I needed to do this morning. It was 8:30 and the phone rang.

"Hello. Caffrey's Investigations. May I help you?"

"Hello Jason. How are you this morning?

"I am fine Catherine."

"I just wanted to call and remind you that we have that meeting with Charlotte today at 1:00."

"Thanks Catherine. I will be there."

"Let's hope that she will be there."

"Maybe she will."

"OK. I will talk to you then."

"Bye. See you then Catherine."

It was time for me to leave and go over to the hardware store. I walked in the door and found Fred.

"Good morning Fred."

"Hello Jason."

"Have you had any activity since I was here the other day?"

"None that I am aware of. I have had some hoodlums in here, but I could not keep up with them. I stay busy most of the time."

"That is good that you have not had anything at least that you know of missing."

"If you had not said something Jason I would have thought you were one of those hoodlums this morning."

"That is good Fred. I do not want people to recognize me."

"Let me get situated and see what is going on today. Maybe we will catch them this morning."

I went on over near the power tools in the section where all the hammers and squares and things like that were. I could keep a good eye on the power tools from there.

I did not get there good until those two same boys that had come in the store the other day came in and came to the power tools again. They looked around. They were looking at the drills today. They finally decided which one that they wanted and took it and paid for it and left.

Fred had hired a new man about two months ago. He came over to the power tools and was looking around. He picked up a skill saw and took it with him. Fred was busy in the office with a very important customer. The new man knew that he was. He took the saw back to the back room with him.

There was a back door easily accessible for the parking for the employees. That is where they all parked and came in and out of the store when they came to work and left. I was very aware of that situation because Fred had told me about it. I had told him that we might need to watch the employees as well as everybody else.

I went out the front door and went around to the side of the building to watch the back door and see if I saw anything or not. In just a little bit the back door opened, and the young man walked out the door with a box in his hand and went to his car and set the box on the back seat. He had it fixed to where that no one would pay any attention to him. He could tell them that he was just putting something in the car that he needed to take home with him and they would think nothing about it.

I walked over and took my credentials out. Showed him who I was and ask him if I could see what was in the box in the car that he just set in there. He told me that it was just some stuff he was taking home today that he needed. I asked him to let me see what was in the box. He did not want to do that, but he knew that I had him.

He finally told me he did not want to but that he would let me look in the box. I opened the car door and looked in the box and found the new skill saw that he had taken to the back with him.

I called Dexter and told him I needed him there at the store and explained to him why. Dexter was there in about ten minutes. I told him what had happened. He put cuffs on Jerry Hicks and took him in to jail for stealing.

I told Fred that I was sorry that it had to be one of his employees. He would never have thought that

Jerry would have done that. He seemed like a very honest person and he just never would have dreamed that it would come down to this.

He pressed the charges and Jerry was sentenced to the misdemeanor with 90 days in jail.

I had to go over to the park now. It was about 10:30. Sarah and Fred usually met at about 11:00 AM. I wanted to be there this morning and follow them to see where they went when they left the park. I figured they went to a motel somewhere.

I got to the park and just parked my car not too far from where they usually met.

In a few minutes she pulled up and just sit and waited in her car this time. In about three minutes he pulled up behind her. She got out of her car and went and got in his car. They left the park headed south towards Fort Williams Street. I followed them. They got to Fort Williams and turned to the right going toward the Jackson Trace Motel. In a little bit they pulled in. He went in and got a room and came back to the car. I had parked in a parking space close by on the grounds of the motel to watch them.

He went around the far end of the drive and parked in front of a room. They both got out and went in. I had my camera with me and I was close enough to them that I could get a picture of them. I took one showing them going in the room together.

I knew they were definitely seeing each other now.

They had gone in the room. I went and knocked on the door. He came to the door and she was standing right beside him. I had my camera ready to take a picture of them. When he opened the door, I clicked the picture of them standing in the doorway of the hotel together. I had all the evidence I needed now.

I left the motel and went back to the office so that I could change into some good clothes. I kept a

William Honeycutt

couple of suits of my regular work clothes at the office, so I would have them if I needed them. It was getting close to 12:30 pm by now. I had to be at Charlie's Steak and Grill at 1:00 pm. I did not have much time to get ready. I had to hurry.

I got my clothes changed and made it to Charlie's at 1:00. I walked in the door and Catherine was already there.

"Hello Catherine."

"Hello Jason."

I sat down and we waited for about ten minutes.

"Do you think she is going to show up Catherine?"

"I really don't think so Jason. I think yesterday scared her out of her mind."

"I have about decided that to Catherine. We can't help her if she does not allow us to."

"At least we are trying Jason."

We called our waitress over to the table. She took our order.

In a few minutes our food was there. We ate our food and chit chatted a little. We finished our lunch and left the restaurant.

I went back to my office and made a few phone calls and got my paper work organized. It was about 3:00. I decided to take off a little early and go by the park for a few minutes.

While I was sitting at the park just enjoying watching the birds and all Jeff was passing by and saw he. He stopped and came over to where I was.

"Hello Jason. What are you doing in the park today?"

"I am just relaxing some right now Jeff."

"I see you are in your old LTD."

"I had to do some surveillance today, so I used it. I am ready for the weekend Jeff. I have had a long week."

"I know what you mean Jason."

"Hey, you remember the time you threw the football and it hit me in the face and you thought that you had broken my nose."

"Yea Jason. How could I ever forget that?"

"It scared mom and then we were all scared that she was going to kill us."

"Yes, I know. We always had fun."

He got a call.

He got up shook my hand and told me he would see me later.

He turned around and left.

It was time for me to go to the tennis courts and meet my nephew. I always meet him on Fridays at 4:00 PM for a couple of games of tennis.

"Hello Jarrod."

"Hello Uncle Jason. Are you ready to get beat?" He said with a big grin on his face.

"Beat me? You hope you going to beat me."

"It will be fun when I do Uncle Jason."

"Yea I know. You think you are good."

"I know I am."

"You going to come and eat with me today and go to the gym with me?" I asked him.

"Yea. I would like that. I would love to see Roxy again."

"I bet you would."

We played a couple of games of tennis. I beat him one game. We left and went to the house in my car. I parked it back in the garage and locked it up.

"Uncle Jason why do you keep this car locked up?"

"I use it when I am on surveillance work Jarrod. I try to keep it to where everybody does not know about it. So, do not tell anyone about it."

"Oh. OK. And I promise I will not tell anyone. It has a fabulous motor in. It really runs good."

"Yes, the motor in it is practically new and it runs at top speeds. It just does not look really good. I do not want people to know that it is a good car. I would race anybody in it. I bet I would outrun them."

"It does look bad, but boy does it run."

We went in the house so see what Alice had cooked today. She had cooked a roast with some potatoes and onions and carrots with it. She had left it on the stove. She also cooked colored butter beans.

We set it on the table and got some plates and got our food and ate.

We got to the gym at 7:00. Roxy was there waiting on us when we walked in the door.

"Hello Roxy."

"Hello Jarrod. How are you tonight?"

"I am doing good."

"I went over to the weights and they went over the do some pull ups."

I let them enjoy their time together while I did my exercises. We stayed about two hours and left, and I took him by the park to pick up his car and I went home.

I went in the house and I fixed a pot of coffee and waited for it to get ready. I poured me a cup when it finished making and went in the living room and sat down in my recliner and leaned back thinking about spending some time with my mom tomorrow. I was excited about that.

CHAPTER EIGHT

Well, there was not much that I could do right now. I turned the TV on to see if I could find something that would take my mind off the things going on in my world right now.

I found the discovery channel and I stopped it to see what was happening on Discover. They were going over the lives of lions and tigers. I love them both. They are such beautiful animals.

About the time I got settled in good the phone rang and it was Jake Simmons. I had not heard from him in a long time. He comes through town about once every three months and he always call me. We grew up together and had known each other the most of our lives. He lives in Wetumpka, Alabama. He was just coming through and would not be here long this time and wanted to come by and see me for a little while. I told him to come by and we could spend some time together.

Jake is a six foot four-inch-tall man. He is very muscular. He has dark brown hair with heavy eye brows. His eyes are dark blue. He has a great smile and is very handsome. He has a long face with a square jaw.

In a few minutes he drove up in the driveway and got out. I went to the door and asked him to come on in.

"Hello Jake. How are you doing?"

"I am doing very well Jason and, how are you?"

"Great man. It is so good to see you. It has been a while."

"Yea. I know. It is nice to see you to."

Jake went over and sat down on the couch.

"Would you like something to drink and a snack? I have carrot cake if you would like some."

"Sure, I will take some and a coke to go with it if you have any."

I went in the kitchen and got us a piece of cake and him a coke and me a barq's root beer.

"My sister made this, and it is very good."

"It is delicious Jason. What have you been doing?"

"Working mostly and playing some tennis with my nephew."

Jake was familiar that I had dreams, but he did not know much about them. I did not want to tell him much about that, so I told him just a little about it.

"What have you been up to Jake? Are you staying pretty busy?"

"I have been pretty busy. I have just come from Tuscaloosa. I have been working on one up there. I think we have it finalized now though."

"Are you staying in Sylacauga tonight or going home?"

"I was planning on staying in Sylacauga and going home tomorrow. I have just not gotten a room yet."

"There is no reason for you to go to a motel. I have plenty of room here. You can stay with me tonight."

"That sounds good Jason."

He went out to his car and got his things out and came back in the house. I showed him where the guest room was. He asked me did I mind if he took him a shower. He took a shower and came back down to the living room.

"We had a lot of fun when we were growing up Jason."

"Yes, we did Jake."

"I wanted to play football. My mom did not want me to. I sneaked around and joined the team anyway. Boy was she mad at me when she found out about it."

"I remember that. I was at your house the night she found out."

It was getting late. We were both a little tired.

I asked him what time he needed to get up. He told me that they were having a birthday party for his mom tomorrow and that he needed to leave about mid-morning sometime.

I told him that would be fine. I would be here. The only thing was that I had to be at my mom's house at 10:00 AM. We had a date and she was looking for me to be there.

Jack went on to his room and lay down on the bed.

I went to my bedroom and turned the lights out and pulled my clothes off and lay down on the bed. I was laying on my back. I was a little tired from the day and was looking forward to a good night's sleep.

I closed my eyes and lay there for a minute and then all of a sudden out of the clear blue I saw Charlotte (who had been in my dream) again. I opened my eyes immediately. I did not want to be dreaming anything right now. I just wanted to go to sleep.

I closed my eyes back again and the first thing I saw was her again. I was hoping it would just go away, but it did not. I got up and went to the bathroom and splashed my face with some cold weather. I knew that would help me from having the dreams or at least I hoped it would.

I went back and lay down on my bed again on my side to see if that would help any. I lay there for a minute and then I closed my eyes and it started all over again. Then I saw the man that had murdered her in the first dream. But I still could not tell much about him just that he was there. He was very vague, but he was there.

I opened my eyes and wondered what to do. I had given her my phone number and told her to call if she had any problems. It was already 2:00 AM. I decided that I would let her call me if she needed me. I hated to call her at this time of the night and bother her. I have these kinds of dreams all the time anyway. Maybe it was just another dream tonight. I sure did hope so.

I lay there for about thirty minutes. I closed my eyes again and saw nothing for a change. That was nice. In a little bit I began to see something, but I was not sure what it was. And then all of a sudden, she was there again. Something was not right about all this.

It was 3:45 AM by now. I decided that I needed to call Dexter and Jeff both and get them to go with me over to her house and see what was going on over there.

I called Jeff first. I told him what was going on and that I was worried that if we did not go over there that something was going to happen to her tonight. He told me he would go to her house and meet me and the Chief. I gave him the address. He told me he would call the chief.

I went to Jake's room to tell him what I was doing.

He was awake wondering what was going on.

I told him.

He told me that he would go with me.

He was already sitting on the side of the bed by then.

He got up and to put his clothes on.

I went back to my bedroom to put my clothes on. I got ready to leave. I knew they would be there

Murder of Grace

fairly quick. We left the house. At that time of the morning there was nothing on the road hardly anyway. I hurried to get there and was there about the same time as they were.

I told them that if she did not answer the door that we may just have to go ahead and break in and see what was going on. The chief knocked on the door and no one answered the door. He knocked again and still no one answered the door or made any noise in the duplex apartment. It was too quiet.

Jeff told Dexter to step back and he would open the door with his lock picks. He got them from his car and had the door open in about a minute. He pushed the door all the way open and still we heard nothing. The lights were off. We eased through the living room and neither saw nor heard anything. Jeff stuck his head in the kitchen to see if he could see anything in there and there was nothing.

We had not turned on any lights yet. We were being very careful to make sure that we did not scare anybody off if that was possible. He told us to open the bedroom door and see if there was anything in there. I was dreading this part because that is where the killer had killed her in my dream. Dexter opened the bedroom door and we saw something on the bed.

Oh my god. It can't be. I know it has not happened. I eased over to the bed and found her mutilated. I walked out of the bedroom. And turned on the lights so we could see what it all looked like. It was awful. There was blood everywhere.

Jeff found that the killer had gotten in the house through the kitchen window. The kitchen window did not have a lock on it that worked. He had torn the screen off the window and had gotten the window up without a lot of trouble and climbed through it.

It was just not right. But it had happened. I was very upset. I just went in the living room and sat down in a chair and put my head in my hands and could not hold it back anymore. I had to let something go. It was boiled up inside me. It had all come to a head by now and I was devastated by the murder. It was so gruesome.

When I looked at the body on the bed the first thing that I looked for was how he had killed her. Her throat been cut from ear to ear. The coroner said that he had gotten the jugular vein and that she died fairly instantly. Then we saw the body parts strewn over the bed where he had laid them when he was cutting her fingers off. He took plastic bags and put the body parts in them and laid them neatly on the side of the bed near the foot of the bed. Then he cut the hands off and put them in a bag and laid them on the opposite side of the bed near the foot of the bed. He had used plastic bags to cover the body parts as much as possible to keep some of the blood from getting on the bed and on the floors.

He was trying to control all the blood as much as possible. The bed was soaked through and through. He was careful to make sure that he had kept as much of the body over the bed as possible to lessen the probabilities of blood being anywhere else except in that room.

He had cut her feet off and had put them in bags and put them at the head of the bed near the side of it. There must have been some kind of message that he was trying to send us, but we did not have a clue yet as to what it was. All I knew for sure is that it was gruesome.

He had finished cutting her head off and had placed it in a bag and set up so that the face would be looking towards the foot of the bed. It was all very gross. Is was sickening to look at but of course that was a part of our jobs.

The Forensics were there gathering blood samples to see if hopefully they could find some of his blood. I was doubtful that they would find any

Murder of Grace

of his blood anywhere though because he had been so careful with everything that he had done so far it looked.

There was some blood on the window seal where he had gone back out of the house. They got samples from there hoping that maybe some of it would be his. They had made sure that they had gotten what they knew would for sure be her blood to make sure if there were any other blood samples that they would know it would be his.

Carlton Brothers (the coroner) was checking everything hoping that he could find DNA which would help to find who the murderer had been. It appeared that he had been very cautious to not leave anything behind that we could find that would give us anything to go on.

That is very hard to do but so far, we were coming up short on finding anything.

Jake came over to me and ask me was I OK. I told him that I was not OK but that I would be alright. I had to get through this. I did not have a choice but that this one had gotten a little personal. I had met the woman who had been in my dream.

I appreciated his concern. We had been friends for a life time though it seemed and that is just the way we did things when we were with each other.

There was blood everywhere in the bedroom. He had been very careful to make sure that he did not get any blood in the rest of the house. He had to have taken trash bags and pulled them over his shoes when he left the bedroom to keep from getting blood anywhere else in the house.

The thing that I was trying to stop from happening had happened. I had done everything that I could think of to do to keep it from happening and it seemed to have done no good.

Catherine and I knew she had left Tuscaloosa to get away from a boyfriend that had been abusive to her. She said it was the only way that she could get away from him. So she came to Sylacauga. I wondered if it could have been him that was doing the killing.

All the departments had been notified. I was on top of things trying to figure out what to do next. I was confused at the moment. I was so upset. I had to go outside and just take a deep breath and get my act back together. It was hard right now. I was sick at my stomach over the dream and in spite of everything that I tried to do to stop it, it still happened.

The chief had already got several of his men there and they had cordoned the place off. It was ready for the investigation to start. They were all taking pictures of the incident. It was very gruesome, but it was things that we had to do.

I told Jeff and Dexter that I would try to find out who her ex was and maybe we could question him and see if he had anything to do with it. Then I could try to find out who some of her friends were from Tuscaloosa. That would at least be a good start on trying to find out something about her.

All we knew was that she was from Tuscaloosa before she came to Sylacauga. Maybe she had moved to Tuscaloosa from somewhere else to escape a stalker. The only way to find out was to start in Tuscaloosa and see what I could find out.

They were all going to work on the case around the Sylacauga area to see what they could find out about her. Maybe she had found a couple of good friends that she shared some thought with. We sure hoped so.

It was 7:00 AM. The morning was going by fast now. They had gotten the body from the house and taken it to the funeral home. There were still some things that Carlton had to get worked out before they could do anything with it.

I told Jeff I needed to go home and get ready to go over to my mom's house. I had to go and see her

I promised her I would be there. Jake was supposed to leave by about 9:00 this morning. I needed to go so that he could get his things and be able to get on the road. It was Saturday morning, and this was going to be a long day unfortunately. I had been counting on just taking it easy, but it does not look like is going to happen. There was not a whole lot right I could do accept just wait till I could get things together.

I got Jake and we left the crime scene and headed toward the house. I decided to go by The Grill and Eggs Breakfast Bar and get something to eat. Jake agreed with that. I was hoping I was going to be able to eat after that scene. It was one of the worst I had ever seen.

We went in sat down and ordered our breakfast. I had ham and eggs and grits with toast and Jake ordered sausage, eggs, and grits with toast. We drank some coffee while we were waiting on our meals to arrive.

"What are you going to do now Jason?" he asked me

"I don't know for sure, but I think I am going to Tuscaloosa and see if I can find her ex and see what I can find out. Maybe I can find a couple of friends of hers that will be able to help us out a little. I am going to see if I can get any leads from that direction." I told him.

"Well, you know how to get in touch with me. If you need me call me and I will come and help anyway I can. Or if you find any leads in my direction let me know and I will check them out."

"I will do that Jake if I see any way you can help."

Our breakfast made it to the table and we ate. It was delicious. It was getting late and we had to get on the road towards my house, so Jake could get on the road. He had a very important engagement that he had to get to.

We got to my house and went in and he went up to the bedroom and got his things. It was already about 9:00 that morning. He told me he would go ahead and get on the road towards home unless I needed him for something before he left. I told him I would be OK. It is not easy, but I have to go to moms in a few minutes anyway.

Jake got in his car and left towards Wetumpka.

I changed into some relaxing clothes.

I got in my car and headed out towards my mom's house.

I got there a little earlier than planned but that was fine. It was home anyway. Mom was busy doing some little things in her flowers. She always had some beautiful ones. Always something a little different. She knew how to grow the most beautiful roses in the world. I think she had every color in the rainbow.

We went in the kitchen and sat down at the table with something to drink. She kept Barq's root there for me when I was there. That is what I had, and she had a glass of lemonade. We were just talking about the day and what it might be like.

I ask her did she remember the dream I had told her I had had. She did. I told her about Charlotte and how that she was the one in my dream. She was devastated that it had happened again. She told me I needed to quit having them kind of dreams. I told her I wish I could quit having them.

She and dad were changing the will some and that was what she wanted to talk with me about. Over the years dad had bought several homes and pieces of land around the area. They wanted to know what I wanted when something ever happened to them. I told mom all I wanted was them. I never did care what I got if I got anything when they were gone.

Murder of Grace

I told her since she was asking that they could just leave me this house. It was the biggest and I was not married yet and I might get married and have a dozen kids one day. She laughed at me for that one.

I told her to do whatever she and dad thought would be the best things to do. She told me that she would like for me to tell them what I really wanted. I told her I would have to think about it and decide what I might would like to have. But it really did not matter to me anyway.

I spent the rest of the morning with her just enjoying being with her. I told her I had some things that I had to do. I had to make arrangements for some place to stay in Tuscaloosa a few days probably. I told her my plans on trying to find some leads concerning Charlotte in Tuscaloosa since that is where she came from when she moved to Sylacauga a few months ago.

"See you later mom. I hate to leave but I do need to go. I have just been so busy lately with work and all. I will come soon and spend the day with you." I told her.

"You have been saying that for a while." She said.

"I know. I know. But I will. I mean it. I will do it soon. That is a guarantee." I told her.

"You just be careful in Tuscaloosa and stay out of trouble. We worry about you a lot. It would have been easier if you had not chosen such dangerous work." She told me.

"Well, I will, and I have got to go for now." I told her.

"OK. Will see you soon I hope." She said.

I went to my car and waved by and left.

I went back by the crime scene to see if anyone was still there. Everyone had left accept they did have a guard posted there for right now. I walked around for a little bit and was checking things out. I asked him would it be ok if I went inside. He let me go. He knew me. I went back in the bedroom to see if I could find anything that maybe we had missed that morning.

I walked around in the house just looking around. It appeared that he had been very cautious in everything. He wore latex gloves to handle things in the house that he had used. He had not left any finger prints that we could find on anything, anywhere. He knew what he was doing. He covered it very good.

I was hoping to find anything that would give us some clue as to who he might me. I did not find anything that looked suspicious I keep looking. I decided to look under the bed and see if there was anything there. I did not see a shred of evidence of any kind that would do us any good.

I looked around in the kitchen to see if there was anything that had been missed. I was being very careful to not disturb anything. The investigation was still in progress. I did not find anything.

I left the crime scene and went on towards my house. I wanted to go and see if I could rest a little and get some arrangements made for sleeping and all in Tuscaloosa.

I got home and got out of my car and went in the house and made me a pot of coffee. I needed some about right now. When it got finished making I made me a cup and took it in the living room and set down in my recliner to make some phone calls. I had several I needed to make.

I got my phone book and started looking for hotels in Tuscaloosa. I called around and I finally made some reservations at the Wingate by Wyndham at 1918 Skyland Blvd E. They were very nice and pleasant.

CHAPTER NINE

I got me another cup of coffee and sat down in my recliner to drink it. I needed somebody to talk with. I had had a bad night and bad day. I was still really upset over the murder.

I picked up the phone and called Rita.

"Hello Jason. What are you doing?" She said when she answered the phone on one ring.

"I am just sitting here drinking some coffee and talking to your right now." I told her.

"I knew you were going to call Jason."

"How did you know Rita?"

"I just sensed that you were. Something is wrong Jason. You needed someone to talk with."

"Are you ready to hear the bad news?"

"I was afraid of that. I had that feeling that it was going to be bad."

"It happened Rita. He did it. He killed her. Last night."

"Do you guys have any idea who it might be?"

"No we have no idea yet."

"How about fingerprints Jason?"

"It looks like he wore gloves. Probably plastic gloves so that there would be no fingerprints."

"Sounds like he has done this before." She said.

"Whoever he is, he is good."

"Maybe they will find something Jason. Anything will help."

"I went back by the crime scene and did some checking and I could not find anything."

"That is no good Jason."

"That means that he is probably going to do it again."

"Yea. Most likely unless you can get something on him."

"Did you have a good day Rita?'

"I did Jason. I am sorry for the awful news you have to deal with."

"I just needed someone to talk with for a little bit."

"I am glad you called Jason."

"I will let you go for now. I will talk with you soon."

I got me another cup of coffee. I decided that I wanted to talk with Catherine for a little bit. She is my best friend around here.

"Hello."

"Hello Catherine. This is Jason."

"What are you up to Jason?"

"Just wanted to see if you had heard the news about Charlotte."

"Yes, Jason I have heard it. I was not expecting it right now."

"I knew it was coming soon Catherine, but I did not expect it last night."

"I was hoping that we could get her some protection before anything happened to her but that did not work out."

"I am going to Tuscaloosa and find her ex-boyfriend and see what I can find out from him."

"That is good Jason. Maybe he will have something that will help to get a lead on the killer."

"I hope he can tell me something that will help."

"Someone is at the door Jason. I need to let you go and answer it."

"OK. I will talk with you later."

I went in the kitchen and got me another cup of coffee and cut me a big piece of that carrot cake that my sister had sent to me. I sat down at the table and ate it.

I called Jeff to see if he knew anything yet.

"Hello Jason."

"Hello Jeff. Do you know anything yet?"

"I talked with one of her neighbors Jason."

"Did they know anything?"

"She told me that she had seen a late model F150 truck in her yard. She said the man looked to be about six foot three inches tall. She said she was guessing at his height, but he was tall. She said it was a dark maroon truck. She said no one answered the door and he left."

"That is better than nothing."

"Yea. Maybe it will get us somewhere Jason."

Jeff told me they were running F150 trucks in the area trying to narrow it down. He said he was hoping to find something related to the description of the truck. He said they would check it out if they found anything.

That is the type truck that Jim Sax has and was the identical description of him. I knew there is no way that it could be him. I hope they do not bother him. Everybody knew him and knew that he had never been in any trouble.

"I should call Dexter and see if he has anything yet."

"That probably would be OK Jason if that would make you feel better."

"Dexter probably does not know anything else right now or he would have contacted you and let you know. I think I will wait until I hear from him."

"Yes, that is about the size of it Jason. I am sure he does not know anything else yet."

"I have arrangements made to go to Tuscaloosa to see if I can locate her ex-boyfriend. Maybe he knows something, or he could be involved in it or have done it himself." I told him.

"That is good Jason. We need to get a lid on this just as quickly as possible."

"I will let you go Jeff. Just wanted to check in with you. Thanks for listening."

"Anytime Jason. You know you can call me."

I made a fresh pot of coffee. I poured me a cup and went back in the living room and sat down in my recliner and turned on the TV to the discovery channel. I kicked my foot rest up and leaned back a little and was drinking my coffee.

The phone rang. I was concentrating. It scared me. I grabbed it and answered it.

"Hello. Jason Caffrey speaking." Staring at the ceiling wishing the phone had not rang right now.

"I am coming to get you." With a muffled voice.

"You better be good then."

"I have been watching you for a long time. You will be easy to get when I get ready to."

"When are you planning on getting me?"

"Anytime now. I am ready." And they hung up.

I did not have any idea who the caller was. I was beginning to wonder if it was the person that has been following me in that 1957 Chevrolet. Maybe I need to talk with the Coosa County sheriff and see if they can find out anything about him. I will do that Monday.

Jim had been home about three days when Charlotte got murdered. He and Jane were just spending some time together. They were very busy people most of the time.

The news was fixing to come on. I went and got me another cup of coffee and sat down to see what they reported on the crime scene. They went over it in detail. They gave a description of the truck the neighbor had seen and a description of the man that she had seen at Charlotte's front door.

I thought that was a great idea. But then I wondered if it were so great an idea. It would give

Murder of Grace

the murderer time to hide and get away for a while if he saw it. I really did not think that they would bother Jim if they traced the truck back to him. They all knew him and knew that he was a very honorable citizen.

It was getting late. I turned out all the lights and locked the doors and went to my bedroom. I turned the covers back and lay down on my bed. I was lying on my back staring at the ceiling hoping that I was going to get a good night's sleep. I was wore out. I needed some good rest.

I closed my eyes and in just a short time I dozed off. I was not fully asleep. I started seeing visions of things that started running together. I tried to open my eyes and I could not. They were beginning to become plainer as I saw them. It was a beautiful tall slender woman with shiny red hair down to her waist. She was the epitome of beauty. Medium dark blue eyes with a long chin. She had long arms and long fingers. A beautiful woman in my dream. I could enjoy this.

Then I saw that she was in her living room. She was standing by the window looking out. She had on blue jeans and a pull over top. The top was red. In a little bit she heard a noise in the house and was looking to see where it came from. It sounded like a window had been pushed up. It scared her, and she tip toed towards the kitchen to see what was going on.

When she got near the door she saw a man standing there and she screamed. He was all blurred out. I could not recognize him at all. I had no clue as to what he looked like. I only saw the image of him. He ran toward her and grabbed her and told her to shut up. She screamed again. He had his blade in his hands ready to kill her with. He did not give her another chance to do anything. He just cut her throat and he laid her body on the table in the kitchen. He began his dissection of the body just as he had the last one.

He carved her up and put her body parts in the same order that he had the last time. But they were on the floor this time. The table was not large enough to hold them. He sat her head up on her body facing towards the feet just as he did the last one.

I woke up. Oh my God. What is happening? Another one of those awful murders is fixing to take place and I bet he will not take much time in between my dream and the murder this time. I knew that it was going to happen. It was about 1:00 AM. I got up and went to the bathroom to take me a long hot shower.

I turned the water on and got under the shower. I got the soap and wash wrag and I bathed my body with soap and washed it off. All I could see was blood. I washed again. It just did not seem to want to come off. I scrubbed and eventually it all came clear. I got out of the shower and dried off.

I needed someone to talk with. It was too early in the morning to call somebody. I could call mom, but I just did not want to wake her up.

I went in the kitchen and made me another pot of coffee. I did not want to close my eyes right now. I wanted to call Rita. I could not stand it any longer. I poured me a cup of coffee and went in the living room and picked up the phone and called Rita.

"Hello Jason."

She always knows that it was me.

"Hello Rita. Sorry to call you at this hour of the night."

"That is OK Jason. You have had another one of those dreams, haven't you?"

"Yes, and it was awful. He is fixing to murder again."

"Maybe you guys will catch him, and he will not get to."

"We will not get him. We do not have enough to go on."

"Are you OK Jason?"

"No. Rita I am not OK. I am really upset. These dreams are getting to me lately. They have gotten much worse."

"I wish there was something I could do Jason."

"Just being my friend Rita means a lot. At least I have someone that I can talk with that understands."

"Are you going to be OK Jason?"

"I will get it together. It is hard, but I will be fine."

"I hope so. It upsets me when you have these dreams. You get so upset and there is nothing I can do."

"I guess I need to let you go Rita. It is so early in the morning. Maybe you can get some sleep now."

"OK Jason. You take care and if you need me call me OK."

"OK I will. Bye for now. Talk with you soon."

"Bye Jason."

I leaned back in my recliner and closed my eyes for a minute and went to sleep. All of a sudden, I heard a strange noise and it scared me. I almost jumped out of my chair. I looked at the clock and it was 8:00. It was the phone ringing.

"Hello. Jason Caffrey speaking."

"Hello Jason. This is Jeff. We have located the owner of a truck with the description that Sarah Davis gave us. We know where the person lives. We are going to check them out early this morning and see what they know."

"Can you tell me who it is Jeff?"

"I would rather not right now Jason until after we check them out."

"OK. That will be alright. But when you find them please let me know who it is."

"OK Jason. I will let you know. I need to go for now. I will talk with you later."

"Thanks for calling Jeff."

It was 11:00 AM. I was wore out. I just wanted some rest. The phone rang.

"Hello Jason Caffrey, speaking."

"Hello Jason, this is Jane." Timidly.

"Hello Jane. What is wrong?"

"Jason, they have come and arrested Jim for the murder of that woman last night."

"They did what?"

"Arrested Jim. I did not know who else to call. I hope you do not mind."

"Of course, I do not mind. They took him to jail?"

"On suspicion of murder I do not know what to do."

"Don't worry about it Jane. I will take care of it."

"I can't help but worry Jason, but I trust you."

"Let me go for now. I will talk with you after I see him."

"OK Jason. Bye."

She was very upset, and she was crying. I did my best to calm her down.

I got dressed to leave the house. I went straight to the police station to talk with Jim to try and comfort him. I asked them to let me go back and see him. They escorted me to his cell. I went in the cell with him.

"Hello Jim. Sorry to see you like this."

"Hell, Jason I have never as much as had a speeding ticket. I have a perfect record. And they come and arrest me for the suspicion of murder. What are they thinking?"

"I do not have a clue what is going on but I know that you did not do it."

"I am glad you believe in me Jason. I need somebody to right now. Dexter knows me, and he knows I would not have done that, but he arrested me anyway."

"I will start working on it today. We will have you out of here by tomorrow some way or the other. If we have to have money for bail, we will get it some way or the other. Just do not worry about it. I know a few people who will help us out here."

"Thank you very much Jason. I really appreciate this. I will repay you some way."

"You do not have to Jim. Just forget it and I will see you tomorrow."

My weekend had fallen apart. I was in disarray right now. I did not know what direction to go. I was confused. It was bogging me down. I had a lot on my plate. I knew one thing for sure. I needed to counsel my trip to Tuscaloosa and go later after I got this mess with Jim straightened out.

I went home to mull it all over and just try to figure what to do and who to talk with first. I knew I needed to talk with an attorney for sure. I had not eaten a bite of anything yet. I was hungry. I called pizza hut and ordered me some pizza.

I sat down with my barq's root beer and waited for my pizza to get there and watched a little TV. The pizza arrived. I ate and it was delicious. It was Sunday, but I needed to talk with Catherine. I did not want to wait till Monday morning.

"Hello Jason. What are you doing?"

"I have something I really need to talk with you about Catherine. They have arrested a very good friend of mine. We have been friends for a long time. They say they think he could be the one that committed the murder. There is no way that he did it."

"Why did they arrest him? What evidence did they have on him to think that he might have done it?" She asked me.

"They do not have anything really except for the description of the truck and the man that this

Sarah Davis saw at about 6:00 PM knocking on her door."

"That is very weak evidence Jason. I would think they need a little more to go on than that before they could arrest him." She said.

"I think they just want to get it under the hat so that people will not be so scared." I told her.

She told me that she would be glad to talk with him and represent him. She told me that if I would meet her at the jail Monday morning that we could talk with him together. I told her I would be glad to be there. She told me to meet her at 8:00. She agreed to represent him on my knowledge because we had been friends for a while now.

Then I told her about my dream Saturday night. She asked me did I think that this one was going to happen also. I told her that it was going to happen and that he would not take as much time to get to this one as he did the last one. She was amazed that things had turned so sour in our area. I was shocked myself. We talked for a few minutes and it was time for us to say bye. I told her I would see her early tomorrow morning.

All I wanted to do for the rest of the day was just to sit down in my recliner and get some sleep. I needed it bad. I hoped that I would be able to. I was sitting there and got to thinking about the person in the 1957 red Chevrolet that had been watching me. I had decided that the person that was making those strange phone calls was the person that drove the 1957 Chevrolet. It looked like that I might not get a chance to see the Sheriff of Coosa County Monday, but I would just as soon as I had a chance.

I am thinking that the person doing the murdering in our little city is the very person that is making the phone calls that drives that 1957 Chevrolet. How do they know me and why are they bothering me? Who Knows? I sure to hell don't know.

Murder of Grace

It was about 3:00 PM. I went out on the porch and sat down on my swing to watch the birds. I was just sitting there relaxing and Dexter pulled up in my yard. He got out of the car and asked me was it OK for him to come over and sit with me for a little bit. Fine, I said.

He came on the porch and sat down in the chair near the swing.

"What are you up to Jason?"

"I have been busy Dexter."

"What you been doing?"

"I went to the jail and talked with Jim."

"Why did you want to bother with that right now Jason?"

"I know that he did not do it and I know that we will have him out by tomorrow sometime one way or the other."

"You might need to wait Jason. We have enough on him for suspicion of murder."

"You really did not have enough on him to even arrest him Dexter, but you did."

"I think you need to cool down some Jason."

"I know that Jim did not commit the murder."

"How do you know that for sure Jason?"

"I have known him all my life. I know that he would not have done it. I just know Dexter."

"I hope you are not making a mistake Jason."

"I am not making a mistake."

"I need to go Jason. I have some things I need to do."

"I will see you tomorrow Dexter. Count on it."

I went back in the house to get me a sandwich. I just plain did not want to cook. I had some ham and cheese in the refrigerator. I made me a ham and cheese sandwich and got my plain chips and sat down at the table with a root beer and ate.

I needed to talk with Susan Hendricks.

"Hello Jason. How are you?" she asked.

"I am fine I guess considering everything. We have not talked in a while and I just wanted to say hello to you and see what you have been up to lately."

"I have been busy working on some cases that have piled up on my desk and they expect me to do them all right now." She told me.

I told her about the woman in my first dream having been murdered. Then I told her about them arresting Jim for the murder.

"Is there anything I can do Jason?"

"Not right now Susan but I appreciate it."

"Well if there is anything just let me know."

"I have a very good attorney friend here in Sylacauga that is going to represent Jim. We are going to talk with him in the morning and do everything we can to get him out of jail tomorrow." I told her.

"Do you think you can get him out at least on bail?" She asked me.

"That should not be a problem. Just how much bail they will want is the problem. Jim does not have much money to put on things like that. He has a family and it takes most of what he makes to take care of the family." I told her.

"Don't worry about it Jason it will all work out in the end." She said.

"I will just be glad when it does."

"It will Jason. I don't have a doubt about it."

"I just wanted to call you and say hello Susan. I guess I will say bye for now."

"Bye Jason."

I called Tuscaloosa and canceled my reservation for the hotel while I had it on my mind. It was dark, and I went back out on the porch just to sit in my swing and enjoy the full moon tonight and watch the stars. That was always nice to watch the things in the life circle of amazement. It always intrigued my mind thinking about how it all got there in such beauty.

I heard the phone ring. I had talked to everybody I needed to talk with I thought.

"Hello, Jason Caffrey, speaking."

"Hello Jason. What are you doing?"

"I was sitting on the porch mom and watching the moon and the starts and enjoying the amazement of creation."

"That is nice. Why have you not called me today?"

I explained to her what my day had been like and she understood.

"I have just been busy mom."

"I just wanted to see that you were OK. I will let you go for now and let you rest. Call me tomorrow."

"I will for sure. Talk to you later."

It was getting late by now and I decided that I would go and lay down and try to get some sleep tonight. Maybe I would be able to since I had had very little in the last three days.

CHAPTER TEN

I turned out all the lights in the house and went to the bedroom to lay down and try and get some sleep. I was lying on the bed when my phone rang.

"Hello." Angrily.

"I am sorry. I have the wrong number." In that muffled voice again.

"Quit calling me." I said. Pissed off.

I did not have enough going on, yet I suppose. Somebody knew me that is for sure that wanted to harass me some way or other. They were doing a pretty good job of it so far.

I closed my eyes and was almost asleep when I saw the woman in my second dream again. I saw the murderer again with a little more vision of him than before but not enough to recognize him if I saw him. These dreams are getting old. But they have been getting old for years. I was tired of it.

The only thing is I had the dreams and I knew that something awful was going to happen. I never could do anything to be able to stop it. That is what really pissed me off most of all. It would not be so bad to have the dreams if I could only just be able to stop the murders from happening. Maybe it would change with this dream.

I needed some sleep. So, I closed my eyes again. I was worn out. I needed some sleep. So far it was good. I was not seeing anything. In a few minutes I was gone.

Murder of Grace

All of a sudden, I heard that strange noise in my room again. I jumped and realized that it was just my alarm clock going off. I turned it off. It was Monday morning. It was 5:00 time to get my jogging shorts on and hit the road with Jane. I always looked forward to running with her.

I walked out the door and she was standing next to my drive waiting on me to come out.

"Good morning Jason."

"Hello Jane and you are all spry and ready to go I see."

"Always Jason."

We took off on our five-mile run this morning. We were running along when the big brown boxer came out to meet us about a mile from the house. We took the time and patted him on the head and went on our way. He was always friendly.

"Did you have a good weekend Jason?"

"I was very busy this weekend. I am sure you saw the news on the woman that got murdered Saturday night."

"Yes, I saw that. That was awful."

"They arrested one of my best friends for the murder and he did not do it."

"That is no good Jason. I am sorry to hear that."

"It has been a very busy one for me this weekend."

We finished our five-mile run and was back at our homes.

"I will see you later Jane. Have a good day."

"See you Wednesday Jason. Bye."

I went in the house and put me on a pot of coffee and went and took me a good shower and got ready to go to work. I put on my new Levi's and bright blue shirt my mom had bought me about two weeks ago.

I went and poured me a cup of coffee and fixed me a bowl of corn flakes with a banana in them. I sat down at the table in the breakfast nook and ate my breakfast. I finished my coffee and it was about time to leave the house to meet Catherine at the Jail.

When I got there, she had just pulled up. It was 8:00 already. We went inside, and she told them that she was Jim Sax's attorney and that we would like to talk with him. They took us to an interview room and went and brought Jim in. He came in the door and was surprised to see Catherine. He knew who she was just did not really know her.

"Hello Mr. Sax. I am Catherine McCarthy"

"It is a pleasure to meet you. Just call me Jim please."

"OK. Just call me Catherine."

"I am going to represent you Jim and see if we can get you out of this mess."

"I don't have the money for an attorney. I will have to use a court appointed attorney."

"Forget that. I am going to represent you. Don't worry about the money."

"Just sit back Jim for a minute and listen. If there is any money needed it will be there for whatever reason." I told him.

I knew that Catherine took charity cases on occasions when she was confident that the person she was representing was innocent and that they could not afford it any other way.

"Where were you the night of the murder being Saturday night?"

"I was out shopping around just looking and doing nothing in particular."

"Was you alone or was someone with you?"

"I was alone. I was just trying to kill some time while my wife was busy at her sister's house.

"I hate to be so forthright Jim, but I have to ask this. Did you kill Charlotte Taylor?"

"Excuse my French, but hell no I did not kill her. I could not ever have done anything like that. I have a perfect record with not even a parking ticket on my record." He told her."

"You have no alibi of your whereabouts that night."

"No. I was by myself. Somebody just has to believe me."

"I do Jim. We just have to prove it now."

"I did not do it that should be proof enough."

"I am taking this case on a gut feeling Jim. I am confident that you did not do it. I know we can get you out of this.

"But I already told you I do not have any money to pay an attorney with."

"You will have a hearing set up soon. I will be there to represent you. If anyone ask you who your attorney is, you tell them Catherine McCarthy."

"Yes mam. I will, and I thank you very much."

"We will talk to you soon Jim."

The hearing was set up for the afternoon. We had to go to Talladega for that. Catherine did not have any cases today. It was set for 3:00 pm. I told her I would meet her there. I did not have to be there, but I was going to be. Jim was a best friend.

We left the jail. She went to her law office and I went to the city to talk with Dexter. I got there, and he was in his office. I ask the secretary if I could see him. She told me to go on in that he was not busy right now. I walked in the door.

"Well, hello Dexter."

"Hello Jason. What are you up to?"

"I just thought I could come and talk with you for a bit. Do you have anything new on the crime yet?"

"We do not have anything new. We are looking for the murder weapon. We are going to search Jim Sax's place and see if we can find it there." He told me.

"Jim did not do it Dexter. I believe that you really know that, and you are just being stubborn.

You want it settled so that people will not be so scared anymore. It was a gruesome murder."

"Yes, Jason we need to get it settled as soon as possible and this is a possibility and a good one at that." He told me.

"Well, I talked with Catherine yesterday and we came over this morning to the jail and talked with Jim. She is going to represent him because she does not believe that he did it and she is taking it on a gut feeling. She is having a hard time believing that he did it." I told him.

"That is good Jason, but she needs to be sure before she takes the case. There is a very good possibility that he did it." He told me.

"NO, he did not do it and I know that without a doubt. The hearing is today at 3:00. She and I will be there for the hearing and get him off on bail someway." I told him.

"OK, Jason if that is what you think you need to do but you need to be careful. You do not want to set a murderer free." He told me.

"You do not know what you are talking about Dexter and I have known you a long time." I told him.

I just wanted to go somewhere and hide in a hole and hope that when I came out all this would just go away. I doubted that it would. I knew that it was all real and that I would have to deal with it.

I went to the office and got my stack of folders down and started looking at them, but I just could not concentrate on them today. Too much had happened. I was thinking about the murder that had just taken place and the second dream that I had just had recently. Then I had the court case on my mind concerning Jim.

The more I thought about that Dexter had arrested Jim for the suspicion of murder the more pissed I got. I could not wrap my head around the

Murder of Grace

fact that he had arrested him on suspicion with so little evidence to go on.

I decided that I might better go to the bank and transfer some money in case his bail was set high. Whoever knows what they will do in court? I was going to give it to him because I knew that he did not deserve to be in jail. He had a wife and kids. They needed him. She did not work. She just stayed home and took care of the kids and him. So I went and transferred $50,000 just in case I needed it.

It was getting about time to head out toward Talladega to be there in time for the hearing. I rode over to Catherine's office and she had not left yet but was getting ready to go. I asked her did she want to ride together. "Sure, that will be good Jason." Jane (his wife) had already gone to Talladega. She left a little early. She was really upset. She did not know what they would do about anything. She was so scared they were not going to let him out on bail. She was worried about the bail money. She did not have any.

We left and headed out towards Talladega. We got there about 2:30. We got in the court house and Jane was there waiting. She looked so upset. We went over, and Catherine hugged her and told her it would be OK. I stayed with her and Catherine went and took her place with Jim. He looked relieved to see her. I told her to not worry about anything because no matter what happens we already had it worked out.

It was time for the hearing to start. Catherine had already taken her place with Jim and was waiting for the Judge. The court session was called to order.

Catherine took her stand and explained how that Jim had an absolutely clean record. He did not even have as much as a parking ticket against him. She explained that all they had to convict him on was circumstantial evidence to begin with. She showed how that they really did not have any proof that he had committed the crime. She told the judge that there was no way that Mr. Sax deserved to be behind bars with so little evidence against him in the first place. She explained that they needed to dig a little deeper and come up with some real proof that he had committed the murder. The state was objecting the whole time, but the judge was over ruling him every time. Catherine had that smile that she used especially in the court room. Everybody noticed it. The judges loved her. She finally rested her case.

The state really wanted to be very harsh. They presented their case and said that there was no way that he had not committed the crime and that he needed to be in jail.

The state took their stand to not allow him to be released on bail. They explained that he would be a flight risk and that he needed to remain in jail until the case was solved in totality. Catherine just stood her ground until it was time for her to speak.

She told the judge that since all they had was circumstantial evidence to begin with and that they did not have any real proof that he committed the murder that they had no right to hold him at all.

It was time for the judge to make his decisions on whether to allow bail. He ruled in the favor of bail at $100,000. He allowed that Jim could continuing working his job as he always did unless that became a problem. He adjourned the court. They took Jim to the Talladega County jail. We met with Jane and told her to just sit tight and do not worry about anything. We still had time to make it to the bank and get the $10,000 money order that we would need to pay the bond with. She said there was no way she had that kind of money.

I told her to forget it and don't worry about it I was going to help them out. She said there would be no way that they could pay it back. I told her to pay

Murder of Grace

me back a $1.00 a week if that was all they could do but I was going to pay the bail. I told her we would have him out within the hour.

We went to the bank and I bought a money and took it back to the bail bond woman and gave it to her and she got the paper work together and we took it to the jail and he was released within the hour.

"We got that part cleared up. Now it is time to eat something." I told them.

"We can eat at Ryan's." If that is OK with Jim and Jane here." Catherine said.

"We can't afford to eat out Jason." Jim said.

"It is on me today Jim. Meet us at Ryan's."

We got to Ryan's and went in. We all got the buffet. It is always good. We sat down to eat our meal.

"Jason I will never be able to pay you back $10,000." Jim said.

"Don't worry about it. You are not going to run and it will all be clear soon. You did not do it."

"No I am not going to run that is for sure. I did not do anything."

"We got through this first phase Jim and we will get through the rest of it. It was pretty obvious that the state does not have much to go on. They had nothing to present in court today." Catherine told him.

"I hope I get out of it."

"Don't worry about it Jim. In the end you will have nothing on your record. I know what I am talking about. Trust me." I told him.

"I can't keep from worrying Jason. I have not done anything."

We finished our meal and left to go home. Sylacauga was not that far away.

I told Catherine on the way home that Jim would be exonerated because I knew another murder was fixing to happen just like that one. We made it back to Sylacauga and went by her office, so I could pick up my car. I told her I would see her tomorrow. She agreed, and we left towards our homes.

I decided that I needed to go over and talk with Jim a little bit because I knew that he was worried about the money and that he would never be able to pay me back for that.

He lived on the north side of town. I rode over to his house. They had not been home long when I got there. He invited me in to have something to drink. I told him I would take some tea if they had any. He got me a glass of tea and himself a coke and told me to come to the porch and sit.

We went out on the porch and sat down in some nice wood chairs that he had bought not too long ago. They were comfortable. He started trying to explain to me that he would never have the money to pay me back.

I told him that if he never had the money to give me back that it would be fine. I had a little bit of money and I could help him out of a situation that he had no control over. It was unfair to him and that he did not deserve that and that is why I did what I did.

He wanted to do something to repay me some way. I told him that life has it ways of solving thing in the end. You were in a need and I helped you out because I knew that you could do it no other way. It will come back to me somewhere. I will have a need of some kind and need help some way somewhere in life and someone will be there for me also. That is how I see things in life. It pays to help when you can. I could, and I did. I would not have done that for just anybody, but I knew that you deserved the help at the time.

Just go about your life now as always and live it to the fullest and do not let this matter worry you down.

Murder of Grace

I have never told you much about my dreams. You know that I have them, but we never talk about them. I will tell you a little bit. Maybe this will help you out. I had another one last night. Another woman is going to be killed. So, just make sure that you have someone that can vouch for your whereabouts until after we find this person committing these murderers.

You mean you had a dream of a woman being murdered and you know that it is going to happen. Yes, I did. And yes, I know that it is going to happen. The one that you were accused of killing I dreamed about that one happening, and it did. I have had these kinds of dreams for a long time and they always come true. Stay close with someone that can prove where you have been and what you are doing so that you will not be picked up for number again. They will be watching you unfortunately, but they will not be anywhere near the scene when it happens the next time and it is going to happen. It will be soon to.

Well, Jason I hope you are wrong, but you probably are not. I will just take your word for it. You know I don't really believe in those kinds of things much anyway, but I have no reason not to either. I will just wait and see what happens.

I told him I understood that he did not believe in them much and that it was OK with me. It will not affect our friendship anyway and that is all that mattered.

"There are only a few people that know about them and I want to keep it that way so just don't tell anyone else about me telling you about my dreams.

"I will keep my mouth shut. I would never put a friend like you in any kind of danger. You have been a life saver for me and I just still do not know how to thank you for it."

"Well Jim it is getting late and I guess I need to go towards the house."

"OK Jason. I will see you later. Thank you for everything."

"You are very welcome Jim and I will see you soon."

We shook hands and I left and went home. I got to the house and parked my car and went on the porch and sat down in my swing.

While I was sitting there that 1957 red Chevrolet went by the house. For some reason I never can get the tag number on that car. Maybe it is not anyone following me, but they seem to always be there when I am. That is why I think they are following me for some reason.

I had a few minutes before I had to leave and go over to the warehouse. I made me a pot of coffee and poured me a cup and went in the living room and sat down in my recliner. About the time I got set down good the phone rang.

"Hello. Jason Caffrey speaking."

"Hello, I am going to still get you. I am just waiting." With the muffled voice.

I was pissed. I hung the phone up. And keep drinking my coffee and eating my cheese curls. The phone rang again.

"Hello." Very pissed.

"What are you doing? It is me again."

"None of your business quite frankly." And hung the phone up.

I decided that it was time to put a tap on my phone. I would do that tomorrow when I had the time to do it. I got ready and left the house and headed toward the warehouses. I got there, and I was right. I could get in the building that they were working in from the back. I got inside and found me a place to hide that no one could see me and waited.

In a few minutes I heard them at the door. They got it open and came in. They came over to where they were working with their drugs. I watched them, and I saw that they had them a meth lab there.

There was surely not anything that I could do tonight. But now I knew what was going on.

They finished their night and left. I gave them plenty of time to get gone and I left the warehouse got my car and went home. I would have to call Jeff in the morning and let him know what is going on at the warehouses.

It was already about 10:00 PM. I turned out all the lights in the house and locked the doors and went to the bedroom and pulled my clothes off and lay down on my bed. I was laying on my back and staring at the ceiling. I did not want to close my eyes. I wished that I could just go to sleep with them open and maybe I would not have any dreams.

In a few minutes I turned over on my side and shut my eyes hoping to go to sleep. I was almost asleep when I saw the woman with the long red hair. Oh shit, I thought. I am having another dream. I could not get her out of my mind. She was there. Something was fixing to happen.

I opened my eyes and got up and went to the bathroom and splashed my face with cold water hoping that would help me to not dream. It never had helped in the past. I do not know how I thought it might help now but I had to try it anyway.

I dried my face off with a face towel and walked into the kitchen and got me a Barq's root beer and the cheese curls I was eating from earlier and took them to the bedroom and sat down on the side of the bed. There was so much going on I was not sure what to think first. But right now, I was thinking about the girl with the long red hair that was fixing to be murdered.

I wanted to do something about it but there was nothing I could do. It did not work the last time. I did not feel that I had time to get things together to stop it from happening.

I finally lay back down on the bed and was able to go to sleep. I woke up Tuesday morning when the clock went off at 5:00. Boy I did not feel like running this morning, but I needed to take my run. I put on my jogging shorts and hit the road. I got back to the house and made me a pot of coffee. I went and took a shower and shaved and dressed for work.

I made me a bowl of corn flakes with a banana in them and ate it while I was waiting for Alice to get there.

I finished eating and poured me a cup of coffee and went in the living room and turned the TV on to watch a little morning news. The doorbell rang.

I opened the door.

"Good morning Jason." Alice said with a big smile as always.

"Good morning Alice. It is good to see you this morning."

"I want to thank you for helping my nephew out the other day. He told you took him home."

"Jeremy. Yea. He told me that his aunt worked for me."

"He seemed like a nice boy.

"He is Jason. They just do not have much. He is trying to find him something to do to earn a little money."

"Maybe he will get something soon Alice."

I decided that I would wait till the boys got there that morning and talk with them a minute.

I poured me another cup of coffee while Alice went about her work. I went back in the living room and sat down. In a few minutes Jim and Austin came in the yard.

I walked back to where they were and thanked them for a very nice job they did on my privacy fence. I asked them to clean the pool for me today. Just the trash off the water and sweep everything for me good.

They told me they would be glad to do it. I always pay them a little extra when I ask them to do things like that for me.

I left the house and went by The Grill and Eggs Breakfast Bar to see if anyone was there this morning. I went in and sat down and ordered me a cup of coffee. I was watching the door. A woman with long red hair came strolling through the door. That was a shock. She looked exactly like the woman in my dream.

She had sat down at a table near me. I got up walked over to the table and introduced myself. She told me that she was not looking for a boyfriend and that she preferred that I just go back to my seat and leave her alone.

Well, I did not want to, but I had to obey her wish. I went back to my table and sat down. I went outside and sat in my car and waited for her to come out of the restaurant. I decided that I would at least follow her and see where she went.

She got in her car and headed out toward the Avondale community. I stayed far enough behind her that hopefully she would not recognize that I was following her. He went into the housing community and turned onto a street very close to where Charlotte had lived. That concerned me. She pulled into a drive and parked her car. I stopped and watched her get out of her car and walk onto the porch. She took her keys and unlocked the door and went inside.

I thought, well at least I know where she lives. Maybe I can get someone to watch the place for any suspicious activity and stop anything from happening to her.

I left and went on back towards my office and decided that I would go by and see Catherine on my way. I stopped in and the secretary motioned me to go right on into her office. I walked in the door and she looked up and motioned for me to sit down in the chair just in front of her desk. She had just hung up the phone.

I asked her what she was doing today. She told me she had a couple of cases that she had to work on and see if she could get everything ready for court.

I told her that I had just seen the woman that was in my last dream and that she lived very close to where Charlotte lived. I told her what had happened and that I followed her. She went to the same community Charlotte lived in. I explained that she had to live there because she had the keys to the house and all. It was a duplex just like Charlotte's.

I need to work on my cases, but I just don't seem to have time to. These dreams are causing me a lot of problems. Don't worry about it Jason it will all come together soon.

I worked on my files. They needed to be organized again. I had not had much time to do that lately. It took me most of the morning to get them organized. It was about lunch time.

I left the office and went over to Charlie's Steak and Grill. As I pulled up I saw Jeff getting out of his cruiser. I called him and ask him to wait on me and we could eat together. He waited, and we went in together and sat down at our regular table. It was nice to be back at Charlie's for a change. I missed it.

Our waitress came to the table and took our order and thanked us for coming in.

"Well Jason what have you been doing?"

"Just working on paper work today."

"Do you have anything new on the Taylor murder?"

"No. It is all about the same right now."

"The second murder is fixing to happen Jeff. I had the second dream the other night."

"You know I do not believe in that much Jason."

"But you know when I tell you about them they always happened. Don't they?"

"Yes. You are always right Jason."

"That means you need to listen to me. I know what I am talking about."

"I understand what you are saying Jason, but I cannot go on just a dream."

"Sure, you can. It is going to happen the same area the last one happened in Jeff."

"How you know that Jason."

"I saw the girl that was in my dream and I followed her to see where she went. She went to the same area that Charlotte lived in. She lives in a duplex the same as Charlotte did."

"Maybe you are wrong Jason."

"I am not wrong Jeff. You watch, and you will see I am right."

"Well, if it happens Jason I might just have to arrest you. You seem to know so much about it."

"You do not want to do that Jeff. That will be a big mistake. You know my mama."

"Yes, I do Jason and I sure do not want to make her mad. I just hope that it does not happen for your own sake Jason. That is concrete evidence"

"When it does, arrest me Jeff. That will be your mistake as sheriff in Sylacauga."

"We will just pray that it does not happen Jason.

"I hope it don't. I do not like having the dreams and I surely do not like the outcome of them. They are horrific."

"Well, we will just see what happens. Let's hope that you are wrong."

"I hope I am wrong, but I will not be and that is what upsets me so bad. I told you about the dream. You know about it now. You know that I know it is going to happen and there is nothing that I can about it. It is all up to you and Dexter now Jeff to see that it does not happen if there be any way to stop it. I know that you do not believe in the dreams and all, but I have them and it is going to happen."

"We will just keep our eyes open. That is all we can do. We cannot do much of anything else. Sorry Jason."

"You could Jeff you just are not going to. That is too simple to figure out. All because you do not believe that someone can have dreams like, and I have never been wrong. Well I am telling you again it is going to happen it always does when I have these dreams."

"I hope you are wrong this time Jason."

"I need to tell you about the warehouses Jeff."

"Did you find out something Jason?"

"Yes I did. There are six guys that go there Jeff. They have a meth lab there. I was able to get in the building from the back like I told you I thought I could. I got in and hid and watched till they got there. I watched them close with my high-powered binoculars. They definitely have a meth lab."

"We need to stop it Jason. I will get on that soon."

"Let me watch a little bit more and make sure there are certain nights that they are always there before you do anything."

"OK. When are you going back?"

"Tonight, unless something comes up and I can't."

"OK we will wait until you are sure of a good time to go in and break it up."

"I will let you know. I guess I need to get to the office Jeff. I will see you later."

"OK Jason. Talk to you soon."

CHAPTER ELEVEN

I got all my paper work and the pictures of Sarah Long and Fred Johnson together and put them all in a folder to take over to Catherine's. Sometimes I wish I had a runner to help me out. I should hire me one but sometimes I don't need anybody although today would be a good day.

I grabbed the folder with the information on Sarah and Fred to take over to Catherine. I took it and gave it to her. She thanked me for it.

"You have any cases today Catherine?"

"I had one this morning Jason. I was representing the young girl who got raped. They put him in the slammer."

"He got what he deserved."

"What you been doing Jason."

"Trying to get my paper work caught up and wondering what is going to happen in my life next."

"You will be OK Jason."

"I guess I will go Catherine. I have some things I need to do. See you later."

"Take care Jason."

I decided that I would hang around the Avondale community and see what was happening with the lady that I had seen in my dream. I parked over on the street close to her house. I could see it well enough to know if anything was going on. I had been there about an hour when she came out the front door and got in her car.

I watched her, and she backed out in the street and drove towards the mill. I followed her. She parked in the mill parking lot. I knew then that she worked at the same place which Charlotte worked. I knew that she probably had a night off tomorrow night since she was working the night shift. That was at least how it worked for Charlotte. So, I did not have to worry about her tonight because she was at work. That was good.

I left the Avondale community and went back towards town. I wanted to stop by the Mexican Restaurant tonight. I got there and went inside and found me a table near the window for the view outside. The waitress came and took my order. I ordered tacos because their tacos would melt in your mouth. They were delicious.

I was waiting for my order. I looked up towards the door and saw Jake Simmons walk in.

"I was passing by Jason and saw your car and I stopped. How are you?'

"I am good Jake. What are you doing in this part of the world?"

"I have to go to Tuscaloosa tonight to be there for tomorrow."

The waitress came to the table to give him a menu. He told her he did not need the menu and to just bring him some tacos with sweet tea.

"What are you doing in Tuscaloosa?"

"We are working a new case that we have just picked up."

"What have you been up to Jason?"

"You do not really want to know Jake. My life has been a mess lately."

"All I have right now Jason is time. Tell me about it."

I told him about the second dream that I had the other night. Then I went on to tell me about how that they had arrested Jim Sax for the murder of Charlotte and how that Catherine and I had gotten him out of jail and all. Then I told him about my conversation with Jeff and how that Jeff told me that if the murder happened that they may have to arrest me because I seem to know all the details about the murders.

He was amazed at the last part of that.

"You do not really mean that he said that he may arrest you for the murders if it happens because you seem to know a lot about them." He said to me.

"That is what he told me. I could not believe that he was saying it in the first place." I told him.

"Everybody knows you Jason. They all know you could never do anything like that even if you really hated them. He is just talking out his ears."

"I know. He don't really want to arrest me for something that I have had nothing to do with. He has never seen my mom mad. She can get very mean when she gets mad and she knows all the right people."

"I have never seen your mom mad either and I don't think I wish to." He told me.

Our food made it to the table. We ate our tacos and they were delicious as always.

"Would you like to come over to the house for a while before you leave for Tuscaloosa?"

"Sure. I need something to pass the time for a while anyway."

We paid our tickets and left the restaurant and he followed me to my house. After we got to the house, we sat down on the porch in the swing. I went in the house and got us something to drink and came back to the porch. I looked out towards the highway and that 1957 Chevrolet was passing by the house. The tag is always at an angle that I cannot see the tag number well enough to make it. I told him about the 1957 Chevrolet following me and about the phone calls at night and that I thought it was the person driving the 1957 Chevrolet.

"You need to get a tap put on your phone Jason."

William Honeycutt

"I have decided that I was going to do that tomorrow."

"Maybe you can keep them on the line long enough to catch them."

"I am going to talk with the Coosa County Sheriff if I ever have time to go to Rockford. I have about decided that the person driving it is the same person making the phone calls because the phone calls are kind of late at night."

"That is a good way to hopefully get that settled Jason. That would be one thing out of your way."

"Would you like to stay here tonight Jake?"

"Yea. It is not that far to Tuscaloosa from here."

"I do have to go to the warehouses to make sure if those guys I have been watching show up tonight or not."

"I just need to call and cancel my reservations for tonight."

We rode over to the warehouses. I parked close enough I could see the warehouse that they were using but out of their sight so that they would not notice me. We sit there for about an hour when the same three men that always showed up first came along. I told Jake that was my men. After the other three showed up and they were in the building, we left and went back to the house.

Jake went to his car and brought his things in and ask me if it would be OK for him to take a shower. I told him to make himself at home.

"Am I sleeping in the same room as last time?"

"That is your room Jake when you are here."

He took his things in the room and finished his shower and came back down to the living room. I was watching the news.

"How is the case going concerning the lady in your first dream?" He asked me.

Murder of Grace

"Well it is at a standstill right now. Nobody can seem to find any evidence of any kind that will tie to anyone that will do us any good." I told him.

"Well maybe you will get something soon." He said.

"I was going to Tuscaloosa and try to find her ex-boyfriend and see if he knows anything about why it happened. And see if maybe he is tied to the murder in any way." I told him.

"Maybe he can at least give you some leads. Tell you about some of her friends from Tuscaloosa." He said.

"That would be nice to find somebody that knew her and just a little bit about her. She may have moved to Tuscaloosa from somewhere getting away from somebody stalking her. Who knows? I don't for sure."

"Something will show up sooner or later Jason. It always does."

"What have you been doing since I last you Jake?"

"I have been swamped with cases that we have been trying to get caught up on."

"That is good. At least you have plenty to do."

"I have been thinking about moving from Wetumpka and expanding my base a little."

"How far out you plan on expanding it Jake?"

"It is all in the future right now Jason. I really don't know."

"You need a good central location for all the major locations around it."

"I am going to need someone to go in business with me Jason."

"Do you have anybody in mind yet?"

"Yes, I do but I have not talked with them yet."

"Keep me informed and let me know what you do."

"I will Jason. You will be the first to know."

Well, it was about 11:00 already.

William Honeycutt

"If you do not mind I am going to lie down."

"Make yourself at home Jake."

"See you in the morning."

"I need to lie down myself."

I went to bed and the next thing I knew my alarm clock went off. I always ran every morning. I went out on the porch and waited till Jane came out and told her I was not running this morning. I went back in the house and went to the kitchen to fix breakfast.

I was fixing some eggs, grits, and bacon for breakfast. About the time I had the bacon cooked he walked in the kitchen.

"What are you doing Jason?"

"I am making us some breakfast."

"It sure smells good in here. You did not have to do that."

"It is the least I can do for a good friend."

I finished getting it ready while he got us a cup of coffee and set it on the table in the breakfast nook. By the time we had finished eating it was 6:30.

"Well Jason I guess I need to get on the road."

"It is about that time. That will give you enough time to get there and be ready for your interview."

"Yes. And I do not need to be late for this one."

Jake got his things and left and went to Tuscaloosa. I went to my bedroom and put on my work clothes. It was still early. I left the house and went to The Grill and Eggs Breakfast Bar to see who showed up this morning.

I had placed my order and was waiting for it to come up. I looked up and Jim Sax came walking in the door. I waved at him to come over to my table.

"Good morning Jim."

"Good morning Jason."

The waitress came over and took his order.

"What have you been doing Jim?"

"I have just been working mostly Jason."

"That is good Jim."

"Jason, I am having a hard time dealing with having been arrested for the murder of that woman. I try not to worry Jane with it. She is so upset over it all." He told me.

"Jim this is going away. The killer will be caught. You will be exonerated, and it will not show up on your record."

"I sure hope so Jason. I do not need this on my record. A murder. I did not do it. I think everybody that knows me knows that I did not do it. I could get a thousand witnesses if I had to. This is about to drive me crazy." He told me.

"Don't let it bother you any more Jim. We have the worst part of it over with already. You are not in jail. The only thing you need to do is be careful right now and be where someone knows you and can prove that you were with them. Cover your ass in other words so that you do not have to worry about being picked up again." I told him.

"OK I can do that, and I have been so far. I do not do anything that I cannot prove where I have been one way or the other." He said.

"That is good Jim."

Our food made it to the table. We ate, and chit chatted some about our lives from our childhood. We enjoy that few minutes remembering the things we used to get into. The trouble that we caused our teachers and the pranks we pulled on our classmates.

Finally, he told me he needed to go and get back home because Jane was looking for him back soon and if he were not back she would worry herself sick.

I left the restaurant and went to my office. I had just walked in the door good when the phone rang.

"Hello. Caffrey's Investigations. May I help you."

"Hello Jason. This is Greg."

"What's up Greg."

"I need to see you today. I have some things for you. What would be a good time for you?"

"Anytime will be OK Greg. I am not busy this morning."

"I will see you in about an hour then."

I called Catherine while I was waiting for Greg to get there. She was busy working on her case that she had to go to court today for. She told me that those pictures I had gotten for her of Sarah Long and Fred Johnson would do what she needed. We talked for a little bit and just as I hung up the phone up Greg came walking in the door.

"Hello Jason. What are you doing?"

"I am waiting on you Greg. I just finished talking with Catherine for a little bit. What you got on your mind Greg?"

"I have been doing a little research trying to find out anything I could concerning Charlotte Taylor. You had told me she came from Tuscaloosa and I checked their starting out. She did live in Tuscaloosa for a short time about two years is all. I found that she moved to Tuscaloosa from Tulsa, Oklahoma. I had a friend of mine to check her out in Tulsa. She lived in Tulsa, Oklahoma for about five years. She was a mover Jason. She moved around a lot."

"Maybe we can find some friend's, people that knew her that can tell us a little about her." I said to him.

"I learned that she moved from Houston, Texas to Tulsa, Oklahoma. What we need to do now is put out feelers for information of people who knew her. That might will help lead us to her killer." He told me.

"That is why I wanted to go to Tuscaloosa and look around and see if I could find her ex-boyfriend and see what he could tell us. He might have some connections to the murder in some way. I still am going if I ever find the time to go." I told him.

"Well, Jason I wanted to let you know what I had found out. I know things have been going bad for you lately. I hope it will help out some."

"You better believe it will." I told him.

"I need to get back over to the office and get some things together. I have to go to court today over this big car theft that has been taking place in Talladega. I think we will wrap it up today. I will be glad to see it over with. It looks like we will win the case." He told me.

He was out the door and gone time he got it out of his mouth. That is just the way Greg is though. When he is ready to go he goes.

I decided that it was about time to go and find me some lunch. I went over to Charlie's Steak and Grill to have me a T-bone steak. I had not had one in several days and I was ready for one. I got to the restaurant and went in and sat down and about the time I got sat down good Dexter came walking in the door.

When I saw him I motioned for him to come over and sit with me. He came over and sat down and ask me what I had been up to lately. I told him that I was trying to get all the loose end of things tied up. He laughed and said he thought all of us had some loose ends lately with all this latest murder in our little city.

I told him that it would all end one day. He told me that it would never end that there would always be something. I laughed and told him how right he was in that.

The waitress came to the table and took our orders. When I ordered my plate, he just told the waitress to make it two of the same.

We sat around waiting on our lunch to get to the table and chit chatted about life and what we had been up to. I filled him in all the details about my latest dream and told him what Jeff had said to me about that he may have to arrest me since I seem to know so much about what was happening with the murders. Jeff laughed and said that there was no way that I was going to get arrested. He reminded me that everybody knows me and knows that there is no way that I would or could do anything like that.

Our food made it to the table. We ate those steaks like we had never had one before. We finished and left the restaurant. Jeff went back to the Sheriff's office and I went over to the park to see what was going on. I sat in the park for a few minutes and got up and left and went over to the phone company and talked with them about putting a tap on my phone to trace calls for a while.

They ask me when I wanted to start it. I told them to start it as soon as possible. They told me that by the time I got home that the trace would be on my phone. I left and went on back by the office and picked up some paper work that I wanted to go over and just had not had time to do it at the office.

I left the office and went on towards the house. I stopped by the grocery store and picked up a few items on the way home. I needed some drinks and some cheese curls for sure.

I finished at the grocery store and went home.

I got to the house about 5:30.

I just sat down on the porch and watched the birds. I always enjoyed that when I had a chance to do it. They were beautiful. I needed to go on in the house now.

I turned on the TV and went into the kitchen and made me a fresh pot of coffee. When it was finished I poured me a cup and went back in the living room and sat down in my recliner and turned the TV to the news channel to see what was going on.

Murder of Grace

They talked a little about the murder of Charlotte.

And then they moved on with all the other local news. Not much was happening right now. That was good. I think it was all happening in my life and I surely was not going to tell them about my dreams. I would be slaughtered.

CHAPTER TWELVE

I was sitting there leaned back in my recliner when the phone rang. I answered it and it was my phantom caller again. I hung up on them forgetting that I had my phoned tapped to try and catch who it was. OK. They will call back. They always do. In a couple of minutes, the phone rang.

"Hello. Jason Caffrey speaking."

"I will still get you. You wait and see." They said to me.

"How are you going to get me?" I asked.

"Just wait and see. It will be a surprise." They said.

"I don't like surprises so just tell me how you plan to get me." I said.

"I will not give out my secret to you, but I will get you. It will not be hard to do. You are an easy one." They said.

"So, you think I am that easy?"

"I am going this time for now, but I will be back." They said.

"No, wait, don't go yet." I said. They hung up anyway.

I was not able to keep them on the phone long enough to get the trace on who it was. Maybe they would call back and I would be able to keep them on long enough to find out who it was. "I sure to hell hope so. This is getting old."

I got up and went to the kitchen and made me a fresh pot of coffee and when it was finished, and I poured me a cup and took it to the living room and

Murder of Grace

sat back down in my recliner and found me a good action movie on TV to pass the time away I hoped.

I kicked the foot rest up and sit back with my coffee and reached over and got my cheese curls and just as I did the phone rang again. I answered it.

"I just have to call you again. I cannot resist it. I figure by now you have the line tapped to try and trace the calls to find out who I am but I am smart." They told me.

"How smart do you think you are? I will catch you sooner or later one way or the other. You can count on that." I told them.

"We will see. Just remember I am going to get you and make you pay for what you have done." They told me.

"I did not know that I did anything." I told them.

"You have done a lot of things and caused a lot of problems. And I am going to make you pay for them." They told me.

"How are you going to make me pay for them?" I asked them.

"That is my secret. I can't tell you that part. If I do it will take the surprise away. And I want you to be surprised." They said.

"Remember, I don't like surprises. They irritate me." I told them.

Then they just hung up the phone. Not quite enough time to get a trace on it.

I hoped that would be it for tonight. I did not want any more of those kinds of calls. I sit back and just got involved in my movie and was thinking about what I was going to do tomorrow, and the phone rang again. I did not want to answer it but I did anyway. Well it was a good thing I did. It was my mom. We talked for a little bit and she told me she had to go that dad wanted her. She said bye, bye and hung up.

I was ready to relax now. I should not be getting any more phone calls tonight. I leaned back in my recliner and was falling asleep when the phone rang again.

"Hello. Jason Caffrey speaking

"Hello Jason. I just wanted to call and say hi to you." Rita said.

"Well, it is good to hear from you Rita. What are you doing?" I said to her.

"Working mostly. What have you been doing Jason?" She asked me.

"It seems like my life is staying upside down right now. Everything wrong is happening it seems like. I just cannot get a day without something going wrong."

"Everything will get better Jason."

"Jeff even told me that he might even have to arrest me for murder if another one happened since I knew so much about them before they happen."

"Wow Jason that is unreal. Do you really think he would that?"

"No. I really don't think he would. I think he knows better."

"How does he think that he could get away with that on just a dream to begin with? He is an officer of the law. He should know better than to even think it."

"I told him that if he arrested me that he would have to deal with my mom and that he really did not want that."

"I would not want to have to deal with your mom Jason if she were mad."

"I need to come back to Manassas and see you soon and get away from here for a day or two. Or maybe you could come down here and spend the week end with me soon. That would be nice." I told her.

"I tell you what I will come to see you this time. I would love to come and see what Sylacauga is like. I have not been there yet." She said.

"Maybe you can work it out and come next week end. That would be nice." I told her.

"I have a little vacation time. Maybe I can come and spend a little more than the weekend." She told me.

"That would be fun." I told her.

"OK Jason I just wanted to call be sure you were alright. I need to go for now."

"I am glad you called. Take care and I will talk to you soon."

We hung up the phone.

It was about 9:00 already. The night was slowly going by. I have had enough drama already tonight.

I went to the bathroom and took a shower.

I needed to be refreshed when I started my day tomorrow morning.

I turned out all the lights in the house and locked the doors and I went to the bedroom and got ready to lay down. I went to the bedroom and lay down on my bed. I was laying on my back looking at the ceiling thinking about the things that I needed to do tomorrow.

The first thing I needed to do was go and talk with the Coosa County Sheriff and see if there was any way that we could find out who owned that 1957 red Chevrolet from Coosa County. In a few minutes I closed my eyes and began to doze off.

I went to sleep and was sleeping very well when all of a sudden, I saw the woman with the long red hair in a dream. Damn dreams. This was getting old. I saw her just as plain as day in my mind. Then, the vision of the person who was going to kill her was in view. Just not enough to recognize who it might be. I could not make out enough to give any description except that he was tall. I woke up. I sat up on my bed and just put my face in my hands and wondered why this dream kept coming up and why tonight. But it was there. And I wanted it to go away, but it would not.

I got up from my bed and went into the living room and sat down in my recliner. I did not want to close my eyes again

I was sitting there, and the phone rang. I did not need a phone call right now. I was not in the mood for it. I just wanted peace. I answered it anyway

It was the muffled voice caller.

"I will get you for sure." They said. It really irritated me, and I just hung the phone up. It was about 1:00 am. I got up from my recliner and went in the kitchen and made me some coffee. I poured me a cup when it was finished making and went back and sat back down in my recliner to get my head back together again. I finished my cup of coffee.

I got up and went back to my bedroom and lay back down on the bed. I was a little tired and disgusted at the same time. All I wanted was my life back.

It did not seem like that was going to happen. I have been strung out for two weeks now and it did not seem to be going away.

I was lying there wondering what I would do now. Again, it was the time of the night that I just did not want to call anybody, but I needed somebody to talk with.

I lay there, and I just wanted to drift away without any dreams or seeing anything.

Finally, I drifted off again. I was having some peaceful moments sleeping very well. Then, she came up again in my dream. She was very vivid. I could see her well. Then all of a sudden, I saw him slice her throat from ear to ear again. I done seen this one time. Is it happening again? Is it tonight? Is

Murder of Grace

she in trouble right now? Don't tell me this murder is taking place right now?

I jumped up from my bed and was on the floor before I could think. I knew that I had to call the police station and get them to get a hold of Dexter for me immediately. It was an emergency. He had to be notified. The murder was happening right now. I just knew it. I would not be having this dream tonight unless the murder was taking place.

I called, and they told me they could contact him immediately and have him to call me. Within five minutes my phone rang, and I told Dexter that we had to go over there now. I told him about the dream and what had happened and told him that it was taking place. The woman is dead already I told him. We need to get there before he gets away.

Dexter told me that he would get some officers out there as soon as possible and see if there was anyone on the outside fooling around and that he would get there as soon as possible. I told him where she lived.

I got my clothes on and headed out for Avondale community to try and be there by the time Dexter got there. We arrived at about the same time. He called Jeff and Jeff arrived with some of his offers just ahead of us. They were all waiting for Dexter to get there so that we could go in the house and see what was going on.

The officers had already gone around the house to see if they could find anyone and were keeping a good eye on the house so that if anyone left from inside they would see them.

We went to the front door and knocked on the door. No one came to the door to answer it. We knocked again. I told Dexter we needed to go inside no matter what. He tried to turn the door knob and the door was locked. He popped the door one time with his shoulder and the door came open. He pushed it back and walked into the living room.

William Honeycutt

Once he was in the living room he turned the lights on in the living room. The officers were outside the house watching all the entrances of the house in case someone did leave they would see them.

He walked over to the bedroom door and looked in and it was empty. That was a good sign that maybe no one was here. I hope that was the case. We all stayed behind him and let him be the lead. He walked over to the kitchen and flipped the light switch which was just inside the door of the kitchen.

OH my God. He said. This is just like the first one except in the kitchen on the kitchen table. I walked up to the door and almost gagged it was so bad. There was blood all over the kitchen. It was horrifying. I could not believe my eyes. It had happened just like I saw that it would. I turned around and went back in the living room and sat down in the closet chair I could find and stuck my head between my legs. I was gagging.

Dexter told us all just to stay back and do not touch anything. We needed to make sure that we found some finger prints or something on this one so that maybe we could stop this before it went any further.

I could not go back in there right now myself. Jeff just walked outside and stood staring in the sky. I was finally able to get up and walk out the door. I walked over to where he was and ask him what we were going to do about this one.

Dexter called the morgue and told them to get Carlton on the phone and have him to come over there immediately. Carlton was there in about a half hour. He walked in the door of the kitchen and was astounded. He said it is so similar to the first one. Everything the same almost except he did this one in the kitchen on the table instead of in the bedroom.

"I believe the killer is trying to tell us something, but I just do not know what it is." Dexter said

"Yes, I believe that is what is happening." Carlton said.

"Why does he set the head up on the body at the top and have it always looking towards the feet? Is there a reason for that?" I asked.

"Yes, there is a reason for it. He did it on both murders." Carlton said.

"What we also see here is that both ladies seem to be tall and slender best I can tell so far from what I see here." Carlton said.

"Yes, it appears that way but the first one had long blonde hair and this one has long red hair. But otherwise they are the same. Only the color of the hair different." I told them.

"So far I believe that it is the same person that did both these murders. Therefore, we know that the killer must be somewhere in the area." Jeff said.

"They both also worked at the mill here in Avondale." I told them.

One of the officers had found her purse and called Dexter over to where it was. Dexter took her purse and found her ID. He told us that her name was Delores Cummings. "Do any of you know her or have you ever heard of her?" He asked.

No one knew her and had never heard of her. Now we wondered how long she had lived here. Charlotte had only been around a few months. Very short time. Was she a newcomer in the area? That was definitely something that we were going to need to check out Dexter told us. I told him I would check on that the first thing in the morning.

Carlton had already gotten his crew out to the crime scene and the place had already been cordoned off They were taking all kinds of pictures of the body and the kitchen where all the blood is. They were taking all their samples of blood and all hoping that the killer had left some sign of DNA. If like the last time, there probably would not be any thing for us to find.

Well, this was number two and I had seen them both before they happened and could not stop either one of them. I was so upset. I wanted to go hide somewhere to where nobody or anything could find me. I did not want to live right now. I was hurt. I was just really upset.

The body had been gathered up with all it parts and put in the ambulance to take to the morgue. There were a lot of things that had to be tied together before anything could be done with the body. That was going to take plenty of time. It appeared that he had used the plastic bags just like the last time to make sure that he had left nothing at the scene that could be traced back to him.

I was afraid that it was going to be just like last time. I sure did hope not. Both took place in the middle of the night one on Saturday night and the other on Wednesday night. It looked like that he only committed the murders at the oddest times.

Several things looked the same which was making it look like we may be dealing with a serial murderer here. I hope that it was not and that this would be the end of it. I had a funny feeling that it would not be though.

I hoped that I was wrong about that part. But I felt that I was not going to be wrong. I was not wrong about the two women going to be murdered. It happened just like I said that it would.

I just wanted to go home for a while and hopefully this would all just go away. Maybe I am having a dream. I hope so. I left the scene and went to my house and the first thing that I did was make me a pot of coffee and then I sat down in my recliner and just sit there wondering what to do next. I really did not want to do anything.

Murder of Grace

The first thing that I was going to do was go to the mill to the employment office and talk with their staff and see if I could find any information concerning her. That might would help some in knowing where she had come from. I don't know if it would or not but it was sure worth a try.

I went back to the kitchen and got me a cup of coffee and came back in the living room and sat back down in my recliner.

CHAPTER THIRTEEN

It was already 5:00. I put my jogging shorts and went out the door and Jane was waiting on me.

"Good morning Jane."

"Good morning Jason. How are you this morning?"

"I am not doing very well this morning Jane."

We started off on our five-mile run.

"What is wrong Jason?"

"If you have not heard it yet Jane, you will. There was another murder last night."

"I have not heard it yet and where did it happen Jason?"

"The same area as the last one."

"That is not good but then no murder is good."

"How are your studies going Jane?"

"They are going very well Jason. I have a solid 4.0 right now. If I can keep that up I will graduate with honors."

"You can do it girl. That is good."

We made it back to the house and I told her I would see her Monday for sure. She went in her house and I went and got me a cup of coffee. I went back in the living room and sat down. All I could think about was what I had seen over at Delores Cummings place after the man had murdered her. The body was on the table. Her hands and fingers and arms and all had been cut off. They were placed in plastic bags and put at the foot of the person. The

Murder of Grace

feet and all had been cut off and placed at the top of the person near the shoulders and the head had been cut off and was set up on the body facing towards the feet. All the body parts were in plastic bags.

Why did he put them in plastic bags? What was the purpose of that other than to contain some of the blood? Why did he kill one on the bed and the other on the table? He did it in the same fashion but just in different places. Either way it was gross. It was actually horrifying.

I could not stop thinking about it. I did not know what was going to happen next. My life seemed to be going downhill fast. All these things going on and why I could not put a handle on it. I could not imagine why people wanted to do such awful things.

It was about 6:00 AM already. I went to the bathroom and took me a long hot shower. I felt a lot cleaner after all that blood I had seen this morning. I went into my bedroom and found me something cherry to wear. I put on my favorite red shirt and my newer blue jeans. That felt good. They all felt clean. I felt better.

The doorbell rang.

I opened the door and it was Alice.

"Good morning Alice."

"Good morning Jason. Have you heard the news about the woman being murdered last night? That is awful."

"I know about it Alice. I was at the crime scene this morning."

"I hope that it does not happen again Jason."

"Maybe it will not Alice."

"Anything special you want me to do today Jason?"

"No Alice. Just do your normal work."

I left the house and went to The Grill and Eggs Breakfast Bar and as I was pulling in Jeff pulled right up beside me. We walked in the restaurant together and sat down.

"How are you feeling about now Jason?" He asked me.

"To tell you the truth, still a little bit disgusted. It is a shame to have to know something about a murder like that and cannot do anything about it." I told him.

"I know what you mean. I am glad it is you and not me." He told me.

"You just learn to live with it but it is not easy to deal with sometimes." I told him.

The waitress came to the table and took our order and left.

"I am going to see if I can find any information on Delores this morning from the mill where she worked. Maybe she has some friends that can tell us something about her." I told him.

"That will be a good start. I am going to ask around town about her and see if anyone knows her." He told me.

"Maybe we can find something out concerning her. I sure hope so." I told him.

"That will at least be a start. I think Dexter is going to run the data base and see if he can find anything on her from anywhere." He said.

"The first thing I am going to do is talk to the hiring staff at the mill and see if they can give me any background information on her. I know they do not have to tell me anything but under the circumstances I am sure they will." I told him.

Our order made it to the table finally. We ate our breakfast and Jeff told me he had a lot to do today and that he needed to go.

"Are you going to arrest me Jeff since you said you would probably have to if it took place?" I asked him.

"No, Jason I am not going to arrest you because without you we would not have known anything until after it happened although we could not do anything before it did." He told me.

"That is good because if you did you would have to deal with my mom and you do not want to do that." I told him.

"I will talk to you later today Jason I am sure. Have a great day."

"I will and you have a great day to Jeff." I told him

We left the restaurant and I went over to see if Catherine was at her office yet. She was there. She said she got up this morning and it was plastered all over the news about the murder. She told me that she could not rest so she just left home early and came on to the office.

I asked her if she had any coffee made and of course she did. We got us a cup and sat down in her office.

"Jason do you have any idea what is going on here?" She asked me.

"No, I do not know anything, but it looks like from all the way things are taking place at the murder scenes that we have a serial killer on our hands." I told her.

"Well, that is not good, we do not need a serial killer around here." She said.

"Well, it happened right in the same area as the first one and you know those people are going to be very nervous now wondering who will be next." I said.

"I would be if I were in their neighborhood for sure. I am nervous and don't even live near that part of town."

"Would you like some more coffee Jason?" She asked.

"Yes I would but let me get us some." I said to her.

I got up and went and got us another cup of coffee and brought it back to the office and we were talking about the things that we could do to try and find out who was behind this.

I told her that the employment service at the mill should be up and running by now and I needed to head that way and see what I could find out about her since that is where she worked.

I got to the mill at about 9:00 that morning. It was Friday. I went in and found the employment service and talked with the secretary. I told her I needed to see the head of the department. She told me that Mrs. Katland Caruthers was in a meeting right now and it would be about a half hour before they would be finished. I told her I would be glad to wait. I really needed to talk with her about some important business. She showed me where I could wait and told me that when Mrs. Caruthers was finished and was ready to see me that she would let me know.

I sat down and grabbed the TV turner and tried to find something that would keep me busy while I was waiting. I was in the middle of a good Western by John Wayne when the secretary stuck her head in the door and told me that Mrs. Caruthers was ready to see me.

I got up and followed her back to the office and she escorted me to her office and showed me in. I walked in and Mrs. Caruthers motioned for me to sit down in the chair right in front of her desk.

"Hello Mrs. Caruthers, I am Jason Caffrey. I am a private investigator and I need to talk with you about a very important matter." I told her.

"I am Katland Caruthers and just what can I help you with Mr. Caffrey?" She asked.

"Please call me Jason Mrs. Caruthers." I told her.

"OK Jason and you may call me Katland."

"Kateland I am here concerning Delores Cumming. I knew that she worked at the mill and she is the lady that was murdered last night in her apartment." I told her.

"Yes, I saw that on the news this morning." She said.

"We do not have anything to go on right now and I was hoping that you could give me some information about her. Usually you would have some in her employment application about her prior jobs and things of the nature. That would help us out some just to know a little about where she came from.

"Sure Jason, I can help you out some. Since you are a private investigator and she was murderer I will do all that I can to help out in any way to find the murderer." She said.

"Thank you and I really will appreciate that."

I asked her since Charlotte Taylor had worked for them also if she could get me the same type information on her. She told me she would be more than obliged to do that for us.

She told me to just wait right there and she would be right back. She stepped out of the office and called her secretary and they talked for a minute and then she came back in the office. She told me that she would have the information for me in a folder in about ten minutes. She told me to just wait outside in the office there and the secretary would give it to me just as soon as she got it copied for me. I thanked her for her time and apologized for bothering her and she told me to forget it.

It took the secretary about fifteen minutes to get it all together for me. When she had it in the folder she handed it to me and told me that she hoped that we found the murderer soon. I told her we would find him as soon as possible. I thanked her and left the building and went back to my office to go over the information that I had.

I got to my office and by the time I had sat down at my desk the phone rang.

"Hello. Caffrey's Investigations. May I help you?" I said.

"Hello Jason. What are you doing?" Rita asked.

"I am just getting ready to look over some information concerning the woman that was murdered last night. It happened Rita. They did not wait long this time. Just a few days from the time I had the dream." I told her.

"I know Jason. That is awful. That is why I called. I have been trying to get you, but I got no answer. I was getting worried." She told me.

"I was away from the office trying to get some information concerning the dead woman well actually the dead women. I got information on them both. I am going to look it over and see if I can get any leads that will help." I told her.

"Well, maybe you will Jason. Is there anything that I can do? I know you are upset." She said to me.

"There is not much anybody can do Rita right now but thanks anyway." I told her.

"I am trying to get it worked out to where I can come up next weekend Jason and spend a few days with you."

"That will be nice."

"Yea. I think I can get it worked out. I have some vacation time and I mentioned it to my boss. He did not say anything and that is always a good sign."

"I will just count on it then Rita. When you get it worked out just let me know."

"I will let you know Jason."

"I will call you tonight and we can talk some."

"OK. I will look forward to it."

"Bye for now Rita."

"Bye Jason."

I opened Delores folder that they had given me from the mill.

Murder of Grace

The first thing that I found that she used for a reference was an uncle. His name was Tom Cummings an uncle she said he was. He was from Norfolk, Virginia. I got on the phone and started trying to see if I could find a Tom Cummings in Norfolk, Virginia. This would be a good lead if I could find him, maybe. I found three Tom Cummings in Norfolk.

I called the first one and he told me that he had never heard of a Delores Cummings. I called the second one and they told me that they knew a Delores but that she lived in Charleston, South Carolina now. As far as they knew she was fine. This is not looking to good so far. I called the third one and the last one.

When I got him on the phone and ask him did he know a Delores Cummings, he told me that he did. He told me that he had a daughter by that name. He said he had not heard from her in over ten years now. This was not good. I asked him did he have any pictures of her and could he describe her to me. He did describe her to me as to what she looked like when she left home. The image that he gave me over the phone was just like what I saw in my dream. This had to be her father. Why would she have called him an uncle? That was interesting.

I told him that the Delores Cummings that I was asking about had been murdered in our little town of Sylacauga, Alabama. I told him that the description that he gave me of her was just exactly what she looked like when I had met her. I told him the whole story about how I had seen her in the restaurant and that she had told me that she was not looking for a boyfriend and that she would appreciate it if I would just tend to my business and leave her alone.

He told me that that sounded like his Delores. He told me that he would come to Sylacauga and take care of any arrangements of any kind. I told him that if he could come and take care of all that it would help us out a lot. He said he would fly to Birmingham and rent a car and that he would be in Sylacauga as soon as he could get arrangements made to get here.

I gave him my phone numbers and told him when he got into Sylacauga and found him a room to stay in to let me know.

That was a good start on that one.

I kept looking through the information and I found another name that maybe would be of help for us. Ray Bradford was in Charleston, South Carolina. She described him as a first cousin. I got on the phone and started trying to find a Ray Bradford from Charleston, South Carolina. They had one that was listed. I called the number and when they answered I asked them if this was Mr. Ray Bradford. They said yes. I explained who I was and why I was calling. He told me that he had known a Delores Cummings from Norfolk, Va. He said it had been about eight years since he had seen her but that they were not cousins. He told me that she was his girlfriend at the time. Why would she call him her cousin if he was her boyfriend? Wow this was getting weird.

I told him what had happened to the one that was here in Sylacauga. I asked him if he could describe the one that he had dated to me. He did and the description that he gave me was exactly like the description that her father had given me. They were definitely the same girl. I had no doubt about it.

I asked him did he mind if I came up and see him and talk with him about Delores. He told me that would be fine. I told him that I would decide the first of the week and let him know when I would be there. I thanked him and hung up.

I learned that she was from Norfolk, Va., and learned that she had lived in Charleston, South Carolina. I am wondering now where else did she

Murder of Grace

live and why did she end up in Sylacauga and go to work at the mill.

It was time to take a trip over to the see Dexter and give him an update on what I have come up with on Delores. I left the office and headed towards City Hall and the first thing I saw was a five-car pileup in the middle of Broadway Ave. and Fort Williams St. I saw Dexter there trying to help get it taken care of.

In a few minutes they had it all cleared out and I pulled up and ask Dexter could we go somewhere and talk for a few minutes. He told me that he was ready to eat some lunch and that we could meet over at Charlie's if I wanted to do that. I told him that would be fine. He said he needed to go by the office first.

I left and went on over to Charlie's and got us a table and told the waitress that I was waiting on the Chief to meet me for lunch. She asked me if I wanted anything to drink while I was waiting. I told her to bring me some coffee for right now. I waited about thirty minutes before he showed up. He came in the door and I waved him over to the table.

The waitress saw him come in and came on over and brought him his menu and we told her we did not need the menu that we already knew what we wanted. We both ordered the T-bone steak dinner.

After the waitress left the table I told him about the Father and that he would be in Sylacauga as soon as he could get arrangements made. I asked him why he thought that she might would have called her father an uncle rather than having referred to him as her father.

He told me that he had no idea why she might have done that but that we might learn something about all that once we saw her father. He told me that when he got in town that he wanted to see him. I told him I would arrange that.

William Honeycutt

I told him about the boyfriend and how that she had referred to him as a cousin instead of boyfriend. I told him this was getting weird. He agreed with me. I told Dexter that I was going to make arrangements the first of the week sometime and go to Charleston and visit with the boyfriend and see what I could learn about her. I am sure he can tell us things that the father will not be able to tell us. Any information that we can come up with will be helpful. It might give us some clues we need in being able to find the murderer.

Our meals came along and we ate them, and chit chatted a little about the weather and all and he told me he had to go to the office and get some reports written up. That was one big mess down at Broadway earlier.

We went and paid for our meals and left the restaurant and I went back to the office to finish looking over the paper work from the mill to see if I could find any other good clues. I think it was about time to call Jake and see if he could help out some.

I opened up Charlotte's file and the first thing I found in hers was that she had referred to her boyfriend in Tuscaloosa. I knew I needed to check this one out. I had a lot going on right now, but he was close to me. I should be able to find him and talk with him this weekend. His name is James Gardner. At least she had called him what he was, her boyfriend.

I haunted for a James Gardner in Tuscaloosa and found two. I called the first one and he had never heard of a Charlotte Taylor. I called the second one and he told me that he knows her and wishes that he could see her. I told him the purpose of my call and asked him if he could describe her to me. He did, and his description matched her perfectly right down to the eyes. I explained to him what had happened to her and he was very upset.

Murder of Grace

I told him that if there was any way that I could spend a little time with him that I would like to meet with him and find out all I could concerning her. He told me that he would be glad to meet with me. We made arrangements for Sunday. I felt that would give me plenty of time to get things worked out with Tom Cummings.

He gave me two telephone numbers that I could reach him when I got to Tuscaloosa. I told him I would see him Sunday.

I was looking over the rest of the information in Charlotte's file when the phone rang. It was Mr. Cummings telling me that he would be in Birmingham at about 8:00 PM tonight. I told him that it was about 45 minutes from Birmingham to Sylacauga. I told him when he had made it to Sylacauga and found him a room to call me and let me know that he was there.

I continued to look over Charlotte's file and found that she had listed her father who was from Houston. What was interesting neither of the girls had ever been married it looked like. They both had had boyfriends but had never married. There has to be something that ties them together someway or other. Her father's name is Jarrell Taylor.

I started checking and found only one Jarrell Taylor that lived in Houston, Texas. I called the number and a woman answered and I ask her if this was the residence of Jarrell Taylor. She told me that it was. I asked her if Mr. Taylor was home. She said he was and got him to the phone.

When he got on the phone I explained to him why I was making this call. He told me that it had been about 10 years since he had seen or heard from his daughter. I ask him if he could describe what his daughter looked like to me the last time he had seen her. He did, and it was exactly what the murdered lady looked like. I told him that the person described to me by him was exactly what the murderer woman looked like.

I asked Mr. Taylor if we could decide for some time next week to meet and talk about Charlotte. He told me that he could come to Sylacauga if that would benefit us. I told him that would help us a lot and if she was actually his daughter that he could make the arrangements to do what he wanted to once it was cleared. I told him we had all her credentials and that would be enough for him to know that it was his daughter or not. He told me he would set up the arrangements and would let me know when he would be in Sylacauga. I told him to give me till the middle of the week if possible I had several people I had to meet within between now and them. He said that would be fine.

It was getting late and it was time for me to leave the office. I left the office and went over to the tennis courts to play at least one game with Jarrod before I went home. He was there, and we caught a game.

"Sorry I don't have much time today Jarrod, but I have some things I have to do."

"It is OK Uncle Jason."

"I am not going to the gym tonight. I do not have time to."

"I think I will go. I would like to see Roxy."

"I am sure she will be glad to see you Jarrod."

"I have to go now and find me a bite to eat. I will talk with you later."

"Ok see you Friday for sure OK."

"Call me and come by the house one-day next week."

"OK I will do that."

I left and went to the Mexican restaurant to get me something to eat. I knew Alice had cooked something and put it in the refrigerator, but I could eat that tomorrow.

CHAPTER FOURTEEN

I had just got in the restaurant and sat down to order my meal when Jim and Jane walked in the door. Jim saw me and came over and ask me did I want some company. I told him that would be fine that they were more than welcome to sit down with me.

They sat down, and the waitress came to the table and brought the menus and ask us would we like something to drink. We all ordered a glass of tea and the waitress left the table.

"Well, Jason did you have a good day today?" Jim asked me.

"I had a very busy day." I told him.

"I saw the news on the lady having been murdered. Guess what! I have plenty of alibis for that one." He told me.

"That is good Jim. Maybe we can get you cleared from the first one now. It looks pretty much like the person who murdered the first girl murdered the second one also. That is not the conclusion yet but will come to that eventually. Once it does then all the charges against you will be dropped." I told him.

"That is good. This has had me so upset. I lost all my respect for the police department in our city because of it." Jane said.

"I understand that Jane. That would be easy to do especially when it gets that close to home." I told her.

"Well, I will be glad when it is all over myself." Jim said.

"It will be soon Jim. You are fixing to be set free of all the charges. I don't think they will ever bother you again unless of course you actually do something." I told him.

The waitress came back and took our orders. While we were sitting around waiting for our food to come. We chit chatted about the weather and all the things going on in our little city and what we thought might be the outcome of some of them. In about eight minutes our food was brought to the table.

We ate our food.

"What are you going to do now Jason that we are finished eating?" Jim asked me.

"I am going home and try to rest for a little while. I have had a very busy day today and I have a meeting later on tonight with someone. I just need a little rest before then." I told him.

"I have got to go home and wash some clothes. I have put it off as long as I can." Jane said.

"I am going to mow the yard when we get home. Maybe it will not be too hot by the time we get there. I put it off till late. It is a small yard anyway and don't take long to mow it." Jim told me.

"You guys have a very good rest of the day and night. Take care and I will see you again soon I hope." I told them.

We left the restaurant and I went home. I pulled up in my drive and parked the car and got out and went upon my porch and sat down in my swing and was watching the birds when I saw that 1957 Chevrolet go by the house again. For some reason I never can see that tag well enough to get anything other than the 22-county number on it.

I got up and just as I stood up Jeff pulled up in the yard. Stuck his head out the window and ask me

Murder of Grace

if I were busy. I told him I had just gotten home and had not even unlocked the door yet.

"Well, I will go then and come back later." He said.

"No that is not necessary. Just get out and come on up." I told him.

"OK I will do that. I needed to talk with you a minute or two if you have time." He told me.

"I have time right now for a little while." I told him.

Jeff got out of his cruiser and walked up on the porch and sat down in the chair he always sits in when he comes by to see me.

"Would you like something to drink?" I asked him.

"Sure, coke if you have any." He told me.

"I will be right back.' I said to him.

I went in the house to get the drinks and while I was there the phone range. It was my muffled caller. I did not have time to try to keep him on the line this time. I just hung up and went on and got our drinks. I was on my way back through and it rang again, and it was him again. I hung the phone up again and went on to the porch with our drinks.

"I can't breathe anymore without something going wrong." I told Jeff.

"What is wrong now?" He asked me.

I explained to him about the phone calls. I told him that I had had a tap put on my line to try to find out who it was. That is who it was on the phone both times when I went to get our drinks.

"That is no good." He told me.

"Well, maybe it will all stop one day. I sure hope so." I told him.

"Dexter told me you had some things on our second lady that might be helpful to us in tracing down who might be killing these girls." He told me.

"I have come up with some important names of people on both of them. I have not had a chance to talk to Dexter since I have them for Charlotte." I told him.

"Is there anything I can do right now?" He asked me.

"No, there is nothing that you can do right this minute but if you would like to talk with the ones that are coming here we can arrange that once they get here."

"I would love to talk with them."

"I found the fathers of both them. They are both coming here to make sure that it is their daughters. In fact, Mr. Cummings is on his way here now. He will probably be in Sylacauga by about 9:00 tonight." I told Jeff.

"You been working Jason."

"That will give you a chance to talk with him."

"I would like to talk with both of them once they are here." He told me.

"Mr. Cummings and Mr. Taylor wants to finalize things while they are here if that is possible."

"I do not think that is going to be a problem. I think that forensics and all is finished with everything on both women now." He told me.

"Do they have enough to be sure that it is the same person committing the murders?" I asked him.

"Yes, I think they do but they just have not made it official yet." He told me.

"Well Jason I need to get on the road. I will talk with you later."

"OK. But before you go. I went over to the warehouse and these guys seem to be going every night."

"We can work out a plan to catch them in the act and clean that mess up."

"They are always there by about 8:00 Pm."

"I will get that worked out Jason and let you know when we are going to take care of it."

"Please do let me know. I want to go with you."

"I will see you later buddy. Take care."

"See you later Jeff."

I went in the house and went to the kitchen and made me a pot of coffee. I needed some coffee now. I had to stay alert for sure. Mr. Cummings would be here after a while and I needed to talk with.

When my coffee had finished making I poured me a cup and just stood there by the coffee pot and drank about half of it thinking about the questions that I might want to ask Mr. Cummings tonight. I filled my cup back full and took it and went into the living room and sat down in my recliner and turned the TV on. I was watching a western when the phone rang.

I reached over and picked it up and when I answered it the voice was muffled again. It was my mystery caller. I was sick of this.

"Hello Jason. What are you doing?" They said to me.

"I am just sitting here right now." I said.

I was going to try to keep him/her on the phone long enough to get a trace if it was possible. So, I was going to make conversation.

"You are and why aren't you doing something?" They said.

"Because I want to just sit is why and it is none of your business anyway." I told them.

"Well, just remember Jason, I am going to get you and I even know how I am going to do it." They told me.

"OK, well when you are ready just come on and do it. I am tired of waiting on you." I told them.

"This is getting exciting for me Jason. You seem to be so calm about it all." They told me.

"I am not scared of you. You should know that by now." I told them.

"I am coming soon Jason count on it."

I had kept him on the line just long enough for a trace to be run on my phone and find out where they were calling from. I hung the phone up. The operator called me and told me that they were calling from a pay phone from the shopping mall on Ft. Williams St. I told them I knew where that was. And I thanked them for it. I told them to keep the tap on my phone for right now until we caught them.

At least now I knew they were calling from a pay phone. I could get someone to watch the mall for me and take some pictures of people on the pay phones. There were three of them in the shopping center.

I called Jerry Underwood a private detective friend of mine from Childersburg, Al.

"Hello Jerry.

"Hello Jason. What are you doing?"

"Trying to figure out who my mystery caller is. What are you doing?"

"Not much right now. You have a mystery caller?"

"Yes. I had a trace put on my phone and they are calling from a pay phone in the mall in Sylacauga."

"You need some help Jason."

"Yes, I need someone to come to the mall and watch the phones and get some pictures of people on the phones. Would you be interested?"

"Sure. I would be glad to do that for you."

"When could you start?"

"Is tomorrow night good?"

"What time do you need someone to watch?"

"I get the calls from about 7:00 on. The one thing I think that will be important is that I think the person making the phone calls drives a 1957 two tone red Chevrolet."

"Do you know if it is male or female?"

Murder of Grace

"The voice is muffled but it sounds like a male."

"Ok. I will be there tomorrow night. If I get anything I will come by the house and give it to you. I know where you live. You do still live in the same place, don't you?"

"Yes. And thank you very much."

It was about 8:00 PM. I needed to talk to my mom for a minute, so I called her. She answered the phone on the first ring. She normally does answer on the first ring when I call her.

"Hello mom." I said.

"Hi, Jason, how are you?" She asked me.

"I am fine just tired." I told her.

"It is good to hear from you." She said.

"Well, I have been very busy lately and am going to be very busy this weekend trying to get information on Charlotte and Delores. I have some very important meetings with people and I will not get to come over this weekend. I hope you can forgive me for that." I told her.

"I understand Jason. Just be careful. I am very worried about you. You have been too stressed out lately. You need to take a break and rest some." She told me.

"I will as soon as I get through this. It is just going to be a long ordeal I am afraid. But Rita is planning to come next weekend and spend a few days with me. I will make sure that you get to meet her while she is here. Maybe I will get a little rest then." I told her.

"That is nice Jason." She told me.

We talked for about ten minutes and said our good byes.

I went to the kitchen and got me a fresh cup of coffee and went back and sat down in my recliner to wait on a phone call from Mr. Cummings letting me know that he was in Sylacauga. At 9:15 he called me and told me that he was at the Jackson Trace

Motel. I told him that I would see him in a few minutes.

I got to the motel and found him, and he invited me in his room.

"Did you have a good trip Mr. Cummings?" I asked him.

"I did and am glad it is over." He said.

"I have a few questions I would like to ask you about Delores if you do not mind answering them." I said.

"I will be glad to answer anything if it will help us to catch the one that killed her." He told me.

"Anything will be a help since we do not have anything that gives us any clues as to why the murders are taking place." I told him.

"Is there more than one that you are dealing with?" He asked me.

"Yes we have two young women and we are sure that it is the same person committing the murders. So, any information that you can give us will be appreciated very much. We need to find whoever it is before they keep going on with more murders." I told him.

"This is very serious then Jason. I am sorry to hear it."

"Mr. Cummings could you tell me what her favorite thing in life was. The thing that she enjoyed the most." I asked him.

"Please just call me Tom. And the thing that she liked most in life was to dance. She took Ballet dancing lessons when she was a little girl. Actually, she became very proficient with it." He told me.

"Did she want to take it up as a profession?" I asked him.

"In fact, she joined a group and followed them and worked in big shows with them with her Ballet. She won awards for her dancing and was very proud of them." He told me.

Murder of Grace

"Do you know the name of the company that she worked with?" I asked him.

"No, that was so long ago I don't remember. Remember I have not seen her about ten years." He told me.

"No I have not forgot that is what you had told me. That is a long time with no communications. I am so sorry to hear that." I told him.

"Now I will never get to see her again. This is tearing my heart out. I loved my little girl." He said.

"I am so sorry. I know this is hard on you right now and I appreciate you taking the time out of your life to help us out. It is very kind of you to do this." I told him.

"I am willing to help all I can." He told me.

"Tom, it is getting late and I know that you are tired right now. Would you like for me to come back tomorrow and talk with you some more?"

"Yes. If you do not mind I would appreciate that."

I left and went home and went to the kitchen and poured me a cup of coffee and went back in the living room and sat down in my recliner. I was thinking about what I had learned about Delores at this point. I wondered what her being a ballet dancer would have to do with her being murdered.

She had won awards Tom had told me. Did that mean that maybe she had become very popular. She traveled with a group and they did a lot of shows according to Tom. She must have been very good. Maybe there will be some other things that will help to understand the reasoning for the murder. My mind is wondering. We know more now than we did.

It was late and I knew that I needed to go to bed and try to get a little sleep. I got up and turned out all the lights and went to my bed room. Tomorrow is Saturday. I was hoping to be able to relax this weekend, but I guess I will not get to.

CHAPTER FIFTEEN

It was time to go to bed. I locked the doors and turned the lights out and went upstairs to my bedroom. Alice had been here today, and boy did it smell good. I pulled my clothes off and lay down on my bed. I was staring at the ceiling thinking about what I was going to do tomorrow. I closed my eyes and was relaxing and was looking forward to a good night's sleep. I started getting very sleepy. Then I saw a young tall slender woman with long dark black hair. I was slipping off into another dream. I hated it so much. The dream was coming no matter what I did.

I could not open my eyes. I saw her just as plain as you could see anyone. She had long dark black hair. Her eyes were dark blue. She had a long face and narrow chin. She had long arms and long fingers. She lad long slender legs. She was very well trimmed and was beautiful.

She was standing by the window in the living room looking out. The street lights were on and no one was in the streets it appeared. I could see it all. It was as if I was in the room with her. Then a figure showed up. Tall slender, muscular figure. I could not tell much about them at all. They were very hazy. The figment was very dull but just enough that I could see they were tall and muscular.

He told the young woman to come and sit down on the couch and she did. She seemed to not fear him although he had a sickle in his hand. He told her he just wanted to talk to her a minute. She said that she did not have much time. He told her he did not need much time.

"All I want you to do is dance for me."

"I can't dance tonight. I don't have any music here."

"You can dance without music."

"I don't dance anymore."

"If you don't dance for me I will have to hurt you."

"I quit dancing.

I knew then that she was a ballet banker. Why is he killing ballet dancers?

He walked over behind the couch and put the sickle to her throat and sliced it from ear to ear and she was dead instantly and he went on and carved the body up just like he had the other two women and I woke up.

Damn. This is getting ridiculous. Another dream of another murder of the same kind. We have a serial killer on our hands. We have to stop him before he gets to her. I did not need this tonight, but it happened anyway. I have been having dreams of the nature since I was a very small boy about six years old.

I went to the bath room and took me a shower hoping that would help me to relax and maybe be able to get a little sleep. I hated to have to think about it anymore. But I could not get it out of my mind. That is about all that I could think about.

I got out of the shower and dried off. I went in the living room and sat down in my recliner. I knew that I was not going to be able to sleep right now. I did not want to close my eyes. I was scared to. I just sat there and wished I had somebody to talk to.

I had been sitting there about ten minutes when the phone rang. I reached over and picked it up and answered it.

"Hello." I said.

"Hi Jason. You have had another one of those dreams tonight." She said.

"Yes I did. And it was awful." I told her.

"That is why I called. I just knew that you had. I woke up from a dead sleep and that is all I could think about. I decided that I should call you." She said.

"Thank you for calling Rita, I needed somebody to talk with." I told her.

Thankfully Rita could see things and she seems to always call at the right time. I was devastated. I really did need someone to talk with and it was just the time of night that I would not call anyone unless it was an emergency.

"Well, Jason I am coming next weekend. I wish I could come now but I just cannot leave right now. We have too much going on in the unit. My boss told me I could have a few days off after next week if I wanted them. So I am going to take them. I need it." She told me.

"I will be so happy to see you. It will be nice to have someone around for a few days." I told her.

"Are you OK now Jason?" She asked me.

"I will be fine. It is not easy, but I can deal with it. This one was a little more detailed than the last two were, but I am getting used to it in spite of the fact that it is so disgusting." I told her.

"I will let you go for now and I will call you again tomorrow sometime." She said.

"I am going to be pretty busy tomorrow and if you call and do not get me just keep calling I will be here sooner or later." I told her.

"Bye Jason."

"Bye Rita."

It was sure nice to hear her voice. I needed that. That at least helped some. Maybe I can just rest some here in my recliner. I did not want to go back to the bed. I was afraid I would surely dream again and that I did not want.

I closed my eyes and went to sleep. I woke up when I heard the clock go off. I had forgot to turn it off for the weekend. But that was ok I needed to get up early anyway.

I went to the bathroom and washed my face in some cold water to wake myself up good. I went to my bedroom and found me some clean clothes and put them on. Then I went to the kitchen and put on a fresh pot of coffee.

I sat down at the table and waited for the coffee to make. When it was finished I poured me a cup. I took my coffee and went in the living room and sat down in my recliner and turned on the TV. The news was on and they were going over both the murders in Sylacauga. They said that since both murders had happened the same way that we must have a serial killer here, but the police just have not concluded that yet.

I turned the channel and found some cartoons to watch for a few minutes.

I decided that I would go out and eat breakfast at The Grill and Eggs Breakfast Bar. I go there and sat down at my usual table. Sally Worthington came to the table to take my order.

"Hello Jason. You never come on Saturday mornings. How are you?"

"I am fine Sally."

"What can I get you this morning?"

"Just bring me my usual Sally and thank you."

Sally normally waited on me when I went to The Grill and Eggs Breakfast Bar. She had medium length brunette hair. She had dark blue eyes and an average build. She was a very lovely lady and had a great smile and was always pleasant.

Just as she left the table I looked towards the door and Tom Cummings walked in. I waved at him and he came over and sat down with me. Sally came back and took his order.

"Did you have a good night tom?"

"I did Jason."

In a little bit Sally brought our food to the table.

"Tom, I actually met Charlotte and Catherine and I talked with her for a few minutes. Catherine is an attorney friend of mine. Charlotte seemed like a very nice lady. We both liked her." I told him.

"Everybody around home really liked her and keep asking me where she is and what she is doing."

"Did she finish school?" I asked him.

"No, she left when she was sixteen years old with the ballet outfit and went on the run to dance. That is all she wanted to do." He told me.

"So, she was a traveler." I said.

"She loved being on the road a lot. She told me the last time she talked to me that when she was back in the area she was coming to see me. That has been a little over ten years ago." He told me.

"She had a boyfriend who lives in Charleston, South Carolina. She had listed him as a cousin on a job application and that is how I found him. I called him and talked with him for a short time. I have to go and meet with him in South Carolina the first of the week sometime. Maybe he will be able to give us some information concerning her. I sure hope so." I told him.

"I never knew she had a boyfriend in South Carolina." He said.

"We are going to follow any and all leads that might give us any information concerning her." I told him.

"I hope you will find the murderer." He told me.

"Tom the Sheriff and the Chief of Police would like to talk with you. Can I call them and set up an appointment for you to meet with them Monday sometime?" I said to him.

Murder of Grace

"Sure, I will be glad to talk with them. Maybe we can get some arrangements for the body and all to be taken care of." He told me.

"I am sure Dexter will be glad to help you get that worked out. I am sure they will meet with you together. That way you will only have to answer questions one time." I told him."

"That sounds good Jason."

"Once I get a meeting set up with them I will let you know when it is."

We left the restaurant and I went back to the house. I called Jeff and told him that Mr. Cummings was in town now and that he was willing to meet with him and Dexter. I asked him if he could set up the meeting with him and Dexter for the same time. He told me he would call Dexter and get it set up and call me right back and let me know when it was.

In a few minutes Jeff called me back and told me that he and Dexter would be glad to meet with him Monday morning at 8:00.

I called Tom at the motel and told him when the arrangements were. I told him that I would meet him Monday morning and we could go see them together and I would introduce him.

"Hello. Jason. How are you this morning?"

"I am fine mom. I will be over in a little while. Are you going to be home?"

"Yes, Jason I am going to be here."

"I will see you soon then. Bye for now."

I left the house to just ride around for a little while.

I got to moms at about 10:00.

"Hello mom. What are you doing?"

"Waiting on you Jason."

She asks me if I wanted something to drink. I told her I would love to have a barq's root beer. We went in the kitchen and sat down at the breakfast nook. She got me my barq's root beer and her a glass of orange juice and asked me did I want a snack. She had some cinnamon rolls and I got me one of them.

"I thought you were not going to be able to come this weekend."

"I got it worked out and I needed to see you mom. You always make me feel better. All I can do lately is dream."

"I am sorry to hear that son. I wish there was something we could do about that."

"I am going to have the dreams no matter what we try to do to stop them."

"I know Jason. We have spent a lot of money trying to help you overcome them and it has done no good."

"I know mom. That is why I know there is no need for me to spend money to try to stop them. They are a part of my life and I just have to deal with it."

"But I still wish there was something that we could do."

"What have you been doing mom?"

"Working in my flowers and a little crocheting lately. What have you been doing?"

"I have been working mostly. Rita is coming next weekend. She told me last night when she called."

"That is good Jason."

"I will make sure that you get to spend some time with her while she is here. You will really her mom. She is super."

"I am sure I will like her Jason."

I left and went back by the motel to see if Tom was OK. He told me that he did not bring enough clothes to carry him for several days and that he needed to buy a couple of suits. I took him to a small men's store downtown and he found two outfits and bought them. I took him back to the motel.

Murder of Grace

It was late and I was ready to go to the house. I told him that I would call him sometime tomorrow and see how he was. I left and went home.

I made me a pot of coffee and I sat down in my recliner to rest some. It was about the time of day for the mystery caller to call. Jerry told me that he would be in Sylacauga today to start checking on that for me. He said if he found anything that he would come by the house and bring me the information. He always did what he said he would do. I knew I could depend on him.

I had been sitting there thinking about the things that I had learned from Tom when the phone rang. I answered the phone and sure enough it was my mystery caller.

"I am coming soon. Very soon." They said.

"Well when are you coming?" I asked him.

"Very soon." He told me.

"You are causing too much trouble right now. I am going to stop it." They told me.

"Make yourself feel real good about it when you do because you will need to." I told them.

"I already feel good about it. You are nervous and that makes me feel good. I like it that way." They told me.

"I am not worried about you. You are too chicken to do anything. I think you have a rubber neck myself." I told him.

"Don't you ever talk to me that way again or I will come a lot sooner." They told me.

"I am not scared of you." I told them.

He hung up. I think I pissed him off. I don't think he liked me talking to him that way. I had just about decided that it was a male making them phone calls and I still think it is the person driving the red 1957 Chevrolet. I was going to catch him one way or the other.

I was sitting there thinking about the phone call that I had just had when the phone rang again. I answered the phone.

"Hello." I said.

"Hi Jason, what are you doing?" Rita said.

"Stewing over my mystery caller calling me again." I told her.

"You just cannot get a breather can you Jason?" She told me.

"It does not seem like that I can." I told her.

"Things will get better Jason." She told me.

"I have a good friend of mine working on trying to find out who the caller is now. At least we know it is from a pay phone at the mall." I told her.

"That is good Jason. Maybe you will catch him now." She said.

"I hope so." I said.

"What did you do today?" She asked me.

I told her about my day and what had taken place. I had had a good day just a long one. She was happy to hear that it had been a good day. We talked for about thirty minutes longer on the phone and finally decided that we needed to hang up. She told me she would call me back tomorrow.

I explained to her that I had to go to Tuscaloosa tomorrow and that when I got back home that I would call her.

We said good bye and hung up the phone. I sat back in my recliner and was ready to get some rest now. I sat there for about five minutes and the phone rang again and it was my mystery caller.

"Hello." I said

"Hey Jason I am getting close now." He told me.

"OK why don't you just get it over with?" I told him.

"I would but I just like making you miserable because I know you look forward to these calls." He told me.

"Of course, I do but just come on or are you just too scared to come and try. You know I have a lot of friends." I told him.

"I will be there soon." He told me and hung up the phone.

I sat there for a few minutes thinking about what I was going to do about my mystery caller. I was tired of him calling me now. I hoped that Jerry had been there tonight and had something on him.

I heard the doorbell ring and I went to the door and peeped out and it was Jerry. Jerry had some papers in his hand. He told me that he had been to the park and watched the phones. He told me about the man in a red 1957 Chevrolet that had come up and got out of his car and went to the phone and made a phone call and seemed to have been on it for a little bit. He had the time written down and it was about the time of the first call he had made to my house.

Then he had the same information with another call at about the same time as the second call had come in. It was the same guy in the red 1957 Chevrolet. He had some pictures that he gave me of the person. They were not great pictures, but they were pictures.

I looked at them and it was someone that I did not recognize. I told him that he did not need to do that anymore that it had been the person I thought it was the whole time. All we must do now is just find out who that red 1957 Chevrolet belongs to.

We talked for a few minutes. He told me that he had been very busy lately. It seemed like that everybody needed him at the same time. I told him I understood that. I asked him if I needed some help could he help me out rounding up information on this murder case going on in Sylacauga. He told me he would help if I needed him

It was getting a little late by now and I was about ready to go to bed and try to get a little sleep.

William Honeycutt

I turned out the lights in the house and made sure all the doors were locked and went to my bedroom.

    I pulled my clothes off and lay down on the bed. It was time to try to get some sleep. I was tired and sleepy

CHAPTER SIXTEEN

I was lying on my bed and finally closed my eyes. I turned over on my side and was almost asleep. I saw the woman with the long dark black hair again. Oh my god, I do not want to dream again. I need to rest in peace for a change. I do not need to dream about this murder again. It is getting more than I can handle. How much longer can I deal with it? I tried to open my eyes and I couldn't. I knew that it was fixing to happen again. I only had the dreams this close together when it was going to happen. Please let me wake up and not see anything else at least for tonight. I turned over on my other side and it just would not go away. She was there no matter what I did.

It was getting worse. I did not know what to do. The tension was building. I wanted to curl up and never wake up.

It was making me go crazy. The dreams would not leave me alone. Finally, I was able to open my eyes.

I got up and sat on the side of the bed. I was shaking a little. This has never happened before. It has never done this to me. I got up and went to the bathroom and splashed my face with cold water. It never really helped that much but I always tried it anyway. It at least made me feel a little better.

I went to the kitchen and made me a half pot of coffee and poured me a cut and sat down at the breakfast nook table. I just wanted to be left alone. I did not want to be bothered anymore. I was getting sick. It was tormenting me. My mind and every part of my being.

I drank my coffee and wondered when the murder was going to happen. I would bet that it was going to be a short time between this one and the last one. He was getting braver by the minute I think. I do not think that he thought we could ever catch him He was good. I will give him that.

I really did need some sleep. I needed to go back to my bedroom and try to get some sleep. I had a long day ahead of me tomorrow. I needed to be rested before I started out towards Tuscaloosa. I need to have my mind clear so that I could ask the questions that I needed to ask. That means I need some sleep.

I went back to the bedroom and lay back down on the bed and was dreading to close my eyes, but I did anyway. It was clear. I did not see anything. I fell asleep. I woke up Sunday morning when the clock went off at 6:00.

I went to the kitchen and made a pot of coffee and went back to the bedroom and put me on some leisure clothes for traveling and went back to the kitchen and got me a cup of coffee.

I called Mr. Gardner to make sure that he would still be able to meet me today. He told me that he would definitely be there. I told him that I would be there at about noon. He told me to call him and let him know that I was there, and he would meet me.

I made me a bowl of cereal with a banana in them and ate me some breakfast. I called Tom at the motel to be sure he was OK. The morning was slipping by. It was time for me to leave.

I left Sylacauga and made it to Tuscaloosa at about 11:30. I stopped at McDonalds and got me something to drink. I found a pay phone and called James to let him know that I was there. I told him where I was, and he told me to just wait and he would meet there. I told him what kind of clothes I had on. I had on my blue jeans with my red button up shirt and my red and white sneakers.

He made it there shortly.

"Hello Mr. Caffrey."

"Hello Mr. Gardner. Just call me Jason."

"OK Jason just call me James please. Is here OK or would you like a place a little more private?"

"This is fine with me."

We got us something to drink and sat down at a corner table. There was hardly no one in the restaurant.

I told him that I hated to have to bring this up, but I knew that she had left Tuscaloosa trying to get away from an ex-boyfriend. That is at least what she told us. He said I am that boyfriend. We were just having a hard time at the time. Things were not going good for neither of us. She had asked me to just go away for a little bit and let her alone. I did not want to go away and leave her alone. I loved her. I wanted to spend all my time with her. She was a very talented young woman. I just wanted to be with her. She impressed me.

So, she was not trying to get away from you because you were being abusive to her. He told me that definitely was not the case. He said he had never been abusive to her. He loved her too much for that.

I asked him what she did. He told me that she worked in the rayon mill not too far from Tuscaloosa. I asked him how long she worked there. He told me that she had worked there about two years.

I asked him did she have any talents. He told me that she was a dancer. I asked him if she was a ballet dancer. He told me that she was and that she was very good at it.

Things were coming together. But why would someone be killing young women who happened to be ballet dancers? I don't know but I hope we find out soon.

I asked him how long she had been a ballet dancer. He told me that she had told him that she had been dancing since she was about five years old. That is a long time I told him.

Did she graduate from school or do you know anything about that? I do not know he told me. But I know that she joined a group that traveled, and she danced all over this part of the country. She had moved around a lot because of her ballet.

I told him I needed something else to drink and did he want me to get him something. He wanted something, and I got us both something.

I ask him did she have any friends who could give us any information about her. He told me that as far as he knew that she did not have any friends in Tuscaloosa that he knew.

I am meeting with her Father in Sylacauga sometime about the middle of the week. I do not know exactly when yet, but we are getting that set up with him. His name is Jarrell Taylor. Have you ever heard her talk about her father? Yes, I have he told me. I knew his name but in I did not know him. It had been a long time since she had seen him she told me. I asked her why and she told me that was none of my business. So, I did not ask her anything else about it.

Is there anything about her that we need to know that you can think of that will help us to tie this murder to somebody? The only thing I can think of that we have not talked about is that she drank a good bit. She had turned to liquor to try to drown out her troubles. Do you drink I ask him? He said that he drank some but not much.

I told him that I hated to have to ask him this but since he was an ex-boyfriend I was going to ask it. He told me to ask anything that I wanted to ask. I ask him did he actually have anything to do with

Murder of Grace

the murder of Charlotte Taylor. He assured me that he did not have anything to do with it at all. He told me that he could not nor, would he ever do anything like that to anybody.

"Well James it is getting late and I need to head back towards Sylacauga. If I need to talk with you can we meet again?"

"Sure. Just give me a call and we can definitely meet."

I left McDonalds and I was hungry now. It was time to find something to eat. There was a little restaurant on the right side of the highway about twenty-five miles outside of Tuscaloosa on the way home that I like to eat at when I was in this area. When I got to it I stopped and parked and got out and went in. It was called Taylors Steak and Ale. I love steaks and they usually cooked a good one.

The waitress came to the table and took my order. She brought my tea back to the table while I was waiting for my steak to get there. I was just relaxing and waiting for my meal to arrive when someone walked up to me and ask me who I was. I ask them what they wanted and why did they want to know who I was. They ask me if I was from Sylacauga. I told them that I was. They said they thought they recognized. The lady looked at me and said you are Jason Caffrey, aren't you? Yes, that is me.

May we sit with you for a few minutes? I allowed them to sit with me. I learned that it was friends of mom and dad's that had known me all my life. I just really did not know them. They said they had not seen them in a long time. We are planning to come to Sylacauga in a few weeks and we plan on looking them up and spending some time with them. Tell them that Jerry and Lisa Weathers said hello. I will tell them for you and I know they will be pleased to hear from you as well.

William Honeycutt

The waitress was bringing my dinner just as they were leaving. I ate my steak and paid my ticket and left the restaurant.

I was driving down the road and there was a hitch-hiker on the road. I don't normally pick them up but I stopped and picked this one up. He told me that he was going to Sylacauga. I asked him what he was doing hitch-hiking on a day like today. He said that he needed to get to Sylacauga so that his mom and dad would not be mad at him.

He had a small back pack with him and he ask me if he could just set it on the floorboard in the front between his legs. I told him that would be fine.

In a few minutes he was piddling in his back pack for something and he pulled out a .22 Remington pistol and stuck it towards me and told me that he wanted me to stop and do what he tells me to do or that he would shoot me. That was a shock. I was not expecting anything like that. He looked like he was about nineteen years old. I slowly pulled over to the side of the road and ask him what he wanted me to do. He told me to slowly get out of the car and that he would be right behind me with the gun pointed straight at me.

I got out of the car very slow and watched him very carefully. He seemed to be just about ready to shoot anybody that did not do what he told them to do. This was not turning out to be a good day after all. He told me he wanted me to carefully take my bill fold out of my pocket and to give him all my money that was in my billfold. I told him he could have what I had but I did not have much in my billfold. He told me to take it out of my sock if it was not in my billfold.

I told him that I did not have any in my sock either. I told him that what little money I had was in my billfold. He did not believe that and wanted me

Murder of Grace

to take my shoes off and pull my socks off so that he could see if I was lying or not.

I finally was able to make my move and I kicked his hand with the gun in it and the gun went flying from his hand and I kicked him in the stomach and he doubled over and went down to the ground. I was really pissed by now. I had my handcuffs in the car where I could get to then. I got them and put them on him and sat him back down in the car in the front seat where I could keep a good eye on him.

I took him all the way to Sylacauga with me because that is where he said he wanted to go. I took him straight to the police station and filed a report on him. They put him in jail. I found out that his name was Calvin Deason. I told him I would see him tomorrow that I was too tired to fool with him right now.

I left the jail and went home. It was about 7:30 by the time I got home. I made me a pot of coffee and got me a cup when it finished and went and sat down in my recliner. It was time to call Rita.

"Hello Jason. How are you?"

"Hi Rita. I am finally home and I am fine." I told her.

"That is good Jason and what are you doing?" She asked me.

"I am just sitting here in my recliner talking to you and taking it easy for a change today. It has been a busy one." I told her.

"I am sure you are tired by now after your trip to Tuscaloosa." She said.

"I am and I am glad to be home."

"Did you have a good trip Jason?"

"I did except that I picked up a hitch hiker and he tried to robe me with a .22 Remington."

"What are you doing picking up hitch hikers?"

"He was a young boy and I hate to see kids out like that and I left sorry for him." I said.

"I guess that taught you a lesson."

"I don't normally do that, but I just could not pass him up."

"You need to be more careful Jason. That will get you in trouble."

"Are you ready to come down next weekend?"

"Yes. I am looking forward to it. I can stay a couple of days longer if that is OK with you."

"You can stay as long as you want to."

"I am sure we can find plenty to do."

"OK I just wanted to call you and let you know I am home and am OK. I will talk with you later."

"Bye Jason. See you soon."

I rode over to the motel to see if Tom was OK.

He told me he was trying to figure out what he wanted to do once he got everything settled with his daughter. His wife had died about two years ago he told me, and he was by himself. He has four children living and they all keep him company most of the time when he is home. He told me he had not taken a trip since his wife had died and that he thought he might need to do that sometimes and just enjoy life.

He said this trip has done him a lot of good. It had helped him coping with his wife's death.

It was getting late. I left the motel and went back to the house to get some rest. I went in and got me a braq's root beer and went back to the living room and sat down in my recliner. I turned on and turned it on the news channel. It was all the same old things as normal. Nothing new.

I locked all the doors and turned out all the lights and went to my bedroom. I knew that I needed to get some sleep if it were possible. I pulled my clothes off and lay down on the bed on my back looking up towards the ceiling wondering what tomorrow was going to be like. It seemed that there was always a surprise for me. I just dreaded to see what it was.

CHAPTER SEVENTEEN

I turned over on my side to close my eyes. I was almost asleep when I saw the woman with the long dark black hair and dark blue eyes in another dream. WHY? Please! I do not need this tonight. My brain is overloaded right now. The stress is getting bad. PLEASE go away.

I tried to open my eyes and I could not. We just had a murder. We did not need another one. The woman with the long dark black hair would not go away. I could not help from seeing her. The image of the man was there but just not much to go on. He had the sickle in hands. She was nervous.

He told her that she had to dance for him or he was going to hurt her. She told him that she did not want to dance and how was he going to hurt her if she did not dance for him. That is my secret he told her. All I want is to see you dance again. I have watched you and I like the way you dance. She told him that she did not have any music and that she could not dance without some music.

He told her that she would regret not dancing for him because she would have to pay the price.

It looked like it was going to be another one of those nights. No sleep again. It was definitely keeping me from getting any rest.

Finally, I was able to get my eyes open. I sat up on the side of the bed to see if I could just get my mind straightened out. I sat there with my head buried in my hands wondering what I should do now. I went to the bathroom and splashed my face with some cold water. It at least woke me up.

I was able to see plain and to move around good without falling all over everything. I went to the kitchen and put on a half pot of coffee.

When it finished making I poured me a cup and went in the living room and sat down in my recliner and turned the TV on. All I wanted to do was find something funny and fun.

I found The Three Stooges and watched it for a few minutes.

I hoped that I would be able to get a little sleep. I sure needed it.

I drank my coffee and got me another cup and when I finished drinking it I went back to my bedroom to lay back down.

I was lying on my bed on my back. I was scared to close my eyes. I just knew that I was going to have the dream no matter what I did. I finally closed my eyes. I was not seeing anything. After a while the alarm clock went off at 5:00. It scared me, and I almost jumped off the bed. I realized what it was and turned it off.

I got up and put my jogging shorts on. I was looking forward to seeing Jane this morning

I walked out the door and she was waiting on me as usual.

"Good morning Jane. How are you?"

"Me. I am good Jason and, how are you?

"I am ready to run this morning Jane. Let's get started."

We started running and about a mile down the road our brown boxer met us and would not let us get past him until we petted him. We rubbed his head and he was happy and went on about his business.

"What have you been doing Jason?"

"I have been working Jane. It seems like right now I just cannot get a break."

"You will be OK Jason."

"A good friend of mine is coming this weekend to spend a few days with me. I am looking forward to that."

"That is always nice."

We were back at the house. I went in the house and put on a pot of coffee and took me a shower and shaved. I dressed and got ready to go to work. I poured me some coffee and drank a couple of cups while I was watching the morning news.

I called Tom at the motel to see if he wanted to meet me and eat some breakfast. He did. We met at The Grill and Eggs Breakfast Bar. Catherine came in We got to the restaurant at the same time. We had been there about five minutes when Catherine walked in the door and saw me and came over to say hello. I asked her did she want to sit with us. She sat down with us and I introduced her to Mr. Cummings and explained to her who he was. She gave him her condolences for his daughter's murder. She asked him how he was doing and how was he handling her death. He told her everything was fine and that he was doing well with it all considering everything.

The waitress came to the table and took our orders.

"What are you doing today Jason?" Catherine asked me.

"I have to make arrangements to go to South Carolina today or tomorrow." I told her.

"Why are you going to South Carolina?" she asked me.

I told her about Ray Bradford being Delores es ex-boyfriend. She told me that maybe all this would be a help.

I told her about having met with Charlotte's ex-boyfriend yesterday and how that I learned that both these ladies were ballet dancers and were in the professionals on top of that.

"Ballet dancers?" She asked me.

"Yes, that was interesting. I am trying to figure why someone is murdering ballet dancers and if we do have a serial killer on the loose around here." I told her.

I wanted to tell her about the third person that I had dreamed about, but I did not want to tell her the details in front of Tom, so I just waited. I was sure I would see her later anyway. I normally did.

The waitress brought our food to the table. We ate our food and it was time to get to work. Tom had a meeting with the Sheriff and the Chief of Police at 8:00 this morning. I told him that I would meet him over there and introduce him to them and he thanked me for that.

We got to Dexter's office and Jeff had just gotten there. I introduced them. I told them that I was going over to the office and that I would be back after a while.

I left and went over to the office. I got Ray Bradford's telephone number out and gave him a call. He answered on the first ring. I asked him which would be better for me to meet him tonight or tomorrow sometime. He told me that tomorrow would be the best time to meet him. I told him that I had to decide and that I would call him back in a few minutes.

I got my arrangements made and called him back and told him I would be there tonight and that we could meet in the morning if that is possible. He told me that would be fine. I told him that we could work out where to meet once I got there. He told me he could be there by 9:00. I told him that would work for me.

Now that was settled. I could move on with the rest of my morning. I went back over to the chief's office to see if they were still in a meeting with Tom. They were. The secretary told me I could go in if I wanted to. I told her that I would just wait till they were finished and then I would go in and talk with Jeff and Dexter.

They were in the meeting for about another half hour when Tom walked out of the office. I saw him and walked over to him and ask him how it went. He told me that they were both very courteous and very nice. He said that they told him that he could do whatever he wanted with the remains of the body.

I asked him how he was going to handle it under the circumstances. He told me that he wanted to have the body cremated and take the ashes home with him. He wanted to have a memorial service with the family and friends. He was almost in tears when he was telling me that part of it. I knew that was hurting him very much. And the sad things were that it had been over ten years since he had seen her. I could not imagine what that would be like to have a daughter that you had not seen in more than ten years and she gets murdered. That would be very hard.

I thought it over and decided that I would call the airport back and set up my arrangements back to Birmingham from Charleston. I chose the 7:50 PM flight to Birmingham. She told me it would leave at 7:50 PM and arrive at 10:56 PM. That was good. That would give me plenty of time to get home and get some rest once I got to Birmingham.

Tom had already left and went back to the motel.

I went over to see Catherine and see what she was up to.

I got to the office and the secretary told me to go on in that she did not have anyone with her right now but that she had an appointment in about thirty minutes. I thanked her and walked on into Catherine's office. She motioned for me to sit down in the chair beside the desk this time. I sat down.

"What are you doing Catherine?"

"I am getting ready for my appointment."

"I have had another dream Catherine. It is a lady with long dark black hair. He is on the move for the third one now. We have a serial killer on the move."

"You think it is going to happen Jason."

"I have had this one several times already Catherine. It is going to happen soon. I do not believe there is anything we can do to stop it."

"That is not good Jason. We should be able to do something."

"It is going to happen in the same area as the last two Catherine."

"How do you know that Jason."

"I just know that it is. It is a serial killer."

"That is sad Jason. I don't know what to say."

"I am leaving tonight to go to South Carolina. I am meeting with Ray Bradford. The boyfriend of Delores."

"You think he will be able to help Jason?"

"I don't know but we will find out."

Her secretary stuck her head in the door and told her that her appointment was there. Catherine told her to tell them she would be with them shortly.

"I sure hope we find out something that will help to catch him."

"I will let you know if I get anything that might do any good."

"OK Jason. Please do."

I got up and told her I would see her later and left.

I went over to talk with Jeff a few minutes to see if they got anything from Mr. Cumming that I did not already have.

I got to Jeff's office and they showed me in.

"Hello Jeff."

"Hello Jason. What you got on your mind today?"

"I have a lot on my mind today Jeff. I have to go to South Carolina today and visit with Mr. Bradford and see if I can get anything more that will give us some leads towards the killer of these two women."

"What time are you leaving today Jason?"

"I am leaving from Birmingham at 3:15. I have got to go home soon and get things ready to go and head out to Birmingham. I do not need to be late for sure."

"When are you coming back?"

"I am coming back tomorrow night. I will get back into Birmingham about 11:00 tomorrow night."

"You will be tired for sure Jason."

"Yes, I will but I will be ok. Maybe I will not have any dreams. That will be nice."

"You do not need to have any more dreams Jason."

"I have had one for the last several nights."

I went on and told him about the dream and what the young woman looked like and told him that it was fixing to happen and there was nothing we could do to stop it. That is what pisses me off so bad is that I have the dreams and see the person that is going to be murdered and cannot do anything to stop it. We did our best to stop the one with Charlotte and it still happened. He told me he understood how that must make me feel.

I told him I guess I had better leave and go on to the house and get my things ready to do.

I told him I would see him later and left.

I got in my car and it was just about 10:30 AM. I decided that I could run by and say hello to Dexter before I went home.

I got to the Police Department and went in and Dexter had just walked into his office when I got there. He motioned for me to come on in. I went in and he motioned for me to sit down in the chair in front of the desk.

We talked about Tom for a little bit. He told me that they would have the remains of the body cremated for him by tomorrow afternoon. They had already called him and told him when he could come and pick up the ashes. I told him that I was headed to Charleston, South Carolina to talk with Delores boyfriend there to see what I could get from him. I told him that I would be back Tuesday night.

I told Dexter I would talk with him when I got back from South Carolina and let him know what I came up with. We just needed one good clue that would help us a lot. Maybe I will get it from Ray when I see him.

I went to the house and I called Alice and told her she knew where the key was to get in the house. I told her that I would not be there Tuesday but I needed for her to do some special cleaning for me because I was having company next weekend. I told her that if she needed to bring someone with her to help her this week to bring them and let me know how much I would owe them. She told me that she had someone that would help her get everything in excellent shape. I told her to use them both days if she needed to.

I went upstairs and put me on some traveling clothes and got ready to head out to Birmingham. I called Tom to tell him I would be gone until tomorrow night. I asked him how long he planned to stay. He told me that he was going to stay till Wednesday and then he was going home. I told him I would see him Wednesday before he left.

I left the house and went towards Birmingham. I got to the airport at about 2:30. I was pushing it. I made it into the lobby and found the ticket booth. I purchased my ticked and the agent told me where to go. I got to the gate just in time to make it on the plane.

I am always pushing time it seems like. But I was there and that is all that mattered. I got on my flight and was sitting in my seat and was waiting for the plane to take off. It set there for a long time before it finally left. I think we were about thirty minutes late leaving the airport. That is OK. I have all night anyway, but I would like to get there and hopefully get a good night's sleep. I knew that I was not planning to do anything except just go to the hotel and rest.

Instead of making it by 7:18 PM as it was supposed to it was about forty-five minutes late. I got off the plane and went and found me a rental car. I got my car and found a Holiday Inn and got me a room.

I went to my room and took my things in. The first thing I wanted to do was find me something to eat now. It was getting late for sure. I found a good steak restaurant and ate me a good T-bone steak and went back to my room and turned on the TV to see what I could find to watch.

I pulled my clothes off and lay down on the bed for a few minutes and got up and took me a shower and cleaned up. I called the desk and asked them to call me at 6:00 in the morning. It was time to make a phone call and work out the arrangements with Ray for our meeting in the morning.

I called him and when he answered the phone I told him who I was. He asked me where I was. I told him. He told me that he could meet me at the Hotel if I wanted to. I told him that would be fine. He told me he would see me then at 9:00 in the morning at the hotel.

I left the TV on and turned it down real low. I just wanted a little noise tonight. I thought maybe that would help me to be able to get some sleep. In a few minutes I was out like a light. I did not have any dreams and I slept like a baby. That was the first good night's sleep I had had in a long time.

I was sleeping tight when the phone rang at 6:00. I answered it and got up. I put on my clothes. They had a restaurant in the hotel. I went over to the restaurant and went in and found me a table and sat down.

The waitress came to the table and took my order.

In a few minutes she brought my order to the table.

I ate it and went and paid for my meal and left the restaurant and went back to my room. It was about 8:30 by now. It was about time for Ray to be there. I just sat down in one of the chairs in the room and sat back and thought about what I needed to ask him.

In a few minutes the phone in my room rang. I answered it and the clerk told me there was a Ray Bradford there to see me. I told them to tell him where my room was and send him around to it. In a couple of minutes someone was knocking on my door. I opened the door and this tall muscular man was standing there looking at me. He had dark black hair and was a very handsome man.

"Hello are you Jason Caffrey?"

"Yes, that is me. Come on in Mr. Bradford if that is you."

"That is me."

He came on in the room I asked him to have a seat. He sat in the chair next to the window. I sat down in the chair on the other side of the table.

"How long had you known Delores?" I asked him.

"I had known her about two years. That is about how long we had been seeing each other when she disappeared." He told me.

"How did she disappear?" I asked.

"She was here one day and gone the next and I never saw her again." He said.

"What did she do?' I asked him.

"She was a ballet dancer. She was tied up with an outfit that did some traveling and she would be gone for a week or two at a time but she always came back home." He told me.

"So, she was a professional ballet dancer then."

"Yes that is all she did." He told me

I asked him did she have any friends that he knew that knew things that would help us. He told me that if she had any friends like that that he did not know who they were.

I told him that I hated to be so blunt with him, but I needed to ask him something that I hated to half to ask. He told me to ask away. I asked him did he have anything to do with the murder in any way. He assured me that he did not have anything to do with it. He said that it had been a while since he had seen her and wondered where she had gone. He said that he kept hoping that she would come back, but she just never showed up.

Then I got that phone call from you telling about how that she had been murdered. I just wanted to help if there was anything that I could do.

We sit around and talked for about another hour and I did not learn anything that I already did not know. I thanked him for his time and he left. It was about 11:00. I had enough time to make it to the airport very quickly. I called to see if I could change my flight. She told me that they had one leaving at 12:45 and would arrive in Birmingham at 2:44 PM. I asked her could she get me on that flight and she told me that would not be a problem.

I rescheduled my flight. Got my things and headed to the airport. I got there just in time to get my ticket changed and make the flight before it left. I was on my way home much earlier than I expected. The flight left on time. That is not normal. But it did. I was in Birmingham at 2:44 just like I was supposed to be.

I found my car and headed home. I was in Sylacauga by 4:15. I went by the Police station to see if Dexter was there and I found him getting ready to leave.

I asked him did he still have Calvin Deason in jail. He told me he did but that he was sure he would be going to the Talladega County jail in the next day or two. I asked him if I could talk with him for a minute. He let me go back to see him.

I walked in the cell and sat down on the side of the bed with him. I asked him why he pulled that gun on me and try to rob me. He told me that his mom and dad were hungry and that they did not have any way to get any food or anything. He said that his dad was not able to work and that they needed something to eat.

I asked him if he was telling me the truth or was that something that he was making up hoping that I would believe it. He told me that it was the truth and if I would just go to his house I would know that he was telling me the truth.

I thought about it for a few minutes. I ask him where his mom and dad lived. He told me they lived in the Avondale community. I could not believe what I was hearing from him. I told him to tell me exactly where the house was and to tell me his mom and dad's first names. I told him I would go by and see them on my way home today and talk with them about him being in jail and why and see what they wanted to do about it.

He told me that they could not do anything about it because they did not have any money to do anything with. I told him I was going to see them. He gave me their names. His mom's name is Dorothy and his dad's name is Jessie. I told him I would see him tomorrow for sure. I would talk with him more about everything then.

I went back to the office and Dexter was still there waiting on me to finish with Calvin. We talked for a little bit and I let him know that Mr. Bradford was not of any help at least for right now. But I told him that it did not feel right and that I was going to hire someone to keep a watch on him and see what kind of a life that he lived. He fits the description of what I thought the killer might look like which was not enough to go on yet.

I just wanted to make sure that we did not miss out on something that we needed to know. I had a good friend in Charleston that was a Private Investigator. I told Dexter that I was going to call her and see if she would help us watch out for him and see what he was involved in. She will do it for me I know. She always has done favors for me when I asked her.

I think I am ready to go to the house and rest for a while. But I have to make a stop on my way home. I am going by to see Calvin's mom and dad on my way home and tell them that he is in jail and why and see if what he is telling me is the truth. Dexter wanted to know what he had told me. I told him I would tell him tomorrow after I checked his story out. I will talk to you tomorrow I am sure.

I left and went towards the Avondale community.

CHAPTER EIGHTEEN

I headed for Georgia Ave. close to Central Avenue. I found it with no trouble. I pulled up in the yard of a very run-down house. I was kind of heartbroken to see people living in those kinds of homes. I got out and went and knocked on the door. A man came to the door and I told him who I was and asked him was he Jessie Deason. He told me he was. I ask him did he have a son named Calvin Deason about 19 years old. He told me that he did but that he not seen him since Saturday. I ask why. He told me that he had gone to try to earn a little cash so that he could buy some groceries because they did not have anything to eat.

I told him that his son was in jail. He asked me why and I told him about how Calvin had ended up in jail. He told me that he did not know that Calvin had a gun. He wondered where he had gotten it. I ask them did they have any food. He told me they did not. I told him I would be back in a few minutes.

I went to the store and bought some groceries and took them to them. I gave them the groceries and told them that I would see what I could do about their son being in jail. I told them I would be back some time tomorrow and talk with them.

I left and went by the motel to see if Tom was OK.

While I was there he told me that since he had talked to the Sheriff and the Chief yesterday that he had gotten really depressed. They told him that everything would be ready by Wednesday about noon. He was going to pick up the ashes he told me. He told me he was going to wait till Thursday to leave.

I left and went home. I went in the kitchen and put on a pot of coffee and went back to the porch to set and watch the birds and enjoy being at home.

Jeff pulled up in the yard and got out of his cruiser.

"Hello Jeff. What are you doing?"

"Was riding around some and thought I would stop by for a minute."

He came up on the porch and sat down in his usual chair.

"Have you got anything arranged on that drug ring in the warehouses yet Jeff?"

"No not yet. I am working on it though."

"We need to get that broke up as soon as possible." I told him.

"Yea. Maybe we can get that done Thursday sometime."

"Have you seen Tom lately Jeff?"

"No."

"I went by on my way home and he seemed to be very depressed."

"I noticed that Monday when we were talking with him."

"I am sure this has been very hard on him."

"Without a doubt." He said.

"Let me know if you get it set up for Thursday and I will go with you guys."

"OK. I guess I need to go Jason. I will see you later."

I went in the house and got me a cup of coffee and looked to see what Alice had cooked today. She made some fried Chicken with green beans and mashed potatoes. I got me a plate full and put it in the micro wave and warmed it up and boy was it delicious.

"Hello Jason. It is good to hear you."

"Hi Rita, what are you doing?"

"Nothing right now." She told me.

"I just wanted to call you and make sure you were still planning on coming down this weekend." I said.

"Yes Jason, I am still coming unless of course you do not want me to come." She said to me.

"Don't be silly. You know I am looking forward to your coming down." I said.

"I will be there with bells on my toes and a ring in my nose Jason, you can count on it." She told me.

"Bells on your toes will be fine I do not mind them but leave the ring out of your nose." I told her.

"OK if that is how you want it then." She said.

"This will be a good time for you to meet my mom. She will be tickled to death to get to meet you." I told her

"That will be nice Jason, I know I will like her." She said.

"Everybody likes my mom." I told her.

"Have you been busy Jason?"

"Busy is not the word for it Rita. I have not had time to think. Let alone anything else."

"Sounds like you need some time off Jason."

"Boy do I."

"Well maybe we can just enjoy the days while I am there, and you not work."

"That is my plans. We will see how it goes."

"It will work out Jason. You wait and see."

"I guess I need to let you go Rita. It is good to talk with you."

"OK Jason. I will talk with you soon."

I went and got me a barq's root beer and sat down in my recliner and tried to find something good to watch on TV.

The phone rang.

"Hello. Jason Caffrey speaking."

"Hello Jason. I just wanted to talk with you for a minute." Tom said.

"What is wrong Tom?"

"I got a little depressed and just needed somebody to talk with for a minute."

"I am glad you called Tom. Is there anything that I can do?"

"Thank you for being a friend Jason."

"Anytime Tom."

He told me that he had made all his arrangements to get back home and that his oldest daughter was going to meet him at the airport. I told him I knew he would be glad to see her when he got there. He seemed a little excited about talking about her.

"OK. I will let you go for now. I will talk to you sometime tomorrow."

"See you later Tom."

I was sitting there drinking my barq's root beer when the phone rang..

"Hello. Jason Caffrey. Speaking." I said.

"Hello Jason. It is me again. I have not bothered you lately." He told me.

Oh my God it was my mystery caller again. I just hung up the phone. It is disgusting.

I turned out all the lights except of course for the night lights that were always on.

I went to my bedroom and walked out on my balcony facing over the pool. I sat down in my chair and watched the stars and the full moon and just enjoyed the night air. I went back inside and pulled my clothes off and turned the cover back on my bed and lay down. I turned the TV and was watching a western.

I was getting sleepy. I turned the TV off and turned over on my side and my eyes were getting heavy. I was almost asleep when the woman with the dark black hair and dark blue eyes lit up like a Christmas tree. She was so plain. WHY? Another

William Honeycutt

dream. I just cannot lie down in my house without having a dream. I tried to open my eyes, but I could not get them open. The dream was there, and I could not stop it. I saw the best image of the murderer that I have seen so far but not enough to make him out. Why was I seeing her so plain and only a glimpse of the killer?

I finally was able to open my eyes. I sat up on the side of the bed and buried my face in the palms of my hands. I did not know if I could bear this tonight. I got up and went to the kitchen and made a pot of coffee and poured me a cup when it was finished. I just sat down in the kitchen at the bar and drank some coffee and thought about it.

I had to go back to my bedroom in a little bit and try to get some sleep. It did not look like I was going to get much tonight though. It had started.

I left the kitchen and went back to my bedroom and sat down on the side of the bed. I wanted to lay down and was kind of dreading to because I was afraid of what I would see when I closed my eyes. I went ahead and lay down anyway and slowly closed my eyes again. There she was again in my vision. I could not get her out of my mind tonight.

The murderer was there. He had his sickle in his hands. He was rubbing in between his fingers and licking his lips. He was enjoying making her miserable.

"I guess if you are not going to dance for me I am going to have to punish you."

"How are you going to punish me?"

"I may have to cut your fingers off first."

She started crying and begging him to not cut her fingers off. He told her that if she did not dance for her that he was going to have to do something to make her pay for not dancing.

She found a knife laying on the table that she had left lying there by accident. She picked it up and threw it at him. The knife hit him but only with the butt of the knife. It did not hurt him at all.

"Why are you throwing knives at me?"

"I am trying to protect myself."

About that time, I finally got my eyes open.

I just lay there with my eyes open. It was about 1:00 AM and I just wanted to sleep. I got back up and went to the living room and sat down in my recliner and closed my eyes to see if I could go to sleep sitting there. I was almost asleep when she popped in my dreams again. For some reason she was there tonight. Is this the night that the murder will happen? I went back in the kitchen and got me some more coffee and heated it up in the microwave. I took it and went back to the living room and sat back down in my recliner. It was about 2:00 AM and I needed to at least rest. I was tired from the day. It had been a long day. I closed my eyes again after I had drunk my coffee.

About the time I had closed my eyes and thought that I was fixing to get some sleep the telephone rang. I answered it and it was Jeff. He told me I needed to come to the Avondale area and told me the address. He said there had been another murder and he needed me to come to the house.

I got there and when I got there. They told me it was in the living room this time. It looked like he had killed her on the couch. They told me the body was carved up just like the other two and the body parts placed strategically around the body just like the other two. The head was placed on the chest facing the feet the same as the others had been. It was all identical except this one was in the living room and she had long dark red hair. I walked in the door and saw the body all laid out on the floor it was just like they described it to be.

The third murder had taken place. They had all happened in the same neighborhood. The bodies were all murdered the same and were mutilated and placed all in the same order. It was a serial killer. No doubt about it. They already had all forensics there. They were taking pictures and getting blood samples and trying to find some fingerprints. They already had it cordoned off.

They had found her ID and Jeff told me her name was Jennifer Watkins. I told Jeff that he did not waste any time this time. He said that he had talked to some neighbors. One of them knew her. They had spent a little time with her when she was home. They said that she worked at the mill and that she had lived in the apartment there for about six months. He told me that Dexter was sending some men out here today to canvass the neighborhood and see what he could find out about her.

The other two were ballet dancers. I wonder if she was a ballet dancer. I will lay my odds on it now that she was. And I bet that she is from up north somewhere. We have one from the east and one from the west I bet she will have come from up north.

I told him that I would go back to the mill and see Katland and see if she would give me some information like she did the last time.

Dexter came out of the house and told us that he thinks that we may have a break this time. He found a box with the plastic bags in it that he used for the body parts. Maybe it will have some fingerprints on it. He also said that they found some string on the back of the couch and maybe it was tied into the murder some way.

I told him that he had been too good up till now and maybe he was getting careless. I doubted that he was, but I was sure hoping that he was.

I told Jeff this was another one from one of my dreams. I knew it was going to happen. I never got to meet her before something happened to her though. I at least had gotten to spend a little time with the first one and had at least met the second one. He told me to quit having the dreams and maybe this would quit happening. I told him I would be glad to not have the dreams. My nights would be much better.

It was already 5:00 AM. It was time to go home for a while and get me on some clean clothes to work in and take me a quick shower. I told him I would see them later.

I left and went home. I went upstairs and took me a shower and shaved. I went and put me on some work clothes and headed out to find me something to eat at The Grill and Eggs Breakfast Bar. I got settled at me a table and Jim Sax came walking in the door. I saw him and motioned for him to come over and sit with me. The waitress came and took our order.

"What are you doing out so early Jason?"

"We had our third murder last night Jim. Where were you?"

"In my bed asleep."

"Once Catherine finds out about this one Jim I am sure she will file a motion for all charges against you to be dropped."

"I am ready for that to be over Jason."

"We do not have a clue yet who the murderer is, but I know that it is not you."

"This will clear me completely want it Jason?"

"Yes. Without a doubt. You will have nothing on your record when it is all over."

The waitress brought our food to the table and we ate. Jim told me he had to go because he was on his way to his next job. It was just in Birmingham though not too far to have to go.

He left, and I went on over to my office early to see if I could get my paper work caught up. I had a few things I needed to do this morning. I was sitting at my desk and remembered that I was going to call Janie this morning. They are an hour ahead of us. I am sure she will be in the office by now. I called, and she answered on the second ring.

I told her that I was calling her to see if she could help keep a watch on Ray Bradford who lived in Charleston. She asks me why and I explained to her the reason. I told her I just needed to know as much about him as she could find out. I told her I had talked with him and things just did not seem right. She told me she would be glad to do that. I gave her his address and his phone numbers. She told me that she would find the rest if she needed anything else.

We talked for a couple of minutes and we both had things that we needed to do so we hung up and I went back to my paper work. I needed to make another phone call early this morning and see if I could get hold of Jarrell Taylor. I had his number. So, I called him and he answered the phone. He told me that he was going to call me but was trying to give me plenty of time to get to the office before he did.

I asked him when he was coming to Sylacauga. He told me that he had a reservation for a flight out of Houston at 4:50 PM today that would arrive at 8:51 PM. I asked him did he want me to meet him at the airport. He told me that he could rent a car and drive it. I told him that would be fine. He told me that he could just stay in Birmingham tonight and come to Sylacauga early Thursday morning.

I told him that would be fine and when he got in Sylacauga Thursday to give me a call and let me know that he was here. We talked for a little longer and then I told him I needed to go and would talk with him tonight when he got in. I hung the phone up. I knew I needed to go over to the jail and talk with Calvin Deason.

I left the office and went over to City Hall. I asked them if I could see Calvin Deason. They allowed me to go in and talk with him. I told him that I had gone over to his house and talked with his mom and dad. I told him that I had went and gotten some food and took it to them and they were not hungry for right now. He told me how much he appreciated it.

I ask him where he got the gun from. He told me that he took it off a drunk who was sitting under a tree in the park in Tuscaloosa. I ask him didn't he know that the gun would get him in some serious trouble. He told me that all he wanted to do was scare somebody into giving him some money, so he could buy his family some food.

I really believed him.

I told him that I would talk with an attorney that I know and see if there is something that we might can do to help him out. I know that you are going to have to pay for the crime some way. But maybe there is something that can be worked out. I will see what I can do although it was me you pulled the gun on. I could just drop the charges, but you would still be in trouble over that weapon that you had on you.

Let me do some talking and I will get back to you. You will not be here much longer. They will move you to the Talladega County jail soon. But I will still come and see you OK and let you know what I find out.

I left the jail cell and went back, and Dexter was there, and I stopped in and talked with him a few minutes. I told him about Ray Bradford and how I felt about it not seeming right with him some way. He may be involved in these murders. I don't know yet, but I have a detective friend of mine working on it. She lives in Charleston. She told me she would see what she could find out.

I left the City hall and went back to my office. I had a few reports I needed to make. I worked on them and had them about finished and the phone rang, and it was Rita. She wanted to know what I had been doing today. I told her I had been very busy. We talked for a few minutes. She told me she needed to go she had to get some reports filled out before she got into trouble but that she just wanted to say hi to me.

It was dinner time. I called Catherine and ask her had she eaten yet. She told me she had not. I ask her did she like Mexican food. She said she did. I invited her to go to the Mexican restaurant with me and I would buy. She accepted, and we met to eat our lunch.

CHAPTER NINETEEN

We went in and found us a booth back in the corner where it would be quite hopefully. We sat down, and the waitress came to the table and took our order. I just wanted me some enchiladas with some good hot sauce to go on them. She ordered a Tostada meal.

"I just did not want to eat alone today so that is why I asked you to come and eat with me." I told her.

"What have you been doing today Jason?"

"I have been trying to get loose ends tied up and get my paper works together. I usually wait till the last minute to get my reports ready. I have been trying to do a little along this week so that I would not have to do it all at one time." I told her.

"That is good. You should always do it that way." She said.

"I know but I am usually on the run most of the time." I told her.

I told her about Calvin Deason over at the jail and the situation with him and me. She was alarmed. I explained to her the stories I had gotten from his family and him. I told her I truly believed they were all telling the truth. I asked her was there any way that she could help to keep him from actually serving time in prison I think I know enough people that I can help find him some work that would help to bring in some money. I am willing to try to help him if there is any way that it can be done.

She told me that she could represent him in court and do her best to get him out of serving time. He would still have the record and would have to report to a parole officer, but I think we can help him if you feel sure that he would be true to what he promised us that he would do. I will have to talk with him and make my decision at that time.

"He is in the city jail right now, but they are going to move him soon to Talladega County jail." I told her.

"I will go over after we finish eating since I do not have any thing pressing me until later this afternoon. Will you go with me?'

"Yes I will go with you Catherine. That way he will not be as scared since he knows me."

After we finished eating our lunch we went over to the jail to talk with Calvin. They brought him out and took us in one of the open offices and let us talk there. I introduced him to Catherine and he was very polite. She told him that she needed to ask him a few questions. He told her that he would be glad to answer them.

"Why did you pull a gun on Jason, Calvin?"

"I was trying to scare him into giving me some money, so I could buy some food for my family. Dad cannot work. He is not able to." He told Catherine.

"Where did you get the gun from? Did you already have it? Why did you think you needed a gun? You know that is dangerous, don't you?"

"No, I did not have a gun. I took it from a drunk man sitting by a tree in the park in Tuscaloosa and yes mam it is dangerous, but we needed some food and I could not get a job for some reason and I had to try something." He told her.

OK Calvin, Jason has checked your family out and we find that it is true in what you have said about no food. I believe your story. I think you are telling us the truth. I am going to represent you in court and try to get it set up to where that you will not actually have to serve time in jail. You will have to report to a parole officer if I am able to get this to work for you. You will still have a record. I will not be able to get you released from all the charges, but you will be free and will be able to work.

He told Catherine that he did not have any money. She told him to not worry about the money that she did this sometimes when she felt confident that the person had a good reason for what had happened in their life. She told him just to tell the truth at the hearing once it was set and that she would take care of the rest.

We left the jail and went on back to her office. I wanted to talk with her a little more and let her know what all was going on. I kept her in touch with all the details of everything at least that I was allowed to. She was my best friend around here anyway.

We talked for a few minutes and I went back to my office and got all my reports for the day finished. I needed to run by the hotel and see how Tom was doing.

I knocked on his door and he came to the door.

"Hello Tom. How are you today?"

"I am fine Jason. I went and picked up the ashes to take home with me today."

"It will all be over soon Tom and then you will be able to move on with your life."

"Yes. It is not going to be easy, but I will be able to handle it. My family will be close and watch out for me."

"I know you will. Have you eaten anything yet Tom?"

"No."

"Would you like to go over to Charlie's and eat?"

William Honeycutt

"Sure."

"Meet me there and we can eat and then I have to go home."

We got to Charlie's and found us a table and just as we were sitting down good Jim Sax come strolling in the door. He saw me and came over to say hello.

"Hello Jason. What are you doing?"

"Hello Jim, how are you. This is Tom Cummings the father of Delores Cummings."

He shook Tom's hand and told him that it was nice to meet him and told him he was sorry for his daughter's death.

The waitress came and took our order. Jim ordered some take outs so that his wife would not have to cook when he got home.

We sat around and jut talked about all the conditions of our little city and wondered what it was all coming to in the end. I told them that we would catch this murderer soon. Tom said that he bet those people living in the Avondale community were scared and worried about everything. I told him that they were and we needed to get this stopped as of like right now. We have a few leads that we are working on. I hope that something shows up soon.

In just a little bit the waitress brought Jim his take outs. He left and went home.

Tom and I finished eating. I told him I would talk with him tomorrow before he left and headed out towards my house. I got home and sat down in the swing and swung back and forth dangling my feet watching the birds and looking at the beautiful flowers growing in my front yard.

I love red roses, so I had a few in my front yard to where I could see them when they were blooming. I hardly ever went in my back yard. I need to though. Maybe I need to put me a swing in the back yard and start spending my time there.

Murder of Grace

While I was sitting on the porch it was getting dark, I saw that red 1957 Chevrolet come by the house. I still could not see the full tag number. I decided that I needed to go to Coosa County and find the sheriff and tell him about this car passing my house and looks pretty much like it is stalking me. I needed to also take him the pictures that I had of the person in a 1957 red Chevrolet and let him see them and explain to him that they have been making these phone calls to my house and see if there was any way that he could catch them. I decided that I would do that the first thing tomorrow morning.

It was time to go in the house and watch a little TV and get some coffee and enjoy another cup before time to go to bed. Some people cannot drink coffee at night and sleep. Coffee does not keep me awake. The dreams is what keeps me awake.

I found a good Patrick Swayze movie and was watching it when the telephone rang. It was the mystery caller again. I was sick of this. I told him that I was going to get him, and he could count on it. He was a little pissed when I said that. I hung up the phone when I told him that.

I knew then for sure I was going to Rockford Al. and see the Sheriff.

It was about 8:30. I called Rita.

"Hello." She said

"Hello Rita. What are you doing?"

"I am just sitting here relaxing from a long day at work." She told me.

"I am doing the same. I had a long one to today." I told her.

"It is good to hear from you Jason." She said.

"I just wanted to talk with you a few minutes and see what you were up to." I told her.

"I have been busy, busy just trying to get everything caught up before Friday got here." She told me.

"My mystery caller called again tonight." I told her.

"What are you going to do about that Jason? It does not seem that they are going to leave you alone."

I told her what I had planned to do tomorrow concerning the mystery caller. She told me that was a good idea. It seemed that my life was filled with problems and that I had to get something done about this one. I was hoping that the Coosa County sheriff would be able to help me out.

Well, we talked a few minutes and I told her I needed to get off the phone. We hung up.

In a few minutes the phone rang.

"Hello. Jason Caffrey speaking."

"Hello Jason, this is Jarrell Taylor. I decided to come on to Sylacauga tonight."

"Have you found you a place to stay yet Jarrell?"

"No. Where is a good place to stay Jason?"

"The Jackson Trace Motel is a clean motel and they are friendly. It is also one of your cheaper motels in the area."

"I will stay there then."

"You have my office number. Call me in the morning some time and we can meet and talk."

"OK. I will do that."

"Come to think of it. It would be better if you called me in the afternoon and we can meet."

"I will. I will talk with you tomorrow."

It was getting late. It was time to try to get some sleep. I turned out the lights and went to the bedroom.

I lay down on my bed. I turned on my TV to have a little noise. I was a nervous wreck about right now. I just did not want anyone to know how much all this really upset me. I have had too much happening lately in my life. I was worn out. I did not know which way to go I just wanted my life to get back to normal. Like it was before all these murders started happening in our little city.

I did not care what was on TV. I just wanted to relax tonight. I hoped that was possible.

I was lying there on my bed watching a good action movie by Mel Gibson. I always love his movies. They were always good. I closed my eyes and was slowing drifting off into sleep. Then I saw a young woman with long blonde hair and beautiful sky-blue eyes. She was sitting alone in her living room watching TV. She was laughing and enjoying her life it seemed like. Then, a tall muscular man it looked like came into the living room from the kitchen and stood there with a sickle in his hands. He was rubbing it in his fingers and licking his lip and looking straight at her. She screamed very loud and jumped up and ran towards the door. She was not fast enough to get to the door before he had his hands on her arm and pulled her very hard backwards. She fell on her back on the living room floor. She was still screaming, and it seemed that no one was hearing her. He grabbed her and jerked her up and slung her toward the bedroom door. She fell through the door and landed just inside the bedroom.

She was still screaming. He got her by her arm and slung her up on the bed and told her that he was tired of her making a fool of herself and that he was going to stop it. He walked over to the side of the bed and she tried to get off the bed and he would not let her. He was a strong man and she had no advantage over him.

She knew that he was fixing to kill her. She was scared out of her mind. She did not know what to do. She tried to get up again and he slung her back down on the bed and told her not to move again or that he would kill her right now.

She lay there hoping that he would not kill her. She hoped that he would just go on and stay away but she knew that he was going to kill her no matter what she did.

She tired one more time to get up. She scrapped him on the arm with her long fingernails. She did not know what else to do. He slapped her and pushed her hard back down onto the bed.

He brought the sickle up close to her throat and told her that if she did that one more time that he would kill her right then.

She lay very still and in a little bit he placed the sickle on her throat and sliced it from ear to ear and made sure that he got the jugular vein. She died instantly.

I still could not tell who the man was. I only had a slight image of him. Could only tell that he was a tall muscular man. That is all I could get.

I woke up. I was shaking all over. This was the worst dream that I had had yet. I could not believe that I had had so much detail of the next murder scene. I was very upset. I was delirious. I did not know what I was going to do. I had to have somebody to talk to. I did not want to be alone right now. I wanted to be where somebody was that I could talk to.

I tried to get up, but I could not. I had to sit back down. My stomach was hurting. I was sick. I tried to get up again and made it up, but I staggered to the bathroom and splashed water on my face. I looked in the mirror and almost scared myself. The dream had scared me out of my mind tonight. It was unreal. I washed my face with soap and water and splashed cold water on it again. I dried off and combed my hair. I felt a little better.

I went to the kitchen and made a pot of coffee and poured me a cup when it finished. I went in the living room and sat down in my recliner. I could not stand it anymore.

"Hello Jason." Very sleepily.

"Hi Rita. I hated to call but I had to talk to somebody and I knew you would understand."

"You had another one of those dreams Jason. How bad was it this time?"

"It was bad Rita. It thinks it was the worst one so far. He is on the move Rita. It is another long blonde headed woman. He is going to make it his fourth victim."

"Jason you are going to have to quit having these dreams."

"I wish I could."

"Jason I will be there this weekend. Maybe that will help."

"I am so glad you are going to be here Rita. I need somebody. This is about to drive me crazy."

"I just had to have somebody to talk with for a minute Rita."

"It is OK Jason. You know can call me anytime."

"I guess I need to let you go."

"Are you going to be alright Jason?"

"Yes, I will be fine Rita. It is just so hard sometimes."

"If you need me again call me. OK."

"Ok I will.

We hung up the phone. I needed to try to see if I could rest now. I got up and went back in the kitchen and got me a cup of coffee and brought it back to the living room. I sat back in my recliner and drank it. I leaned back in my recliner again and closed my eyes. I did not see anything and that was nice. I needed some sleep. In a few minutes I was asleep. My alarm clock went off at 5:00 as it normally always does. I got up and went upstairs and turned it off and put on my jogging shorts and walked out the door. Jane knew that I ran every day and she was waiting on me this morning.

"What are you doing out this morning Jane?"

"I decided that I would get in an extra day Jason."

"It is good to have you this morning to run with."

She smiled and told me it was nice to see me. We ran our five miles and got back to the house. I told her I would see her in the morning. I went in the house.

CHAPTER TWENTY

I went upstairs and took me a shower and got dressed. I went and made me some coffee and drank a couple of cups while I watched the morning news. They had found out that the ladies were ballet dancers and were calling him the Ballet Casanova. They can always come up with something. It was the most talked about story on the news right now.

I left the house and headed towards Rockford to talk with James Watkins the Sheriff of Coosa County. I needed me some breakfast and there was a little restaurant in Stewartville, Al. called Faye's Fabulous Kitchen. When I got to the restaurant I pulled in and parked. I went in and found me a table and Sally Perkins came to the table."

"Hello Jason." She said.

"Hello Sally. How in the world are you doing? It has been a long time since I have seen you." I told her.

"I am doing great." She said.

"May I take your order?" she asked.

She took my order and turned it in to the cook. She came back over and told me that she was not busy right. She asked if she could sit and talk for a little bit. I told her that would be nice. She told me that she was married and had two children and her husband was a truck driver and he was on the road a lot. She said she just worked some to have something to do while the children were in school. She told me that she did not have to work but it did give her a little extra money to buy extra things for the kids.

I told her what I was doing and that I had a very busy schedule most of the time. She asked me was I married yet. I told her that I was still single and was still not in a hurry.

The cook called out my order and she went and picked it up and brought it to me and asked me did I need anything else. I told her I could use some more coffee

I ate my breakfast and left the restaurant and headed towards Rockford. I got there at about 8:45 and went into the Sheriff's office and asked if Sheriff Watkins was in. They showed me into his office. I shook his hand and introduced myself to him.

He motioned for me to have a seat in the big chair beside his desk. I sat down. He asked me what I was doing in Rockford this morning. I told him I needed to talk with him about a 1957 Chevrolet and a mystery caller. I am hoping there is something you can do to help me out.

He told me he would do whatever he could. I explained to him about my mystery caller and the 1957 red Chevrolet coming by my house and how that it looked very suspicious that they were stalking me.

He told me that he could find out who the person was that owned the car. I gave him my phone number and told him when he found out something to please call me and let me know. I told him I would come and press charges at that time. He told me he would. I thanked him for his time and left and headed back to Sylacauga. I made it back to Sylacauga by about 10:00. I went home. I knew that I had that meeting with Mr. Taylor today.

I called his motel room and told him that we could meet sometime this afternoon, but I just did not know what time yet. He told me that he would just wait on me to get there.

I left the house and went to the office. I knew I had to find out if Calvin had been taken to Talladega yet and when his hearing was. I called and talked with them at the police station and they told me that he had been moved to Talladega. I called the Talladega County jail and talked with them about when his hearing was. They told me that the hearing had been set for Monday at 2:00 PM. I thanked them and hung up the phone.

I called Catherine to see if she knew what was going on. She told me she had not checked yet. So I told her what was happening with Calvin. She told me that she did not have to worry about anything because I did her work for her. We both laughed, and she thanked me for it.

I asked her had she heard anything from the courts about Jim Sax yet. She told me she had just gotten a letter from them today and that she was going to have her secretary type up a letter for Jim and get it in the mail no later than tomorrow. She told me that they had dropped all the charges and that Jim was free. I told her Jim was waiting on that letter because all this still had him and Jane very upset. I told her I would talk to her tomorrow sometime. We hung up the phone and it was time to go and see if I could find some lunch.

I left the office and went over to Charlie's to get me something. I was sitting at my table and Dexter came in and saw me and came over and sat down. I ask him if he was going to eat. He said he sure was.

The waitress came to the table and took our orders.

"Well Jason, what have you been doing this morning?"

"I have been to Rockford to see the Sheriff this morning." I told him.

"That is good. Did he give you any good news?" He asked me.

"Yes he said that he could find out who was driving that 1957 Chevrolet and when he did he would let me know." I told him.

"Maybe you can get that cleared up Jason." He said.

"Well, I hope so this is getting old and I am just tired of it. Dreams and mystery callers and robbers are just too much to be going on all at one time." I told him.

"Have you found out anything concerning Jennifer Watkins from the neighborhood folk?"

"Yes. They told us that she is a ballet dancer."

"Another ballet dancer. I knew she would be. That is his MO Dexter."

"Hopefully we will find out something that will get us a lead on him."

"I have had another one of those dreams Dexter. He is going for his fourth victim."

"No way. This is enough. We have to stop him some way."

"The only image I get of him is that he is tall and muscular. It looks like the hair may be black, but I am not sure of that."

"Well maybe you will get a really good picture of him if you have another dream Jason."

"This is the fourth one of them dreams. She was blonde headed. That means that the rotation of hair color is staring over. I am disgusted, and I just want it all to stop. I hope you get something from the neighbors concerning Jennifer Watkins that will give us a clue to who it is killing these young women."

The waitress brought our food to the table. We ate, and chit chatted for a few minutes and got up and shook hands and left the restaurant. I needed to go home for a while. It was getting about time for Tom to leave to go the airport. I needed to say bye to him before he left and thank him for coming and helping us get some things cleared up.

I went to the motel to talk with him a few minutes before he left. He thanked me for everything that we had done and for me be so nice to him while he was here. I told him that if he ever came back through the area to give us a call. He told me he would. It was about time for him to go. I told him goodbye and left the motel.

I went by Jarrell's room and told him that I had some things that I had to do this afternoon and that it would have to be tonight before I would be able to get with him.

I went back to my office and got all my paper work lined up. It was getting late. My days were going by too fast lately. It was time to go and find some dinner. I left the office and rode over to the Mexican restaurant and Jeff was already there. He saw me and waved for me to come over and sit with him. He had not ordered yet. The waitress came over and took our order.

I told Jeff that these dreams were getting too much for me. I told him about the new dream of the lady with the long blonde hair. I told him that it looked like it was a cycle. Three with different color hair and then the fourth with the same color hair as the first one. I told him that Dexter had told me that they had found out that Jennifer Watkins really liked ballet dancing.

All three of them were ballet dancers. Why was he killing ballet dancers? What had these women done to him? Did he follow them on road trips and scope them out and find them so that he could just kill them? Did he hate ballet dancers? Or did he just hate dancer's period? It was so shocking. Is this fourth lady that I have dreamed about a ballet dancer? I bet she is.

I guess we will find out. Maybe I can find her before anything happens to her and maybe we can stop this one. He is doing things so much closer together than what he was. I do not know if I have time to do anything.

I was going over to the mill today and get any information concerning Jennifer that I could, but I just did not have the time to do it. I will go the first thing in the morning and take care of that. Maybe I can get some information that will do us some good. I sure hope so.

We chit chatted for a little longer and drank some tea. I told him that I had to go to the motel and talk with Mr. Taylor and see if he could give us any information that would help us with leads towards the killer. If it goes like it has so far, I might not get anything. I am sure you and Dexter will want to talk with him. It is Charlotte's father. He told me that they would want to talk with him. I told him when they got something set up to meet with him to let me know. I told him I need to go and see him later.

It was time for me to go and talk with Jarrell. I got to the motel and told him if he had time we could talk now. While we were getting ready to get started the phone rang. Jarrell answered it. He handed it to me. It was Jeff. He told me that he and Dexter could come over to the motel and we could all talk with him at one time and get it over with tonight. I asked Jarrell would that be OK with him and he said that would fine.

While we were waiting for Jeff and Dexter to get there I asked him what kind of things Charlotte liked to do in life. The first thing that he told me was that she loved to ballet dance. He said that she had done that from a very small child. She loved sports, but she just did not have time for them much because she loved ballet more than she did sports.

We just talked a little while we were waiting for the sheriff and chief of police to get there. In a few minutes they knocked on the door and Jarrell opened the door. They came in and we all found us a place to sit.

I asked him was there anything that she liked to do other than ballet that she was involved in. He said that if there was that he surely did not know what it was because for the last ten years he hardly ever even heard from her. I told him that I was very sorry to hear that and that must be very hard on him.

They told Jarrell that they were so sorry to barge in on him this way but felt that we could do this with one meeting and make it easier on him than to have three meetings and him have to answer the same question several times. He thanked them for that and told them it was hard enough just being here under the circumstances and he appreciated their concern.

I told them about her enjoying ballet from a small child and that she had been raised up in Houston. Jeff asked him did she have any friends that he knew of that knew anything about her that he might not would have known otherwise. He told Jeff he only knew of one person that she knew that would know a lot about her, but they lived in Tuscaloosa, Alabama. I asked him did he know their name. He told me his name was James Gardner. I asked him did Mr. Gardner live in Tuscaloosa and come to Houston to visit her or was he from Houston originally. He told me as far as he knew that Mr. Gardner was from Houston originally but followed her when she left Houston.

Dexter ask him did she have any girl friends that kept up with her and what she was doing. Did she belong to any clubs or groups? He told us that she had joined a dance organization that traveled around. I asked him did he know the name of it. He told me that he did not have a clue what the name of it was.

He asked them was there any way that they could have the body cremated and that he could take the ashes back with him when he went home. They told him that could be done with no problems. He ask them what was the soonest they could have that ready for him. Dexter told him that per request he could get that done tomorrow and have them ready by about 4:00 pm for him. He told him that they did not usually get it done that fast but that he could get it expedited in the case of an emergency and that he considered this an emergency. He told Dexter that he would come by his office and pick them up.

We talked with him a good bit longer and finally Jeff and Dexter said that they needed to go. I told them that I would talk to them tomorrow. They thanked him for his time and for him being so polite with them. They left.

I told him I had to go home it was getting late and that I would talk with him tomorrow.

I got to the house and put me on a pot of coffee and poured me a cup and went and sat in my recliner. The phone rang.

"Hello. Jason Caffrey speaking." I said.

"Hello Jason." Rita said

"What you up to girl?" I asked.

"Just wanted to call you and let you know when I would be in Birmingham." She told me.

"When will you be in Birmingham?" I asked her.

"I will be leaving here at 6:00 pm and will be there at 9:33 pm tomorrow night." She told me.

"OK. I will be at the airport waiting when you get there." I told her.

"What have you been doing today?" she asked me.

"Well let's just say I have had a very busy day. Mr. Taylor from Houston is in town and we just finished a meeting with him." I told her.

"Well I will let you go for now. I will be there tomorrow night at 9:33 and please don't forget. OK." She said.

"Don't worry I will not forget. I will see you when you get here. Bye for now." I told her.

We hung up the phone.

It was about 10:00. It was getting on the late side already and I was worn out. I left and went to my bedroom and stretched out on my bed. Boy did it feel good.

CHAPTER TWENTY-ONE

I was just lying there looking up at my ceiling and wondering when all this was going to end. I was thinking about tomorrow night. I had to go to Birmingham and pick up Rita. That was the most exciting part of my week yet. I was looking forward to that.

I just wanted to rest and relax and get some good sleep. I was tired. It had been a long day. I was trying to figure out in my mind if we actually needed to get someone to watch James Gardner. I thought that maybe we needed to put a tail on him since he followed Charlotte from Houston. He did not tell me he was originally from Houston.

I turned over on my side. I had a detective friend in Tuscaloosa who I could get to help me out. He owed me some favors anyway. I decided that I would call him tomorrow. Bryan Richardson was his name.

I was slowly getting sleepy. I closed and eyes and was relaxing pretty good when the tall slender long blonde-haired lady popped up in my dream. I opened my eyes immediately. I did not want to have to deal with this tonight. I just wanted to sleep.

I turned over on my other side and lay there for a little bit thinking about what I was going to do about my mystery caller. It was time to get his butt put in jail. That would stop him at least for a while. I wanted to know who he was and why he was harassing me.

Murder of Grace

Finally, my eyes closed. I did not see anything. It seemed to be peaceful for a change. I was drifting away. My eyes were heavy now and I was almost dead asleep when I saw her again. I could not open my eyes. I was too far gone this time. She was there begging him to please not kill her. I saw her begging him over and over. That is all I could see tonight. I knew this murder was fixing to take place soon because the dreams would not leave me alone. I could not get any break from them.

Finally, I was able to open my eyes. I was awake. I sat up on the side of my bed. I was shaking again this time. These dreams up until recently had never left me shaking like this. Why were they making me shake? Was it because it was scaring me?

I decided that I was going to go to sleep no matter what was going on. I lay back down on the bed. The shakes had gone away. I closed my eyes and I saw a neighborhood, but it was not in Sylacauga. I recognized the neighborhood. It was in Talladega. That is where I recognize it form. Then she came in my dream again. I jumped up off my bed and left the bedroom. I went to the bathroom and washed my face in cold water.

I went down to the kitchen and made me a pot of coffee. I knew that my night was over. When it was finished I poured me a cup and sat down at the table in the breakfast nook. I needed to try to drown out my memories if possible.

My dreams were back to a blonde headed woman. Was he changing his location? It looked like he was according to my dream. I wondered why I had seen that location in Talladega He was going to leave Sylacauga and go to Talladega now. That was why. I had to talk to somebody about it and inform Talladega that they were fixing to have a murder in that location and what the lady looked like.

I finished my cup of coffee and went and poured me another cup and went in the living room with it and sat down in my recliner. I was disgusted. I was very upset. I did not like to call anybody at 3:00 AM. That was just too early, but I needed somebody to talk to with. I had to hear a human voice tonight. I could not wait till the morning.

I knew that he would be pissed at me but I also knew that he would forgive me, so I picked up the phone and called Jeff. He answered the phone on the fourth ring.

"Hello." Very groggily He said.

"Jeff I am sorry I called you, but I had to have somebody to talk to." I told him.

"What in the hell is so important that it could not wait a little while longer Jason?"

"I was so upset after I had another dream tonight. It concerned the last lady I told you about but it is not going to happen here. It is going to happen in Talladega. I saw the neighborhood and all. I saw her begging him to please not kill her. It left me shaking again this time. These dreams have never done this to me before." I said to him.

"Well Jason there is nothing that we can do right now. We will have to wait till later on this morning."

"I am sorry to have called you, but I had to have somebody to talk with. I cannot talk to just anybody about these dreams. I can always talk with you." I said.

"OK. But I am a little pissed at you right now, but I will get over it Jason."

"I had to hear a human voice Jeff. The only person I knew that I could call right now was you. I appreciate you not just hanging up on me."

"I would never hang up on you Jason."

"I will let you go back to sleep I will be OK now I think. I feel a little better since I have talked with you. I just needed to talk to somebody. Thanks Jeff."

"OK Jason. Talk to you later."

I had finished that cup of coffee and I went and got me another cup and went back to the living room and sat down. It was 4:30. I had to get myself together. I had a very busy day today. I turned on the TV to see if I could find anything that would get my mind off the dream. I found The Three Stooges and watched them. It gave me a few laughs. It made me feel a little better.

My alarm clock went off. I got up and went and turned it off and put my jogging shorts on and headed out the door. Jane was there waiting.

We started immediately on our run.

"Did you have a good night Jason?"

"I did not get much sleep last night."

"Why?"

I was surely not going to tell her the real reason.

"Just one of them nights. You know how that is."

"I have had them Jason. I know exactly what you are talking about."

Not really. She does not have a clue what I am talking about. She don't know about the dreams and I am not going to tell her.

We found our big brown boxer and petted him, and he was happy. We finished our run. I told her I would see her Monday. She told me she always looked forward to it.

I went in the house and made me a pot of coffee and went took me a shower and shaved and went and got ready to go to work.

I poured me some coffee and went and turned the TV to the morning news. They were talking about the Ballet Casanova. They had it down pat. Or at least they thought they did.

William Honeycutt

The doorbell rang, and I went and opened the door.

"Good morning Jason. This is Florence Henderson."

"Hello Alice and it is a pleasure to meet you Mrs. Henderson."

"It is a pleasure to meet you also Mr. Caffrey."

"Just call me Jason."

"She is going to help me get everything spic and span for you Jason. Who do you have coming?"

"Rita from Virginia."

"I will make sure it all smells really good and looks fabulous."

"Be sure to change the sheets on the bed in the bedroom with the king size bed That is where she will keep her things."

"I will be sure that is done Jason. Are the boys coming this morning?" She asked me.

"Yes, they will be here, and their check is with you Alice."

"I will have to write Hrs. Henderson's out for her before I leave this morning."

"Is there anything in particular you need me to do Jason?"

"Give it extra special care and dust everything. If you need to work longer please stay as long as you need to."

"Do you want me to pay you tomorrow Mrs. Henderson or is your fee enough for the time?"

"Today will be fine Mr. Caffrey. I will be very satisfied."

"We will get to work Jason."

"There is a check there Alice if you need supplies go and get them."

I talked with Alice and asked her how much I was going to owe Mrs. Henderson. She told me, and I wrote her check and handed it to Alice.

Murder of Grace

I left the house and went to The Grill and Eggs Breakfast Bar. I went in and sat down close to the window. Jeff walked in and came over and sat down with me.

"Well, Jason. Is thing going any better for you right now? You sure look cheerful this morning."

"Everything is about the same Jeff, but I will be alright. I had a bad night. Of course, you know about that I called you early this morning."

"It is OK Jason that is what friends are for."

"I appreciate you not being mad at me I just had to have someone to talk with. It helped a lot. I was able to function after I talked with you."

The waitress came to the table and took our order.

While we were waiting for or food to come Jeff told me that the only thing that we could do was go to Talladega and talk with the Chief of police and tell him what you saw in the dream and explain to him that you have these dreams and when you have them they come true.

We will need to tell him about the three that you have had prior to this one so he will maybe believe you Jason. Maybe that will help and maybe he will put a watch in the neighborhood.

I told Jeff that it was fixing to happen and that it could be as soon as tonight. I explained to him that when these dreams were like this and I had them so close together that the murder was fixing to happen.

He told me that we would go to Talladega today. He said he would call the chief of police in Talladega and set up an appointment to meet with him. He told me that he knew his private number in his office and that he would talk directly with him.

I told him that I really did not want to tell him about the dreams, but I guess I would have to because it was going to happen whether he believed me or not and there was nothing that I could do about it. He told me to not worry about.

He told me that since he did not have a chance to get it worked out to go the warehouses Thursday that maybe we could do that Monday night.

Our food came to the table and we ate our food. After we finished eating we sat around and chit chatted for a few minutes and he told me that he needed to go and that he would get everything set up for today and would let me know what time.

We went and paid for our meals and left the restaurant. I went to the office to see what was going on. The first thing I did was call Catherine to talk with her. She answered the phone on the second ring.

"Hello Jason. What are you doing this morning?'

"Hello Catherine. I am just getting to the office. I thought I would call you and say hello."

"Jason the secretary got the letter in the mail to Jim Sax yesterday afternoon. He should get it today."

"I know he will be relieved when he gets it and knows that he is free and clear of all charges."

"I know he will be glad to see it." She said.

"Thank you very much Catherine for representing him. I know that he appreciates it and if he ever needs an attorney you will be the first person that he will think about."

"Well I have a busy day today Jason. I have to go to Talladega and see what I can do to get Calvin out of jail. I am sure we can work that out. Are you going to be there?"

"I cannot be there this time. I have a very busy day today. Jeff and I are going to see the Chief of Police in Talladega. Catherine the next murder is going to take place in Talladega."

I told her about my dream last night and told her why Jeff and I were going to see the Chief of

Police and talk with him. Maybe we can get a break this time. I sure do hope so.

I told her that I had found out from Mr. Taylor that James Gardner from Tuscaloosa was from Houston originally and that he followed Charlotte when she left Houston. I told her that I was calling a friend of mine in Tuscaloosa and get him to follow him. There is good possibility that he may be involved in these murders some way or the other.

I told her to call me this afternoon when she got back from the trial and let me know how things went. I ask her did she think that he was going to have to have any bail money. She told me that she did not think that would be necessary. She felt confident that he would get out of jail today and get community service whatever the judge deemed necessary.

I told her that if he could be released that I could come and pick him up. She told me that if I felt confident enough that she would let him ride with her and she got to Sylacauga I could pick him up and take him home. I told her just to let me know how it worked out.

I had not talked to my mom in a couple of days. I think that is all it had been. I knew I needed to call her and tell her I still love her.

"Hello Jason."

"Hi mom. I am sorry I have not already called you, but I have been tied up these last few days."

"It is ok Jason. How are you doing?"

"I am doing fine mom. I am still having those awful dreams. I guess I will always have them."

"You probably will Jason. You have been having those most of your life now."

"Have you heard from the rest of the family and how are they doing?"

"They are all doing good and they all told me to tell you hello and tell you to call them."

"I will mom when I have time. I know nobody understands but I have been tied up. It has been constant lately. The type work I do keeps me snowed under most of the time."

"What are you going to do this weekend Jason?"

"Rita is coming in tonight. She will be in Birmingham at 9:33. I have to be there to pick her up."

"I know you are looking forward to that Jason."

"Yes I am."

"What are you two going to do? Are you going to take some time off work and enjoy a few days? You need it by, now don't you?"

"I am sure going to try my best to. I could use the time off. I have a couple of loose ends to tie up. May not get them all done before tomorrow morning sometime."

"Just take a break Jason. You need to. You need to rest some."

"I need the rest mom that is for sure."

We chit chatted for a few more minutes and I told her that I had to go for now and that Rita and I would definitely see her sometimes this weekend. She told me it would be nice to get to meet her since we seemed to be very, very good friends. We said our good byes and hung up the phone.

It was about 9:30 and the phone rang just as I hung it up. Jeff told me that he has set up an appointment with Chief Manuel Neighbors for 2:30 PM. I ask him what time he wanted to leave Sylacauga. He told me to be at his office at 2:00.

I called the motel to see what Jarrell was doing. He told me that he had talked with the Chief of police in Sylacauga and that Dexter told him that the ashes would be at his office no later than 4:00 PM. He told me that he was going to go ahead and plan to fly back to Houston tonight. I told him that I had a very busy day ahead of me and that I did not see any way that I would be home before probably 6:00 PM. I told him that I had his number and when we did catch the murderer that I would call him.

I still had to go to the mill and see Katland this morning and it was getting late. I left the office and went to the mill. I got there just in time to see her before she left. She was getting ready to leave for the day.

I told her what I was there for and she accommodated me with the information just as she had the last time. I thanked her for being so kind to us in helping. She told me that she hoped we caught him soon. I told her when we did I would let her know for sure.

I left the mill and took the information back to my office. I did not bother with looking it over right now. I had too many things going on today. Maybe there would be something in Jennifer's file that would help us.

I left the office and went over to Charlie's to eat me something. I was nervous about having to go and tell a total stranger about my dreams.

Just as I got there Dexter pulled up and we walked in together and sat down at a table and the waitress came and took our orders.

"How are thing going Jason?"

"It could better Dexter. I have been snowed under lately."

"You need to slow down Jason. Take a breather."

"How can I when everything is happening at one time? These dreams are driving me crazy Dexter."

"Just slow down and take it easy someway Jason. You need to."

"I will when we catch this murderer. Maybe the dreams will stop then."

In just a short time our food came to the table. We ate our food and chit chatted some while we were eating. We talked about what it would be like to live in a town that there was no crime in it. That would be nice if that could happen. I would like that a lot.

We finished our food and sat around talked for about five minutes. We left the restaurant and I went back to the office. I had to call Bryan and talk with him and see if there was anything that he could do to help us out with James Gardner.

I found his number and called him. He was in his office and answered on the first ring.

"Hello and who might be calling me now." Bryan said.

"Hello Bryan, it is me Jason."

"Well, Jason what in the world are you doing."

"Snowed under right now Bryan. I needed to talk with you and ask you for a favor."

"Well, Jason what kind of a favor do you need? You old rat."

I explained to him why I was calling him and ask him if he could help us out. He told me that he would be glad to. I gave him the information that he needed to be able to find James Gardner. He told me that he would get on top of it today. He said that he would do the investigating himself to make sure that it was done properly.

I told him when and if he found out anything to give me a call. I asked him did he still have my office phone and home phone numbers. He told me that he did unless they had changed. I told him they had not changed. He told me when he found out something that he would me know.

We talked about another ten minutes and we both needed to get off the phone. It was about 1:30.

I did not have time to do anything else before I had to leave to go and meet Jeff. I just left the office and went on over to the Sheriff department.

Murder of Grace

Jeff was there when I got there. He told me that he would be ready in a little bit

He finished up in his office and we headed out for Talladega. We were there at the Chief's office at 2:25 PM. We went and told the clerk what we were there for and they checked with the chief to see if he was busy. They escorted us to his office and we went in and Jeff introduced me to the chief. He motioned for us to sit down in the chairs in front of the desk. We sat down, and he and Jeff chit chatted for a little bit and then we got down to business.

I told him about my dreams that I had been having and what was happening. Of course, he knew about the murders in Sylacauga. They had been the top of the news lately. He did not know about my dreams though because they all kept that quite for me and I appreciated that. I told Chief Manuel that I did not like telling people about my dreams but that Jeff and I both felt like we needed to talk with you and tell you because the next murder was going to happen in Talladega.

He asked me how did I know that. Jeff told him that I had the dreams and that when I had the dreams that it happened just like it was in my dreams. Chief Manuel did not want to believe that it was going to happen in his city. I told him that unless somebody tried to help stop it that it was going to happen.

He told me that he did not see how that he could put someone on watch on just a dream that I had had. Jeff told him that three murders had happened in Sylacauga. He told him that because of the dreams that they knew about the murders before they happened. I told him that the murders happened just like I told him that they would happen.

I described the neighborhood that they were going to take place. He was familiar with the neighborhood. I told him that he would not have to have a watch very long because it was fixing to happen soon. It could even be tonight. He only kills the women at night I told him.

I described in detail how he killed them and how he placed all the body parts so that when he saw the crime scene that he might believe me next time. I knew it was going to happen and that they were not going to be able to stop it.

He said that he would put a cop in the area to keep a watch to see if anything suspicious was taking place in the area. He said that would be best that he could do. I thanked him for at least considering that. Maybe that would give us an edge.

I told him that he needed to trust us and give us all the help that he could. Unless we could catch the murderer before the crime that it was going to happen in his city and could be as early as tonight. I guaranteed him that it would happen before the weekend ended.

He told me that I could not do that. I told him that I could because the dreams gave me that much information by the way they occurred. He said we would see. I told him I knew that I was right and before the weekend was over that he would believe me.

Jeff thanked him for his time and told him that if anything happened to call him and let him know. He and Manuel were very good friends. He would not have even listened to me if it had not been for Jeff.

We left Talladega and headed back to Sylacauga. It was already 3:30. I told him that if he did not mind I could surely use something to drink. He stopped at a convenient store and we got us something to drink. We were back in the Sylacauga by 4:00. I got in my car and went to my office.

I got in the office and finished my paper work. I went back to get ready to leave and the phone rang. It was Catherine. She told me that everything went well. He was released from jail today and that he would have to serve community service to work off his time. He would have to meet with his parole office every week and not get into any trouble and everything would be fine for him.

She told me that he was at her office now. I told her that I would come over and pick him up and take him home and talk with him for a few minutes. I told her I was going to talk with some friends of mine and see if we could help to find some work. I believe that if he could work that he would stay out of trouble. I will let you know what happens.

I called Dexter to see if Jarrell had been by to pick up the ashes from his daughter. He told me that he had and that he told him that he was leaving tonight to go home. He told me that he told Jarrell that he did not need anything else right now but if we needed anything that we would give him a call.

It was time for me to go over to Catherine's office and pick up Calvin and take him home. I got there, and he was walking around outside. He saw me and came over to where I was and thanked me for helping him out. I told him to not worry about it.

I told him to wait on me that I just wanted to talk with Catherine for a minute and I would be back. I went in and thanked her for bringing him to Sylacauga. She told me that he was just as nice and polite as she could have asked anyone to be. I told her I needed to go I had a lot to do before I left to go to the airport to pick Rita up.

I left her office and went back outside and told Calvin to come with me that I was taking him home. We got in the car and I ask him would he like to work for me. I decided that I was not going to talk with anyone else about helping him get a job because I needed someone anyway. He said he would like that. I told him I needed someone to answer the phone and help with planning for meetings. I needed someone to help locate people and just run errands for me sometimes. I told him how much I would pay him a week to work for me.

We had a long talk on the way to his house. When we got there, I told him that I would see him Wednesday. He asks me where my office was. I told him I would pick him up Wednesday.

I went to the tennis courts to meet Jarrod and catch a couple of games with him.

"Hello Uncle Jason."

"Hello Jarrod. Are you ready to get beat today?"

"I am going to beat you again Uncle Jason."

"In your dreams Jarrod."

We played a couple of games. I told him that I could not got to the gym today. I had to get ready to go to the airport to pick someone up. He told him he would go because he wanted to see Roxy.

I went to the house and looked in the refrigerator to see what Alice had cooked me today. She had cooked lasagna and it looked delicious. I got me some and put it on a plate and heated it up in the micro wave and got me a barq's root beer.

I ate that, and it was getting about time for me to leave to pick Rita up. I headed out to the airport. This was the trip that I was looking forward to. I was ready to see her. It was nice to have her coming to spend a few days with me. I got to the airport a little early. I just went to the gate and waited for her.

It had been about a half an hour and her flight arrived. She got off the jet and I saw her and hollered for her, so she would see me. She came over to where I was, and I reached down and put my arms around her and picked her up and gave her a big kiss with her arms around my neck. I told her it was really nice to see her.

Murder of Grace

We left the airport and headed towards Sylacauga.

CHAPTER TWENTY-TWO

"I made it Jason! It is so nice to be away from work for a few days."

"I have been excited Rita knowing you were coming."

"It is exciting Jason. We can really enjoy this time together."

"Have you eaten yet?"

"I ate a little snack before I went to the airport."

"Do you want to spend the night in Birmingham or go to Sylacauga and stay at my house?"

"I think we should just go to Sylacauga Jason."

"I have some lasagna that Alice, my maid, made today and it is delicious. Do you like lasagna?"

"I sure do."

"We will just go home and eat then."

"Sounds good to me."

"Remember the boy I told you about that pulled the gun on me and tried to rob me?"

"Yes, how could I forget it Jason."

"Well Catherine got him out on community service and I hired him to work for me."

"You did what? You are gullible Jason."

"I checked him and his family out. He was telling me the truth."

"Are you sure he is going to be OK Jason?"

"I really believe that if he has a job that he will never do that again."

Murder of Grace

"Did you have a busy day Jason?"

"Yes, I did. How about you."

"I had a busy day trying to get all my paper work together and filed before the day ended."

We made it to the house about 10:45 and went in. I brought her things in with us and took her up to the big room with the big king size bed in it. I told her this could be her room. I set all her things in the bedroom and we went to the kitchen.

I got the lasagna out and set it on the counter and found some plates. We both fixed us a plate and put them in the micro wave and heated them up. We ate, and she told me that was some of the best lasagna she had had in a long time. I told her that Alice was a great cook and that she always cooked me a meal on Tuesdays and Fridays when she was here.

I gave her a tour of my house. She asks me why I wanted such a large house. I told her that I might get married one day and I wanted something that my family would be comfortable in.

We went in the living room and sat down on the couch. I put my arm around her shoulder and told her that I was so proud to have a great friend like her.

"Well someday maybe this will develop into more than just a great friendship Jason."

"Who knows? It could. I really like you a lot. I have liked you a lot from the time I met you."

"I like you a lot to Jason. That is why I came down to see you."

We turned on the TV to see what was on.

"Jason, I have had a rough day today. I think I would like to lay down and get some rest."

"Sure. I think I need to do the same thing, but I am just excited, and it is going to be hard for me to sleep."

I made sure all the doors were locked and turned out all the lights and we went upstairs to our bedrooms. She went in hers and closed the door. That was a little disheartening that she closed the door.

I went to my bedroom and lay down on my bed and was lying there thinking that it was so nice not to be by myself right now. Maybe one day I will never have to be alone anymore. That would be nice.

In a few minutes I heard someone knock on the door. I looked up and she was standing there in here bright red nylon gown. It was low cut and boy did she look nice.

She told me that she could not go to sleep and ask me if she could come in my room for a few minutes. She came in and sat down on the side of the bed. I told her to just lie down and maybe she could go to sleep on my bed.

She lay down and put her arms over my waist and asked me could she just sleep right there. I told her she could sleep anywhere that she wanted to. She snuggled up close and I put my arms around her and gave her a big kiss and we both went to sleep.

All of a sudden, the alarm clock went off and I woke up and turned it off. "Damn I forgot to turn it off last night." It was only 5:00. She did not wake up. I lay back down close to her. I just watched her. She was beautiful, and I finally went back to sleep. It was nice to have someone in the house with me. I did not have a dream and boy was that nice.

I woke up at 7:00 and got up and went to the kitchen and put on a pot of coffee. By the time the coffee was ready Rita came in the kitchen.

I walked over and put my arms around her and picked her up and looked at her straight in the eyes and told her that she was the most beautiful thing I have seen lately. She blushed and told me to quit talking like that. I kissed her and set her back down on the floor and ask her did she want a cup of coffee.

I got some cups and poured us some and we sat down at the breakfast nook table to drink it. You could see my back yard well from there. She told me that those roses in my back yard were beautiful.

We were watching the birds in the back yard feeding off the flowers. We talked a lot about nature and how beautiful it was and how it would be nice if the whole universe would be that way and that there was no crime or anything. We of course were dreaming. There are evil people in the world and that is just the way it is.

She told me that she was going to take her a shower and clean up and put her on some clean clothes and then we could go and do whatever we wanted to.

I told her that we would go to Birmingham and go to the Vulcan Park and to the Birmingham Zoo and to the Galleria mall if she wanted to. She told me that sounded like a lot of fun.

We got dressed and we left the house and stopped by The Grill and Eggs Breakfast Bar to eat some breakfast on our way to Birmingham. We were sitting at our table and Jim Sax came walking in the door. He saw me and came over to the table. I introduced him to Rita. He ask me could he sit down for a minute that he had something he wanted to tell me.

I told him to sit down.

"Guess what Jason."

"What's that Jim?"

"I got a letter from Catherine telling me that all the charges had been dropped and that I did not have to worry about that anymore. That was the best relief I have had in a long time. That had just about driven me nuts."

"That is good Jim. That mess is over now."

"Thank you so much Jason for helping me. I will repay you someday."

"You do not owe me anything Jim.'

"I know Jason, but I will repay you. I will go and let you and Rita enjoy your time."

"I will catch you later Jim. Take it easy.

"Wow Jason. he is a nice person." Rita said.

"I have known Jim the most of my life Rita. He is a very nice man. He was the one that they arrested in the beginning when these murderers started. Catherine helped get him out of all that mess."

"They tried to ruin an innocent man Jason."

"Unfortunately, it happens and the bad guy gets away."

Our food made it to the table and we ate our breakfast and chit chatted some and headed towards Birmingham to take in the Zoo the first thing.

We made it to the zoo and went straight to the tigers and lions. They are astoundingly beautiful. Or at least that is what I think.

"I just want to touch one of them Rita."

"I would like to touch one of them to Jason."

"They are one of the most beautiful animals in the world."

"And can be very vicious to." Rita said.

We left and walked over to see the birds. I believe there was every kind of bird that you could think of. We enjoyed looking at all the different spices and the different fabulous colors. They were amazing. I always loved looking at the birds.

We went to the alligator swamp and checked out the alligators. The morning was slipping by kind of fast. I ask her was there anything else in particular she wanted to see. She told me she wanted to see the monkeys.

We went over to see the monkeys and they were swinging all over the trees and making faces at us. "I wish I had a banana to give them." I said.

"That would be fun Jason. They are too funny." They looked like they were having fun. It was a very busy morning in the zoo. We checked out the Zebras. We had gotten tired and decided that we would leave the zoo and go over to the Vulcan and enjoy that for a while.

We left and went to the Vulcan Park and Museum and studied the history of the Vulcan from 1903 to the present. We went up to the observatory and looked around for a while and enjoyed that and the day was slipping by fairly fast. We were ready to leave the Vulcan. I asked her was there anything any particular she wanted to do. She told me that that she loved Museums.

We looked up museums in Birmingham and we found the Alabama mining museum and we went and checked it out. It was fun and we enjoyed it. It was time to find us something to eat. We found us a hot dog stand in downtown Birmingham. We got us some chili cheese dogs with French fries. They were delicious and a little messy but boy were they fun.

She knew about the Riverchase Galleria shopping mall in Birmingham and she wanted to visit it more than she wanted to do anything else. When we finished eating we headed to Hoover to visit the Galleria. She was excited. It is the largest enclosed shopping mall in the state of Alabama. It has everything that you could want.

We got there about 2:00 PM. We found us a parking place. We went inside, and we were both astounded at how beautiful it was. It was enormous. She told me she just wanted to look around and have fun and buy her some new clothes.

We went into some ladies' shops and she looked and hunted and found her a beautiful sky blue pants suit that she fell in love with. She tried it on to make sure that it fit her, and it did and boy did she look good in it. She told me that we could go

William Honeycutt

ahead and purchase that because she was through in here. She told me that she wanted to go to Macy's.

We finally made it to Macy's and she looked around and found her several new outfits that she liked and we bought them and by now we were loaded down with packages that we had to lug with us. She still wanted to do some more shopping. There were a lot of ladies specialty shops and she just wanted to look around.

We went to a couple of men's shops. I bought me some new blue jeans and a couple of shirts. Blue jeans were about the only thing that I wore anyway. It was getting late and we were tired. We decided that it was time for us to leave the mall and go find us a good restaurant.

We left the mall and rode around just looking and enjoying the sights. I ask her what she would like to eat. She told me that she wanted a nice juicy steak tonight.

I ask her had she ever eaten at a Longhorn Steakhouse. She never had. There was one on highway 280 in Hoover. I took her there to eat. We got in the restaurant and the hostess led us to a table and seated us and told us our waiter would be right with us. We thanked her and sat down.

The waiter came to the table and took our order and brought our drinks back to the table. We sat around and talked while we were waiting on our lunches to get to the table.

He brought us our chef salad. It was almost a meal in itself. In a few minutes he brought our steaks and baked potatoes to the table. She told me that was one of the biggest T-bone steaks she thought she had ever seen. The baked potato was huge.

We ate our delicious meal that we had ordered and just sat back and enjoyed being there. We finally finished everything, and we left our waiter a very nice tip and thanked him for his professional mannerisms and told him we would be back again. He took our credit card and paid for our meal and brought my credit card back.

We got up from the table and left the restaurant. Now we had to decide what we were going to do. It was getting late and we were both very tired. I asked her did she want to do anything else or was she ready to go to the house now. She told me that she was ready to go to the house.

We left Birmingham and went back to Sylacauga We got home about 9:00 PM. We went in the house and took all our new things we had bought with us.

I told her I needed to call mom and tell her we would see her tomorrow.

"Hello Jason."

"Hello mom. What are you doing?"

"Just sitting here and wondering when I was going to hear from you and when you were bringing Rita over to visit."

"That is why I am calling. We are coming over tomorrow. Is there any time that will be best for you?"

"Anytime will be OK Jason. I am looking forward to meeting her."

"We will come over at about 10:00 in the morning if that is OK."

"That will be fine Jason. Did you guys have fun today?"

"Yes, we had a lot fun. We went to the zoo and to the Vulcan Park and to the Galleria. We ate at Longhorns Steak House. It was superb as always."

"Sounds like you guys did the town in."

"Yes, we had fun. I will see you in the morning at 10:00. Bye till then."

"Bye Jason."

I turned on the TV just for the noise mostly. I ask Rita if she wanted anything to drink. She told me to bring her a coke. I got her a coke and me a barq's root beer and took them in the living room and we were just sitting there talking and resting up from the busy day that we had.

The phone rang, and it was my mystery caller. I thought I was going to get away from all that this weekend.

Rita looked over at me and ask me was that your mystery caller you been telling me about. I told her it was but that I think we can get him taken care of real soon.

The news came on and so far, nothing major had happened in the county. Thank goodness.

We decided that we would go to the bedroom and lay down on the bed and turn the TV on and talk for a while. I turned out all the lights and made sure the doors were locked and she followed me upstairs and she came in my bedroom with me.

We jumped on the bed and turned the TV on.

"Well Jason I am just going to sleep with you tonight again."

"OK." I put my arms around her and kissed her and told her she could sleep with me any time she wanted to.

CHAPTER TWENTY-THREE

I turned over on my side and snuggled up close to Rita. I was just thinking how nice it was to have her with me. I was thinking about going over to moms tomorrow and what she would think about Rita. I was hoping that she would like her. Why was I thinking about all these things tonight? I needed to be trying to get me some sleep.

I closed my eyes and was almost asleep when I saw her in my dreams. The woman with the long blonde hair was there. I saw that same community again. It was the same as last time, Talladega, Al. I was having another dream. OMG. Why tonight? I do not need this tonight. I could not get her out of my mind. I could not open my eyes. I did not want to sleep anymore. I finally was able to open my eyes and set up on the side of the bed.

Rita set up right beside me and put her arms around my shoulder.

"You are having one of those dreams again aren't you Jason?"

"Yes. It is so disgusting. I was hoping to get through a few days without anything happening."

My life was turned upside down.

I want my life back.

"Is there anything I can do Jason?"

"No, there is nothing anybody can do Rita."

She put her arm around my neck and rubbed me on the side of the face and told me that she could at least be there with me this time.

"I hope things get better Jason."

"They will not until this murderer is caught."

"Maybe you guys will find him soon and then you can get a break."

"I need it."

We lay down. I did not want to close my eyes. I did not want to see anything else in a dream. All I wanted to do was just sleep right now. We had had a long day and I was tired.

I turned over on my side and snuggled up close to Rita and closed my eyes. I was almost asleep when the blonde headed woman was there again. I could not get my eyes open. I was disgusted.

She was standing there in her living room and he came in from the kitchen. He had his blade in his hand. He was rubbing the blade with his fingers and licking his lips. He was tall and muscular. I could tell that much. He looked like he had dark black hair but I was not sure about that.

"I am here. I am going to punish you for your being bad."

"Please do not bother me."

"I want to bother you. You deserve it."

"What have I done to you?"

"You ignored me."

"I do not know you. I could not have ignored you."

"You always turned me down. I tried every time I saw you."

"What did you try every time you saw it and what was I doing?

"I always tried to get you to go out with me and you always turned me down. You were dancing."

"I don't dance anymore."

"But I want you to dance for me."

"I can't dance for you. I do not have any music."

"If you do not dance for me tonight I will have to hurt you."

"How are you going to hurt me?"

"I will probably start by cutting your fingers off."

She was getting very scared by now. She was shaking all over. He knew he had her where he wanted her and he was happy. He grabbed her and drug her in the bedroom and threw her on the bed and dared her to move. She tried to get up and he shoved her back down on the bed. She screamed. He put his hand over her mouth and told her if she did that again that he would just kill her and be done with it.

He drug her to the side of the bed and he put her in a sleepers hold and she was out light a light. He put the blade to her throat and sliced her throat from ear to ear making sure that he got the jugular vein so that she would die instantly. She was dead. It was over.

It is going to happen tonight. I just knew it was. I would not be having this dream tonight if it were not going to happen. I saw the Citizens Baptist Medical Center very clear. I knew tonight was the night. I could not open my eyes.

I was finally able to get my eyes open. I sat up on the side of the bed. I was shaking. It makes me tremble and shake now. It is only getting worse. I went to the bathroom to wash my face in cold water. While I was washing my face, Rita came to the door.

"Are you OK Jason?"

"I am OK Rita, but the dream just will not leave me alone. I told her.

"It is going to happen soon, isn't it Jason?"

"Yes, Rita it is going to happen tonight. The Chief told me he would put a watch in the area and have it patrolled for suspicious behavior. I am going to call the Talladega Police and tell them they need to watch it very close tonight because the murder is going to happen tonight.

"I think that would be a very good thing to do Jason especially if you are that convinced that it is going to happen tonight."

"When I have these dreams this close together and that detailed of the area it happens. What I am afraid of is that it has already taken place, and no one has seen anything."

We went in the living room and sat down, and I picked up the phone and called the Talladega police. I told them that they needed to put more than I car in that area tonight because that murder was going to take place tonight. They told me they would have to get permission from the chief.

"Wake the chief up then." I told them.

"I can't wake the chief up unless I have proof."

"Don't be a fool and have to face having a murder on your hands tomorrow morning when someone finally finds it and calls it in." I told them.

"What proof do you have that a murder is going to happen because there has not been any activity except normal the patrol has told us." They told me.

They refused to call the chief and tell him I had called and told them what was going on. There is nothing else that I can do. I was pissed. I just hung the phone up and forget about trying to get them to do anything.

"How far is it to Talladega?" Rita asked me.

"It is only about twenty miles Rita."

"We could go and see if we can see anything.

"I do not really want to do that. I think I will just wait here and see what happens."

"In a few minutes my phone rang, and it was Jeff."

"Jason?"

"What Jeff? What is going on?"

"Manuel just called me and told me that they had a murder in the location of town you told him that it was going to happen."

"I knew it was going to happen tonight Jeff. I had another dream about it tonight."

"We can go up in the morning and talk with Manuel." He told me.

I told him that Rita was spending the weekend with me and that I had to be at my mom's house at 10:00. I told him that I did not want to go today. He has all he needs from me. They can get all the pictures and let me see them Monday. I will verify that it is the woman that I saw in my dreams.

The only thing that I would like to do is find out who she is and run some checks on her and see if she carries the same profile as the other three. Then we will know for sure that it is the same person doing the killing.

He told me that he could work that out with Manuel. I told him that I was going to go back to bed and try to get a little sleep. Tell him I will come Monday and verify everything. That way we will know if it is identical to the ones here.

I got off the phone and Rita was so upset. She had heard the conversation and knew, of course, that the murder had taken place. We left and went up to my bedroom and lay down on the bed. She snuggled up close to me and put her arms around me and gave me a big kiss and told that she would see me in the morning.

We went to sleep. I must not have moved an inch. I was lying in the same position I was when I went to sleep. It was 7:30. I got up and went and made a pot of coffee. I needed it this morning. Just as I got to the foot of the stairs Rita was there coming down. I waited on her to get down and when she got to the bottom step she stopped. I put my arms around her and gave her a kiss and told her I was going and take me a shower.

We both went upstairs and took us a long hot shower. I put on my new blue jeans that I had bought and my bright red button up shirt with my red and white sneakers.

Rita put on her red pants suit that she had bought with her bright red sneakers. She had on some bright red lip stick. She walked into the kitchen where I was pouring us a cup of coffee. Wow! She looked smashing. She was hot. I knew my mom was going to love her.

"Wow Jason great mind think alike. We are dressed in the same colors."

"And boy do you look sexy this morning."

"Well thank you Jason."

We sat down at the breakfast nook table staring out at the back yard watching the birds suck the juice from the flowers.

"Jason you have a swimming pool. You did not tell me about it."

"Yes, I do. I don't get to use it much. I don't have much time. I need to start using it every day. It is good exercise."

"Maybe we can take advantage of it while I am here."

"I don't see why we can't Rita. Do you want to eat here or go somewhere and eat?"

"I think we should get out of here Jason. I am not in the mood to cook neither watch cook."

We left the house and went to Sarah's Country Breakfast. I told her that there should not be anybody there to bother us. Most of my friends did not come there and I just did not want to be bothered this morning by anybody.

It was right in the middle of town and I parked my car in the back so no one could see us. We went and found us a table in the corner so that hopefully nobody would pay us any attention. The waitress came to the table and took our order and thanked us for coming by to eat with them.

We sat and talked a little about last night. I told her that I mostly just wanted to think about today and what we were going to do. I was going to have to be enough involved tomorrow

In a few minutes she brought our breakfast to us. I had ordered me a short stack of pancakes. I did not want much. We were going to eat lunch with my mom and dad. She ordered one eggs with bacon and some orange juice to go with it.

We finished our meal and we left the restaurant.

We rode around just so that she could see what Sylacauga was like. There was not much there. It is a small city but nice. I took her out to show her where the marble quarry was and let her get a taste of that. She loved marble. She told me that she thought it was so beautiful. I told her most people thought that about marble.

It was getting about time to go to my mom's house.

I told her I was not going to tell her anything about what anything looked like. I wanted her to see it without any preconceived ideas. I knew that it was going to be a surprise for her to see what kind of home I was raised up in.

We got to the drive from the highway to my family home. We were pulling up in the drive. She was in awe of the beauty of the place. She could not believe that it was such a large house. The porch was from one side to the other side of the house. It was a 5000 square foot house with eight bedrooms.

We got out of the car and mom was standing on the porch waiting for us. She had to be watching and see us coming up the drive. She always is. We got on the porch and the first thing mom said was hello.

"Jason, who is this beautiful woman you have here? Is it Rita?"

"Yes, mom this is Rita."

"Hello Mrs. Caffrey. It is a pleasure to meet you."

"I am so glad to meet you also Rita. I have heard a lot about you since Jason met you."

"Would you like to sit on the porch Jason or go inside?" Mom asked me.

"We can sit out here and look at all these beautiful flowers especially these roses for a few minutes."

Rita and I sat down on the swing and mom sat in the rocker next to the swing.

"Rita, Jason tells me you are an FBI agent."

"Yes, that is what I do Mrs. Caffrey."

"Do you plan on making that your career or do you have other plans in the future?"

"Never know what the future holds for sure. I enjoy my work. I probably will always be in law enforcement some way maybe just not the unit I am working with now. That could change." Rita told her.

"Do you guys want to go in the house where it is cooler? I need to go in and check on my lunch. I am making a good dinner for today."

"Yes, mom, I expected that, and I think I am ready to go in for a while." I told her.

We went in the house and Rita and I sat down in the living room while mom went to the kitchen to check on her lunch.

"This is one large home Jason."

"Yes, it is Rita. It has eight bedrooms."

"What kind of work did you mom and dad do Jason?"

"Dad was the vice president of the quarry and mom was the secretary for the President."

"Wow. That is amazing Jason. I am learning a little about you a little at a time. You never told me all this."

"I don't talk about it Rita. Everybody knows my family."

"It is nice Jason."

We were sitting on the leather couch and mom came and sat down in the big chair right beside the couch. Rita was admiring the beautiful scenery picture that was on the wall next to the fireplace.

Mom told her that was one of her mom's favorite pictures in her collection. When her mom died she had willed it to my mom and mom had it in the living room because it was one of her favorite pictures in the house. It was an Autumn forest and river scenery picture painted by one of her favorite artists.

We sat around and talked. In a few minutes a car came up in the drive. It was dad. I had not seen him in a while. I got up and went on the porch to say hello. Mom and Rita sat in the living room talking.

"Hello Jason. Been a while since I have seen you. How are you?"

"I am fine Dad. It is good to see you."

"I hear you have a beautiful young lady with you today."

We walked in the living room.

"Dad this is Rita Barnett. She works for the FBI."

"Well son, you do have good taste. She is a beautiful young lady."

"Thank you, Mr. Caffrey. It is a pleasure to meet you."

He sat down in his recliner that he usually sits in when he is in the living room. I sat back down next to Rita.

"Well Rita where are you from?" My dad asked her.

"I am from Atlanta, Georgia. I live in Manassas, Virginia close to Quantico."

"That is where you work. You work for the big time FBI." My dad said.

"How long have you been there Rita?" My mom asked her.

"About three years at Quantico."

"I wish Jason would get out of law enforcement. We worry about him all the time. But that is what he likes to do." Mom said.

"It is a dangerous job Mrs. Caffrey but it is also rewarding. I really enjoy my work and I know Jason loves his."

"Here comes Katheline Jason. I was not expecting her today."

She came in the living room and was surprised to see me. It had been a while since I had seen her. I got up and went over and gave her a big hug and kiss and told her I still loved her.

"Katheline, this is Rita Barnett."

"Hello Rita, I am Katheline. Jason's oldest sister. Well I am the oldest period."

"Hello Katheline. It is a pleasure to meet you."

"It is nice to meet the young lady that my mom has been telling me about that Jason is seeing. You are everything she told me you were."

Rita did not know what to say so she just smiled.

"What have you been doing lately Jason?"

"Working mostly." I told her.

"You need to come by every now and then. I miss seeing you."

"I am sorry, but I have been snowed under lately Katheline."

She understood. She and mom went in the kitchen and talked a few minutes. They came back in the living room and Katheline left.

We sat around and talked for a few minutes. Mom told us that she needed to go to the kitchen and get the lunch on the table. She ask Rita did she want to go in the kitchen with her so they could just chit chat a little. Rita left and went with her and dad and I sat in the living room

He asked me what was going on with all these murders taking place and when were we going to catch the killer and get him in jail. I told him that it was a serial killer and we were hoping that it was going to end soon. I told him that we were working hard at finding him but did not have many leads to go on right now.

He asked me if I was still having those damn dreams. I told him that I was and probably would for the rest of my life. He just did not understand that. He told me that maybe I should go to a psychiatrist and let them help me to get over them. I told him that it was a part of my life and that a psychiatrist could not help.

I told him if he did not mind I would rather not talk about all that and just enjoy my time getting to spend with them.

In a few minutes mom came in the living room and told us to come to the formal dining room, so we could eat.

Mom had cooked a big roast with potatoes, carrots, and onions. It looked delicious. She had some green beans and corn also. We all sat down and fixed our plates and dad ask the blessing over the food and told us to enjoy it. My mom was a fabulous cook. Rita told her she did not think she had ever eaten a roast that tasted like that one. Mom thanked her and told her that it was nothing to it.

She had baked a chocolate cake with her thick icing on it almost like fudge. It was the most delicious chocolate cake I think I have ever eaten. She cut us all a piece of it and ask me did I want some vanilla ice cream to go with it. I told her that would be nice. She asked Rita would she like some to go with hers and Rita took her up on it.

We finished eating and got up from the table and went back into the living room. We sat around and talked for a while. It was getting late. I told mom and dad that we needed to go. Dad ask me what we had to do that was so important. I told him nothing. Well he convinced me to hang around a little longer.

Well I did not have anything to do that is for sure except just spend some time with Rita.

He asks me to come out on the back porch with him, so we could just talk some. He asks me was I going to continue doing the work that I am in now. I told him that I enjoyed it although it was trying at times but that it was what I liked doing. He told me that he worried about me a lot.

He told me that Rita was a beautiful young lady and then he asks me when were we going to get married. I told him that we had no plans of getting married that we were just very good friends. Then I told him of course that could change. I do like her a lot. She is a very intelligent young woman and that we liked a lot of the same things and enjoyed spending time together. The only problem was we were just so far apart.

He told me that he was waiting for me to get married. He asks me if I was ever going to get married. I told him to not worry about it that I was going to but just not right now.

We went back in the kitchen and mom and Rita were there putting the food up.

I told Rita that we needed to go so that we could ride around some and she could see some of the community outside of Sylacauga.

We got ready and left and I headed out towards Weogufka. I wanted to show her the country. I wanted to take her and show her where we all got into trouble. I took her to double bridges. It was a fun place back then to go.

It was getting late and we were both wanting to go home and just sit around and enjoy being together.

We went to the house and walked up on the porch. Jeff pulled up in the yard. He got out and came over and asked me who this beautiful young woman was. I introduced him to Rita and told him that she was an FBI agent from Quantico. He asked me what I was doing with an FBI agent from Quantico. I told him that we met and liked each other and just have enjoyed spending some time together. We sat down on the porch and chit chatted for a few minutes.

He told me that he had talked with Manuel and that if possible he wanted to see me tomorrow. I told him that would be fine. He told me he would go with me if I wanted him to. I told him that would be nice. I told him I wanted Rita to ride with us also.

He told me that he was passing by and saw us and decided that it would be best to just stop and let me know that Manuel wanted to see me and that he would go on home He told me what time he thought would be a good time to go to Talladega. I told him we would be there.

Jeff left, and we went in the house and went in the kitchen and found us something to drink and sat down at the table in the breakfast nook. We sat there and talked for a while and drank our drinks that we had.

I got up and made a pot of coffee. I was ready for some now. When it finished I poured us both a cup and we took our coffee and went in the living room and I turned the TV on and sat down in my recliner and she lay down on the couch and asked me what we were going to watch on TV. I told her anything that she wanted to watch was OK with me.

William Honeycutt

CHAPTER TWENTY-FOUR

I was sitting in my recliner and she had found a game that we were watching when the telephone rang.

"Hello Jason. I am back."

"I advise you quit calling me." I hung up the phone."

I told her that was my mystery caller again. I told her that I had already talked with the Sheriff of Coosa County.

"He told me he could find out who it is. I had all the proof I needed to get him behind bars."

"Do you have these incidents a lot Jason?""

"Since I spent the weekend with you it has gotten worse."

"You never get a break. It keeps you wore down most of the time."

"Nobody knows. I just don't tell everybody everything. They would be depressed if I did.""

"Jason the sooner you can get the mystery caller taken care of the better off you will be."

"Nothing I have done so far has stopped any of it. I am dealing with some brave people Rita."

"I know Jason, but you never get a break. You have dreams and you told me that they only get worse. Then you have someone calling your house threating you. You have a busy enough life with your job. You do not need other things to go with it."

"Unfortunately, it does not look like I am going to get a break anytime soon. I know I will not until that murderer is caught. I wonder if my mystery caller has anything to do with the murders."

"That is possible Jason. Maybe that is why he is harassing you."

We were sitting in the living room. All of a sudden there was a gunshot and it splattered the glass in the window facing the couch. The bullet came within an inch of my right ear and blasted the wall right behind me.

"My God Jason. Did that hit you?"

"No Rita but it scared the hell out of me."

We both jumped up and walked over towards the door being very careful hoping there would not be any more shots. It is a good thing Rita got up. He fired another shot and it belted the couch right where she was setting. I opened the door and the 1957 red Chevrolet squealed off from down the road. It looked like they were waiting to see if anyone opened the door. I knew that it was them that fired the shot. It had to be.

I called the police department and told them about the shooting. They came out to the house. Gregory Davis was the officer that came out and took the report. He checked out everything and told me that he would get everyone on it and see if they could find out who did it. I told him I knew who did it. I just did not know their name. He asked me who it was.

I told him about my mystery caller and told him about him squealing off when I opened the door. I knew that it had to be him that did it. We have the bullets that were fired. We will find out what type gun they were fired were fired from and maybe we will catch him soon.

"Well Jason. You have an exciting life."

"Yes, I do Rita. That is just another addition to my drama."

"I know it gets old."

"You got that right. I am just sick of it. I don't even tell mom and dad about these kinds of things. It would drive them crazy if I did."

"Your mom told me in the kitchen that she was always on her toes being worried about you. She said she was so scared that you were going to get hurt or killed."

"They want me to get out of law enforcement. But I enjoy what I do. I do not want to do anything else. I know that being a private investigator is dangerous. We are snoops. We are in everybody's business."

It was getting late. I had some thick plastic that I used to put over where the glass had been shot out on the window. I turned out all the lights and made sure the door was locked. We went upstairs to go to bed.

We went in the bedroom. I walked over to the door that led out on the balcony over the pool and opened it and walked out and she followed me.

"Wow Jason. I have not even noticed that you had a balcony out here. This is nice."

"I don't use it much, but I like having it here."

There was a full moon and the heaven was full of stars. It was beautiful tonight. I put my arms around her and lifted her up and gave her a big kiss and told her I was so happy to have her here and that I hoped we could do this often.

"We might be able to. You never know Jason. So far, I like the area. It is a nice little town."

We lay down on the bed and snuggled up close together. I closed my eyes and the first thing I saw was Rita in my dreams. That was a nice for a change. I was thinking about how beautiful she was and how relaxing it was for her to be here. I am starting to like her more every time I see her. Of course, this was only the third time I had seen her. For some reason it appears I had known her all my life.

Murder of Grace

I was slowly drifting away into dark sleep. Then suddenly, I saw a woman with long dark red hair. She was tall and slender with long arms and long slender fingers. She had long legs and was very trim. She had dark deep blue eyes and her hair was curly. She had it pulled back in a ponytail. She was in her bedroom standing in front of the mirror piddling with her hair brush.

She turned around and had a big smile on her face.

I was dreaming again. These dreams were driving me crazy. I could not keep from it happening. I did not want to dream again. It was too much.

She walked over close to the door and looked out of the bedroom and saw someone in her living room. She asks them what they were doing in her living room. The person was a man very tall with dark black hair and he was very muscular. I did not get a good image of him as I did her. But the two things that I did not have a doubt about was the dark black hair and that he was very muscular.

He told her that he just wanted to talk with her. She ask him why did he have that sickle in his hand. He told her that he carried that with him most of the time because he never knew when he would need it.

She went into the living room and tried to get close to the phone, so she could pick it up and he stepped in between her and the phone. He told her he just wanted to talk with her is all he wanted to do.

She told him that she did not want him in her house and told him to just leave.

He told her than he would not leave because he wanted to talk with her first.

She asks him what he wanted to talk about.

He asks her where she worked.

She told him that she worked at the mill in Sylacauga.

He told her that was a good place to work.

She asks him what else did he want.

He told her that he knew that she liked ballet dancing and that he had seen her dance before and wanted to see her dance again.

She told him that she was not dancing right now and did not plan to any time soon.

He told her that she could put on a record and dance for him.

She told him that she did not want to do that.

He told her that if she did not that he would have to make her pay for it.

She ask him what was he going to do if she did not dance for him.

He told her that he would have to cut her with his sickle. And when he told her that he stepped over closer to her. She backed up and he stepped closer. She went around to the back of the chair close to the couch. He stepped in front of it.

She asked him why he didn't just leave and she could go back to her bedroom and rest.

He told her that he was not going to leave until she danced for him.

He told her to go into the kitchen that he had to talk with her in there.

She told him that she was not going in the kitchen right now because she did not want to.

He told her that was what he wanted her to do and that she was going to do it.

She would not move.

He grabbed her by the arm and pulled her towards the kitchen.

She screamed at him and told him to leave her alone.

He jerked her hard and she almost fell over the chair that time.

Murder of Grace

He pulled her around the chair and she was screaming.

He was not going to leave her alone and she knew that. She grabbed the huge ashtray on the table beside the chair and threw it at him and it hit him upside the head.

He grabbed her by the arm and told her if she did that again that he would just kill her and be done with it.

She knew that he was going to do that anyway. Why didn't he just do it and get it over with. He pulled her into the kitchen. She was fighting and screaming trying to get away from him, but he was a big man and she could not get away from him no matter what she did.

He got her into the kitchen and he grabbed her around the neck and put her in a sleeper hold and she became very limp. He took the sickle and sliced her throat from ear to ear and laid her on the big table in the kitchen. He carved her up just like he had all the rest of the women he had killed.

Rita was shaking me trying to wake me woke. She could not get me awake. I was trembling, and she was scared. I finally woke up and she grabbed me around the neck and looked at me straight in the eyes and told me she was scared to death.

"You were having one of those dreams and I could not get you awake. I was sacred Jason."

"Yes, it was awful. I saw the whole thing this time. I just did not see the location or get a good image of him other than he has dark black hair and is very muscular."

After we sat on the bed for a few minutes, I told her I needed to go and take me a shower because I felt so dirty.

She would not let me go by myself. She went with me to made sure that I was OK.

She went to the kitchen and made some coffee and we drank a cup.

"Jason lets go to my room. Maybe you will sleep better there."

"OK we will do that and maybe I will not have any more dreams."

We went to her bedroom and lay down on the bed. I did not put on my pajamas. I just went to bed with my briefs on. I was not in the mood to put on clothes.

We were lying on the bed and I told Rita that I run five miles every day except on the weekends. I ask her did she want to run with me in the morning. She told me that she did not think she could run five miles in the morning.

We snuggled up close and I kissed her.

The next thing I knew my alarm clock was going off at 5:00 as normal. I got up went and put on my jogging shorts and left and met Jane and we ran our five miles. I came back in the house and Rita was up and had made some coffee. She poured us a cup and we sat down at the breakfast nook table.

We went and put on some clothes so that we could go and find us something to eat. It was a little early and we did not want to cook. We went to The Steak and Eggs Breakfast Bar. We found us a table by the window. We sat down.

I looked up and Dexter and Jeff walked in the door at the same time. They never came at the same time but they did this morning. They saw me and came over and sat down.

"Dexter this is Agent Rita Barnett from Quantico. She works for the SCU. She is my friend that came to stay a few days with me."

"Hello Chief. How are you? It is a pleasure to meet you."

"Wow Jason. How did you find such a beautiful young woman like this that would have anything to do with you? And I am fine agent Barnett."

"It is not hard Dexter when you are as good looking as I am." I told him.

We ate our breakfast and Dexter excused himself. Jeff told me that we needed to leave at 9:00. He told me that would get us there in plenty of time.

"Jason, I have it set up to go over to the warehouses tonight and break that drug ring up."

"OK Jeff. I will go with you guys. I definitely want to be part of that. I can't wait to see their faces when we get there."

"You said you can get in the warehouse from the back and hide until they got there. I would like for you and me to be inside before they get there."

"I like that Jeff."

"I will have the officers to come in through the door they use to get in. They will come in at exactly 8:30. You and I will already be inside, and we can keep them from going to the back of the building."

"What time do you want to go in the building and wait for them to get there? They are usually there at about 8:00. They will definitely not be expecting anybody."

"We can have someone take us there at 7:00. They can leave, and we will have a ride once it is over."

"That sounds like a pretty good plan Jeff."

"I will meet you at your house. Rita would you like to take us over to the warehouse and drop us off?"

"I don't like it but I will." She told Jeff.

I told him that I would see him at 9:00. We left and went over to my office and sat around and talked until it was time to go over to Jeff's office.

We met him at his office and left and made it to Manuel's office at 9:30.

We got to Manuel's office at about 9:30. Rita told me that she was going to shop around in some shops close to the police station while we were talking with the chief. I told her that when we were finished I would find her.

Jeff and I went to the Chief's office and he motioned for us to sit down in the two chairs in front of his desk. He told me all he needed for me to do was to identify the girl in the pictures that it was her that I saw in my dreams and that the body was mutilated the same as the ones in Sylacauga. He got the pictures out and laid them all on his desk. I told him that it was her and that the body was carved up just like the three in Sylacauga and that all the body parts were placed the same as the ones in Sylacauga.

He told me that if that were the case that we had a serial killer on the run. I told him that was definitely the case. I took her name so that I could see if I could find out anything about her. Her name was Becky Doorman.

Jeff told Manuel that if there was anything that we could do to help to please let us know. We needed to all work together to try and find this murderer. He had already killed four women now.

I told Manuel and Jeff about the dream that I had just had. I told them how detailed it had been. I told Manuel that it was probably going to happen in the same location as the one that just happened. He told me there was no way that I could know that. I asked him was I right the first time. He told that that I did some good guessing on that one. I told him that I did not guess about it and that I had dreams and that is how that I knew that it was going to happen.

I told him that if he did not put a watch and have more than one car in the area that it was going to happen again. I told him that it might even happen if he had dozen cars there because it seemed that this guy was good at what he did.

He told me that he would catch the man who did it and that he would not have another chance to kill anyone else in his city.

Jeff told him that we would talk with him later and that if he needed anything to just give him a call. We left his office and when we walked back into the secretary's office Rita had just walked in the door and sat down in a chair.

She got up and we left and headed back towards Sylacauga.

Jeff was not interested in talking much this time. We just rode back home and got to his office. He seemed to be upset over something. I did not know what it was. Before Rita and I left his office, he told me that he wished that Manuel would just listen sometimes but that he was a very hard headed man and did not want to listen to anybody. I told him that before this was over he would be willing to listen to somebody because another murder was fixing to happen in Talladega in the same area just like I told him it was.

I told Jeff we were going to go because I still had to talk with the Coosa County sheriff to get this situation with my mystery caller taken care of.

We left and went back to the house. I called Rockford to see if the sheriff was in. I made arrangement to meet with him.

Rita and I got ready and headed towards Rockford. We were there in about a half hour. We went in the sheriff's office. I gave him the information I had, and he ran it and got the man's name and I filed the charges to have him arrested. The sheriff told me he would take care of it and let me know when they had him and I could come back down and take it from there.

We left, and I asked Rita what she wanted to do the rest of this day. She told me that we could just ride and look around that she was enjoying the countryside. We left Rockford and went to

Alexander City, Al. and we rode and looked and talked about life in general. I told her I was tired of all this stuff going on in my life. I needed a break from it all. She told me that I should just go back with her to Manassas when she left. I told her I wish I could.

We finally made it back to Sylacauga about 5:30 that afternoon. We had enjoyed just riding and looking at scenery. It was beautiful country. I asked her did she want to eat something before we went to the house. We were both ready to eat. I took her to Charlie's.

We got to Charlie's and went in and sat down at my usual table. The waitress came to the table and took our order.

"One day I am going to get married Jason. I am looking forward to having a family."

"Me to Rita. I just don't think I am ready for it right now."

"I don't think I am either Jason. But I do look forward to it."

"Jason, I did not realize that your life was so busy."

"It is and I love it that way."

"I wish it was busy in a different way Jason. You have too much other things going on." She told me.

"Don't let me forget to call the insurance office in the morning. I have to get them out to the house to check the window for me."

"I will remind you Jason. You need a secretary that is for sure."

"I have just hired Calvin. Maybe he can help take care of a lot of things for me."

"I sure hope he works out Jason."

"I believe he will Rita. I have a lot of confidence in him."

The waitress brought our big juicy T-bone steaks to the table. We ate them and left and went to the house. It was time to rest. We had had a busy day.

We went in the kitchen and made a pot of coffee and took us a cup and went to the living room. I sat down in my recliner and kicked it up and she lay down on the couch and stretched out and turned the TV on and found a game show to watch.

The doorbell rang. I went to the door and opened the door. Jeff was standing there.

"Are you ready to go Jason?"

"Yes, I am ready Jeff. I almost forget we were going tonight."

Rita jumped up and we got ready and we headed out towards the warehouses.

CHAPTER TWENTY-FIVE

We got to the warehouse. I gave Rita the key to the house and told her that I would be home as soon as we got this taken care of. She left and went back to the house. Jeff and I sneaked our way to the back of the warehouse and got in the building and went and found us a place to hide.

He stayed quite so that no one would know we were there just in case someone had come in early. That was not likely, but we wanted to be safe. In a few minutes we heard a noise at the door. It opened up and the six men came walking in. They went over to the little area where they had their meth lab set up and started working on their drugs.

I looked at my watch and it was 8:15. It was just about time for the officers to come in the building. Jeff and I were ready for the bust. I had my weapon ready to use if I had to. Jeff was prepared for anything.

In a few minutes the front door opened. The men in the meth lab were alarmed and one of them grabbed his gun and fired it at the officers coming in. Gregory Davis yelled at them and told them to stop and do not move or he would shoot them.

One of them tried to run. Jeff shot him in the leg just below the knee. And he fell down and grabbed his leg yelling "Why in the hell did you do that?" "We told you to stop and not move but you did not listen to us." Yelled Gregory.

Another one them decided that he wanted to make a break for it and Gregory shot him in the arm just below the elbow. He grabbed his arm screaming "You bastard." "Maybe I am a bastard, but I don't have a meth lab." Yelled Gregory. "Put your firearms down and drop to the ground with your hands behind your back or we will shoot you." Jeff told them.

Four of them hit the dirt and put their hands behind their backs and the officers were on them time they hit the ground putting handcuffs on them. The other two wanted to run and tired but they were taken down with shots to their legs. The officers did not want to kill them. They just wanted to stop them.

They were on the ground and four of the officers grabbed them and slung them around and jerked their arms behind their backs and put the handcuffs on them. They were all taken out and loaded in the patty wagon and taken to jail.

We called in all the force and they were there soon and had the crime scene cordoned off. They were getting everything they needed for being able to charge them with the felonies they deserved to be charged with.

Gregory ask me did I want him to take me home. I told him that I was ready to go. We got in his car while the rest got in their vehicles and we all left the crime scene.

I got to the house and Rita met me at the door.

"I was scared Jason that you might get hurt. Are you OK."

I thought it was nice to have someone that cared about me to meet me at the door. I had never had that before since I have been on my own.

"Yes Rita. I am fine. We got them. They are in jail now."

"That is good Jason. Now that is one more meth lab broken up."

"And just how many more are there?" I said.

"Only God knows. But you can bet there are thousands."

She had made some coffee. She went and poured me a cup and brought it to the living room.

We were sitting in the living room drinking our coffee and discussing when she thought she might go home. She told me she had several days and that she had told them she would be back Thursday. I told her she could stay as long as she wanted to. She told me that he was going to stick to her original plans and stay till Wednesday.

She called the airport and make her reservations for Wednesday leaving at 12:34 PM and to arrive at 5:21 PM. She told me that would give her some time to rest before she had to go to work Thursday morning.

She got up off the couch and came over to my recliner and plopped down on my lap and told me that she was tired of sitting by herself. We both laughed, and she kissed me and told me that she hoped that this would not be the last time that we met and spent some time together. I told her that it would not be.

She got up and went back over and set down on the couch and we were watching a game show and just talking. Someone knocked on the door. I got up and went to the door. I peeped out and see who it was, and it was Catherine. What was Catherine doing at my door? She never came by my house.

I opened the door and she came in. She came in and told me that she really needed to talk to me. I introduced her to Rita. I told her what Rita did and she was impressed. She told me that she had just left from her fiancé house and that he asked her to marry him. She said that she was not expecting that right now.

Murder of Grace

I asked her did she accept the proposal. She told me that she had told him to let her think about it for a couple of days.

She said she wanted to marry him but that she did not know if she wanted to get married right now or not. I told her that she could tell him of course she would marry him but that she would like to wait a little while before they had the wedding. She said that sounds like a good idea.

She asks me did I mind if she stayed until she kind of got over the shock. I told her she could stay as long as she needed to. Rita told her that she probably never would get over the shock and we all laughed.

In a few minutes Catherine told me that she was going to go home now and hope that she could get some sleep tonight after that. I told her after she got home and relaxed that all the shock would be gone and that the excitement would be there.

She left, and Rita and I sat back down in the living room. I did not plan on doing anything tomorrow. It was Tuesday and it was the last day she would be here. I wanted to spend it with Rita. We were not in a hurry to go to bed tonight. We sat in the living room watching TV and just enjoying being together.

I got up from my recliner and went over and set down on the couch beside her and gave her a big kiss. I told her that when she left I was going to really miss her. She told me she would miss me also.

It was getting late and we were enjoying the evening together and watching TV. I got up and went and made sure all the doors were locked and turned out the lights and we went up to my bedroom to lay down. We walked out on the balcony and looked at the full moon and it was beautiful. I put my arms around her and lifted her up and gave her a big kiss and told her I did not want her to leave. I sat her back down and she smiled and told me that she would stay if she could.

We stood on the balcony staring at the beautiful stars and moon in the sky and admired the beauty of their creation. We walked back into the bedroom and I closed and locked the balcony door.

We pulled our clothes off and lay down on the bed. We snuggled up close to each other and the next thing I knew the alarm clock went off. I decided that I was not going to run this morning. I hit the snooze button and went back to sleep till the clock went off again. I got up and went and put on a pot of coffee.

I was fixing us a scrambled egg, bacon and pancake breakfast when Rita came strolling into the kitchen.

"What are you doing Jason?"

"I am making us some breakfast."

"It sure smells good."

When I got our breakfast finished we ate it. It was delicious. We finished eating and went and put on some clean clothes and came back to the living room and just sat down and turned on the TV. The doorbell rang. I went to the door.

"Hello Jason."

"Hello Alice."

She came, and I introduced her to Rita.

"Where did you find this beautiful young woman Jason?"

"Birmingham when she was working on a case there. She is from Manassas, Virginia."

"It is a pleasure to meet you Rita. I think you found the best there is in Sylacauga. We all love Jason."

"I think he is pretty good Mrs. Alice."

"Jason, Jeremy fund him a little part time job at the gym. He does not have a way to get there so he ask me if he could stay with me for a while. He is staying at my house right now.

Murder of Grace

"That is good Alice. I hope you do not have any trouble from him."

"Oh, I want Jason. He is a good boy."

"I liked Alice. He seems like a good boy."

"Anything special today Jason?"

"No. Just your normal work Alice."

"OK. I will cook you a special dinner today for the two of you."

"Thank you, Alice. I appreciate that. Rita and I are going to hang around here for a while."

We went in the living room and sat down on the couch and turned the TV to cartoons. We did not want to see anything serious. We had had enough of that lately in our life. We just wanted to enjoy being together without being bothered. We just enjoyed the morning being together. It was slipping by fast.

We decided that we would go somewhere and find some something to eat. I told her we could go to a little restaurant in Stewartville and eat. It would be kind of quiet and that we would not be bothered by anybody.

We got in the car and headed for Faye's Fabulous Kitchen. We got to the restaurant and we were the only ones there. Sally came to the table and took our order. I introduced her to Rita and told her that she was my best friend.

In a few minutes Sally brought our lunch to us and it sure looked delicious. I ordered a hamburger steak smothered in onions with a baked potato and a green salad. She ordered beef tips with a baked potato and a green salad.

We were in the middle of eating our lunch when the Coosa County sheriff came in. He saw me there and came over and told me that they had the man in the 1957 Chevrolet in jail. He told me they had just picked him up. He told me his name is Samuel Colander. I told him that I would come to his office Wednesday afternoon and take it from there. He told me that would fine and walked away from our table.

We finished our lunch and left the restaurant. I decided that the only way that I was not going to be bothered was just to ride around and enjoy looking at the sights. That is what we did. I just headed out going towards Birmingham the back way.

We talked some more about what it would be like to have a family. I told her that I think I would love to have a dozen children and maybe mom and dad would leave me their big home to raise them in.

The afternoon was slipping by fast. It was getting late. But we were not in a hurry to do anything, so we just kept riding and enjoying being together. This would be our last day to get to spend tougher.

I was a 6:00 and we decided that it was time to go home and see what Alice had cooked for us. We got to the house and went in the kitchen and found a roast with baked potatoes. She made a chef's salad and had made a chocolate cake for desert. I do not know how she found the time to do all that and get all the cleaning done that she has to do but she does.

We heated everything up and set it on the breakfast nook table and sat down and ate that delicious dinner that Alice had cooked. We finished eating and went in the living room and turned the TV on and found us a good movie to watch and sat on the couch and talked and enjoyed the evening together.

It was getting late. We locked the door and turned out all the lights and went to the bedroom. She wanted to go back out on the balcony for the last time. We did and enjoyed it a lot. We sat at the table and talked about our jobs and what we wanted to do for the rest of our lives.

She told me that if she ever left the FBI that she might consider private investigation. I told her that I loved what I did. It was dangerous, but I enjoyed it.

We went back in the bedroom and lay down on the bed and the next thing I knew the alarm clock went off and I got up and put on my jogging shorts and went and met Jane and we ran our five miles and I came back in the house and Rita was up and had some coffee made.

I turned on the TV to see what was on the news. They were talking about the Ballet Casanova and that the police had not found him yet and were still looking for him. The morning was going by fast. Rita already had her things ready to go. I got them and put them in the car. We left the house and headed out towards The Grill and Eggs Breakfast Bar. We ordered our breakfast and ate and left.

I had to pick Calvin up. I promised him I would. We got to his house and he came to the car. I introduced him to Rita. He was impressed and ask me how I found a beautiful woman like Rita. Rita laughed and told him that she was not that beautiful. I corrected that very quickly.

We got to the office and I explained to him that all I needed him to do this morning was just to take telephone calls and get the messages. I explained to him that he did not need to tell them where I was but that I would be back after lunch sometime. I told him that I had to take Rita to the airport. If I need to return calls just tell them I will call them as soon as I get back to the office.

I told Rita that we could leave and ride towards Birmingham and take in some sights this morning while we were waiting for time for her to leave. That was the only way I knew that we would definitely not be bothered.

We left Sylacauga and went towards Birmingham. I told her I dreaded to see her go. I wished she could stay longer but of course I understood why she couldn't. We passed the morning off lust riding and taking in the sights. It was time to go towards the airport.

We made it to the airport at 11:30. That gave her plenty of time to get checked in before time to leave. It was almost time for them to call her flight. I hugged her and pulled her up close to me and told her that I would see her again soon. She told me that she looked forward to it.

I kissed her said bye and that I would see her soon. They called her flight for boarding. I kissed her one more time and she left going to board the big jet. I stood there watching her going towards her flight to board. Just before she got there she turned around and waved a big good bye to me. I waved back and threw her a kiss and watched her till she boarded the jet. I turned around and left the airport and went to find my car.

CHAPTER TWENTY-SIX

I found my car and headed towards Sylacauga. I had a lot to take care of when I got there. I made it back to the office at 1:15.

"How has your morning been Calvin?"

"It has been nice. I have mostly answered some phone calls."

"Did I have any important calls?"

"You have some you need to return."

"OK. We will go eat first and then I will call them."

"I can't afford to go and eat out Mr. Caffrey."

"Just call me Jason and I am going to pay for yours today."

I looked at the list of calls and it was my friends that I had asked to check on some people for me. I told Calvin to come with me and we would go and eat.

We left and went over to Charlie's. Catherine came in the door and saw me and Calvin and came over and sat down.

"Is it ok if I sit with you guys Jason?"

She knew it would be that is why she sat down.

"Hello Calvin. How are you?"

"I am fine. Now that I have a job thing will get better."

"Where are you working?"

"For Jason."

Catherine looks at me with quizzical eyes as in you have not told me you hired somebody.

"I did not know you hired anybody Jason."

"I know. I have just not had the chance to tell you."

"But you have been needing some help for a while."

"I have been kind of putting it off."

"That is good that you have someone now."

The waitress came to the table and we ordered our meals.

Catherine was impressed. I told her I needed someone to answer my phone for me when I was not at the office and someone to run errands for me at times. I thought that might be some good experience for Calvin. This way it gives him something to do and someone to help me out.

The waitress brought our meals to the table. I asked Catherine what she had been doing since we saw her the other night. She told me that she had made up her mind that she was going to tell him yes, she would marry him. I congratulated her, and I told her I looked forward for the day.

We finished our meals and Catherin left and went back to her office and Calvin and I and went to our office.

We got to the office and I told Calvin to sit down over in the chair beside my desk. He sat down. I explained to him exactly what I needed him for him to do. I told him that things would change some as he learned things and became more familiar with everything. I told him that I wanted him to work Monday thru Friday from 8:00 AM till 5:00 PM with an hour lunch break. I explained to him that he did not have to take it at any certain time just when he had time.

He ask me why I hired him and not let him find a job somewhere else. I told him that I had been thinking about hiring someone to help me out and that now was a good time to do it.

I told him that I would pay him $400.00 dollars a week starting out. He said that is a lot of money.

Well to me that is not a lot of money but it was a good starting salary for a young man. To him that would be a lot of money though because he comes from a very poor family. I told him that would help him to help his family get on their feet some.

I had to make some phone calls now that we had talked some. I told him just to sit there and look over a couple of folders that I gave him to study and see what he thought about them.

I picked up the phone to call Janie Worthington in South Carolina. She answered the phone and I ask her what she was doing.

"Hello Jason. Not much right now. I called you this morning and I see you have someone working for you now."

"Yes I hired him last week."

"That is good." She told me.

"Yes, I decided that I needed a little help. What is going on?"

"I need to talk to you about Ray Bradford. I have been checking on him. I have watched him go and come from the airport. He has been flying somewhere. I checked it and found out that he has been going to Sylacauga, Alabama. I learned that he uses another name when he flies. He has some fake ID's."

"Do you know what his fake ID is Janie?"

"He has one I know that he uses by the name of Johnathan Harvey."

"I am thinking that he has something to do with the murders. We just had one to take place in Talladega, Alabama. It is the same one that murdered the women in Sylacauga."

"Maybe this will help. I will continue keeping a check on him to see what else I can come up with Jason."

"Thank you very much Janie and I will do some checking on him and see what else I can find out. I have a very close FBI friend in the SCU in

Quantico. I will get her to run some things on him and see if anything comes up. She will do it as a friend for me. I know she will." I told her.

"Remember the police do not like the FBI involved Jason."

"I know but they never would know that I ask her to help me out. I would tell them that a good friend of mine who told me to not mention their name helped me to find the information."

"Maybe you could get away with that Jason." She said.

"What else have you been doing Janie?"

"Just working and trying to keep my head above water."

"Well, I just wanted to call you back and see what you had come up with. I knew you had something when I knew you had called."

"Thanks Jason for getting back with me."

"Have a great rest of the day Janie and I will talk with you again soon. I have a couple of more calls I have to make. Bye for now."

"Bye Jason. Talk later."

Well that was putting things a little better in order. I still think he had something to do with the murders whether he committed them or not.

I got Ryan's number and called him back

"Hello Jason."

"Hello Ryan. What have you got for me?"

"Jason, I have learned that James Gardner has a long record. He has misdemeanors and felonies both on his record. He robbed a bank in Houston and left Houston and went to Colorado for a short time and robbed a convenient store there. He was picked up and put in jail and was released because they decided to drop the charges on him. He left there and went to Tulsa, Oklahoma. I have been watching him and he goes towards Sylacauga every week about the middle of the week most of the time and comes back on the weekend usually."

"OK. It sounds like he may be involved in the murders. He could be the one doing it."

"I have talked with several women that know him and they claim that he is stalking them. They say they do not want to press charges yet because they think he is just fooling around anyway."

"OK Ryan I really appreciate it. We do not have enough on him yet to pick him up on suspicion of murder, but I wish we did."

"I will keep my eyes and ears open Jason and continue watching him and see what else I can find out. Just wanted to let you know what I had so far which is not much."

"Thanks for calling me Ryan and I need to get off here. I will talk to you again soon."

"Sure Jason. I will catch you later then."

It was about 3:45. I asked Calvin did he have a car. He told me that he did not. I asked him did he have driver's license. He told me he did. I ask him how he was going to get back and forth to work. He told me he guesses he would have to walk. I told him I would take him home today and pick him up in the morning and we would talk about that tomorrow.

I told him that I was going over to the hardware store to talk to Mr. Jackson and see how thing were going for him.

I left and when I got to the hardware store I ask Fred how he was doing. He told me he was doing fine. I asked him had he had any more trouble with robbery in the store. He told me so far nothing that he could see.

I went back to the office. I told Calvin that it was time for us to go home. I took him home and told him I would see him in the morning at about 7:45.

I went back up to Charlie's to get me something to eat. I was sitting there and Jeff came in and saw me and came over and ask me could he sit down. I told him to make himself at home. He did. He asked me what I have been doing lately. I told him I had not been doing anything much.

The waitress came to the table and took our orders. Jeff ask me had I had any more dreams. I told him that he knew about the last one and that so far nothing has happened but that it would happen anytime now.

I told Jeff that I thought we might have a lead or two, but I would tell him more about it when I got some more information on it.

The waitress brought our food to the table and we ate. I told him I would talk to him tomorrow sometime. He told me bye and that he would see me later.

We left the restaurant and I headed towards my house. I realized that I had not called the Sheriff in Coosa County. I would just have to do that the first thing in the morning. I have been snowed under lately and did not have time to hardly think.

I got home and went in the house to the kitchen and made me a pot of coffee. I needed that about right now. I did not have to worry about my mystery caller tonight. He was in jail now. I would see him tomorrow sometimes and maybe I could get a handle on why he was harassing me.

When my coffee finished making I poured me a cup and sat down in my recliner expecting to have a very peaceful night. That would be nice. I could use that. I do not get many of them.

Time was going by. I decided that Rita should be home by now. I called her to see how her flight went. She told me that she had a nice flight.

We talked for a few minutes and I told her I would talk to her again soon. She told me that if I had another one of those dreams and I needed someone to talk with to call her no matter what time of the night it was. I told her I would if I needed someone to talk with. We said good bye and hung up the phone.

I went back in the kitchen and poured me another cup of coffee and sat back down in my recliner and about the time I got set down good the phone rang.

"Hello." I said.

"Hello Jason. Just wanted to call you and see what you were doing." Mom said.

"It is good to hear from you mom. I have been busy today getting Rita off to the airport and getting my new employee settled in."

"You hired someone to help you out Jason. That is good you needed someone. Maybe that will help you to slow down some."

"I doubt it mom. He will only be answering the phone and running errands for me and doing things of that nature. I will still be doing all the work."

"Anything that might help you will be a help Jason." Mom said.

We talked for about ten minutes and she told me that she had to go, and we hung up the phone.

I was just thinking about what I needed to do tomorrow. I had to go over my flies and look at a couple of new cases that had come in and get started on them. Catherine had one that she needed me to work on for her and I needed to get that one started.

It was getting a little late, but I wanted one more cup of coffee before I lay down. I went back in the kitchen to get me a cup of coffee. Just as I got it poured and turned to go back in the living room the doorbell rang. At 9:00 at night? That never happens at my house. I was alarmed. I set my coffee down on the table beside my recliner and went to the door and peeped out and it was Jake Simmons.

I opened the door and ask him what in the world was he doing at my house at this time of the night ringing my doorbell.

"Were you asleep?" Jake asked me.

"No, I was getting me a cup of coffee. I wanted one more cup before I went to bed. Would you like something to drink?"

"Yes, I will take a coke." He told me."

"OK. I will be right back."

"OK." He said.

I went to the kitchen and got him a coke and came back in the living room and sat down in my recliner.

"I needed to talk with you about the murders that are taking place. I have been doing a little investigating on my own when I had time and I found a couple of things that might be of interest to you and may help you get to the killer." He told me.

"What have you found out Jake and thank you for trying to help out some?" I told him.

"Well I have been staying in Sylacauga for a few days and I was watching Ray Bradford to see what kind of schedule he kept. I know that he goes to Sylacauga once a week about the middle of the week."

"That is interesting because Janie told me the same thing and she told me that he used a fake ID when he made the trips." I told him.

"That is good that we both have the same information. He was the boyfriend, wasn't he?" Jake asked.

"Yes, he was, and I have had a suspicion that he has something to do with the murders in some way or the other." I told him.

"I wanted to come by and talk with you about it." He told me.

"I appreciate it very much."

"You are very welcome Jason. I know you guys are ready to get this one over with. It is all over the news and I have been watching and keeping up with it."

"I think everybody has. I think it has made the people here a little less worried now that it has moved out of Sylacauga, but they are still worried because who know where it will be next." I told him.

"I guess I will go back to the motel and get some sleep." He told me.

"You can stay here if you like for the rest of the time that you are here in Sylacauga."

"OK I think I will do that Jason. I am tired of the motel anyway."

He went out to the car and brought some things in that he had not taken in the motel room. He told me that he would go to the motel and check out in the morning after we got up.

"Jason there is something else that I wanted to talk with about." He told me.

"OK and what is that Jake?"

"You know I told you I have been thinking about expanding my business and getting a partner to work with me."

"Yes, I remember that." I told him.

"Well I think I am about ready to do that Jason. What I wanted to know is if you would be interested in joining with me and us being partners." He said to me.

"Well now Jake, that is a big decision." I told him.

"I know, and I have been thinking about it. I like Sylacauga. It is a nice little city. It is centrally located to Birmingham and Montgomery." He told me.

"Yes, it is Jake. And I would like that. I just need to think about it a few days and get my thoughts together on it. I have just hired someone to help out some with paper work, phone calls, and errands." I told him.

"They could do that for both of us if we joined together as partners."

"Let me think about it a few days. I just need to collect my thoughts right now."

"OK I am not in a big hurry to do this. I just wanted you to be the first one I ask to join me."

I told him that he could sleep in the room that he always sleeps in. It was getting late and I told him that he could stay up as late as he wanted to but I was going to bed.

We both got up and I made sure the doors were locked and turned out all the lights and we went to our bedrooms.

I pulled my clothes off and lay down on my bed. I was lying on my back as usual and I closed my eyes for a minute and it started all over again. These dreams. Oh my God. I am tired of them. I opened my eyes and just sat on the side of my bed for a minute trying to clear my head so that I could get some sleep.

I lay back down on my side and was just lying there with my eyes open not really wanting to close them when I floated off into dream world and could not open my eyes. The lady with the long dark red hair was in my dream again. I could not get her out of my mind. She was there. I could not open my eyes. I did not want to see anymore. It was horrifying. I tried to open them, and they just would not open. I needed to get free from this. I did not need this happening to me tonight.

I saw him again and the only thing that I could make out was that he was tall and muscular with dark black hair. That was the only features I could see. I could not get anything else.

I saw him grab her and jerk her into the kitchen. This is the second time I have seen this. The dream is fixing to come true. I was finally able to get my eyes open. I sat up on the side of the bed. I was shaking all over. I could not get myself together. I got up and went to Jake's room and called him. He asks me what was wrong. I told him I had a dream again and that the murder was fixing to happen if it had not already happened.

I told him I needed someone to talk with so that maybe I could get my mind controlled and be able to think clearly. Right now, I just could not think too well. I was off in space wondering why this was happening to me. Nothing new in my life but I did not want it there.

He got up from his bed and ask me if I wanted some coffee. I told him if I could make it to the kitchen I would love some. He went to the kitchen and made a pot of coffee. It finished making and he poured us a cup and we sat down at the table in the breakfast nook. He told me that I needed to drink the coffee and maybe I would quit shaking.

I told him that the murder had happened and that we would hear from it real soon. He asks me did I know where it was. I told him it was in the same location as the last murder in Talladega.

In a few minutes the phone rang, and it was Jeff. Jeff told me that they had found the body of the woman in the same location as the last one and that the body had been carved up just like the last one. He told me that Manuel wanted to talk with me again tomorrow if that was possible. I told him that I would go only if he went with me. Jeff told me that he would take me.

I told Jeff I would not go by myself to see him because he did not believe anything I said. I ask him why Manuel even wanted to talk with me because he was not going to believe me anyway. This was the 5th victim. Somebody needs to listen. I know what I dream, and I know that they will come true when I have them. I warn people and they just will not listen to me. If they would just listen and take my advice we might could catch the killer.

Jeff told me that maybe Manuel was looking at what you said more closely than he did the first time since you had told him it was going to happen again, and it did. I told Jeff that would not be likely. I asked him did he remember that he told me that he might have to arrest me for the murder since I knew so much about it. He told me that he did, and he was definitely listening to me about the murders because they had all happened just like I said they would.

You get it set up with Manuel and let me know when we will be going, and I will be there. He told me he would let me know when. We talked a minute longer and then we hung up the phone and I told Jake what was going on. I told him I bet that she worked at the mill in Sylacauga and that she was a ballet dancer.

"Why is he killing ballet dancers was what I wanted to know?" I told Jake.

"There has to be some reason for it. Maybe it is not just because that they are ballet dancers but maybe they were successful somehow and he does not like that." He told me.

"Maybe he wanted to be a ballet dancer himself and he was not good enough to make it." I told Jake.

"That is a possibility or maybe he just hates women." Jake said.

"That is possible." I told Jake.

"How do you feel now Jason? Are you OK? What are you going to do now?"

"I am very upset. I will not be able to sleep anymore tonight. I will be OK. I am getting used to being destroyed with dreams and phone calls."

"I am glad I did stay with you tonight." He told me

"I am glad you did to. I do not think I could have stood it if I had been alone tonight." I told him.

"We can watch TV and drink coffee and see if we can find something to get your mind off everything for a while."

"That would be nice, but I doubt I will be able to get my mind off these murders. They are too close together."

"We will see what we can do. Maybe we can find something."

I was sitting in my recliner and he was lying on the couch changing the TV trying to find something interesting and funny. I ask him when he was going back to Wetumpka. He told me that he did not know yet but that it would be fairly soon. He had some things that he had to take care of before he went.

I had leaned back in my recliner hoping that I might be able to close my eyes and get a little bit of sleep. In a little while I woke up when I heard my alarm at 5:00. I got up and went to the bathroom and took me a shower and when I finished Jake had woke up and made us some coffee. While he took a shower and cleaned up, I drank me some coffee.

He came in the kitchen and poured him a cup and we both drank our coffee. It was about time to leave the house and go pick up Calvin and take him to work. I had a full day today and a lot to do. Having to go to Talladega did not help matters.

I told Jake that I needed to go. We both left the house. He told me that he would come by the office later on today and make sure everything was OK.

CHAPTER TWENTY-SEVEN

I went and picked Calvin up and ask him if he had eaten any breakfast yet. He told me that he had not. I took him and went to The Grill and Eggs Breakfast Bar. We went in the restaurant and sat down and just as we got set down Jeff walked in the door and came over to the table and sat down with us. The waitress came to the table and took our order.

Jeff told me that he had talked to Manuel this morning and that he told me that he was going to be in the office all morning and that we could come anytime. He asks me when I wanted to go. I told him that after we ate breakfast and I took Calvin over to the office and got him situated that we could leave and go and get that over with.

The waitress brought our food to the table. We ate our food and we got ready to leave the restaurant. I told Jeff that I would see him in about thirty minutes. I left and took Calvin over to the office and got him situated and told him I would see him as soon as I got back from Talladega.

I went over to the Jeff's office and he was ready to go when I got there. We got to Talladega about 9:30. We went in and found Manuel waiting for us.

He motioned for us to have a seat. I sat down in the chair in the corner of the office facing towards him and Jeff sat down in one of the chairs in front of his desk.

"Good morning gentlemen." Manuel said.

"Hello." I said.

"Hi Manuel." Jeff said.

"We have had our second murder now Jason and you told me that it was going to happen because of a dream that you had." Manuel said.

"Yes, I told you that a murder would happen and that you needed to put extra people in the area and did you do that." I said to Manuel.

"I could not do that on a dream. I do not have the man power." He said to me.

"I told you that because of the dream that I had that it was going to happen. And it did." I told him.

"I should arrest you for the murder." Manuel said.

"I don't think that would be a good idea Manuel since you have no proof other than he told you it was going to happen because of a dream. We can prove that it happened three time in Sylacauga and that he told us it was going to happen and can even prove that he was at home when all three murders took place." Jeff told him.

"I didn't mean I actually was, but it was a thought." Manuel said.

"Quit thinking that way and listen to me when I tell you it is going to happen and try to help catch the killer by posting someone like I ask you to and maybe we will catch him." I told him.

"What I know is that everything was the same as the last one. The body was carved the same way and placed in the same places just like the last time. It was a very bloody and disgusting situation just like last time." He told us.

"I figured that it would be since I saw it that way in my dream. He is not changing his MO. He is doing it all just exactly the same just in a different location in the house each time. That was what you found in the second murder. It was in the kitchen not the bedroom like the first one." I told him.

"How did you know that it was in the kitchen Jason?" Manuel asked me.

"That is how it was in my dream. That is how I know. If you would just listen to me and do what I ask you to do before it happens we might can catch him. But you do not believe in dreams and that I could have the dreams and that this could happen in your city but it did and I have the dreams and they come true." I told him.

"OK. If you have another dream concerning anything in my city no matter what it is I think I will listen to." Manuel said.

"OK. If I have another dream, of which I hope I never do, I will let you know if it concerns your city." I told him.

"Do you think you have any clues this time Manuel or is it cold as before." Jeff asked.

"Right now, we do not have a thread of evidence of any kind that will do us any good at knowing any possibility of who the killer might be." Manuel said.

"Maybe we can get a handle on this soon. We are doing everything we can do to get some kind of evidence on him, but it seems like almost impossible right now. He will make a mistake somewhere along the way sooner or later. Let's hope it is sooner." Jeff said.

"I am working on a few things and I hope something breaks soon. I am checking out people with possibilities that maybe might help us get something on the killer." I told him.

"OK gentlemen I appreciate you coming up and talking with me. If I get anything that might do us any good I will let you know." He told us.

"Thank you, Manuel, and if we get anything that will do you any good we will let you know."

We all shook hands and we left and went and got in our car and headed for Sylacauga. We got back in Sylacauga about 11:30 AM. I went back over to the office to see what was going on. Calvin told me that it had been very slow. He told me that the sheriff of Coosa County had called the office and that he told him I was out of town this morning. He told me the sheriff wanted me to call him as soon as I could.

I picked up the phone and called him and talked with him. I told him that I could not do anything before Monday. I had a very busy schedule right now. He told me that would fine.

I ask Calvin did he want any lunch. He said he did not have the money to buy anything with. I told him to come with me and we would go to Charlie's and eat that he could pay me back one day when he had some money.

We left the office and went over to Charlie's to eat. We went in and sat down, and the waitress came to the table and took our orders. In a few moments she brought our food back to the table.

While we were eating, I asked him if he had a car would he make the payments on it and take care of it. He told me that he could not get one because he did not have any credit, and nobody would sell him one. I told him that I had some friends and that is what we were going to do after lunch was go and see about getting him some transportation.

When we finished eating I took him over to the Ford dealership in Sylacauga and talked with Jeremy Childers. I told Jeremy that the boy needed a car and that I would stand good for him if he would let him have one. I explained to Jeremy that Calvin was working for me and that he needed transportation.

Jeremy told him to go out on the lot and look around and see if he could find something that he liked. Calvin was excited. He walked out on the car lot and started looking around for something that he liked. He saw a Ford Mustang convertible. He walked over and was looking at it and he had already decided that he could not afford it.

Jeremy saw that he had been looking at it and we walked out where he was standing looking at the Ford Mustang. Jeremy asked him did he like that car. Calving told him that he loved it. It was solid red, apple red. It had a rag top, black. Jeremy ask him did he want to drive it.

Calvin could not believe he was being ask did he want to drive the red convertible Ford Mustang. It was a hot car. He was in love. It was in his eyes. I told him to drive it if he wanted to and see if that would be the car that he wanted. He told me that he did not have to drive it because he knew that was the car that he wanted. I told him you never buy a car that you do not drive first.

Jeremy got the keys for the car and handed them to him. He told him to get in and that we would ride with him. Calvin started to take off from the parking lot and pushed the gas a little too hard and it spun a tire and he stopped. Jeremy grinned and told him to go ahead.

He pulled out on the road and was grinning from ear to ear. He was in love. No doubt about it. We rode down Broadway and came back up to the car lot and got out of the car. Jeremy ask him was that the car that he wanted. He was still grinning from ear to ear and he told Jeremy that he wanted that car but that there was no way that he could buy it. He told Jeremy that he did not have any money and could not pay anything on it until after he had worked for a while.

I told him to forget all that and just listen to Jeremy for a minute. Jeremy told him that he was going to sell him the car with no down payment and that he would work out the payments for him so that he could afford them. Calvin was shocked. He could not believe that somebody was going to help him. I told him to not worry about it that one day he could pay all these people back for helping him. He told me that he would never be able to repay anybody that we were all being too good to him.

Jeremy told him to come in the sales office with him while he got the papers worked up and he would go over everything with him about the payments and all. We followed him in the office and when he had the papers ready he went over them with Calvin and told him that all he expected from him was that he makes the payments on time. He told him if he did that when he got it paid for and needed another car that he would be able to help him.

When Calvin had signed all his paper work and was finished I told him to go out and wait for me that I needed to talk with Jeremy for a minute. Calvin left. I thanked Jeremy for helping the boy out and that if anything happened that I would take care of it. He told me that he felt confident that the boy would pay for the car. I told him that was why I asked him to help him out if there was any way possible.

I thanked him, and we shook hands and I went out and told Calvin to meet me at the office. We left the Ford dealership and went back to the office. I wrote him his check for the week. I paid him for the full week and told him that I would see him Monday morning at 8:00 AM. He told me he would be there.

He left and headed towards the bank to cash his check. He was so proud of his new car. I was sure he was going to show it off to his friends this weekend and brag about it. He looked like a new person.

I went and got me some dinner and went home. I had a very nice evening. It was getting late and I went to bed. I heard a strange noise in my bedroom and realized that it was my alarm clock. I got up and put on my jogging shorts and went out the door and Jane was waiting on me as usual.

"Good morning Jason."

"Good morning Jane. Are you ready for these five miles?"

"I am always ready Jason. Have you been busy?"

"Yes, I have. I guess I always will be."

We were running, and our brown boxer came out to meet us and he will not let us pass him until we play with him for a minute. We petted him and finished our five-mile run and I went back in the house.

I took a shower and cleaned up and made me a pot of coffee. I went in the living room to see what was on the news this morning. They were talking about the serial killings in Sylacauga and Talladega. They were still calling him the Ballet Casanova.

The doorbell rang, and I went to the door.

"Good morning Jason."

"Good morning Alice."

"I guess I need to get started Jason. I have a lot to do today."

"OK Alice. How is Jeremy?"

"He is fine, and he is enjoying his job at the gym. He told me that he met Jarrod. A boy that comes in the gym and he said he really likes him."

"That is my oldest nephew Alice. I play tennis with him every Friday afternoon."

"If he is like you Jason, I understand why Jeremy likes him."

"Your check is there where I always leave it Alice. I am taking today off work. I have decided to just take it easy. I am going to hide and meet my nephew and play some tennis with him and go to the gym tonight. That is about all I am going to do."

"You need to do that every once in a while, Jason. It is good for you. I will get to work."

Murder of Grace

I went in the kitchen and found me a cinnamon roll and drank me another cup of coffee. I went to my bedroom and just lay down on my bed and forgot about the world for a while.

It was getting late in the day. I knew I had to get up and get out of the way because Alice would be in my room soon to clean it.

I went downstairs and ask her was there anything she needed. She told me that she was fine. I got me a glass of orange juice and went out on the porch and sat down for a while. It was getting about time to meet Jarrod.

I left the house and went to the tennis courts to meet my nephew.

"Hello Uncle Jason."

"Hello Jarrod. How are you?"

"Are you ready to get beat today Uncle Jason."

"You only hope you are going to beat me Jarrod."

"I have confidence Uncle Jason."

We played a couple of games. I beat him in one of them today. He usually wins. We went to McDonalds to get us something to drink and talk for a few minutes.

He told me that he had met this boy that works at the gym named Jeremy Whitcomb. I told him that was my maid's nephew.

"He told me, Uncle Jason, that there was this person that has been following him every time they see him."

"It must be the same one that was following him the night I took him home."

"I am going to take him, and we are going to follow them and see if we can find out why they are chasing him."

"If you find out anything let me know. Just do not bother them. Let me know what is going on and if I have to we can get behind them and maybe stop it."

We left McDonalds and went over to Charlie's to get a bite to eat. We went in and sat down, and Dexter walked in the door. He saw me and came over to the table and ask me could he sit down. Of course, I told him that he could. He sat down and ask me what I had been doing today. I told him about our meeting with Manuel over the 2nd murder in Talladega.

The waitress came to the table and took our orders. We ordered the T-bone steak, baked potatoes, and green salads. We sat around and talked about the things that we might could do to get a lead on the killer.

In a few minutes the waitress brought our food to the table. We ate our food and chit chatted while we ate.

"What are you going to do this weekend?" Dexter ask me.

"I am going to try to take it easy and rest mostly and not do much of anything." I told him.

"I am going fishing tomorrow. You want to go with me."

"I have not been fishing in a long time. Sure, I will go with you." I told him.

"We will go to the Coosa River and hide out and fish for a while. Maybe nobody will bother us that way." He told me.

"That would be nice, and it definitely would be fun." I told him.

"I plan to leave at about 8:00 in the morning. You want me to come by your house and pick you up on the way down." He said.

"That will be good. I will be ready." I told him.

We finished eating and he told me he would see me in the morning. It would be something different for a change. We got up to leave and shook hands and I told him I would be ready when he got there.

We left the restaurant and I needed to do some grocery shopping before I went home. I went to Winn-Dixie to buy me some groceries. Jarrod left and went to the gym.

I was walking around in the store looking for some things that I needed when I looked up and saw a man with a gun holding it in a cashier's face. The manager was over by the office door near the cash registers and he was astounded. He was telling her to give him all the money she had in her register and that if anyone tried to stop him that he would shoot her and them to.

I eased around closer so that I could get a good look at him. I carried my .44 magnum Smith & Wesson with me, but I did not see how that I could get it and do anything with it without causing big problems. He could not see me. I was behind some displays near the front of the store close to her register.

He told her to give him the money now or he would shoot. She was not fast enough for him and he fired one shot up in the air in the top of the store and busted out a light in the ceiling. He told her that the next one would be for her. She was scared and shaking. She got the money out of the register and threw it at him. It went everywhere. He was trying to get it and keep the gun on her at the same time.

I was able to get my gun and ease over a little closer. He did not want to leave any of the money. He looked about 21 years old. He had turned his back on me still looking at her. I was able to get over close enough. I jumped in behind him and stuck my Smith & Wesson on the back of his head and dared him to move. He froze. He was not expecting that.

Then he ducked and turned and swung at me. When he did I knocked his gun out of his hand. The manager of the store came running over and grabbed the man's gun and held it on him. He turned and tried to run, and I kicked him in back and he fell flat on his face and the manager put the gun on his head and told him not to move.

I took the gun and had the guy where he could not move and told the manager to call the police. About the time I got that out of my mouth the sirens were blaring outside the store. Four officers came in the door with their weapons pointed and they were crouched down looking to see what had happened.

I motioned for them to come over where we were. I told them what had happened. They arrested the guy that had tried to rob the store and took him outside and put him in the police car. One of the officers came over to talk with the manager and the young waitress about the incident so he could file his report.

In a few minutes everything was back to normal in the store. The customers were a little nervous and was ready to get their things and go home. The officer finished his report and left and went back to the police station.

I found out that the young man who had robbed the store was from Sylacauga and that he had a felony record. This was not the first place that he robbed.

I left the store and went to the house. I was ready to forget about everything.

CHAPTER TWENTY-EIGHT

I got to the house and pulled in the garage and walked up on my porch and turned to look back and Jeff was pulling up in the yard.

"Hello Jason."

"Hello Jeff."

"Thought I would stop by for a few minutes and say hello."

"It is nice for you to stop by Jeff."

"What is going on in our little city here lately?" He asked me.

"I do not know Jeff, but it seems like we can't get a break."

I went in the kitchen and got us something to drink and sat down on the porch with Jeff.

"That was an interesting situation you had at Winn-Dixie Jason."

"You never know what is going to happen that is for sure Jeff. I am just glad I was there when it happened."

"We have too much going on around here right now."

"Tell me about it. I hope it stops soon."

"I will go for now Jason. I will see you tomorrow I am sure."

"OK Jeff. Thanks for stopping by. Have a great evening."

We shook hands and he left. I went in the house and made me a pot of coffee. I did not finish my grocery shopping. I will do that tomorrow sometime if I have time to.

When the coffee finished making I poured me a cup and went in the living room and sat in my recliner. In a few minutes Jake came walking in the door. He got him a cup of coffee and came back and sat down on the couch.

"Did you have a busy day Jason?"

"As normal. We even had a little incident in the grocery store today on my way home."

"What happened Jason?"

"Somebody tried to rob a cashier."

"Seems like everything is happening in Sylacauga right now Jason."

"Yes. We will get a break one day."

We were watching TV and about the time I got interested in a good movie the phone rang.

"Hello. Jason Caffrey speaking."

"Hello Jason. What are you doing?" Mom said.

"I am sitting here in my recliner drinking a cup of coffee. What are you doing mom?"

"Nothing right now. What are you going to do this weekend Jason?" She asked me.

"I am going fishing in the morning with Dexter. We are going to Coosa River and fish for a while."

"That sounds like fun. I am sure you will enjoy that." She told me.

"It has been a while since I went fishing and I am kind of looking forward to it." I told her.

"Are you coming over this week end? I would love to see you."

"I will be over there either tomorrow evening after we get back from fishing or sometime Sunday. I do not know for sure yet which but I will be there."

"OK. I will let you go for now. Talk to you later Jason."

"OK. Bye for now. Talk to you soon mom."

Murder of Grace

I went and got me another cup of coffee and sat down in my recliner to drink it. I leaned back to watch a movie that had just came on and I drifted off and went to sleep. I woke up in a little while and looked at the clock and it was 11:00. Jake had already gone to bed.

I got up and made sure the doors were locked and turned out all the lights and went to my bedroom. I pulled my clothes off and lay down. I was lying on my side when my eyes closed, and I was drifting away. The next thing I knew I was in dream world.

I tried to open my eyes, but the dream was there and I couldn't. I saw a tall slender young woman with long dark black hair. She had long arms and long fingers and she had long legs and was very slender. She was beautiful. Her hair was very curly and was pulled back with a banana clip. She was in the living room sitting in her big leather chair by the fireplace. She had the TV on and was watching a movie.

I could see her laughing and then all of a sudden, she looked around towards the kitchen. There was a man standing in the door way with a sickle in his hand. He was rubbing it in between his fingers and licking his lips. She screamed and ask him what he was doing in her house. He told her that he wanted to see her dance. He told her he enjoyed watching her in the shows that he had seen her in. He told her he hunted her until he found her and now he wanted to see her dance again.

She told him that she was not in the mood to dance. He told her that if she did not dance for him that he was going to make her pay for being so rude. She was crying by now and was scared to death. She got a hold of herself and quit crying. She did not know what to do. It was devastating for her to see a man in her living room now with a sickle in his hand.

William Honeycutt

She told him that she did not have a record player. He told her that she did not need any music that she could dance without it. She got up from her chair and walked around behind the big leather chair she was sitting in. There was a fire poker sitting close enough she could reach it.

He moved into the living room a little closer to her. He told her that he wanted her to dance right now. She told him that he would have to give her time that she had not danced in a while. He told her that she was good and that she could dance for him now.

She reached and got a hold of the fire poker and told him that if he came any closer to her that she would poke him in the throat with it. He told her that she would not be fast enough to get him. She told him that he did not know what she could do because he did not know everything about her. He told her that he knew more than she could imagine. He told her he had been watching her for a long time and keeping up with what she had been doing.

She was scared and was trying to keep him from seeing how scared she was. She gripped the fire poker in her hand to keep it from shaking. She stepped to the side of the chair. He came in a little closer to her. She had the poker in her hands and was ready to use it.

He reached out to grab at her and she slung the poker at him and caught him on the side of the face. It brought blood. She was happy. At least she had hit him and hurt him. It really made him mad. He told her that he would kill her now for sure.

She told him that he would have to catch her first. He reached for her a second time and she hit him on the other side of the face with the fire poker. He was really pissed now. He reached up and rubbed his face and when he looked at his hand he found that she had brought blood a second time.

Murder of Grace

He reached out and grabbed her arm and jerked her and she got away from him that time. He told her that he was going to get her and that she would pay for having hit him with the fire poker and making him bloody.

She told him that if he touched her again that she was going to punch him just as hard as she could in the stomach with it. He stepped up a little closer to her and was watching her very carefully so that he could dodge the fire poker if she tried to use it again. She reached out and she slung it again at him and hit him on his arm and knocked the sickle out of his hand. He grabbed it up and told her that was it. He told her he was tired of fooling around with her and that he was just going to kill her and get it over with.

She ran over behind the couch which was sitting away from the wall. He came towards her again and she threw the lamp, which was sitting on the table, at him and hit him in the stomach with it. He jolted and jumped back and got his thoughts back together and told her that he had had enough and was going to make her suffer before he killed her.

He reached over the couch and tried to grab her. He could not reach her. He jumped up on the couch and reached for her and grabbed her by the hair of the head and jerked her. She fell over the couch into the floor. He grabbed her up and put her in a sleeper hold and she was fighting him with everything she had.

All I could see of him was that he was tall and muscular and had dark black hair. I could not get anything else that would do me any good for recognizing him.

In a little bit she was gone. He put the sickle to her throat and sliced her throat from ear to ear and made sure he got the jugular vein and she died immediately. He carved the body up and placed it just like he had the other five women that he had murdered. The living room was bloody.

He forgot about the fire poker with his blood on it when he left. He did not take it with him or get rid of it. It was lying on the floor behind the couch.

I woke up and was shaking all over. It was horrifying. I was devastated. I did not know what to do. I knew I had to talk with somebody though. This was the sixth woman that I had dreamed of and so far, we have nothing. I could not take any more of this.

I went to the kitchen and put me on a pot of coffee shaking the whole time I was trying to get going. I was so upset. Finally, it finished making. I was starting to calm down a little. Some of the shaking was going away. I poured me a cup of coffee and took it to the living room. I had to hold it with both hands to get it in there without spilling it. I sat down in my recliner and picked up my phone and called Rita.

"Hello Jason. You have had one of those dreams again." She said.

"Yes, and it was a really bad one this time even worse than the others have been. They just seem to get worse and harder to deal with." I told her.

"I am glad you called me. I was having a hard time sleeping anyway. Now I know why." She told me.

"I am still shaking but not as bad as I was."

"Are you going to be alright?" She asked me.

"I will be alright. It may take a while for me to get calmed down." I told her.

"Do you need me to come down there? I can if you need me to." She told me.

I told her I would be fine after a while and that I would be able to deal with it but I was just real upset right now and needed someone to talk with. She told me that we could talk as long as I needed to.

Murder of Grace

We talked for a long time and finally I told her I guess I needed to let her go so she could get some rest. She told if I needed her to call her back. She said she did not have anything planned. We hung up the phone.

I went to the kitchen and got me another cup of coffee. I was settled down from what I was. At least I was not trembling anymore. I was able a hold my cup in my hand without spilling the coffee everywhere.

I went back in the living room and turned on the TV and sat down in my recliner. I just wanted to forget that the world existed right now and definitely not have any more dreams.

I drank my coffee and I closed my eyes and I went to sleep. I woke up at about 5:00 and got up and made me some fresh coffee. I poured me a cup and drank it. After I had drank my first cup, Jake came in the kitchen and got him a cup and sat down with me at the table in the breakfast nook.

He asked me what I was going to do today. I told him I was going fishing this morning with Dexter. I asked him did he want to go with us. He told me that he couldn't because he had some surveillance that he had to do this morning. He told me that he was going to leave late this afternoon and go home.

I told him I if I did not see him before he left that I would call him by the middle of next week and tell him what my decision would be on going in partnership with me. He told me he looked forward to that call and hoped that I would make the decision to join him.

It was getting close to 8:00 and Jake told me that he was going to go and find him some breakfast before he had to go work this morning. I told him I would see him later and he left.

At 8:00 Dexter pulled up by the curb and parked his car close to the street. I went out and got

William Honeycutt

in and we left. We got to the Coosa River between Stewartville and Weogufka and found us a nice place to fish. We got our hooks in the water and he caught a big catfish before we got started good.

We fished all morning. We had a great day fishing and it was about dinnertime. We had got several good messes of fish. We decided that we were tired and was ready to leave the river. We left and was on our way back to Sylacauga and we were both hungry. We stopped by Faye's Fabulous Kitchen in Stewartville.

We went in and the waitress came and took our order. We sat around waiting on our meal chit chatting about all the things happening in our little city. I told him about my dream last night. I told him that the next murder was fixing to happen very soon.

I told him about what I saw in reference to the fire poker and how that she had struck him on the face with it and brought blood and how that he did not think about the fire porker and that she had dropped it behind the couch when she was there before he killed her. He said that would be a good way to get some DNA on him if that actually does happen. I told him I had to talk to Manuel the Chief of Police in Talladega and tell him what I knew so far. That way when they get to the scene they will know to get the fire poker and get blood samples from it. It will be his blood for sure.

The waitress brought our food to the table. We ate our food and went back to Sylacauga. He dropped me off at my house and ask me did I want any of those fish we caught. I told him to take them with him. It had taken my mind off things for a while.

I went in the house and got a Barq's root beer and went back into the living room to my recliner. I found the number for the TPD and called them and ask them to please call the chief and have him to call me that it was very important. They assured me that they would get a hold of him and have him call me.

In about thirty minutes the phone rang, and it was Manuel. I told him about the dream. I told him that the murderer was not going to put it off very long I was sure. I told him I would not be surprised if it happened this weekend. He told me that he would put three cars in the area and have them watch it very close. I told him I did not see the area but the three in Sylacauga happened all in the same area. I told him he would probably do the same there.

Manuel thanked me for calling and told me that we would get him this time. I told him I hoped that he was right. We did not need for this to continue. This will be number six I told him. That is way too many. One was too many. We talked for a little bit and I told him that I would talk with him later. He told me he would let me know if anything happened. I told him I appreciated it and we hung up the phone.

I got a cup of coffee and went back to the living room. I sat down in the recliner and kicked the foot rest up and was watching TV when my doorbell rang.

I got up and went to the door and looked out to see who was there. It was Jeff. I opened the door and he came in. I went in the kitchen and got us something to drink. I sat back down in my recliner.

"What have you been doing today Jason?"
"Dexter and I went fishing."
"Did you catch anything?"
"We caught enough for several good messes."
"That is good. Did you keep any?"
"No, I told Dexter to take them all with him and enjoy them. What have you been doing Jeff?"
"Nothing much. Just taking it easy and I plan on not doing anything tonight either."

William Honeycutt

He asks me had I had any more dreams lately. I told him about the one I had last night. He asks me did I think it was going to happen anytime soon. I told him that it was surely going to because I never had them that detailed that it did not happen soon.

I was really expecting the murder to take place tonight or tomorrow night. That is about the way it usually went. I told him I had thought about going to Talladega myself and posting watch and see if I could see anything. Manuel told me that he was going to post three cars in the area to keep a watch. I hope he puts unmarked cars there, so the murderer will not know that they are there.

"I was just out roaming around some Jason and just wanted to come by and see you for a minute and see how you were doing."

"Thank you, Jeff, for coming bye. These dreams are about to drive me crazy."

"Maybe they will go away here soon, and you will not have to worry about it." He told me.

"I probably will have dreams just as bad as these concerning something else when the murderer is caught." I told him.

"What are you going to do tomorrow Jason?" He asked me.

"I am going and spend some time with mom tomorrow." I told him.

"That is good." He told me.

"I think my wife wants to go to the park and have a picnic and just enjoy the day outside the house roaming around and just having fun." He told me.

"I hope you have a lot of fun." I told him.

We talked for a few more minutes and he told me that he needed to go. He got up and we shook hands and he left.

I went back in the kitchen and got me some more coffee and came back in the living room and

Murder of Grace

sat down. The phone rang. I answered it. I knew it was not going to be my mystery caller.

"Hello." I said.

"Hello Jason." Mom said.

"Hi mom. What are you doing?" I said.

"I am just calling to make sure you are coming tomorrow."

"I will be there mom. Don't fret."

"I just really wanted to talk to you is all I wanted."

"What did you do today mom."

"I went shopping and picked up a few things that I needed and splurged and bought some things that I did not need."

"I know you had fun mom. You have always enjoyed shopping."

"I got some surprises to." She told me and laughed.

"What kind of surprises did you get?" I asked her.

"It is none of your business right now." She told me.

"Why did you tell me then?"

"Just to make you wonder." She said.

We talked for a few minutes and said our good buys and hung up.

I picked up the TV remote and tried to find me a good movie to watch. I decided that I would just relax in my recliner. I found a good action movie by Mel Gibson and was watching it when I fell asleep.

CHAPTER TWENTY-NINE

I finally woke up and realized that it was already Sunday morning. I had slept in my recliner. I did not have any dreams last night. Maybe I will just sleep in my recliner from now on.

I went to the kitchen and made a pot of coffee. I went and took me a good long hot shower and shaved. I put me on some clean clothes and went in the kitchen and poured me a cup of coffee. I took it in the living room to watch a little TV.

I left the house and went to The Grill and Eggs Breakfast Bar. Just as I got in the restaurant and seated Jim Sax walked in the door. I saw him and waved for him to come over and sit with me.

"Hello Jim."

"Hello Jason. What are you doing?"

"I decided that I would get me something to eat this morning." I told him.

"I am on my way home from Knoxville. I have been working up there for a while. I decided to eat so that Jane would not have to cook when I got to the house." He told me.

"You must have traveled last night."

"I did. I did not want to wait till this morning. I will be home for four days and I have to go back." He told me.

The waitress took our order. We chit chatted about the things that had been going on in our lives.

The waitress brought our food to the table and we ate and talked some while we were eating. We finished eating our breakfast and he told me he needed to get home. I told him it was nice to see him and that I would talk to him later. We shook hands and Jim left.

I got up and left and rode over to Calvin's house to see what he was doing this morning. I pulled up in the yard and he was outside.

"Hello Calvin."

"Have you been in the house since you got home with that new car?" I asked him.

"Yes, I have just come out to ride around some." He told me.

"Did you show it off all day yesterday?"

"Yes and my friends want one like it."

"Maybe one day they can buy them one."

"They are jealous of me now. They asked me how I came up with something like this." He told me.

"How did you tell them that you came up with it?"

"I told them that I just went and bought it. Well, I did. I signed all by paperwork by myself. I know you helped me by talking with the owner of that place and that is why that I was able to get the car but I did not tell them that part of it."

"That is good Calvin. I was hoping you would keep that between us."

"Is that a garage in the back there Calvin?"

"Yes, it is but I have to get it cleaned out and then I am going to keep my car in it and keep it locked when I am not using it."

"That is good. I just hope that you take very good care of it."

"I will." He told me.

"I just wanted to come by and see you for a minute Calvin. I am going over to my mom's house for a while. I will see you in the morning at the office."

"OK. See you then." He told me.

I left and drove down by the park and it was empty. I parked and got out and walked over and found me a bench and sat down. I just wanted to sit and watch the birds for a few minutes before I went over to my mom's house. I sat there for about thirty minutes and left and went to my mom's house.

As I was pulling up in the driveway she walked out on the porch and waved at me. I waved back at her and got out of the car and went up on the porch and gave her a big hug and kiss and told her I still loved her.

"I love you more than you love me." She told me.

"I do not know how that is possible because I know I love you more."

"There is no way Jason you can love me more than I love you. I am your mama you know." She told me.

"OK. I give up. You win."

"I know." She said.

"Would you like something to drink Jason?"

"A Barq's root beer would be nice."

"Let's go inside and sit at the table in the breakfast nook and I will get you one."

"OK."

We went inside and went to the kitchen and she got me a Barq's root beer and her a coke.

"Did you have fun fishing yesterday Jason?" she asked me.

"I did and look forward to the next time whenever that may be." I told her.

"What are you going to do today when you leave from here?"

"I don't know yet. It depends on what time I leave."

"Are you going to eat with us today?"

"I plan on spending most of the day with you." I told her.

Murder of Grace

She told me to come with her to the den because she had something that she wanted to show me. We went to the den and she picked up this big bag handed it to me. She told me it was mine.

I opened it and looked inside. It was two new pair of Levi's and two shirts and a pair of new sneakers. A red shirt and a blue shirt. I hugged her for them and gave her a big kiss and told her that I loved her. She told me that was the surprise she was talking about but did not want to tell me about it. I thanked her for it again.

We went out on the back porch and sat down in the chairs and mom was telling me all about her plants and what all she had had to do to them to make them so beautiful. We were just enjoying our time together.

We went to the kitchen where she could check on her dinner that had been cooking all morning. She was fixing a roast beef with potatoes, onions, and carrots cooked with it. She had fixed that fabulous chocolate cake that she was so famous at that everybody loved and she had some ice cream to go with it when it was time to eat.

We walked out on the front porch and sat down in the swing and were talking about how beautiful it was this year and dad drove up in the front yard. He got out and came up on the porch and sat down in the chair next to the swing.

"Hello Jason."

"Hello Dad. How are you?"

"I am doing really well son. What have you been doing?"

"I went fishing yesterday with Dexter and we caught a bunch of fish. And just trying to keep my life together." I told him.

"It is getting about time to eat. The food is ready, let's eat." Mom said.

"Sure I am." Dad said.

We went in the kitchen and mom put the dinner on the table while dad and I talked and enjoyed being together. I did not get to see much of him. He was gone a lot when I came over.

We ate lunch and went into the living room.

"Well, Jason what are you going to do this week coming up?" Dad asked.

"I am going to work and get my new man I hired trained and hopefully he will be a lot of help to me." I told him.

"You hired someone to help you?" He asked.

"Yes, I needed someone to answer the phone while I was gone and to run errands for me so that I would have time to work on my cases." I told him.

We sat around and talked for a while. It was getting late and was about time for me to go home. I told mom and dad that I needed to go. Dad asked me why I had to be in a hurry. I told him that I just needed to go home and relax for a while.

We got up and walked out on the porch. I gave them both a big hug and told them I loved them and that I would see them soon. Dad told me to be careful.

I left and started towards home. I still had not finished doing my grocery shopping yet. I had to stop by the store on the way home and finish that or I was going to run out of things that I needed. Especially my coffee and coffee creamer. It was getting low.

I stopped by Winn-Dixie and bought the few items that I needed and headed towards the house. I got home and took my groceries in and put them up. I made a pot of coffee and went in the living room and called Rita.

"Hello Jason."

"Hello Rita. What are you doing?"

"Nothing right now except talking with you." She said and laughed at me.

"I just wanted to call you and talk with you a little bit."

"Are you OK Jason?"

"Yes, I am fine Rita."

"Good. I was thinking about you today and was hoping you were OK."

"I had a great night last night and I spent the day with mom and have not been home very long."

"That is good."

We talked for a few more minutes and I told her I would let her go for now and that I would talk with her again soon.

I turned on the TV and found me a good movie to watch and kicked my foot rest up and leaned back in my recliner to just rest some and enjoy the movie.

After a while I woke up and looked at the clock and it was 10:30. I had been asleep for about three hours. That was nice. Maybe everything was going to be good tonight because I did not have one of them dreams.

I went to my bedroom and put me on some pajamas and went back to the living room and sat in my recliner and leaned back.

CHAPTER THIRTY

I sat in the living room till about 12:30 AM and it was time to go to bed and try to get some sleep. I went and lay down on my bed. I was staring at the ceiling thinking about what I needed to do.

I finally was able to close my eyes. When I was almost asleep I saw the woman with the dark black hair in my dream. I wanted to open my eyes because I did not want to dream anymore. I could see her very well. I could see exactly what she looked like. I saw the murderer. I could only see that he was tall and muscular with dark black hair.

The dream was there. I could not stop it. I saw him grab her and her fall over the couch on the floor in front of the couch.

Finally, I woke up and I was shaking. I was so upset. I knew the murder had taken place. I had no doubt that it had happened tonight.

I called the TPD and told them to have Manuel to call me ASAP that is was very important.

In a few minutes the phone rang. I told Manuel that the murder had happened. I told him that he needed to go and see if he could find where it was. It told him that it was in the same location that the other two had been and that it happened in the living room this time.

He told me that he would get the officers on it immediately and would let me know what they found.

I went in the kitchen and made me a pot of coffee. I knew that I was not going to get any more sleep tonight. When the coffee was finished I poured me a cup and took it in the living room with me. The dream had not gotten so detailed tonight as it had in the past. I was not as upset from the dream as usual. I was upset over the murder but not the dream.

I was sitting in my chair and my phone rang.

"Hello. Jason Caffrey speaking."

"Hello Jason."

"Hello Rita. What are you doing?"

"You had the dream again didn't you and the murder has already happened."

"Yes, and Yes. I am upset over the murder. The dream did not last long tonight though. It ended quickly, and I am not upset over the dream. I am not trembling or shaking or anything like that this time."

"That is good Jason. I saw it and I knew you might need someone to talk with, so I called you."

"I have not heard from the TPD yet. They are searching for the crime scene and I expect to hear from them anytime now. I spoke to Manuel and told him what had happened. He has men searching the area now hoping to find it. He will find it."

"You are confident Jason."

"If you had these dreams like I do you would understand why I am so confident."

"I know. I knew when I called you that the murder had happened. I saw it and when I see these things I have no doubt about them either. I just don't dream about them. I only visualize them in my mind."

"You have the ability to see what is happening in the present and the future."

"Yes, and sometimes it is very scary."

"I know. I wish I could just see it that way and not have these dreams, but I have the dreams instead."

"Are you going to be OK Jason?"

"Yes, I will be fine."

"The one good thing is that she struck the murderer with the fire poker on the face and it brought blood. The fire poker has his blood on it and they will find it behind the couch where she dropped it before she fell over the couch."

"That is good Jason. They can get some DNA that way on him and maybe it will lead to catching him."

"I have a feeling this will be the last one in this area and that he will move on down the road farther away. He will eventually realize that he made a mistake by forgetting about that fire poker with the blood on it."

"If he crosses the state line Jason the FBI will have to get involved."

"I know. I have a feeling that is what he is going to do this time."

"Maybe they will send me to help investigate if that happens."

"I know they are going to want me to come because they will know that I know about it because of the dreams. When I dream of it I will have to call the PD where it is going to happen and inform them that it is coming to pass. I cannot just sit back and wait for it to happen and then tell them I knew that it was going to happen."

"That will be hard on you Jason."

"Yes, it will be because I have already been threatened twice, once by Jeff here and Manuel in Talladega that they should arrest me because I seemed to know so much about it."

"Yes, and that is no good."

"Can you imagine what a PD will think of me if I call them and give them such detail on a murder case that has not happened yet but is going to happen and it actually takes place just like I tell them that it will?"

"What are you going to do Jason?"

"I am going to call them and talk with them. Fly there and tell them about it if I need to. I will do whatever I have to do to try to prevent it from happening. It probably will not do me any good. I have not been able to prevent six from happening yet but maybe somebody will listen to me sooner or later."

"I know what you mean. I do not tell anybody about my ability to see the future and what is going to happen. I do not know anybody other than you that I trust right now. I know you understand because of the dreams."

"Yes, I do understand Rita and I wish that these dreams would quit haunting me."

"I know what you mean."

We talked a little bit longer and she told me that she needed to go and try to sleep the rest of the night because she had a long day ahead of her tomorrow. I told her I would call her tomorrow night and let her know the details. We hung up the phone.

I went back in the kitchen and got me another cup of coffee and went back in the living room and sat down in my recliner. Just as I got set down good the phone rang.

"Hello. Jason Caffrey speaking."

"Hello Jason."

"Hello Manuel."

"I just wanted to let you know that we found the murder scene and it was the lady with the long black hair just as you had said it would be. Was done just like the other two. The bodies were mutilated, and body parts put like they had been the last two times."

"I am sorry Manuel. Do you need me to come there tomorrow?"

"No Jason but if I need you for anything I will call you. You need to find out Manuel if any of the neighbors knew her and knew anything about her.

See if she breathed that she was a ballet dancer. They have all been ballet dancers so far."

"We will be sure to ask that specific question when we talk with her neighbors and see if they have seen anyone lurking around her place looking suspicious and all."

"Maybe we will get him this time. Be sure to look behind the couch and find the fire poker. It will have blood on it Manuel. It will be his blood. She dropped it before she fell over the couch and he never thought about it again because he was too concentrated on killing her."

"That is good that will give us some DNA evidence. We found her ID and her name is Sylvia Brown"

"Yes, it will and maybe it will lead us to him."

"OK Jason just wanted to let you know what was going on. I will talk with you later and if you ever do tell me anything else I am just going to believe you."

"OK Manuel. I will talk with you later.

I kicked up my foot rest to my recliner and leaned back and closed my eyes to rest and when I did I fell asleep.

CHAPTER THIRTY-ONE

I woke up at 5:00 when my alarm went off. I pulled on my jogging shorts and walked out the door to meet Jane.

"Good morning Jane. How are you this bright and cheerful morning?" What a die that was. I was depressed. I was not going to tell her that though because if I did, then I would have to tell her why and I do not want to do that.

"Good morning Jason. I am great and how are you this beautiful day."

"I am great Jane. We are going to have a good time this morning."

"We always do Jason. And boy are you cheerful this morning."

"Just trying to get my day off with a great start."

We ran our first mile and petted our great big beautiful brown boxer. He was extra friendly this morning too. I wonder if he had a bad night and was trying to get his day started with a bang.

"Our boxer was over friendly too this morning Jason. Did you put a bug in his ear?"

"I guess he must have had a great night."

We ran our five miles and got to the house and I went in and put on a pot of coffee. It went and took me a long hot shower and shaved and got ready to go to work. I wore my bright red button up shirt that my mom had just bought me and my new Levi's. I felt worthy again.

I left the house and headed for The Grill and Eggs Breakfast Bar and was sitting by the window and Catherine walked in the door and saw me and came over and sat down.

"What have you been doing Jason?"

"I have been dreaming Catherine. What are you up to?"

"I thought I would stop in this morning and get me something to eat since I did not want to cook."

The waitress came to the table and took our order.

We both ordered two eggs over easy with bacon and a short stack of pancakes.

"I am going to the office and get ready to go to court today. I have a big case starting this morning." She told me.

"Have you heard about the last murder in Talladega yet Catherine?" I asked her.

"No. When did it happen?"

"It happened last night."

"I did not turn on my TV this morning. I just wanted to get ready and leave the house early."

"I had that awful dream and knew it was going to happen and called the TPD and had Manuel to call me. I told him that the murder had happened and when they found the crime scene he called me back and told me they had found it just I told them they would.

"That is awful Jason. Why are these things going on around us right now? I wish they would stop."

"Well it will stop when we catch him. At least we have a little more to go on now than we had before. She struck him with a fire poker and it brought blood and he forgot about the fire poker because he was concentrated on killing her. They will have that in Talladega to go on. That will help. Maybe we can catch him before he does it again."

"What are you going to do today Jason?"

"I am going over to the office and see if I can get a computer set up for Calvin and see what he knows about computers. I have one set up but I do not want anybody messing with it. I do not need any of my files tampered with."

"You think he knows much about computers Jason?"

"I don't know, but I am going to find out this morning. I think I am going to have to go and buy one though. I don't think the old one I have is going to work too good."

"Have you tried it lately?"

"No, I think I will just take him and go to the store and buy one and then I will not have to worry about it. I hope that he is computer literate. Then I will not have to teach him much."

"Well, maybe it will work out that way. That will good."

The waitress brought our food to the table. We ate breakfast and sat around and talked for a while and she told me that she needed to go and get things ready for court. I told her I would see her later.

We left the restaurant and I went to the office. It was 7:45 AM. I went in the office and the telephone rang. It was Janie.

"Hello Jason."

"Hello Janie. What you got on your mind this morning?"

"Jason, I do not know what is going on but Mr. Bradford left Saturday night and went to Birmingham. I had someone to follow him and see what he did. They told me that he rented a car in Birmingham and headed south. They followed him, and he went to Talladega. I just heard on national news that is where the last murder just took place."

"It is where it happened. That is number six Janie and we need to get it stopped now."

"That is all I know right now but my follower will let me know what else they find out and when they do I will let you know."

"I don't know if he is actually committing the murders or not, but I believe that he is involved some way or the other."

"Maybe we will soon find out."

"Well at least they will have a blood sample on the murderer this time because she hit him with a fire poker on the face and it brought blood. That will help. We may need to get a blood sample from Mr. Bradford and see if he ties into it that way. If not, we need to find out how he fits in these murders. I just believe that he does."

"OK Jason I will go for now, but I will be in touch real soon."

"Talk to you later Janie and thank you very much for calling."

Just as I hung up the phone Calvin came walking in the door. He was on time. It was 8:00 AM. I told him to get ready and let's go to Walmart's and get a computer. He was excited about that. I asked him did he know how to work one. He told me that he did.

We got to Walmart' and found an HP. I bought it and we took it back to the office. I ask him did he know how to get it set up. He told me that he did. I told him to have at it and have fun that I was going to run over to the SPD for a few minutes.

I left and let him take care of the computer. I went over to see if Dexter was in the office. The clerk showed me to his office and told me to go in. I walked in the door and Dexter motioned for me to sit down in the chair in front of the desk.

"Hello Jason."

"Hello Dexter. How are you today?"

"I am fine Jason. What are you doing?"

Murder of Grace

"I just wanted to come over and talk with you for a little bit. I know you have heard about the sixth murder now."

"Yes, I have and it is about time that we get a good handle on this and get it stopped before it happens again."

"I sure wish we could. I would like that a lot."

"Well maybe he made a mistake this time and left us something that will help us."

"He did. She struck him with the fire poker on the face and it brought blood. When she was behind the couch she dropped it before she fell over the couch. I told Manuel about that so that they would be sure to look behind the couch and find it. They can get a blood sample from that."

"That is good Jason. We can get some DNA from that and if he is in the system we can find him."

"I think that Ray Bradford the boyfriend of Delores in Charleston, South Carolina has something to do with the murders. He could be the murderer. I just felt like he was not telling me everything when I had that meeting with him. It all seemed a little strange the way he told it."

"You may be on to something Jason."

"What have you been doing today Dexter?"

"I had to go and testify in a case for Catherine earlier today."

"The one with the car thieves?" I asked him.

"Yes. That one. I am sure they will be convicted."

"I went to Walmart's and bought a new computer for the office. Calvin is setting it up. When I get back to the office I am going to see just how much he knows about computers. I hope he knows a lot of tricks on research and all. That way he can get information for us that we have a hard time getting otherwise."

"You think he might know Jason."

"I don't know but I will find out soon. What are you going to do this afternoon Dexter?"

"I have to go over to the court house today and help them with the security for a while."

"Well I just wanted to come by and talk with you a little bit if you had time. I guess I need to get back to the office and see how things are going for Calvin."

"OK Jason. You take it easy and I will talk with you later."

I left the SPD and went back over to my office and Calvin had the computer set up and ready to go. He was playing around with a game.

It was time to go and find some lunch. I ask Calvin did he like Mexican food. We went over to the Mexican restaurant. The waitress came to the table and we ordered our meals. I ask him what he wanted to do for the rest of his life. He told me that he wanted to work in law enforcement some way.

I ask him would he be interested in detective work. He told me that sounded like it might be something worth looking into. I ask him did he graduate from school. He had graduated from Sylacauga High School. He told me that he was an A, B student. He said he mostly made A's. I ask him what had happened to him since he graduated with honors like that.

He told me that after he graduated that his father became disabled and that the family was having a very hard time and that he tried to find jobs to where that he could help out. He told me that nobody wanted to hire him.

I ask him why. He told me that he did not have the money to buy nice looking clothes to where that he could look nice when he went on interviews. He told me that he just could not get things going in his favor.

Murder of Grace

The waitress brought our food to the table and set it down and asked us if we needed anything else. We told her we were fine.

We ate our food and talked some. When we finished eating we went back to the office. I told him to sit down at the computer and show me what he knew about them. I found out fairly quick that he was pretty smart when it came to computers.

I had to go to Rockford, Alabama and talk with the sheriff and get the charges filed and signed against my mystery caller. I told Calvin I would be back after a while.

I got to Rockford about 1:30 PM. I went in to see the Sheriff to file and sign the charges on Samuel Colander my mystery caller. He had all the paper work ready and I signed it. He asked me what was going on in Talladega County with the murderer. I told him that we had a possible chance to get some DNA on them this time. I told him about her fighting back and hitting him with the fire poker on the face and bringing blood.

He told me that would be good. He said that he sure hoped they stayed out of Coosa County because he had enough on his hands and surely did not need that. He told me that he would let me know when the hearing would be for Mr. Colander.

I left and headed back to Sylacauga. I got back to Sylacauga about 3:30 PM and went over to the office. Calvin told me that a Jake Simmons had called and ask me to call him back when I got back in Sylacauga.

I had been thinking about what I might do. I had decided that I would go in business with him if he would move to Sylacauga because I did not want to move anywhere else. Everything was going well for me the way it was.

I called him and that was what he wanted to ask me about. I told him my thoughts and he told me that he liked Sylacauga and that would be a good central location for the area. He told me that he would come to Sylacauga soon and we could spend the day and work out all the details. I told him that would be fine, and I looked forward to it.

We talked for a few minutes and I told him I needed to go and that we could talk again soon. It was about 5:00 PM. It was time to go home. I asked Calvin was he going to eat with me or was he going home. He told me that he was going home and eat because he had bought some steak and his mom was making him one tonight and he was looking forward to it.

We went out the door and I locked the office and we left. I went over the Charlie's and went in and sat down and the waitress came and took my order. I got me a T-bone steak, well done, a baked potato and a chef salad. I was hungry tonight for some reason.

In a few minutes the waitress brought me my food and I ate it. When I finished eating I left and went home.

I made me a pot of coffee and poured me a cup when it was finished and went in the living room and sat down in my recliner.

Just as I got relaxed the phone rang.

"Hello. Jason Caffrey speaking."

"Hello Jason."

"Hello Ria. What are you doing?"

"Nothing much. Just wanted to call and see how you were."

"I am fine so far. Did you have a good day?"

"Yes, I had a very good day just a busy one is all."

"Jake called me today and he wants us to go in business together. I am thinking about takin him up on it."

"That is good Jason. I am glad to hear that."

Murder of Grace

"We both have our friends that we rely on when we need help on things and that will be beneficial to both of."

We talked for a few minutes about our lives in general and finally she told me she needed to go and take care of some things before she went to bed tonight. I told her I would talk to her later.

I was sitting watching a John Wayne movie when the doorbell rang. I went to the door and looked out the peep hole and it was mom and dad. What in the world were they doing here? I opened the door and told them to come on in and gave mom a big hug and kiss and asked her what they were up to. I hugged dad and told him it was nice to see him.

We sat down in the living room and dad ask me what I was going to do this week end. I told him I hoped that I was not going to do anything. He told me that they were having a family get together and that I needed to be there. He said they had some things they needed to discuss with the family.

I told him that I would there.

I went in the kitchen and got us all something to drink.

We sat in the living room and talked for a while and mom and dad told me they had to go but that they would see me Saturday. I told him I would be there.

They left, and I went and got me another cup of coffee and came back and sat down in my recliner and was wondering if the fire poker had made a difference or not. I had not had a chance to talk with Manuel today and make sure that they found it. I was sure they did though.

It was getting late and I was getting sleepy. I got up and went to my bedroom and pulled my clothes off and lay down on the bed. I was slowly going to sleep. I needed to. I was tired.

CHAPTER THIRTY-TWO

I turned over on my side. I closed my eyes and was almost asleep when I saw the city limit sign for Atlanta, Georgia. What am I doing in Atlanta? The car I was in was driving towards a beautiful sub division in South Atlanta. I could not see the driver of the car. All I could see was an image at the time.

The car pulled into a beautiful big house with a front porch all the way across the front with a swing on the right end of the porch. It had a big humungous entrance door. It was bronze with stained glass. The home was a red brick home with white trim. It had a double garage. The car pulled up and stopped without going into the garage.

All I could see was an image of a woman getting out of the car and she went on the front porch and unlocked the door and went in the house.

The living room was large. It had a three-piece leather, dark brown, living room suit with three beautiful wood tables.

When I looked around at her again she was there. She was a tall slender woman. She had long, curly blonde hair. She had long arms and long slender fingers. She had long slender legs. She was beautiful. The same as all the other six women who been murdered that I saw in my dreams. But I am in Atlanta this time. Why am I in Atlanta? Is it going to happen in Atlanta?

She went over to the couch and sat down and picked up a magazine and about the time she picked up the magazine she heard an awful noise in the

Murder of Grace

bedroom. She jumped as though it had scared her. She jumped up off the couch and there was a man standing in the doorway of the bedroom with a sickle in his hand looking directly at her.

As in the other six dreams of the murdered women I could only see an image. It was a man. He was tall and very muscular just like the rest of them had been. He had dark black hair.

He told her he had come to see her because he had been watching her for a long time. She asked him what he wanted. He told her that she was a ballet dancer and very professional with it. He said that he wanted to see her dance again.

She told him that he could come to her next concert and watch her dance. She told him where it would be. He told her that he did not want to go there that he wanted to see her dance tonight. She told him that she preferred not to dance tonight.

He told her that if she did not dance for him tonight that she would have to pay the price for not doing what he had asked her to do. She asked him what that would be, and he told her that he would have to hurt her really bad.

He took a step out of the bedroom into the living room and showed her the sickle and told her that he knew how to use it and that he would. He told her that he did not want to hurt her but that he would if she did not dance for him.

She told him that she did not have music at home for that.

He told her that she had to practice somewhere.

She told him she did that at her classes that she took.

He told her that was ok because she could do it for him now.

She told him that she needed some time and it was hard to do it without music.

He stepped into the living room a little closer to her. She backed up towards the kitchen. He told her not to move. By now she was scared. There was a table sitting at the end of the couch with a drawer in it. She kept a .22 magnum handgun in that drawer. She was hoping she could get to it.

He moved a little closer to her and she stepped back a step. She was beginning to shiver just a little, but she did not want him to see that. She tried to contain it so that he would not notice.

He moved in a little closer to her. She did not want him with that sickle close to her. He told her that if she did not dance for him now that he was fixing to make her pay for it.

She was so nervous by now that she knew she could not dance for anybody. She knew that what he meant by hurt you or make you pay for it was that he was going to kill her. She did not know how that she was going to get away from him if she could not get to her handgun. She did not see any way to do. She was scared, very scared by now.

He was getting mad at her. She was shaking. It was very noticeable now that she was scared. He told her that she better do something and do it now. When he told her that she fainted?

He grabbed up and put the sickle to her throat and sliced it from ear to ear. And after he killed her he dragged her to the bedroom and laid her on the bed and he cut her to pieces just like he had the last six and spread the body parts in plastic bags just like the last ones and cut the head off and placed it up at the top of the body facing her feet.

It was always looking down. Why did he always have them looking at their feet? Made no sense.

I woke up abruptly. I was shaking all over. I was really upset. I was having a hard time even sitting on the side of my bed. My stomach was churning something awful. It was like a washing machine churning the clothes around and around. I started gagging. This one really made me sick. I was having an awful time.

I tried to get off the bed to go to the bathroom and it was all I could do to stand up without doubling over I was so sick. I was hurting in my chest. I felt like a tractor trailer had run over me. I felt like I was going to collapse before I could get to the bathroom.

I made it in the bathroom finally. I stripped off my clothes, what I had on, and climbed into the shower and finally got the water turned on. I stood under the cold water hoping that would help me be able to compose myself. It started getting easier to stand up straight.

I was finally able to get my shower and when I finished I dried off and stood in front of the mirror and wondered how I had survived that ordeal. I needed somebody to talk to. The only person I knew that I could call at this time of night that would not get mad at me was Rita.

I went and made me some coffee and poured me a cup and went in the living room and sat down. I had to hear a human voice now. I did not want to do it but I called her anyway.

"Hello Jason. I know you had another one of those dreams."

"Yes, Rita, I did. And it was awful. The worst one so far."

"Are you alright Jason?"

"Yes, I am fine now, but I was sick as a dog earlier."

"I woke up right before you called me, and I knew when I woke up that you had had another dream."

"I just wish they would go away."

"What did you see this time Jason."

"It is going to happen in Atlanta this time Rita or at least that is what I saw. So far I have not been wrong."

"If it happens and it all comes out like the six that you have told me about in Sylacauga and Talladega there is no doubt that it will definitely be a serial killer and being that it would have crossed the state lines the FBI will have to get involved."

"Maybe that would be a good thing Ria. So far, we have not gotten anywhere. At least the FBI has data bases that we do not have and maybe they could tie in some things that we have not gotten a hold of yet."

"Yes, maybe my boss will send me that way and see what we can come up with to help you guys out."

"Well, I can tell you this much for sure Rita, Dexter does not want the FBI here. I know that for sure. But of course, despite that he will still be polite unless of course they piss him off."

"Most local police do not want the FBI in their faces Jason. And I understand that. We just have to do our jobs when we have to get involved."

"I can tell you this much Rita, and you know I have not been wrong on six accounts, it is going to happen, and it is going to happen in Atlanta."

"I am sure you know what you are talking about Jason."

"I am hoping when I talk with Manuel tomorrow that he will tell me that they got the blood samples and that they tested it and found a name to go with it. That would be great."

"Maybe that will be the case Jason."

"The only thing is, Rita that is not going to stop the next murder because it is fixing to happen real soon. Probably in the next day or two at the most. Probably no later than by Wednesday night."

"Maybe Manuel will have a lead on the killer, a name that we can all start looking at when it does happen and that will help us to track him down quicker."

"The sooner the better. I do not need to have any more of these dreams. So far he has murdered six and fixing to murder the seventh person. He is working in a cycle by doing a blonde headed, then a red headed and then a black headed.

We talked for a few more minutes and I told her I would be fine. She told me she would check on me tomorrow. I told her that if I was not in the office Calvin would be. We said our good byes and hung up the phone.

I leaned back in my recliner and closed my eyes and hoped that I could go to sleep and sleep till the clock went off. I knew I could not go back to the bedroom and get any sleep.

All of a sudden, I heard this strange noise and realized that it was my clock. I got up went to the bedroom and turned it off. I put on my jogging shorts and went in the kitchen and put on a pot of coffee and headed out the door to make my five-mile run.

I got back to the house and took me a shower and shaved and got ready to go to work. I got me a cup of coffee and went in the living room and turned the TV on and all they were talking about was the Ballet Casanova. I changed the channel to cartoons and the doorbell rang.

It was 7:00. I went to the door to let Alice in.

"Good morning Jason."

"Good morning Alice and what are you doing this morning?"

"I came to work for you Jason. What are you doing?"

"I am ready to go to work Alice. I think I have a busy day today."

"Jeremy really does like Jarrod that boy that he met at the gym."

"That is good Alice."

"He told me that they have been riding around together lately and that Jarrod is really smart."

"He is smart Alice. He has always been on the bright side all his life."

"Maybe he will be the best thing that has happened for Jeremy."

"I am glad they are getting along good Alice. Maybe it will be good for both."

"Well I guess I better go to work Jason. I have a busy day I know. I always do when I work for you."

"If you ever need to bring any help with you Alice do not hesitate to do so. Just let me know when you do."

"OK Jason. I will.

I left the house and went to the Grill and Eggs Breakfast Bar. I got there and sat down, and Calvin came in and came over and sat down with me. The waitress came and took our order. Dexter came in the door and came over and sat down with us.

"Hello Calvin. I have heard about you working for Jason. How do you like it so far?" Dexter said.

"Wow. It is nice. I like my job."

"That is good Calvin. What do you do?"

"I answer the phone and run errands for Mr. Caffrey." Calvin said.

"Just call me Jason, Calvin."

"OK. Jason bought me a computer and I am getting my feel of the computer back. I can operate it fine, but it had been a long time since I had got to use one."

"I have already determined that he is a whiz on the computer Dexter." Jason said.

"Maybe he can help us find this killer. Maybe he can learn how to run the data bases and find information for you Jason that will help out in all your cases."

"Yes, that will be nice for sure. I have my nose stuck in a lot of things most of the time."

I asked Dexter had he heard anything about what was going on in Talladega. He told me he had not heard anything yet but he needed to talk with Manuel and see what was going on.

I told him that they should have the blood sample analysis by now and that if the persons DNA was already in the data base that we would be on his trail from there.

He agreed with me and I told him that would get us closer to catching the killer.

The waitress came and brought our food. We sat around and talked and ate. We finished our meals and it was time to go to the office. I told Dexter I needed to go to the office and get some paper work done this morning and that I would talk with him later.

I got our tickets and paid for them and told Calvin to meet me at the office. I did not get in the office good until the phone rang. It was the Sheriff from Coosa County. He told me that the hearing for my mystery caller was on Wednesday afternoon at 2:30. I told him I would be there. He told me if I wanted them to do anything with the man that I needed to be there otherwise they would have let him go.

When I hung up the phone it rang again. Calvin answered it and it was Jake. He handed me the phone.

"Hello Jason."

"Hi Jake."

"What are you doing tomorrow Jason?"

"I don't know yet."

"I will be coming through tomorrow. I can stop by and we can talk about our going in business together."

"OK. What time will you be coming through?"

"I will be in Sylacauga about 10:00 AM."

"OK. I will keep my schedule open for you for the morning then."

"See you in the morning then at 10:00 AM."

We hung up the phone.

William Honeycutt

Write it down on the calendar Calvin for me to meet Jake here in my office at 10:00 tomorrow. I told him anytime that I had appointments to write them on the calendar so that we could keep up with them. I told him to keep me reminded so that I did not forget someone when I had an appointment with them. He smiled and told me he already had been doing that and showed it to me. I had not really paid it much attention until then. I see so far, I have hired me a very smart young man.

The morning was slipping by fast and it was about lunch time. I told him that he could go and find him something to eat if he wanted to. He told me that he had brought him a brown bag lunch for today. He was he was going to try to save some money if he could.

He went over to the convenient store close to the office and got him a coke and brought me back a barq's root beer. I told him that I was not going to eat lunch today that I was just going to take it easy in the office and work on some cases that I had to get finalized.

He ate his lunch and found him a game on the computer to play while he was on lunch break. I just worked on paper work getting it all organized.

I ask Calvin did he want to ride on a surveillance job with me. I need to see what was going on with some kids who had been accused of stealing hubcaps. It was about the time of day that they were usually up to their shenanigans. He told me he would love that. We left and rode over to the east side of town near a park where the hubcaps had been going missing.

I told Calvin to keep his eyes open and watch very closely so that if they were there today that we could catch them. We were sitting and watching. In a little while a young boy with red hair came walking by the car and strolled over near the restrooms where he met a couple of more boys. They all looked about sixteen years old.

I asked Calvin did he know them. He told me that he did not. He said he had seen them around. I moved from where I was parked to a different location so that we could see them in the rear-view mirror. In a little while one of the boys walked over to a Lincoln Continental and popped the hub cap off the car and they took it to the bathroom and hid it by a dumpster. They did that till they had all four of the hubcaps off the car.

I waited till they got the last one. Calvin and I got out of the car and walked over towards them. They kind of walked to the other side of the restroom talking as if they were leaving. I spoke to them and ask them what they were doing today. They told me they were just fooling around.

I told them yes, they were just fooling around stealing hub caps off people's cars. They assured me they were not doing that. I told them we sat there and watched them steal them. And then I showed them where they had hidden them until they could get them in their vehicle and take them to sell them.

I pulled my credentials and showed them who I was. I told them they were under arrest and that the police would be here any minute.

They told me that we could not take them to jail that we did not have any proof. I told them that Calvin and I both watched them take the hubcaps off the Lincoln and they would go to jail at least until they could make bond.

The police got there and loaded them in the car and took them to jail with the evidence. I found the person that owned the Lincoln and told them they would get their hubcaps back today sometime.

We left the park and went back to the office. Calvin ask me was that all there was to being an investigator. I told him absolutely not that was just one of the simple things we did. He said that would not be hard to do. I told him we would talk about those kinds of things later on as we went along. I explained to him that there is training that he will have to have for the job.

The afternoon was gone. It was time to go home. We left the office. I went over to Charlie's and Calvin went home to eat with his family. He was proud that he had a job and could earn some money to help his family out. I was proud of him because he was turning out to be a great kid.

I finished my meal at Charlie's and left and went by Winn-Dixie to pick up a few grocery items before I went home. I got through shopping and headed towards the house. I pulled up in my garage and got out and got my groceries and went in the house. I made me a pot of coffee and poured me a cup and went and sat down in my recliner.

It was time to take a break from the day and just relax. I turned on the TV to the news to see what was going on. They were talking about the murders in Talladega and how that they had the DNA from the fire poker and how that it had matched some DNA in the data base. That was good to know I thought.

I called mom.

"Hello mom."

"Hello Jason. What are you doing?"

"Nothing right now. I just wanted to talk with you for a minute and see what you were up to."

"Not much Jason. Just resting some from the day. I have been working in the flowers today and I am a little tired from it but they are so beautiful."

"Well do not work too hard in them flowers. You do not need to."

"Don't worry about me Jason. I can still out do you anytime."

"You think. Huh."

"Yes. I know."

Murder of Grace

We talked for a few minutes and said our good byes and hung up the phone.

I found me a movie and watched it and it was time to call it a night. I went to my bedroom and pulled my clothes off and lay down on the bed. I was hoping I would get some sleep tonight. I was a little tired from the day.

CHAPTER THIRTY-THREE

I turned over on my side and closed my eyes. When I did I saw the woman with the long blonde hair. Oh my God. I just did not expect it tonight.

I wanted to open my eyes, but they were so heavy. I could not get them open. She was in my dream. The image of the man that I could not make out was there. The only thing I could see of him was that he was tall, muscular and had dark black hair.

He told her he wanted her to dance for him.

She told him that she did not want to dance for anybody.

If you do not dance I am going to have to make you paid for it.'

How do you plan on making me pay?

You see my sickle. I know how to use it. I will start by cutting your fingers off.

She told him that he would have to get to her to do that and that she would run.

He told her that she could not run very far because he would catch her.

She was scared, and she wanted to get away from him. She ran to the other side of the room and he followed her. She threw a vase at him and hit in on the head with it. He jerked. It hurt.

He told her to never do anything like that again or that he would just kill her.

She knew that he was going to kill her anyway. She threw another vase at him and hit him in the stomach with it and he yelled at her and told her to stop it or he would get this over with now.

He wanted her to dance and she would not.

He grabbed her and put her in a sleeper hold and she passed out. He sliced her throat from ear to ear with the sickle and then he mutilated the body and placed the body parts in the same position as he had the other six.

I woke up and was very upset. I was trembling all over. I could not hardly sit on the side of the bed. It was hard. I tried to get up and I had to sit back down. My stomach was hurting. I could not hardly breathe. I just wanted to roll over and forget that I was alive for right now. I finally was able to make it off the bed and made it to the bathroom.

I splashed water on my face to see if it would help me to calm down. It did not help much. I was very upset. I need to talk to somebody and I needed to talk with them right now.

I went to the living room and sat down in my recliner and I called Rita. I had to hear a human voice now.

"Hello Jason. You had that dream again tonight didn't you?"

"Yes, I did. It was awful Rita. I am going to have to do something. The murder is fixing to take place soon. Somebody has to know about it. I just do not know right now what to do."

"I understand how you must feel Jason. Sometimes I see the future of things and I know that they are going to happen, and I have no control over them. I am scared to say anything to anyone because people laugh at people who do these things and I sometimes am not sure about it myself."

"I know what you mean Rita. I am glad that you can share it with me. It helps to have someone that understands you. A lot of my friends know about my dreams and because of these murders a few more people know about them. They do not necessarily believe in them, but they are at least listening to me." I told her.

"What we need, Jason, is a small group of people that have the abilities like we have and that would make it a little easier even if they were in different parts of the country."

"That would be nice and then we would have someone that would believe in us and someone to help in cases like these when they were happening. Maybe we could find someone that could pick up on the things that I can't see in my dreams and give us more information to go on." I told her.

"You know Jason, one day maybe we can have our own investigative team that will focus on the paranormal abilities. That is a dream at least."

"So, you would be willing to leave your safe house from Quantico and branch out into a business."

"One day I will leave Quantico and move on. I have no doubt about that Jason."

"Would you be willing to come to a small city like Sylacauga?" I asked her.

"It is not the size of the city or town Jason, it is if you like the city or not and so far, I like Sylacauga."

"Personally, I think it is a great little city and I love it a lot and I know I am not going to leave here. I am glad you like it here so far."

"That is good Jason. Maybe you will find someone one day soon that will marry you and you can have a great family and a great life."

"I am not in a hurry to get married. I want it to be the right person when I do get married. I hate divorces. I would not want to get married and have to be in a divorce before we were married very long."

"I hate divorces to Jason. I think it should be a lifelong decision when people make it."

"What are you going to do tomorrow Rita?"

"I am going to work on some new cases that I have to get started."

"I am going to meet with Jake tomorrow here at my office and we are going to talk about our going into business together."

"That is good Jason. I hope it all works out for you guys."

"It will and is fixing to be in the process. I am going to start looking for us a building to rent for our office because the one I am in here is too small. I am not going to let Calvin go. I am going to keep him. He is a very smart young man and a good worker."

"You guys will need somebody to help you when you get combined that way." She told me.

"Yes, we will and I think Calvin will be the right one. He is computer literate and is very smart. He catches on fast to things when I ask him to do them. He is not a lager. I do not regret hiring him. I was hoping that I was not making a mistake and I have learned that it was the smartest move I have made lately." I told her.

"Sounds like you have it all thought out fairly well Jason and that you are ready to get it started."

"I do have it thought out well. I already have us a name picked out if Jake likes it." I told her.

"That sounds interesting. What is it Jason?"

"Master's Investigators. I will explain to you later why I am suggesting that title for our name of the company."

"I like that Jason. That is a nice name."

"Thank you very much Rita. After we talk about things and get it worked out, I will let you know what happens."

We talked for a little bit longer. Then we said our good byes and hung up the phone.

It was about 4:30. I closed my eyes to see if I could get a little sleep.

CHAPTER THIRTY-FOUR

I heard my alarm clock go off. I went and turned it off and slipped on my jogging shorts and went out the door. Jane was waiting on me as usual. We ran our five miles and enjoyed it. I got back in the house and put me on a pot of coffee.

I went upstairs and took me a shower and shaved and got ready to go to work. I went downstairs and poured me a cup of coffee and sat down at the breakfast nook table and drank it.

I grabbed my things for work and headed out the door for The Grill and Egg Breakfast Bar. I was getting out of my car when Jeff pulled up right beside me and stuck his head out the window and ask me what in the world I was doing this morning.

"I came to get me some breakfast. What are you up to Jeff?"

"I am here for the same reason."

We went in and sat at our usual table and the waitress took our order.

"What have you been doing Jason?"

"Dreaming."

"You still having those dreams Jason."

"I had a dream concerning the 7th victim. She is blonde headed. It is a cycle Jeff. He killed a blonde headed and then a red headed and then a black headed in Sylacauga and Talladega. He is going to start over in Atlanta just like he has already done."

The waitress brought our food to the table and asked us did we need anything else. I asked her to just keep a watch on our coffee for us.

"Maybe we can catch him before he makes it to Atlanta Jason."

"We probably will not catch him Jeff. I have already had the dream and you know my dreams always come true."

"It is possible Jason that maybe we will be fortunate to catch him."

"I hope so. He needs to be stopped. Of course, you know that if he crosses the state lines that the FBI will get involved Jeff."

"I know and that might be a good thing. We seem to be having a lot of trouble finding enough information to get to him. Their data bases are much larger than ours and they can get to more information than we can."

"Well, we will see but maybe we can stop him before he gets to Atlanta. I sure hope so, but I am not expecting that to happen because of my dreams." I told Jeff.

We finished eating our breakfast and I told him that I needed to get to the office and work on a few cases that I had to finalize the details on. He told me that he needed to get to the office."

We left the restaurant and I went to my office and when I got there Calvin was already there. He had made a fresh pot of coffee.

"Would you like some coffee Jason?"

"I sure would Calvin. Thank you very much."

He poured me a cup and brought it to me and sat it on my desk.

"What are we going to do today Jason?"

"You are going to answer the phone and take some paper work over to Catherine for me today. I have to meet with Jake at 10:00 this morning to discuss some business."

"What kind of business are you going to discuss Jason?"

"I will let you know later just not right now."

"OK that will be alright I suppose." He said.

"I suppose it may as well be because that is how it is going to be."

"When do you want me to take the paper work over to Miss Catherine?"

"I will have it ready in a few minutes. I want you to get on your computer and look up ballet dancers and ballet companies and see if you can find a Linda Moore that was a ballet dancer. Can you do that?"

"Yes, Jason I can do that. What do you want me to do with the information when I find it?"

"Take notes of what you find and when you finish I will look at it and we will decide what to do with it after you get it."

"OK. You want me to do that now?"

"You do that while I am working on the paper work for Catherine."

I started working on my paper work for Catherine and he got on the computer. He loved it when he could work on the computer.

It was about 9:30 and I had the paper work ready to send to Catherine. I gave it to him and told him to take it to her and tell her that I would talk to her sometime today when I had time to call her or either come by.

He told me he had some things concerning Linda Moore. I told him just to hold it until after I had the meeting with Jake and then we could discuss that.

It was about 9:50 when Jake walked in the door.

"Hello Jason. How are you?"

"I am fine Jake and, how are you?"

"I am a little tired from the trip this morning, but I am fine otherwise. Are you ready to talk business?"

"Good and yes I am ready I have thought this thing over since we have talked about it and I have made my decision."

"That is good Jason. Now we can get started then if you have made the decision that I hoped you would make."

"And what do you think that decision is Jake?"

"That you are going to go in business with me."

"That is what I have decided, and I have even thought of us a good name for the business." I told him.

"I have not gone that far yet Jason but what have you come up with?"

"What do you think about Master's Investigations?"

"I like that Jason. That is a good name."

"How soon do you want to get things rolling in that direction Jake?"

"I have a few things that I have to get together before I can leave Wetumpka."

"Do you want me to go ahead and start looking for us a building here in Sylacauga?"

"Sure, if you want to do that."

"We definitely cannot stay in this building. It is too small. I intend to keep Calvin and I think I would like a much bigger space than what I have here. In fact, I would like to go ahead and find something big enough that we can expand it without having to move again."

"That is good thinking Jason. I like that idea. Maybe we will grow and need some people to help us out."

"I know we will. I know that Rita is going to eventually leave Quantico and move out on her own some way. I would like to ask her to join us when she decides that is what she wants to do."

"That will be nice. We could use some ladies around for sure."

"I will start working on finding us something that will meet our needs then."

"I believe we have this all worked out Jason."

Calvin walked in the door just as we had finished discussing those things. He told me that Catherine ask him if he could take some paper work to the courthouse for here in Talladega. I told him to call her back and tell her that he could.

"What are you going to do for the rest of the day Jake?"

"I do not know yet Jason. I must be in Tuscaloosa in the morning at 9:00 AM. I may just stay here in Sylacauga and rent me a motel room."

"If you stay in Sylacauga, you can stay at my house if you want to."

"OK. I will do that then and we can spend the rest of the day and talk over other things about the business."

Calvin had called Catherine and told her I said it was OK for him to go and take the paper work for her. I asked him when he needed to go. He told me that she told him anytime today would be fine. I told him to call her back and tell her that after his lunch break that he could take it for her.

He called her, and she told him to come over and pick it up and she would give him instructions on what to do once he got to the courthouse. She said she was taking the afternoon off.

"Would you like to go get something to eat Jake?"

"Yes, I could use some lunch about now Jason?"

"Go and pick up the paperwork and meet us over at Charlie's Calvin and eat your lunch and then you can take that paper work to Talladega for Catherine."

"OK. I will be there in a few minutes."

Jake and I left and went over to Charlie's to eat. We went in and sat down, and the waitress came and took our order.

"What is going on with the murders Jason? Do you guys know anything yet?"

"I had another dream and the next one will be in Atlanta. That is all we know right now."

"That is not good Jason. Three in Sylacauga, and three in Talladega, and how many is it going to be in Atlanta?"

"Let's hope that we catch him and there will not be any in Atlanta."

"That would be nice Jake, but it is not going to happen that way. I have no doubt about it. It is because of the dreams. If I had more to go on in the dreams that just the area and the description of the woman then maybe we could catch him before he does anything. Unfortunately, I do not have more to go on."

"Well maybe if you have any more dreams you will see the house in the dream."

Calvin made it to Charlie's and came and sat down with us. The waitress came over and took his order.

"I did this last one but there will be a million houses like it in Atlanta. I need more specific information and then it will be helpful. So far, the dreams have only given me one clue that might help. that was when the lady hit him with the fire poker and brought blood and dropped the fire poker behind the couch before she fell over the couch. He forgot about the fire poker and the police found it after I told them about it. That is the only clue I have had for tracing the killer so far."

The waitress brought our food to the table and asked us could she do anything else for us. We told her we were Ok for now and she left.

"Maybe it will be good in your next dream Jason. Maybe you will see the street and then see the house and then the police can be there before it happens."

"That would be nice Jake if it happens that way."

"You never know that is for sure Jason."

"No, the dreams are always a little different. If I have another dream I can tell you now she will be red headed with long hair. That will be the same. He has not changed his MO. It has remained the same."

We sit around and finished our meal. Calvin told me that if I did not mind that he was leaving for Talladega and take Catherine's paper work for her. He told me that he did not want her to be disappointed with him.

Jake and I left and went back to the office. I told him we could just sit around the office for a while and wait for Calvin to get back and then we could go to the house and spend the rest of the day there.

While we were waiting for Calvin to get back I called to see if I could talk with Katland at the mill. She was not there. They told me she had taken off for the afternoon. I thanked them and told them I would call her tomorrow.

In a few minutes, Calvin came walking back into the office. I asked him did he have any trouble getting the paper work delivered. He told me that it was a piece of cake. He said there was nothing to it. That was good. That means he knows how to get around in the courthouse. The more I learn about him the more impressed I am with him.

He told me that he had the information concerning Linda Moore. I told him that we could discuss that in the morning. I asked him would he like to go home early today. He told me he would like that because he had some things his mom wanted him to do and he had not had time to do them for her.

I closed up the office and Jake and I went to my house and Calvin went home.

We got to my house and walked around to the back yard and sat down in the big chairs. I asked him did he want something to drink. I went in the house and got us something and came back out and sat down.

"I will start looking around for a building for us to use just as soon as I have some time. I know where a couple are and I will go and look at them and see if they will be of any use for us." I told him.

"That is good Jason."

"Do you want to come and look at them before I lease them?"

"No. That is not necessary. I am sure you will do a good job in finding something suitable."

"Ok. If I find something I will go ahead and lease it or would you like to buy it instead?"

"If we could buy it that would be good and then if something happens we can sell it."

"Well nothing is going to happen Jake. We will have it for as long as we want to do business."

"That will be a long time Jason. We are going to set this up to be around for a long time."

"Well, I will look for something that we can buy then."

"That will be good."

"How are we going to set this thing up Jake? We will be business partners. You can be the President and I will be the Vice President. You like that?"

"I will be happy either way Jason. I trust you or I would not have ask you to go in business with me."

"I trust you to Jake or I would not have agreed to it."

"So that is what we can do then. I will be the President and you the Vice President Jason."

"That will work for me Jake."

We sit around in the back yard for a few minutes and talked. We decided that it was time to go in the house. I told him that we could eat something at the house tonight. He told me that he did not know much about cooking. I told him I could cook some and I would fix us a meal.

We were sitting in the living room and the phone rang.

"Hello Jason."

"Hello mom. What are you doing?"

"Just wanted to call you and say hello and see what you were up to."

"I am just sitting here at the house right now talking with Jake. We are going in business together."

"That is good. You will have some help that way. Maybe you will have a little more time than you do now."

"We will probably get busier and I will have less time than I have now."

"I guess you could hire someone then to help out so that you could take some time off and we could see more of you."

"Well mom, maybe somewhere in the future that will be possible."

"What are you going to do the rest of the afternoon Jason?"

"I think Jake and I are going to sit around here and talk and work things out for our new business. It will be the same as we are already doing just that we are going in business together."

"I just wanted to call and say hello mostly. I will let you go for now. Take it easy the rest of the day."

"OK mom. I will talk with you later. You have a great rest of the day."

"Bye Jason."

"Bye Mom."

It was getting about time to cook something. I asked Jake what he liked. He told me anything would be ok with him. I decided that I would cook some cubed steak in gravy with some cream potatoes and some colored butter beans. That sounded good to me.

While I was fixing our dinner, Jake came in the kitchen and sat at the bar, so we could talk some. I got the steak cooked and ready to go in the gravy and sliced the onion. My potatoes were ready to be put in the mixer for the cream potatoes. I went ahead and got everything to make my gravy with and got it ready and put the meat and onions in the gravy to smother them for a few minutes.

After I got the meat cooking in the gravy, I put my potatoes in the mixer and made the cream potatoes. The only thing that I needed to do now was get the colored butter beans ready. So, I opened them and put them on the stove and got them ready. By the time everything else was ready the steak had smothered long enough.

I sat the table in the breakfast nook and put our food on the table and we sat down to eat.

"My God Jason where did you learn to cook like this?"

"From my mom. She is a great cook."

"I can cook if I need to. I just do not do much of it."

"That is good that you can Jason."

"I should do more of it and save some money, but I just don't seem to have the time for cooking or maybe I just do not want to take the time."

We finished our dinner and we cleaned up the kitchen and went into the living room and turned the TV on to see what was on the news tonight.

They were still talking about the murder. They were calling it the Ballet Casanova. What a title. The media always seems to come up with a good one.

We were watching the news and the doorbell rang. I went to the door and opened the door and it was Jeff. I invited him in. He came in and sat down in the wing back chair close to my recliner.

"What are you guys doing Jason?"

"We are talking about our new business that we are going to open."

"You are going to open another business Jason?"

"Jake and I are going in business together here in Sylacauga."

"You will have some help Jason. That is good."

"I hope I am busier than I am now not that I really need to be but it still would be nice."

"Where are you from Jake?"

"I am from Wetumpka."

"Are you moving here or are you going to work out of Wetumpka?"

"I am moving here. It is a good central location for all the larger cities for us that we work in mostly."

"We will be glad to have you here Jake." Jeff said.

"Yes. I am looking forward to it. Jake and I have been friends for a while now and it will be nice to have him around to help me when I need someone." I said.

"Well it may be a while yet before we can get it going but I need a little time anyway." Jake said.

"I am going to see what I can find in a building that will be suitable for us just as soon as I have some time. We are going to be looking for something we can buy. So, if you hear of anything Jeff, please let me know."

"There are several empty ones around Jason. I do not know if they are for sell or for lease."

"I know where a couple are that I am going to check out. We needed it to be kind of large. We want to grow some."

"That should not be hard to find Jason." Jeff said.

"How big you plan on us growing Jason?" Jake asked.

"I don't know. I guess time will tell that part."

"I am sure it will Jason."

"What are you doing tomorrow Jason?" Jeff asked.

"I have to be in Rockford at 2:30 tomorrow afternoon. They are having the hearing for my mystery caller. I have to be there as a witness for the hearing."

"Well maybe that will be the end of your mystery caller. Of course, it is not a mystery anymore."

"No, it is not, and I am very glad to have that over with. The only thing that I would like to know is why was he doing it in the first place? Is he tied into these murders some way? And if he is why was he only bothering me with just telephone calls and passing by my house and two gunshots into my house one time? There are a lot of unanswered questions to this scenario."

"Maybe you will find out tomorrow Jason." Jeff said.

"I sure hope so because I would like to know."

"I just wanted to stop by and see what you are doing. I will go for now. Will talk with you sometime tomorrow."

"Take it easy Jeff. See you tomorrow."

Jake and I sat around and talked for a while. He went out to the car and got his things and brought them in the house. He told me that if I did not mind that he would like to take a shower tonight. He left and went upstairs and took himself a shower. When he finished he came back down stairs and ask me where he was sleeping. I told him the same bedroom that he always sleeps in.

It was getting late. I got up made sure all the doors were locked and turned off the lights and told Jake I would see him in the morning and went to my bedroom and pulled off my clothes and lay down on the bed. I was hoping for a good night's sleep. I turned over on my side and closed my eyes and very soon I was dead asleep.

CHAPTER THIRTY-FIVE

I was dead to the world when I began to see the woman with the long blonde hair. All I wanted to do was sleep. Why was I having this dream tonight? This was the third dream on her. It seemed like my whole world was collapsing from under me. I tried to open my eyes and they just would not open. I could see her so plain.

She saw the killer and he ask her to dance for him again. He knew that she was a ballet dancer. He had seen her dance before. He knew what she could do. He told her he wanted her to do it one more time for him.

He told her that if she did not dance for him that she was going to pay a price. She asked him what the price was that she had to pay if she did not dance. He told her that it would be very bad. He was holding the sickle in his hands and licking his lips and he help it up and told her that he would use it on her.

She told him that she did not want to dance that she was not in the mood. She moved back away from him and he moved in towards her.

She was beginning to get worried by then. She was shaking just a little bit by now. He told her that the best thing she could do was dance for him or she would have to pay the price. She told him that she needed music and that she did not have any. He told her she could do it without music.

She walked over to the table near the couch hoping that she would get to her gun. He told her not to move towards that table again. She asked him why. He told her she looked like she was trying to get to something and that could be the worst mistake she made all night.

She stood still and asked him what he was going to do if she moved towards the table again. He told her that she would pay a price if she did. He hesitated but she still stepped closer again. She was very close to the table now. He was getting pissed at her. She did not know what to do right now so she just stood there.

H looked down towards the floor and when he did she grabbed the drawer and tried to get the handgun from the drawer and he grabbed her and jerked her. She fell on the floor. He grabbed her up and put the sickle to her throat and sliced it from ear to ear. She was dead immediately.

I woke up. I was trembling and shaking all over. I was so upset. These dreams were draining me it seemed like. I wish they would stop. I did not need any more of them. I tried to set up on the side of the bed and just could not move. In a little bit I was able to get my feet and legs off the bed and was able to brace myself on my elbow and raise up a little bit.

When I raised up some I felt my stomach sink to my toes it felt like. I was sick. I could not straighten up right then. I had to lay back down for minute. I was finally able to sit up on the side of the bed. I tried to stand up and when I did I bent double from the pain in my stomach.

I finally was able to stand up. I got to the bathroom and when Jake heard the water running he came out of his bedroom and came over to the bathroom and ask me if I were OK. I told him that I was not.

He asks me had I had another one of those dreams. I told him that I had and that it had made me deathly sick. I was able to wash my face in cold water. That made me feel a little better. I was still trembling some. I still had not gotten myself back together yet.

I told him that I was going to the kitchen and make a pot of coffee if I could get there. He went with me and made the coffee. When it was finished making he poured us a cup and we took it to the living room. I had to hold mine with both hands to keep from spilling it all over the floor.

It was only about 2:00 AM. I told him that maybe when I drank that cup of coffee I would be OK, and we could try to go back to sleep. He told me that we could just try to sleep in the living room. He told me he could rest on the couch. I told him that would be just fine.

We finished our coffee and I leaned back in my recliner and closed my eyes. In a few minutes I was asleep. I heard a strange noise in the house and then I realized that it was my alarm clock. I went and turned it off. I decided that I would not run this morning. I went and took a shower. I called Jake and ask him was he ready to get up. He got and went to the bathroom and washed his face and came out and went and put him on some travel clothes.

I ask him did he want to eat some breakfast before he left for Tuscaloosa. We left the house and went to The Grill and Eggs Breakfast Bar We got to the restaurant and went in and sat at my usual table. It seemed to just about always be empty. I guess everybody was leaving it for me. They must have known I liked sitting at that table.

The waitress came to the table and took our order.

"Jake, when I find the right building I will go ahead and get the process started and when I get to where paper work has to be singed I will let you know so you can come and sign it."

"OK. Do you think that you will find anything soon?"

"I do not have a doubt about it. I know about two places that I am going to check out just as soon as I have time to get a hold of the owner and have them to meet me."

"I need to see the inside because I do not know how they are laid out but we can remodel if we have to or at least get someone to remodel for us."

"Maybe Calvin knows how to do that." Jake said and laughed.

"Yea really, that would be nice, but I doubt very seriously that he would know how to do that. He is a very young man right now." I told him.

The waitress brought our food to the table. We ate our breakfast and he told me that he needed to get on the road because he had just enough time to get to his appointment on time.

I took the tickets and paid for them and Jake left and went towards Tuscaloosa and I headed for the office. Just as I pulled up in my parking space Calvin drove in.

"Good morning Calvin."

"Good morning Jason. It still doesn't seem right to just call you Jason."

"That is OK Calvin, I want you to do that. I am not that much older than you are. "

I unlocked the office door and we went in and Calving turned the lights on and sat down at his desk and turned his computer on. He reminded me that he had found some information on the woman that he looked up yesterday.

"We will look at that in a few minutes. I need you to take some paper work over to the SPD."

"When do you want me to go?"

"I will have it ready in about ten minutes."

He asked me did I want to him make us a pot of coffee. I told him that would be nice. He made the coffee. Just as he came back and sat down at his desk the phone rang.

"Hello Caffrey Investigations. May I help you?"

"Hello. Is Jason in the office?"

"Yes mam he is."

"May I talk with him?"

"Hold on just a minute."

He told me the phone was for me and that he thought it sounded like Miss Janie. I took the phone.

"Hello."

"Hi Jason. How are you this morning?"

"I am fine Janie and how are you."

"I am doing very fine Jason. I just wanted to let you know that I have tracked Mr. Bradford and he left for Atlanta last night. He bought a round trip ticket and he will be coming back to Charleston Friday evening sometime."

"Wow. Thank you, Janie. That means that the murder is going to happen tonight in Atlanta. That is no good. That is of course if he is involved in the murders in any way. I still think he is involved but I am not sure how yet."

"I thought I needed to call you and let you know what was going on with Mr. Bradford. It sounds a little suspicious from the way he travels around. Of course, they could just be business trips and he just happen to be in the locations at the time. That is always possible."

"Yes, that is possible, but I do not think that it is business trips unless it is business trips pertaining to these murders some way."

"You may be right Jason. I guess I need to go I have some paper work I need to do this morning. I just wanted to call you first.

"Thanks Janie for letting me know."

"You are very welcome. Talk to you later."

"Thanks. For sure we will talk again soon I owe you a big favor.

"Bye Jason."

"Bye Janie."

I sat back in my chair. It looked like things were starting to come together on who might be killing the young ballet dancers.

"Take these papers over to the SPD and make sure they understand they are to go to Dexter. He needs them as soon as he can get them. If you can hand them to him in person that will be even better."

"I think they will let me give them to him and I will if he is there."

Calvin took the paperwork over to the police station like I asked.

"Hello mam."

She looked up at Calvin and smiled.

"Hello sir. May I help you?"

"I have these papers from Caffrey Investigations that needs to be given to the Chief of police. Is he in?"

"Yes he is in but he is on the phone right now."

'May I wait on him and give them to him?"

"Yes you may. Just sit over there in that chair if you like. He will be free in a little bit."

"Thank you very much mam."

Calving went and sat down in the chair she had told him he could sit in.

"Sir." She called to Calvin

"Yes mam."

"The Chief is ready to see you."

Calvin took the paperwork and went to the Chief's office. He walked in and the Chief got up and shook his hand and ask him to sit down in the chair in front of the desk.

"Hello Calvin. I remember you. How are you doing?"

"I am doing fine sir. Jason ask me to bring these papers over to you and to hand them to you in person if there were any way that I could do that. I appreciate you letting me come in."

"Since your incident with Jason how are you doing?"

"I am doing really good sir. Jason offered me a job and I have been doing really well since. I really like him a lot. He is a really nice person."

"Yes, he is a very nice person. Sometimes I think he is too good but that is just the way Jason is. I am glad to see you doing so good after all the mess you were in. I am proud of you."

"Thank you, sir. I will do my best to never get into any more trouble. Never again."

"I am sure you can accomplish that. All it takes is just not doing it."

"I know sir."

"Is that all you needed?"

"Yes, Chief that is all I needed to do was bring this paperwork to you."

"Thank you very much Calvin. I appreciate that."

"You are welcome Chief. And thank you for being so nice to me."

Calvin got up and they shook hands and he left.

He got back to the office and told me about his conversation with the chief and how nice he had been to him. He told me that he thought he really liked him and that he seemed like a really nice person.

"Hello. Caffrey Investigations. May I help you?"

"Hello. Is Jason in the office?"

"Yes, he is. Did you want to speak with him?"

"If I may please."

"May I ask who is calling?"

"Tell him it is Bryan from Tuscaloosa."

William Honeycutt

Calvin told me that a Bryan from Tuscaloosa was on the phone. I took the phone.

"Hello Bryan. How are you?"

"I am fine Jason. What are you doing?"

"I am just working on my paperwork this morning."

"I wanted to call you and let you know that I have been keeping a close watch on James Gardner and he left last night and went to Atlanta, Georgia. He bought a round trip ticket and will be returning back to Tuscaloosa some time Friday."

"Oh wow. What is going on here? I never tied him to the murder of the women."

"I have been keeping close tabs on him. I have had a man watching him. I learned that he was in Talladega during the time of the murders there. I just wanted to call and let you know what was going on and what I know."

"I appreciate you calling me. Things are starting to unfold some I think."

"Ok. I will let you go for now. I will talk to you again as soon as I find out anything else."

"Ok. Thank you very much Bryan for calling me.

"Bye Jason."

"Bye Bryan talk to you again soon. I really owe you for this."

"I am just trying to help out some because these murders need to stop."

"And I really appreciate it a lot."

"See you buddy."

"See you."

The morning was slipping by fast. It was already 10:30. I ask Calvin if we had any more coffee. He told me he could make us a fresh pot. When it was finished he went and got us a cup and I told him that I just wanted him to sit back and think about these murders and the things that were going on concerning them and see what thoughts he could come up with to make any sense.

I wanted to see if he could think with an investigative mind and who knows he might come up with something that would be very beneficial to us towards the murders.

I laid it all out for him and told him to take notes because while I was gone this afternoon that was what I wanted him to do was to think about these murders and see what he could come up with.

He was kind of excited that I cared enough to let him in on the details. He was grinning from ear to ear. I knew that he was a smart young man and I wanted to see if there was anything that we could do to help get him on the road to being more than just a person that answers the phone and runs errands.

After I had gone over everything with him I told him that he needed not to say anything to anyone except me about these things. He told me that he could keep a secret. I told him it was really not a secret but that I was starting him in a little training towards becoming an investigator. He really liked that.

It was almost 12:00 noon. I told Calvin that we needed to go and eat us something. I asked him what he wanted. He told me that he would like to have some Mexican food.

We left the office and went over to the Mexican restaurant and found us a table. The waitress came and took our orders.

"Why do you think that I might can be an investigator?" Calvin asked.

"I don't know yet that you can, but I think you have the mind to do it if that is what you decide you want to do."

"Well it is getting interesting that is for sure. I never knew that investigative work could be so interesting."

"It can get very involved at times and sometimes you find things that are almost impossible to deal with, but it is worthwhile in the end."

"I am looking forward to learning all I can about it. I think I might would like it for sure."

"I really enjoy it myself. It just keeps me on my toes most of the time."

The waitress brought our food. We ate and chit chatted a little. We finished eating and left to go back to the office. I pulled up in the parking space and Jeff pulled up just as I got out of my car.

"Hello Jason."

"Hello Jeff. What are you doing?"

"I just came by to talk with you a few minutes."

"Let's go in the office where it is cool and talk."

"OK."

I opened the door and went in the office and sat down.

"What you got on your mind Jeff?"

"I was just wondering if you had anything different than what you had on the murders."

"I have had two of my investigator friends working on some things for me. They have found the two boyfriends of the first two girls in the area where the murders took place during the time of the murders. Ray Bradford the boyfriend of Delores was in this area during the time of the murders and he is in Atlanta now."

"Do you think he is the murderer?"

"I believe that he is the murderer or involved in them one way or the other. I am not sure yet which way I lean but I know he is involved."

"That is interesting."

"Yes, it is. I also learned that Mr. James Gardner in Tuscaloosa is also in Atlanta now. I never suspected him for the murderer, but this is not looking good for him."

"Why is that Jason? Have you had other ones of those dreams?"

"Yes, I have, and the next murder will happen in Atlanta tonight."

"How do you know that Jason?"

"Because of my dreams and the thing going on concerning the murders."

"OK. I understand."

"Watch the news in the morning. It will be all over TV. When it happens in Atlanta and the FBI knows of it they will be there before the water gets cold. The APD will be really pissed at them but they will be there. It is a serial murder."

"Yes, they will definitely be there."

"They will be all over this case in a minute. They will be here and in Talladega gathering all the information they can get from any of us concerning the case. They will want to know everything that we know."

"It is fixing to get nasty Jason for us when this happens."

"No. It will not be that bad Jeff. It just sounds like it will be. The murder is going to happen tonight. There is no doubt about it."

"We will know tomorrow morning for sure. I am going to make sure I watch the news"

"It will be there Jeff. That is the sad part. I even know it is going to happen and still nothing I can do about it. That is what upsets me so bad. I wish that I did not know anything."

"I understand what you mean Jason. The only thing that we have going for us now is that Manuel has the results from the blood sample. He just has not released the name of the person that he has because he is hoping that they can find him before he does anything else. The sad thing is he is not going to find him before it happens. I even have two names and have had the dream, but I do not have enough information to call the APD and tell them anything. They would have no idea where to start looking in Atlanta. I even have a description of the house, but I do not know the area. I did not get enough in the dream to give them the area."

"Well maybe it will not happen, and you will have another dream concerning the murder and you will have the location and it can be stopped."

"It is not going to happen that way for this one Jeff. It is going to happen tonight. There is going to be seven and nothing I can do about it. I only wish there was."

"We can only hope that it will." He told me.

"Maybe what would be good is that the Chief here and in Talladega and me called the APD and tell them that it is going to happen and how it will look once they get to it after they know about it."

"That might be a good idea Jason. I could also call and tell them that would give them four calls to the Chief in Atlanta informing him. He is probably going to think we are all crazy."

"Well at least when it was over he would know that we were not crazy and then he would want to know how we all knew that. Then it all will fall back on me because I am the one that has the dreams and knows that it is going to happen."

"That will make it hard on you Jason if we do that."

"It is ok because all I want is the mystery solved. Why don't you call Dexter and Manuel and ask them to do that? It is almost time for me to leave to go to Rockford. I have to go to court against Samuel Colander. You know, my mystery caller."

"Yea. I remember you talking about your mystery caller. OK I will call them and talk with them. I think I can persuade them to do that. I will call after a while myself.'

"OK. That will be good."

"OK Jason, I will go for now and I will talk with you later and let you know what happens."

"Thanks Jeff. I think this might benefit us for the next murder when I have the dream. Maybe they will listen to me when I call them and tell them it is going to happen."

"See you later Jason."

"See you Jeff."

Jeff left and I told Calvin that I had to go to Rockford. I told him to not say a word to anybody about what he had just heard Jeff and me talking about. I told him that was privileged information. He seemed to understand what I meant by that.

I left and went to Rockford. I got to the court house just in time for the case to start. When they called me to the stand and ask me why I had pressed charges against this man. I went through the whole process and explained to them how that I had hired my friend to come and check it out for me.

They called him to the stand and asked him why that he had been making these calls to me and harassing me. He told them that he knew who I was and that he did not like people like me messing around in people's lives. He thought their life was a private thing and that others did not need to mess around in other people's lives.

It ended up being about a twenty minute trial and they convicted him and he was charged with a misdemeanor and ninety days in jail. When it was over I headed back to Sylacauga.

I got back to the office about 4:30 PM. Calvin told me that he had thought about the murders and he was ready to go over it with me. I told him that we could discuss that tomorrow morning when we got to the office. It was already late. He told me that we still had not talked about Linda Moore yet either. I told him I knew that but today had been a very busy day and that we would talk about that the first thing in the morning.

We left the office and went over to Charlie's to get us something to eat. We got there Dexter walked in the door and came over and sat down with us. The waitress came and took our orders.

"Jason, Jeff talked with me about what you had told me concerning the murder in Atlanta tonight. I called the chief as you two had suggested might be a good idea."

"That is good Dexter. What did he say to you?"

"He told me that there would be nothing that he could do and even if there was that he could not do anything without more proof than just a dream."

"That is what they always say."

"He listened to what I told him. He told me that if it all happened the way that I told him that it would that he would call me back and let me know what had happed."

"I told him I was sorry to have to call him and tell me but that after the first one happened we were hoping that it would give them good reason to listen to us when we called them and told them about the next one and I explained to him why I had said that to him."

"Maybe it will all work Dexter. I hope it will. We need to catch this man someway. I wish Manuel would give us the name of the man that he has so that we could start checking him out but he just does not want it to get out that he has anything. He will not tell anybody the name."

"I understand that. People don't usually keep their mouths hushed and he is afraid that it will get to the press someway and he sure does not want the press to have it." Jeff said.

The waitress brought our food to the table. We sat around and talked for a bit and ate our food. Calvin was sitting there listening to everything Jeff and I were talking about. He seemed to have been really interested.

"Jason can I ask you a question?"

"Sure Calvin."

"What kind of dreams are you talking about?"

"I will talk with you tomorrow about that when we get to the office. We have a lot of things to talk about tomorrow."

"OK. Thank you."

It was getting late and it was time for me to go home and see if I could get some rest. I got home and made me a pot of coffee and got me a cup and went to the living room and sat down.

I turned on the TV and kicked my foot rest up and leaned back a little to drink my coffee.

CHAPTER THIRTY-SIX

By the time I got my chair leaned back the phone rang.

"Hello."

"Hello Jason. What are you doing?" Rita asked.

"I have just sat down in my recliner and leaned back a little to drink a cup of coffee. What are you doing?"

"You have had a very busy day Jason. Haven't you?"

"Yes, I have."

"Are you doing OK?"

"Right now, I am doing fine."

"I mostly called to see how you were doing. I am glad you are doing very well Jason. I miss you."

"I miss you to Rita."

We talked for a few minutes. I told her about the murder fixing to happen in Atlanta. I told her that we all had called the chief of police in Atlanta and told him that it was going to happen. I told her that I wanted some way for someone to believe me when I told them something about this murder.

She told me that she believed me. I told her I had no doubt about that. I told her that is was going to happen tonight and there was nothing that I could do about this one but maybe we could stop the next one before it happened. That would be nice.

She told me that she would let me go for now but that she would keep in touch with me. I told her that when they had to get involved that maybe they would send her to Sylacauga. I told her if they did and they wanted to rent her a room to tell them that she had a place to stay in Sylacauga. She knew that was my place. She told me that she would do that if they sent her.

We said our good byes and hung up the phone.

I sat back in my recliner and thought about that I needed to call mom and tell her I did not think that I was going to have time to make it to the meeting for this weekend.

"Hello mom."

"Hello Jason. What are you doing?"

"I just needed to call you and let you know that I am not going to be able to make it to the meeting this weekend. Is there any way you can postpone it for a couple of weeks?"

"If you are certain that you cannot come we can do that."

"Well I am certain."

I went on and explained to her why I was certain that I would not be able to make it. I knew that the FBI would be involved and that they would be here by the weekend and wanting to know everything they could find out as soon as they could get it out of us. She understood and told me that they would cancel it and let me know when the meeting would be.

"Well I just wanted to talk with you a little bit. I will go for now and talk with you soon."

"OK mom I will talk with you later."

We hung up the phone and the doorbell rang. I got up and went to the door and it was Jeff. I opened the door and invited him in. He told me came by to let me know that he had talked with Manuel and Manuel had told him that he would call and talk with them.

I thanked him for doing that and told him that I had already seen Dexter and that he told me that he called them. He told me he could not stay long that he needed to go home and get some things done before it got dark on him. He left, and I went to the kitchen and got me another cup of coffee and went in the living room and sat down in my recliner. I was tired. It had been a long day.

I was ready to rest if that was possible.

I leaned back some in my recliner and finished drinking my cup of coffee.

I sat the cup down on the trivet and leaned all the way back in my chair just to watch a little TV and try to get some rest.

In a few minutes my eyes closed, and I was almost asleep. I shook my head and got up and went to the bathroom and washed my face. I really did not want to go to sleep. I was afraid that I was going to have another one of those dreams. I knew that the murder was going to happen. I just did not want to dream.

I went to the kitchen and made a pot of coffee and when it was finished I poured me a cup and took it to the living room. I sat down in my recliner and turned on the TV. I was drinking my coffee and watching TV. I was sleepy. I did not want to close my eyes. I did not want to see anything. I finished drinking that cup of coffee and went and got me another cup.

I sat back down in my recliner and kicked up my footrest and leaned back a little to drink my coffee. In a few minutes my eyes were heavy. I was sleepy. I decided that if I was going to sleep I would just sleep in my recliner. I pushed all the way back and closed my eyes.

In a few minutes I was almost asleep when I saw the long blonde headed woman in a dream. I could see her so plain. I saw the man better this time than I had in the past. He was tall and muscular. He hard big arms and big hands. He looked about six foot and four inches tall. I still could not get a good image of his face.

He looked at her.

"I want to see you dance again." In a very rough sounding voice.

"I can't dance tonight. I do not have any music." She said very faintly.

"You can dance anytime you want to dance." He said with a big smile on his face.

"How do you know that I dance and what kind of dance do you want me to do?" She asked him with a quiver in her voice.

"You are a ballet dancer and you have awards for it. I have watched you for a long time." He said with excitement.

"I just cannot dance tonight. I do not have my music at the house." She said hoping that it would make a difference.

"If you do not dance for me I will have to hurt you." He said to her holding the sickle up in one hand with his other hand on the blade of it looking at it and licking his tongue on his lips.

"How are you going to hurt me?" She asked him frighteningly.

"It will be in ways that you will regret not dancing for me." He said to her demandingly.

"Where do you want me to dance at?" She was starting to tremble a little bit by now. She was scared, and it was beginning to show.

"Anywhere will be OK. It really does not matter." He was still holding the sickle up in one hand with the blade in the other hand licking his licks with passion.

"I am not going to be able to do a good dance without my music." She said to him looking at him dead in the face and grabbed the heavy crystal ashtray sitting on the table next to where she was standing. She threw it at him hoping that would get his attention away from her long enough for her to get the gun from the drawer in the table.

"That was a big mistake. You hit me with that and I do not like that." He said with a lot anger in his voice. He had a big grin on his face as to say you will never do that again.

"What are you going to do kill me because I threw it at you?" She asked him and was trembling. She knew that he was going to kill her. She had seen the news on the other women and she had not been worried because he was nowhere near Atlanta.

"I just might do that. You have really pissed me off now." He yelled it at her.

She had moved over closer to the table and was able to open the drawer and get her gun out. She stuck it out at him and pulled the trigger and it did not fire. Then she realized that she had forgot to put bullets in it after she had cleaned it the last time.

"Now you have really made a big mistake. You should have never got the gun out." He said to her with a very pissed off voice. "I will definitely have to make you pay for that one. I might would have let the ashtray go but not now." With a big grin on his face and he waved the sickle in the air and told her that would hurt her in ways she did not want to be hurt.

"I do not want to be hurt at all. Why are you killing all these women? Why do you have to be such an animal? Why don't you live a decent life?" By now she was screaming at him. She could not hole it back any longer. She knew she was going to die and that there was nothing she could about it.

"I like what I do." He told her. "It is a pleasure to me to do what I do." Waving the sickle in the air and coming closer to her.

"That is the kind of animal you are. You do not know how to be a decent person. I am going to get away from you some way. How, I do not know, but you are not going to kill me." She screamed it at him.

Murder of Grace

He got close enough to her that he could grab at her arm. He tried to reach her but she was able to keep him from getting a hold of her. She moved backwards and to her right side towards the kitchen hoping that she could make it in the kitchen and get out the back door.

He followed her realizing what she had on her mind. He was getting very mad. He knew that she was not going to try to dance for him and he did not like that. He was very upset that she was not going to dance.

She tried to run for the kitchen door, but he grabbed her arm and slung her back into the living room. She fell on her side and hit her left arm on the table next to the chair close to the kitchen door. He went over to where she was lying on the floor and stood over her and waved the sickle in the air. "You will regret this you stupid idiot. You should have just danced for me and this might not would have happened to you." He was very mad. "You were going to kill me whether I danced for you or not. I knew that, and I knew I was not going to try to dance for anybody right now." She told him.

"You are going to pay for it now and it will be awful."

He reached down and got her by the arm and she was fighting him the whole time. He was a very strong man and he could handle her with no problem. He pulled her up from the floor and he got behind her. He told her it was time to get this over with. He put her in a sleeper hold and in a short time she was out.

He dragged her to the bedroom and laid her on the bed. He mutilated her body and carved it up. He placed the body parts in all the same locations as he had all the rest of the women he had killed.

He left the house out the bedroom window and I finally woke up. I was trembling all over. I was very sick. My stomach was hurting. It was all I could do to get my feet off the bed and be able to even set up. I was devastated. I had to pull myself together, so I could go and make me some coffee and hopefully make it through the rest of this night.

The murder had happened. It would be all over the news this morning and I knew that.

I was finally able to stand up and make it to the bathroom. I washed my face in cold water. I washed it over and over hoping that it would help to wash away all the awful things that I had just seen and that maybe it was just a figment of my imagination. I knew that it was not going to be. I already knew that the murder was going to happen.

I dried my face with the face towel hanging next to the sink. I was finally able to make it to the kitchen. I made me a pot of coffee and when it finished making I poured me a cup and took it and went to the living room. I had to hold it with both hands because I was still nervous and shaking some.

I got to the living room and sat down in my recliner. I knew it was over and that I was not going to get any more sleep. I would not be able to lay down in the bed or in my recliner and close my eyes any more tonight.

While I was enjoying my cup of coffee. The phone rang. It could not be anybody but Rita.

"Hello Jason."

"Hi Rita. What are you doing calling this time of night?"

"Jason, I had to call you when I woke up and saw you so upset."

"I am glad you did call I need somebody to talk to and yes I did have another one of those dreams. He killed her tonight. The murder has already happened."

"It has crossed state lines now Jason. The FBI will be involved from here out. We will catch him soon."

"I hope they send you here. I could use somebody right now."

"I will ask Sherman to let me come to Sylacauga where the murders started. I know they are going to use me in this one. He will probably get involved in this one directly. If he does he will come to Sylacauga since that is where it started."

"You can both stay at my house if you want to. I have plenty of room." I told her.

"I know. I have seen it. You have a big house and it is very nice to."

"Thank you, Rita. I think it is."

"Jason are you going to be alright?"

"Yes, I always make it through these things. It is just hard when it happens. I just wish I had more information than what I get on either the location or the man so that I could give a description of one or the other that would make it easier to catch him."

"Well maybe in your next dream you will get the address of the house and then we can have someone there in the house or at least around the house and will be able to stop him."

"I hope so. You know it is going to happen again. He kills three women in each location. I will probably have another dream no later than tomorrow night on the next victim. What is so sad, I get an excellent image of the woman and I can describe her to exactly what she looks like and can get very little on the man."

"That is the way it goes Jason. You never know."

"Although I did get a little better image of him this time than I have in any of my dreams. If I could have only got a good image of his face I could give a decent description of him."

"That is good Jason. You have more to go on than before."

"Just not enough to stop it."

"Maybe it will happen the next time Jason. I sure hope it does."

"Me too. I want this to end. I am sure when it does there will be something that will take its place though. I have had these dreams all my life."

"What are you going to do tomorrow Jason?"

"I am going to have a long talk about this murder with Calvin and see what he thinks about everything. I am going to start training him some in the investigative work, so he can start getting used to it. I think I am going to set it up to where he can go and take his classes and get certified as an investigator if he wants me to do that."

"Sounds to me like you really like him Jason."

"He is a very bright young man. He catches on very fast and is a very good worker. He never hesitates to do whatever I need him to do. He knows his way around and can do just about anything he is asked to do."

"That is good. I am glad you found someone like that to help you out."

"Jake and I are going in business together. There are a couple of buildings here I am going to look at and see if either of them will be good for us to use or not just as soon as I have a chance to get a hold of the owner and have him to meet me there."

"You do have a lot going on Jason. I wish I was close enough to help out some."

"Well maybe one day you will be." I said and laughed with a big smile.

"You never know Jason. It could happen."

"Yes, it could Rita."

"OK Jason, if you are going to be alright I will let you go now and maybe you can get a little bit of sleep before the morning."

"Thanks for calling me Rita. I really needed somebody to talk with."

"You are welcome Jason. I will talk to you tomorrow sometime."

"OK. Talk to you soon. Bye."

I got up and went back in the kitchen and got me another cup of coffee and went back to my living room and sat back down in my recliner. I drank that cup of coffee and leaned back in my chair. My eyes closed, and I did go to sleep.

CHAPTER THIRTY-SEVEN

My alarm clock went off. It was Friday morning at 5:00. I put on my jogging shorts and went out the door.

"Good morning Jason."

"Good Jane. We are ready to roll I see."

"I am always ready Jason. Let's get started."

We ran our first mile and found our big brown boxer. He let us pet him and he ran with us for about a half mile and went back home.

"Have you been working hard Jason?"

"I stay busy most of the time Jane. Of course, that is good."

"I have some exams coming up. I dread that. It takes a lot time when I have to study for exams."

"You will do well Jane."

We finished our run and I went in the house and put on a pot of coffee. I went to the shower. I needed it bad this morning. I felt so dirty from last night. I finished my shower and put on my bright red button up shirt and my blue jeans with my red and white sneakers. They always made me feel bright.

I poured me a cup of coffee and went in the living room and turned the TV on. The news of the murder in Atlanta was their top priority this morning. They were calling him the Ballet Casanova.

The doorbell rang.

"Good morning Alice."

"Hello Jason. How are you this morning? You look really sharp today."

"Thank you, Alice. And I am fine."

Alice went about her cleaning and I left and went to The Grill and Eggs Breakfast Bar and Jeff walked in the door. He saw me and came over to the table.

"May I sit down?"

"You sure may Jeff. What are you up to this morning?"

"Getting ready to go to work. Did you see the news this morning Jason?"

"Yes I did."

"It has crossed the state line now. The FBI will be here today." He told me.

"Yes, there will definitely be someone here sometime today."

"You can bet they have kept up with it just in case it did cross the state lines." Jeff said.

"Will Jenkins from Birmingham will probably be here before the morning ends. He is over the SPC unit in Birmingham. I have known him for a while."

"That is all we need now when we may have the case just about solved. Manuel has a name, but he will not release it because he does not want the media to get a hold of it. They have pressed him but he refuses to give them any information. He is very stubborn when he wants to be."

The waitress came to the table and took our order.

"What are you going to do today Jason?"

"I think I am going to see if I can get a hold of the owner of those two buildings that are empty that might be suitable for mine and Jake's business and try to see them today."

"You are changing businesses Jason?"

"No, Jake and I are going in business together here in Sylacauga."

"That is good Jason. Are you going to keep Calvin?"

"Yes, I cannot let him get away from us. He is excellent. He is a computer whiz and a very good worker. I have not regretted hiring him."

"Sounds like everything is getting better for you Jason."

"It is and that is a good thing. If I could just quit having these dreams now everything would be great."

"Yea. I understand that. I used to not take much stock in dreams Jason. But these murders have made me think about it a lot. Every time you have told me you had one it happened just like you said that it would. There has to be something to it. I have got to where I just take your word that it is going to happen."

"I don't like it Jeff, but I cannot control the dreams. I wish I could. I would have all good dreams and these things would not happen, at least not from my dreams."

The waitress brought our food to the table. We ate and chit chatted some and when we finished our meals and we left.

I got to the office and Calvin was already there and had a fresh pot of coffee made.

"Good morning Calvin."

"Good morning Jason. How are you this morning? I watched the news and it was awful. There was another one of those murders but it happened in Atlanta."

"I am fine Calvin. That was the 7th one. It is way too many. Maybe we can catch him before he goes any farther. I sure do hope that we can."

"What do you want me to do this morning?"

"We are going over the things you found about Linda Moore and see what you came up with. And then we are going to discuss these murders and see what you think. That is if we do not get snowed under."

"OK. I am ready anytime you are Jason."

"Get your information on Linda and let's see what you have."

"I found out that she moved to Talladega about eight months ago and that she came from Chicago to Talladega."

"It seems that they have come from all over the country." I told him.

"She moved from Portland, Oregon to Chicago about six months before that. She traveled with a group when she left Portland but when she got to Chicago she changed and joined a professional organization in Chicago. That is about all I know on her. Does that help any?"

"All information is very helpful. We never know where it may lead us but it is always good to have anything we can find. Right now I am going to call Rusty Golden and see if I can get a hold of him and see if he will meet me at a one of his buildings and see if we can use it for our business."

I looked him up in the phone book and called him.

"Hello Rusty. This is Jason Caffrey."

"Hello Jason. How are you doing? It has been a long time since I have heard from you."

"I am fine Rusty. You have a couple of buildings that I would like to see."

"OK. Jason I will be glad to meet you. Which ones is it you would like to see. You have one that is in on Broadway Ave. downtown. I would love to see it. Is it for sell or just for lease?"

"It is for sell Jason. Are you interested in buying something?"

"Yes, I would like to buy something."

"When would you like to come and look at it Jason?"

"Now will be fine Rusty if you have time to meet me."

"How long will it be before you can be there Jason?"

"Give me about thirty minutes."

I took Calvin and we left the office and headed out towards the building on Broadway Ave. We got there and Rusty was there waiting on us.

"Hello Jason."

"Hello Rusty."

"Come in Jason. I have kept the power on."

I was looking around and I liked what I saw. It had a big office when you walked in the door. It was a good place for a secretary and plenty of room for a few chairs. There was a hallway from the front office that led to the rest of the offices. There were five offices down the hallway. There were two on each side of the hall way which were large enough for a nice desk and a couple of chairs for clients to sit in.

At the end of the hall was one big office that was big enough for a big desk and room for a couple of big chairs to each side and plenty of room for a couple of chairs in front of the desk if they were needed.

There was a small room off the front office to the right side that was just right for file cabinets. The building was perfect for what we needed. I really liked it a lot.

"Well, Rusty, this one looks perfect for what we need. We will be hiring some investigators later on as we grow. How much are you asking for this one?"

"Being where it is Jason it is a little high. It is an older building, but it is in excellent shape. We are asking $500,000 for it."

"Just tell me what the one on Jackson street looks like and how many offices are in it."

He told me about the one on Jackson Street and from what he told me I knew that I did not need to see it. It would not be large enough.

"I do not need to see it Rusty. This one will be just what we need. I will call my friend and talk with him and I will get back with you today and tell you what we want to do."

"That will be fine Jason. It is so good to see you. Have you been working hard?"

"I have been very busy the last few weeks with all these murders taking place."

"Maybe they will catch him this time. I saw the news this morning. It was awful."

"Well Calvin, what do you think? Do you think this will be sufficient for our new business?"

"Yes Jason. I think it will work fine. I think that big office will be just right for you." He said with a big grin on his face.

"OK Rusty we are going to go for now. It was nice to see you again. I will talk with you soon after I talk with Jake."

"I look forward to hearing from you."

"I am sure he will tell me to do what I think is best but I just want to tell him about it first."

Calvin and I left and headed back to my office.

We walked in the door and by the time we set down good the phone rang.

"Hello. Caffrey Investigations." Calvin said.

"Hello. Is Jason in the office?"

"Yes sir, he is. Did you wish to speak with him?"

"I do."

"May I ask who is calling?"

"Will Jenkins."

"Hold on a minute."

"Jason it is a Mr. Will Jenkins. He would like to speak with you."

"Thank you, Calvin."

"Hello Will."

William Honeycutt

"Hello Jason. How are you this morning?"

"I am fine Will. What you got on your mind?"

"I will be coming that way after while Jason. I need to talk with the Chief of Police and I definitely want to talk with you."

"I knew I would be seeing you sometime today."

"I have never met the chief Jason. What is he like?"

"He is very nice but is also very stubborn. You will like him Will."

"When I get to Sylacauga I will let you know I am there."

"Are you coming to see me first or the Chief."

"I think I want to talk with you first Jason. You seem to have more than anybody else. You know I don't take much stock in dreams, but you have been dead on with them."

"We will talk when you get here. I will be at the office unless it is lunch time. If I am not at the office come to Charlie's. I will be there."

"OK. I will see you sometimes after a while."

"I will see you when you get here."

I hung up the phone and looked at Calvin and told him things were fixing to get interesting.

The phone rang.

"Hello."

"Hello Calvin. This is Rita. Is Jason there?"

"Yes mam he is."

"May I speak with him?"

"Hold on a minute."

"Jason, it is Rita. She wants to talk with you."

"Hello Rita."

"Hello Jason. How are you?"

"Other than busy, I am fine."

"We will be in Birmingham tonight and in Sylacauga in the morning." Rita told me.

"Well I will look forward to seeing you just not under the circumstances."

"I know what you mean Jason. I wish it was under different circumstances also. Maybe we can get this settled and over with soon though."

"I sure hope so. That would be nice."

"I will call you tonight and let you know where we are going to stay."

"If you want to come on to Sylacauga you can stay with me."

"I will talk with Sherman and see what he says. It is not very far from Birmingham to Sylacauga. He may agree to do that. I will call you back and let you know what he decides."

"Do you know what time you are getting in?"

"We will be getting in Birmingham at 8:51 PM. on Delta."

"That would give you plenty of time to get here before midnight."

"Yes, and I know how to get to your house. I will see if he wants to do that. I will call you and let you know for sure."

"OK. Talk to you in a little while then."

"OK Jason. Talk with you soon."

Well it was about time to go and fine us something to eat or order something and have it brought in. I decided that pizza would be good today. I called Pizza Hut and had them to deliver us two medium supreme pizzas.

The young man brought the pizzas to the office and we ate them, and boy were they good today. About the time we finished eating our pizzas the phone rang.

"Hello. Caffrey Investigations. May I help you?"

"Hello Calvin. This is Rita. Is Jason there?"

"Yes mam he is. Hold on just a minute."

He handed me phone.

"Hello Rita."

"Jason I just wanted to let you know that he told me if you had plenty of room that we would come to your house. He said that would be much more comfortable."

"That is good. I will look for you guys at about 11:00 tonight then.

"OK. I must go for now. See you tonight."

"Bye for now."

The day was going by fast. It seems like it just got started and over half gone already.

I told Calvin I would be back after a while. I wanted to go over to see Dexter and tell him that Will would be down this way this afternoon sometime. I did not want it to be a big surprise. I knew that he would keep his mouth shut and not tell them that he knew they were coming. He is good at that.

I got to his office and he was on the phone. I just went in and he motioned for me to sit down in front of the desk. He hung up the phone.

"Hello Jason. How are you?"

"Hello Dexter. I am fine. And what are you up to today."

"My head is knee deep in paper work right now."

"What you got on your mind Jason?"

"I just wanted to come and let you know that Will Jenkins from the Birmingham SCU will be here this afternoon. He is going to want to talk with you."

"I don't want to talk with any FBI Jason. You know that."

"It has crossed state lines Dexter and the FBI have to get involved now. Sorry. I just wanted to let you know that he would be here. And also, that Sherman Hickman and Rita will be here tomorrow. They will be in Birmingham tonight and they are coming to Sylacauga and stay with me."

"Jason they can just talk with you about it. You know more than any of us. You saw all the murders in your dreams."

"I know Dexter, but you know they are going to want to talk with you. I hate it, but they will be here. I just wanted to let you know that they were coming in. starting this afternoon. Maybe they will be the only ones you will have to deal with."

"I will just suck it up and move on. I don't like it but there is nothing I can do about it."

"Well I need to get back to the office. Will is coming to my office when he gets into town."

"Since Sherman Hickman and Rita will be here to tomorrow, I am going to see if we can have one big meeting with everybody involved tomorrow sometime."

"That would be good if you could work that out Jason."

"I am going to try. Well I got to go. Talk with you later Dexter."

"Later Jason."

I left and got back to my office. Will was waiting on me.

"Hello Jason."

"Hello Will. How are you today?"

"I am fine. Just a little tired from the ride is all."

"Where are we going to start Will? Sherman and Rita from Quantico will be here tonight. It would be nice if we could just have one big meeting with everyone and then we would not have to go over the same details a dozen times."

"Maybe we can work that out Jason. I can stay in Sylacauga tonight if I need to. What time will they be here?"

"They will be in Sylacauga at about 11:00 tonight. That was the earliest flight they could get."

"We can just spend a little time together. I have not seen you in a few weeks now. And when they get in tonight we will see what we can get worked out. I am sure they will go along with that."

"I don't know about Sherman, but I know Rita would. I will meet him tonight when he gets in. You can stay at my house if you want to Will. I have four bedrooms."

"OK Jason, I will do that. That will make it easier on all of us I think. Sherman is fairly laid back. He is usually cool with things. He is not hard to deal with at all. I think he would go along with having one meeting with everyone involved."

"I know we can get it worked out. We can call the Chief's early in the morning and have them to meet us for the meeting." I told Will.

"That sounds like a good plan Jason."

"What are you going to do the rest of the afternoon Will?"

"Spend it with you unless you are too busy."

"The day is almost gone anyway. I will just close the office and we can go to my house."

I told Calvin he could take the rest of the day off and I would see him in the morning. I told him we would have a very busy day tomorrow and to get plenty of rest.

I locked the office and Will followed me to my house. We went in the house and I made a pot of coffee and poured us a cup and we sat down in the kitchen at the breakfast nook table and chit chatted until it was time to find us something to eat.

I ask him what he wanted to eat. We left and went to Charlie's Steak and Grill because I wanted me a T-bone steak. He told me that sounded like a good deal.

Just as we got set down good Jeff walked in the door and saw us and came over and sat down with us.

"Hello Will. I have not seen you in a while. What are you doing here?"

"I had to come to see what we can get going on this murder spree."

"We are all ready for it to be over with."

Murder of Grace

"We have to gather all the information we can to see what all ties in with his having taken it to Atlanta."

"They are all ballet dancers." I told him.

"We will discuss all this tomorrow."

"Since Jeff is the Sheriff and knows a lot about what is going on, we could use him to help us out Will. Is it OK if he comes to the meeting tomorrow?"

"Yes, we need all the information we can get. We need to get this stopped some way, fast."

The waitress came and took our orders. We all orders a T-bone steak and a baked potato with a chef salad.

In a few minutes the waitress brought our food to the table. We ate and chit chatted some about life in general and what we were going to do tomorrow. I told Jeff once I knew what time the meeting would be I would let him know. I told him it would probably be the afternoon since we needed time to get everybody to the meeting.

He told me that would be OK and that he would be there when and where ever it may be.

We paid our tickets and left the waitress a very handsome tip. We left and Will and I went back to my house.

I made a pot of coffee and poured us a cup when it was ready and we were watching the news when the phone rang

"Hello. Jason Caffrey speaking.""

"Hello Jason. What are you doing?"

"Drinking some coffee and talking with an FBI agent from Birmingham. He is staying at my home tonight."

"Sounds like you are having fun."

"I don't know about fun, but I have not seen Will in a while and it is nice to see him."

"Are you talking about Will Jenkins?"

"Yes mom."

"Tell him hello for me. You know it has been a long time since I have seen him. How is he doing?"

"He is doing fine mom."

"I got the meeting rescheduled for two weeks from tomorrow. Everyone said that would be fine."

"Thanks mom. I am glad you got that taken care of. I am going to be very tied up. It looks like I will be working all weekend so far."

"What else is going on Jason?"

"Rita and her boss from Quantico will be here at about 11:00 tonight. They are staying at the house also. You know since these murders have crossed state lines that the FBI has to get involved. They are all coming here.

"Oh. So you are going to be tied up all weekend it looks like."

"Yes. I will probably will not get to come over this weekend. But if I get a break maybe Rita and I came come and see you for a little while. She likes you and I know she is going to want to see you."

"I would love to see her again. I really like her. Of all your girlfriends which I have met, I like her the best."

"Thanks mom. We are not dating. We are just really good friends right now. You never know though. I really do like her a lot. She is super."

"Well I just wanted to call and talk with you a little and see how you were."

"Thanks for calling mom and tell dad hello for me. And when you talk with the others tell them I am sorry for the delay of the meeting."

"I will and bye for now."

"Bye mom."

CHAPTER THIRTY-EIGHT

"How is your business doing Jason?"

"It is great. You remember Jake I am sure."

"You mean Jake Simmons. It has been a long time since I have seen him."

"He and I are going in business together here in Sylacauga."

"What type of business Jason?"

"The same thing we are doing now. We are just combining our forces."

"That sounds interesting Jason. Maybe you guys will need some help later on. I may leave the FBI and go on my own one day."

"We will probably need some help later on. We plan on growing and as we grow we will need people."

"Sounds like you have really thought this out Jason. You were always that way in school. You seemed to always be thinking ahead on everything."

"I like to plan ahead. It keeps things more in order most of the time. I just wish I could plan these dreams."

"Remember the time that I put the worm in a box and gave it to Jeanie and when she opened it she screamed and threw it at me."

"Yes, I remember that Will. You were very devious."

"And it was so much fun. I still am devious when I get to chance to be."

The evening was going by kind of fast and we were really enjoying some nice leisure time. We had not got to do this in a long time. The telephone rang.

"Hello. Jason Caffrey speaking."

"Hello Jason. We are in Birmingham. As soon as we get our car rented we will be on our way to Sylacauga."

"Good. Have you guys eaten anything?"

"No we thought we would find something when we made it to Sylacauga."

"Would you like for me to order some pizza's."

"Hold on a second and let me ask Sherman if he wants pizza or not."

"OK."

"He said that would be fine."

"I will have them here by the time you get here."

"OK Jason. We will see you soon."

"OK. See you when you get here."

We hung up the phone.

"They will be here within the hour Will."

"I am looking forward to getting this over with myself."

"You are not the only one that is for sure."

"I am going to order pizza, so they can eat when they get here."

I called the pizza hut and ordered the pizza. I told them that I needed them here in about forty-five minutes.

I poured us another cup of coffee and we sat in the living room and drank our coffee.

The doorbell rang. I got up and went to see who it was and it was the pizza boy. I paid him for the pizza and took them in the kitchen and set them on the counter. I knew they would be here anytime now.

I sat down and just as I got set down good the doorbell rang again. I got up and went to the door. I knew it had to be Rita and Sherman. I opened the door and it was.

"This is agent Sherman Hickman Jason."

We shook hands.

"It is a pleasure to meet you Agent Hickman."

"Just call me Sherman."

"Hello, Agent, Will." Rita said and introduced him to Sherman.

"Hello Agent Hickman."

"Just call me Sherman."

They came in and sat down and we talked for a little bit. I asked them if they were ready to eat. They were ready. I told them the pizza had just gotten there and it was still hot.

We all went in the kitchen and I found us something to drink. I got my big pizza cutter and cut the pizza while Rita got the plates down.

We ate our pizza. It was getting late. Sherman told me that he had some questions that he would like to ask me but that could wait till the morning. We were all getting tired and we all needed some rest.

I told Rita that she could sleep in the same room that she slept in last time. I showed Sherman and Will where they would be sleeping. It was getting late. Everyone was tired and ready to lay down and try and get some rest before the morning came.

I told them I had three full baths and that they could either take a shower tonight or wait till the morning whichever they preferred. They all decided that they would wait till the morning. I asked Sherman and Will what time they would like to get started. They told me that they would like to be up by 5:00. I told them that would fine.

They all got their things and went to their bedrooms and I told Rita that I would see her in the morning and gave her a big kiss. I left and went to my bedroom and set the alarm clock for 4:45.

It was late. All I wanted to do now was lie down and get some rest. I slipped on my pajamas and lay down on the bed. I was looking up at the ceiling thinking about what tomorrow would be like. I knew it was going to be a long day and that I would be asked five hundred questions.

I turned over on my side and closed my eyes. I was almost asleep when I saw a tall slender, curly red headed, and dark blue-eyed woman. She was beautiful. She had the long arms with the long slender fingers and long legs. I wanted to wake up, but I could not. I was not able to open my eyes. The dream was there, and I could not stop it.

"I am here." He told her.

"What do you want?"

"I want to see you dance."

"I do not want to dance." She told him.

He was holding the sickle that he always used up in his hand rubbing the blade of it in between his fingers and licking his lips and slobbering. "I will use this on you if you do not dance for me." He told her.

"How are you going to use it on me?" She asked him.

I could only see the image of the man as always. He was tall and slender and very muscular and had dark black hair. But this time I could see a ring on his finger. It looked like a Mason's ring. I started seeing a clearer picture of the ring and it was definitely a Mason's ring.

"I will hurt you really bad with it. I might even carve you up if you do not dance for me."

"I do not want to dance, and I do not want you to hurt me either."

"You have to make up your mind which one you want the worst. If you dance for me your chances of not getting hurt are much greater."

She was scared by now. She was shaking.

I woke up. I was trembling, and I sat up on the bed. I heard a light knock on at my door. I told them to come in.

"Jason are you OK?" Rita asked.

"No. Rita I am not OK."

"You had another dream. Didn't you?"

"Yes. She is red headed."

"Did you get anything else this time Jason?"

"I did get one thing that I have not gotten before. I saw a ring on his finger. It was definitely a Mason's ring."

"You say you suspect Ray Bradford in the murder some way Jason. Maybe we can find out if he is a Mason. We can get on that in the morning and see what we can find out."

"If he is a Mason, Rita, we can almost be positive that he is the murderer."

"Sounds pretty much like that would be the way it would be Jason."

"If I just had more to go on it would help to be able to catch him." I told her.

"You always have three dreams before the murder actually happens. The last one the night of the murder. You will surely have one more before he actually murders her."

"If it goes as it normally has, I will have one more before he murders her. Maybe I will get some information that will help us to be able to get to the victim before he murders her. Or maybe I will get a good description of him and we can find him first."

"That would be nice if it works that way."

Sherman heard us talking and came to the door to see if everything was OK.

"Are you guys OK here?" Sherman asked Rita and me.

"Yes and no." I said.

"Do we need to talk?" Sherman asked.

"You will probably not believe a word of it but yes we can talk." I told him.

I asked him, and Rita did they want to go to the kitchen and get something to drink. I told them I needed a cup of coffee before we started talking about anything. They agreed with me that a cup of coffee would be nice.

I went to the kitchen and made a pot of coffee. By the time the coffee had finished making Will came strolling into the kitchen and ask us what we were all doing up this time of the morning. I asked him did he want a cup of coffee. Rita and I fixed us all a cup of coffee and we sat down at the table in the breakfast nook.

"OK Jason what is going on here?" Sherman asked.

"I had another one of those dreams. There will be the eighth murder unless we can find some way to stop it."

"Dream?" Will and Sherman said at the same time with a frown on their faces like what are you talking about.

"Yes, I have had these type dreams all my life in some way or the other. This time it concerns women who will be murdered. They have all up to this point been ballet dancers. The dream that I had tonight showed her as being a ballet dancer. And she has dark red curly hair and is tall and slender with long arms and slender fingers and long legs."

"Really! You get that in a dream about the women Jason." Will asked.

"Yes, I get very little on the man. Only that he is tall, muscular and has dark black hair. Except that this time I saw a ring on his finger. It is a Mason's ring."

"That is not much to go on." Sherman said.

"I know. I wish I had more to tell you about the killer or at least the exact location where the murder is going to happen but unfortunately I do not."

"He always has dreams before the murders happen." Rita told them.

"Yes always three dreams. Maybe I will get lucky this time and see much more details that will give us what we need to be able to stop him before he murders the woman."

"Have you had these dreams on all seven of the women which have been murdered up to now?"

"Yes, and never enough to give us anything to go on."

"I was going to have a meeting tomorrow with everybody involved with the murders, but it looks like I may not need to. I can probably talk with the Chief in Talladega and get what information I need from him on the phone." Sherman said.

"I can go to Talladega and talk with Chief Manuel myself if you would like for me to do that. He might be more willing to co-operate if someone is there in person than he will over the phone." Will said.

"Knowing what I know about Manuel. That is probably how it will work with him." I told them.

"You can do that and maybe we can get it all together by early tomorrow afternoon." Sherman said.

Rita was sitting back listening to everything that was said. She knew everything anyway. I had discussed most of it with her at one time or another.

"I am going to go with Will and we can talk with him together. Is that OK with you Sherman?" Rita said.

"Yes, that will be alright Rita. I think that might be good to do it that way. Jason and I will talk with the Sheriff and the Chief here in Sylacauga." Sherman said.

We all went back to our rooms and lay down. Sherman told me to change the time to about 6:30 instead of 5:00.

I was able to close my eyes and get a couple of hours sleep before the clock went off.

I got up and went to the bathroom and washed my face and went to the kitchen and made a big pot of coffee and went and knocked on everyone's door and told them it was time to get up. I laughed and told them I was up and that it would not hurt them to get up.

I asked them did they want to cook and eat breakfast at the house or would they rather go to a restaurant. They all told me they would rather go out and eat. We all took showers and cleaned up and got ready to leave the house. We left and went to The Grill and Eggs Breakfast Bar.

We got there and went in and found a big table and sat down. The waitress that usually waited on me came to the table and asked me did I bring the army with me this morning. I told her that it was just as good as the army. She gave us all menus and ask us did we want something to drink while we were looking at the menus. We all ordered coffee.

While we were looking at the menus Jeff walked in the door. He saw me sitting there with all these people and came over and ask me who in the world all these strangers were at my table.

"These are the FBI Jeff." I introduced him around the table to each of them and ask him did he want to sit with us. He shook all their hands and told them it was a pleasure to meet them.

"You are the Sheriff." Sherman said.

"Yes. And where are you from Sherman?"

"I am from Quantico. I am the Director for the Special Crimes Unit at Quantico." Sherman said.

"I am the Director of the Special Crimes Unit in Birmingham." Will told him.

"That is where I thought you were from Will." Jeff said.

"How have you been doing Sheriff?" Rita asked.

"I am doing well and am getting better knowing that these murders are going to end soon one way or the other. I have confidence. I want it over with. I want the trash put under the prison and to never be let out to see the light again."

"Maybe that will happen soon." Rita said.

The waitress came to the table and took our orders.

We chit chatted for a few minutes talking about everything under the sun except for the murders for a change. That was nice. I was tired of talking about them right now. I had had a bad night and did not want to talk about it anymore.

The waitress brought our food to the table.

"Do you think that we can have a meeting with you and the Chief this morning and go over the murders?

"Sure. I am sure that Dexter will be glad to work that out." Jeff said.

We finished our meals and we went and paid for them and left the restaurant. I told them that we could all go over to my office. It is small, but we can work out the details and make the phone calls we need to make and get things set up.

We went over to my office. Calvin was already there. I introduced them all to Calvin. They shook his hand and he had a smile on his face from ear to ear. He was excited to meet all the FBI at one time like that.

"Jason, we need to get an appointment set up with the Chief in Talladega for this morning as soon as possible." Sherman said.

"I will have Calvin to call and arrange something ASAP for this morning." I told him.

"We need to also get something with the Chief and Sheriff here and get these meeting out of the way." Sherman told me.

Calvin called Talladega and got their meeting set up for 9:30 AM. I called Dexter and told him to call Jeff and work out a time that they could meet with Sherman and me this morning. He called me back in about fifteen minutes and told me that 9:00 would be a good time for them at his office.

We had our meetings set up and it was time to see what we could figure out on what to do about catching this killer.

"When we get back from Talladega, I will call a friend of mine who is a Mason and see what he can find out about Ray Bradford being a Mason or not." Rita said.

"The one thing you need to press Manuel on is that he has a name from the blood sample that he got from the poker that the young woman hit the killer with. We need that name. That will be a good start."

"I have a good idea I know who the name is going to be but he would not give it out. He said that he did not want it to leak out to the press. He did not want anybody to get a hold of it because he was hoping that he could find the person before the media got the name." I told them.

"We will get it out of him. We have to have it. That way you can put a tracer on him and see where he is from and maybe find him some way." Will told us.

It was about 8:45. It was time for Sherman and me to leave and go and see Jeff and Dexter. Will said that he and Rita would go on to Talladega and get that settled.

We all left the office and I told Calvin to just watch the phone and play on his computer or whatever he wanted to do this morning. I reminded him to tell me to be sure and call Jake today and talk with him about the building.

Sherman and I got over to Dexter's office and Jeff was there. I introduced him to Sherman. They shook hands and said hello.

"Chief, can you tell me a little about what you know about the murders here in Sylacauga."

Dexter went over the details fairly thorough with him on the names of the women and what they looked like and how the murderers had happened.

He told Sherman that I had those dreams and that I had told him about the murders. He told Sherman that he did not take too much stock in that kind of thing until these murders. He said he now pretty much believes whatever I tell him because everything that I had told him about these murders had happened just like I told him that it would.

We sat around, and chit chatted for a few minutes. Sherman thanked them for their time and told me that he had all he needed from them and we could go to the house.

Sherman told them that if there was any way possible that another murder was not going to take place.

We got to the office and Rita and Will had gotten back from Talladega. I told them that if it would be more comfortable that we could go back to the house and work out all the details from here.

"That is the best idea you have had all day Jason." Sherman said.

"Thank you, Sherman." Jason said.

"Let's get the ball to rolling then." Rita said.

"Yeah." Will commented.

"Ok. Let's go. I am going to let Calvin come with us. It that OK with you guys." I asked them.

"He can be our gopher boy today. We will need plenty of coffee today to keep us awake since we got very little sleep last night. Thanks to you Jason." Sherman said.

We left the office and went to the house.

CHAPTER THIRTY-NINE

I had a twenty-cup coffee pot. I went and got it and made a pot of coffee. I showed Calvin how to work it so that when it got low he could make some more coffee. I told him how everybody liked their coffee and told him when it finished to pour everybody a cup. In a little bit Calvin brought us all a cup of coffee.

"Jason there has been seven murders. Right?" Sherman said.

"Yes, there has been seven up to now and the eighth is fixing to happen unless we can stop it." I told him.

"We have some news you guys might be interested in Jason." Rita said.

"Let us hear it then Rita." Sherman told her.

"The name that Chief Manuel had for us in Talladega is Ray Bradford. He believes that he is the killer." Rita told us.

"I had a feeling it was him, but I had no proof. The only thing I had was that I had met him and that he is a tall muscular man with dark black hair. There are a lot of tall muscular men with dark black hair. He is a mason and he does wear that ring." I told them.

"Do you know where he lives Jason?" Sherman asked me.

"All I know for sure is that he lives in Charleston, South Carolina." I told him.

"We can find him then or at least where he lives." Sherman said.

"I will make the phone calls and get that started now if you want me to Sherman." Rita told him.

"I will run some checks and see if he has any kind of record, He is bound to have something on him since that he is a serial killer." Will told us.

Rita made the phone calls and got the tracer out to find out where he lived in Charleston while Will got on his lap top and went to work in the data base trying to find out anything about Mr. Bradford.

We had to get everything going as fast as possible. With Jason having these dreams and a murder fixing to take place we need to stop him before he goes any further. Sherman was thinking.

Rita came back with an address for Mr. Bradford. He lives at 16136 South Charleston Avenue, Charleston, South Carolina. "I will call the Chief of police in Charleston and tell them the situation and have them to go out and arrest him if they can find him." Rita said.

"OK. The sooner you get that phone call made the better." I told her.

"We will wait and see what happens once Rita gets to the Chief of police in Charleston." Sherman said.

"At least we are pretty sure we know who the killer is now." I told them.

"You were right all along Jason. Just a shame we had nothing to go on that was proof enough to do anything about it." Rita said.

"That is usually how it goes. You know just enough not to be able to do anything but know that you are right. You just feel it in your bones and can't do anything." Will said.

Rita got on the phone to the Charleston Police Department. She explained to the chief what was going on and ask them to please go out and see if they could find him and arrest him on suspicion of murder.

William Honeycutt

He told her he would go out and check and if they found him they would arrest him and would call us back. Rita thanked him for being so kind and willing to help out.

It was way past time to eat a bite of something. I asked them what they wanted for dinner. I told them that I could get Charlie's to bring us our dinners. Sherman told me that he would like that. They all agreed with him. We did not have time to go out unless we had no choice. Calvin called and ordered the meals.

The phone rang.

"Hello Jason."

"Hello mom."

"What are you doing Jason?"

"I am talking with my colleagues trying to figure out what we are going to do to catch this piece of trash killing all these young women."

"I just wanted to call and say hello and see how you are doing. I was worried about you."

"You worry too much mom. You do not need to worry about be I will be fine."

"I will always worry about you Jason. You know that. I am your mom. I have to worry about you."

"I know mom. I am really busy right now and will be all weekend it looks like."

"What is going on Jason?"

"I can't tell you right now mom."

"You will find out soon though. Trust me. Just watch the news."

"OK Jason. I will do that. I will let you go for now."

"OK mom. I love you. You take care. Bye, bye."

"What are we going to do while we are waiting for the police to call us back and tell us they have him?" Rita asked.

"We are mostly going to sit and wait for that phone" Sherman said.

In a few minutes our food was at the door. We brought it in the house and we took time and ate our lunches.

In a few minutes the phone rang.

"Hello. Jason Caffrey speaking."

"Is Rita in?"

"Yes. She is."

"May I speak with her?"

I handed her the phone and her eyes got wide when he started talking. She had a big frown on her face. She looked like she had lost her only friend. He asked her did she want him to put an APB out on him. She told him that we would take care of that.

Sherman put out a national alert on him. We were hoping that we would find him someway and be able to stop him from killing anyone else. He told them to keep it out until he told them that we had him in custody.

"OK. It is time to sit back and wait now. Not much else we can do Jason. Do you mind if we stay here a couple of days if we need to?" Sherman said.

"You can stay as long as you need to." Jason said.

"I think I am going to the front porch and sit in my swing for a while. I have not been out there lately" I told them.

"I think I will go out and sit with you if you do not mind Jason." Rita said.

We walked out on the porch and sat down on the swing. It was nice. We could not do much now but just sit and wait to hope to hear something soon.

"I bet you my life on it Rita, that he is in Atlanta right now somewhere. One of my investigator friends found that he has a fake ID that he uses when he needs it. It is Johnathan Harvey.

Maybe we need to check that out and see if he has rented a car in that name in Atlanta." I told her.

We walked backed in the house and talked to Sherman about that possibility. He told us that would be a good idea. Rita got on the phone and made a call to the Atlanta airport and found out that he had used his fake ID and rented a car in Atlanta on Thursday afternoon.

We knew we were on his trail. I bet he did not have a clue that we were. He had been very good up till he forgot the fire poker with his blood on it.

It was time to put out an APB on that vehicle. She had gotten the license plate for the vehicle. Sherman put out a full alert in Atlanta and the surrounding area for the vehicle.

Rita and I went back on the front porch and sat on the swing and chit chatted about life in general.

"Rita, do you really like Sylacauga?"

"Yes Jason, it is a nice small city. I like what I have seen so far. I can see why you like it and would not want to leave."

I told her I had to go and make a phone call. I needed to talk to Jake for a few minutes. I got up went inside to make the phone call.

"Hello Jake."

"Hello Jason."

What are you doing Jake?"

"Nothing much right now. I am coming through Sylacauga tomorrow sometime."

"I just wanted to call you and let you know that I have found us a building for the business. It is very nice. It has a large front office and five other offices. They are all plenty big enough for what we will need."

"That is nice Jason. Is it for sell or lease?"

"It is in the middle of town. It is $500,000."

"Wow Jason. Can we afford that?"

"We can afford whatever we want. It is a very nice location and I plan on being there for a long

Murder of Grace

time. What do you think about it Jake? You want me to go ahead and tell him we want the building?"

"If you think it is suitable and that we can afford it, I do not have a problem with it." Jake said.

"I told him I would let Rusty know we wanted it."

"Just let me know when you need me to come to sign some paper work Jason."

"I will Jake. I will get it all set up and let you know."

"Talk with you later Jason."

"Sure Jake. Bye for now. Talk to you soon."

I called Rusty and told him that we wanted the building, but it would be sometime next week before I would be able to come over and take care of everything. I told him why and he was very understanding.

I went back to the porch and sat down with Rita. Will and Sherman and Calvin had sat down in the living room chit chatting and waiting for a hopeful phone call any time now.

"Well Rita, it is a wait game right now. I wish there was something that we could do." I told her.

"Yeah. I wish there was to. We have done all we can do right now." Rita said.

It was about 3:30 PM. The afternoon was passing by slowly.

Jason and Rita got up and walked around the house and sat down in the swing on the back porch. They chit chatted and looked at the beautiful roses that Jason's mom had put in his yard for him. She told him how beautiful they were.

"Jason, this is a nice place you have. I really like it a lot."

"Thanks Rita. I love it."

"Would you have gone in business with Jake if he had not wanted to do it in Sylacauga?"

"No."

Rita smiled, and her eyes lit up. Thinking she would not want to leave here either.

They went in the house and Jason ask Sherman what they wanted to eat for lunch. They all got ready and left for Charlie's Steak and Grill.

They got to the restaurant and sat down at a big table. Just as they sat down Jeff and Dexter both walked in the door and saw them and came over and asked if they could sit with them.

The waitress came over and took their orders and told them it would be a few minutes before it would be ready. They thanked her and she left.

"How are things going Agent Sherman?" Dexter asked.

"We have an APB out on Ray Bradford and on a vehicle that he leased with his fake ID. Maybe something will show up soon." Sherman told him.

"We are going to get him. I felt that it was him some way all along, but I just did not have enough to accuse him with." I told them.

"We are going to get him now though." Will commented with a big grin from ear to ear as in there is no doubt about it.

"Things are looking better right now than they have since from the beginning I believe." Sherman said.

"Here she comes with our food." Rita said.

"I am hungry." Calvin said.

The waitress set their food on the table for them and left.

"This is one big juicy looking steak." Sherman said.

Will could not wait to cut into it and taste it. "Wait till you taste it agent Sherman. It will melt in your mouth. One of the best ones I have had in a long time."

They all ate and finished their delicious meal and they got up and shook hands with Dexter and Jeff and told them they would see them tomorrow sometimes they were sure. They all went and paid for their meals. I would not let Rita and Calvin pay for theirs. He took care of it for them.

They all left and went back to the house. They unlocked the front door and told them to just make themselves at home that he and Rita were going to sit on the porch for a while.

"We might can do a lot of this one day." Jason said.

"Who knows? It could happen Jason. It would be nice. I really like you a lot." Rita told him.

"I like you a lot to. You are probably my most favorite person in the world right now." He told her.

"That is so sweet Jason."

"Thank you."

"Do you want to watch the news and see what is going on? She asked him.

"No. I know enough. They have not caught him because we have not gotten a phone call yet."

Jason asked her did she want something to drink. She told him she would take a coke. He took Calvin in the kitchen with him and they got everybody something to drink. He told Calvin to make a fresh pot of coffee.

Calving had never had anyone to treat him like Jason treated him. He did not know what to think about it. He really liked Jason a lot. He liked working for him. He told Jason that he was taught that you always ask for something when you were in somebody else's house. Jason told him he understood and that he was taught the same way but that now he could get what he wanted without asking because he had told him it would be OK. Calvin was proud.

Jason left and went back out on the porch where Rita was waiting. He sat down and put his arm around her shoulder and gave her a big kiss and told her that he really did care for her a lot. She kissed him back and told him that he was growing on her. He reached over and kissed her again and told her he was sure that would not be the last time that happened. She grinned. Thinking that it definitely would not be without saying a word.

Calvin ask Jason if he could sit on the porch with them.

"Calvin, have you thought about what you would. like to do for the rest of your life?"

"Yes, Miss Rita, I have."

"Just call me Rita. And what would that be."

"I want to work in law enforcement. I am just not sure yet what I want to do, but I like what all you guys do. I have been watching Jason I like working for him. I am learning a lot. Maybe I could do that."

"That is very good Calvin. Maybe you can take the training you need and be an investigator. Jason will have all the information you need. Or if you decide that you want to be an FBI agent he will help you find the information you need." She told Calvin.

"He has a misdemeanor on his record. I know the judge. He thinks he can get his record cleaned up. He is a good man. I studied and learned why all the things has happened in Calvin's life the way it has. Everything that he told me was the way he told me it was." I told her.

Calvin was listening to all that and he was really liking what he was hearing. Jason had worked with his parole office and got him out of that with just a phone call to report in to his parole officer.

"I hope that that incident does not keep me from being able to work in law enforcement. I have always wanted to." Calvin said.

"I am sure we can get that worked out Calvin." Jason told him.

They got up and went in the house.

It was getting kind of late. They were all tired and worn out from the day. They were all ready to get some rest if that was possible.

Jason and Rita went in the kitchen and poured them a cup of coffee and sat at the bar to drink it and talk some more before they went to bed.

"I think I would love to live in Sylacauga Jason. It is nice here."

"Well if you ever leave the FBI, you can come and join Jake and me in our business. We could use somebody like you."

"That is sure a possibility. I would have to do something with my place in Manassas before I could leave." She told him.

The others had gone to their bedrooms. They finished their coffee and went toward their bedrooms. He followed her to her bedroom and hugged her and kissed her one more time before she went to lay down and told her he would see her in the morning.

Jason went to his room thinking how nice it would be to have someone like her around a lot more. He wished that she lived closer so that they could see one another more often. Unfortunately, she lived in Manassas, Virginia.

He went to his bedroom and put on his pajamas and lay down. He turned over on his side and closed his eyes to go to sleep.

CHAPTER FORTY

His eyes were getting very heavy. He was slowly drifting thinking about what it would be like to have someone to spend the rest of his life with. He really liked Rita. She was always so nice. He knew that if he was going to spend the rest of his life with someone it would have to be somebody like her.

In a few minutes he was asleep. Then the thoughts of Rita disappeared from his mind and he saw the tall slender dark red headed woman in a dream. OMG not again he was thinking. Please I do not need this tonight. I need some sleep.

He could not turn the dreams off and on. When they came he had no control over them.

He saw a nice sub division and he saw a house. It was a beautiful brick home with red shutters on the front. It had a brown roof with a big window in the living room. The house number was on the column on the porch. He could not make it out at first. Then he was able to make it out. It was 16135 Chestnut Street.

"I have come this last time to make you dance for me." The killer told her.

"I am not going to dance for you." The woman told him.

"You will dance for me or I will hurt you." The killer told her.

"I would but I am not able to stand on my tip toes and do any of the pivots that I need to do to be able to dance well." She told him.

"You can dance for me or pay the price."

Murder of Grace

"I will try. I do not want to be hurt."

She went over to the entertainment center and turned on some music.

"That is not the kind of music I want to hear. That is not the elaborate music that you dance to."

"All my good music is at the dance studio where I practice." She told him.

"You better find some here. I do not like that. You are better than that." He told her.

"I do not have any." She said with a quiver in her voice.

He recognized that she was getting a little worried by now. "So you better find something better than that. I have watched you dance for several years now and I know you dance to better music that that."

"Where have you watched me dance at?" she asked him.

"That is none of your business right now. I have watched you and all the rest of the ones that I like, and I decided that if I could not have you that nobody else would have you either." He said to her.

"So, you are the serial killer out killing all these women. They have all been ballet dancers."

"Yes, that is me." He told her.

Jason woke up with sweat all over him. He was shaking from head to toe. Just as he was able to get himself up on the side of the bed sitting Rita walked in the room. She walked over to the bed and sat down on the side of the bed and put hers arms around him and told him that it would be alright.

He told her that just as soon as he got himself together he had something that they all needed to hear. It was something that might help to catch the killer. "He will not kill her tonight but the next time I have one of these dreams concerning her he will kill her. We have to do something before he gets to her and we have only hours to get it done."

"Let's go to the kitchen and get some coffee if you can make it to the kitchen." Rita told him. "I will make it one way or the other. I have to get myself together."

By the time we got to the kitchen Sherman was right behind us. He had heard the noise. He was a very light sleeper. He came in the kitchen and looked straight at Jason.

"Did you have another dream tonight?"

"Yes."

"Did you get anything that will help us out?"

"Yes. I just have to get myself together so that I will be able to think.'

Rita had poured him a cup of coffee and ask Sherman if he wanted any. He told her he did. She poured them a cup and they sat down at the table in the breakfast nook.

Just as they got set down good Will walked in and poured him a cup of coffee and came and sat down.

"OK. What is going on here" Will asked.

"Jason had another one of those dreams." Rita told him.

"Everybody just be quite for a little bit and let me get my head to working. I need to be able to think about it. I saw the address of the house that she lives in. I will have to get it focused back in my mind. I can't think right this minute."

In a few minutes Jason told them he thought his mind was clear enough that he could think. He started trying to think about the address that he had saw in the dream.

"I got it. I remember it. I can see it as plain as day now. It is 16135 Chestnut Street in Atlanta."

"OMG that is Jasmine Woods's address. I know her. We have been friends since we were in college together. She was my roommate. She was majoring in performing arts and I was majoring in English." Rita told us.

"Maybe we can stop him this time, but we only have hours to get things set up before he will be there. I promise you he has it all scoped out. He already knows where she lives and just exactly how to get in the house. He has done his homework. He will show up just before and in time to get in the house just before she comes home." I told them.

"My dad is a judge in Atlanta. Maybe he can help us get things arranged. I know her telephone number. I am going to call her and have a talk with her. She will listen to me. We trust each other." Rita said.

"That will be good Rita. Maybe we will get him this time. We could have the police in the area in unmarked cars in plain clothes so that it would not be suspicious." Sherman said.

"I will call my dad the first thing in the morning and see what he can do to help us out. I am sure he will do anything to help us stop a murder."

It was going to be another one of them nights that they all did not get any sleep. It was 2:30 AM.

"We could go back to bed and try to get a little sleep." Sherman told them.

"Well, I know I will not get any sleep. Not tonight. I will be restless the rest of this night." I told them.

"I know I will not get any more sleep either." Rita said.

"I am sure going to try to get a little sleep." Will told them.

They went back to the bedroom and Rita and I went in the living room and sat down on the couch and turned on the TV. She sat down beside Jason and put her hand on his leg and told him that she would just keep him company because she knew that he needed someone to be close to him right now.

"I guess we can watch a little TV and just sit here and enjoy being together." I told her.

"Yes. We can do that. I am going to call dad and wake him up early in the morning." Rita said.

In a few minutes they had both closed their eyes and they were asleep sitting next to each other.

Jason had his clock set in his bedroom for 6:30 and it went off. He jumped when the alarm sounded and got up and went and turned it off. He went back, and Rita was sitting on the couch looking very sleepy. He went to the kitchen and put on a pot of coffee. This was going to be a long morning.

Rita told him that she was going to call her dad.

"Hello dad."

"Hey baby." That is what he had called her all her life.

"What are you doing this morning?"

"I am drinking a cup of coffee and reading the morning paper." He told her.

"What are you doing?"

"Dad I have something very important that I need to talk with you about." She told him.

"What is that baby?"

"You are familiar with the serial killer. The one killing the ballet dancers I am sure." She told him.

"Yes I am and I surely wish they could catch him and end this mess."

"That is what I want to talk with you about dad.

"OK. Go ahead. Let me hear what you have to say."

"I know that you are familiar with the person that has the dreams and knows about the murders before they happen. His name is Jason." She told him.

"Yes, I am familiar with that."

"Well we are staying at his home dad. Sherman and I and Will from Birmingham." She told him.

"That is good." He said.

"He had another one of those dreams dad last night and he actually saw the address of the woman

Murder of Grace

to be murdered and it is my friend Jasmine Woods's home dad." She told him.

"How can you be so sure that it is her home dear? You know I don't take a lot of stock in dreams of that nature. I need more proof than that." He told her.

"Well dad this is the eighth one and he has dreamed of all the murders so far concerning the ballet dancers and he has not missed. He knew enough about the situations that he could describe how it was going to happen before it happened." She told him.

"Is that right? How can you be sure of that?"

"It has all been proven. The Chief of Police in Sylacauga where the first three happened and the Chief of Police in Talladega where the second three happened knows that he had the dreams and knows that it happened just like he said it would." She told him.

"OK. So, what do you want from me baby."

"I know the woman dad. She is my very good friend. We were roommates in college. Jasmine Woods. You have heard me talk about her. I was hoping that you could help us get some protection in some way for her so that she does not get killed." She told him.

"I could get about anything that I want done. What do you want me to do? I will do this because it is you."

"Sherman suggested that we might could get some police in plain clothes to be in the area. I was hoping that you could help us out there. They could keep a watch on the area and watch for anything out of the ordinary that might look suspicious." She told him.

"Yes, I could do that. The FBI of course is in on this and it would need to be FBI but not dressed up in their fancy suits and all. I think I could handle that for you." He told her.

"I want Jason and me to go to her house today. I do not know how we are going to get there yet. We have not discussed it."

"It is not that far from Sylacauga to Atlanta. You could drive it in about three hours." He told her.

"You are going to get it set up with some FBI agents in the area in plain clothes then."

"Yes, I am going to take care of that. It will happen shortly. I have a good friend in the FBI here. I will call him, and he will do it for me." He told her.

"Can you call be back when you get it set up. I am going to call Jasmine and talk with her this morning and tell her that a friend of mine and I are coming to see her after a while." She told him.

"Yes, I will call you and let you know what is going on."

Rita gave her dad Jason's and Jasmine's phone numbers and told him that if she was not at Jason's that she would be at Jasmine's.

She got on the phone and called Jasmine and told her that she needed to come to see her today. Jasmine told her that she did not have anything to do and that it was OK. Rita told her she was bringing a friend with her.

They were all sitting in the living room trying to decide what to do to get to Jasmine before the killer got there but they also needed to catch the killer.

"What we need to do Rita is plant you and Jason in her house with her and Will and I can stay outside to where we will be close if anything happens and be can be there in an instant." Sherman told them.

"I think that would be the best idea Sherman. My dad is going to call the FBI and get a friend of his to have some plain clothed FBI agents in the area to keep a watch out." She told them.

Murder of Grace

"That will be good. We will just need to know who they are so that we can make sure they know us when we get there. I will probably know them anyway. I know most of the ones from that area." Sherman told them.

"I am not going to tell Jasmine what is going on until we get there. I don't think it would be a good idea to tell her on the phone." Rita said.

"I agree with you on that." Jason said.

"I think what we need to do is get all our things in the vehicles and head out toward Atlanta." Sherman said.

"I think that will be a good idea." Will commented.

"Call Jasmine and tell her we will be there by lunch time and to have us a big meal cooked because I will be very hungry." Sherman said kiddingly.

Rita called Jasmine back and told her as soon as they got everything together that they would be there somewhere around lunch time. Jasmine told her that she would be waiting. They had not seen each other in a while. They had talked on the phone but just had not had a chance to visit.

They all got their things together and put them in Jason's car. They decided that it would be easier to just travel in one car that and Jason and Calvin could turn in Rita and Sherman's car when they came back to Sylacauga.

They headed out for Atlanta about 8:30 that morning. They arrived at Jasmine's house at about 12:30 pm. Jasmine came to the door.

"Hello Rita. You said you were bringing a friend not an army." Jasmine said.

"I will explain once we are inside Jasmine." Rita told her.

Jasmine invited them in her home. They all went in and she motioned for them all to have a seat somewhere.

"Please tell me what is going on Rita. This is very much unexpected."

"It concerns the serial killer Jasmine that is killing ballet dancers. I know you are a ballet dancer and have done it all your life just about." Rita told her.

"What does it have to do with me Rita?" Jasmine asked.

"That is what I am going to explain. That is why that we are all here. Will and Sherman are FBI agents. In fact, Sherman is my boss. Jason here is a private investigator." Rita told her.

Jasmine politely looked at them and said that she was very concerned that they were all there to see her.

Rita went on and explained to her about Jason and the dreams that he has. Jasmine was very concerned about someone having dreams and them be true. Rita told her that they wanted to be there with her to stop it from happening. She explained to her that whether it happened or not that they needed to be prepared for it because so far everything that Jason had said had happened just like he said that it would.

By now Jasmine was getting a little nervous and Sherman noticed it.

"Jasmine that is why we are here. Will and I will be outside somewhere. We will not be in the house. We will be keeping a watch on your place to hopefully catch someone before they get in your house.'

"So, you guys think that I am his next victim." Jasmine said.

"I know that you are Jasmine. I saw it in my dreams. I even saw your house and the address in my dream this time. And when I told them what the address is Rita was shocked. She told us she knew you very well. That is why we came here." I told her.

Murder of Grace

"What we need to do now is get this worked out so that the murderer actually gets in your house Jasmine to where that we can catch him in the act and then we will have him. I will explain to you how we would like to do this and keep you safe at the same time." Sherman explained.

"Now you guys are scaring me. That does not seem very safe. Maybe the best thing for me to do is just leave." Jasmine said.

"He has killed seven other women Jasmine. I am sure that if you just leave that he will hunt you down and find you." Rita said.

"Yes, he probably would. He would probably never leave me alone." Jasmine said.

"We need to catch him Jasmine and we can get him and keep you safe at the same time. That will not be a problem. You can fire a handgun I hope." Will said.

"Yes, I know how to shoot a gun."

"That is good. That is a step forward." Rita said.

"What I would like to do if it is possible Jasmine, is put Rita and Jason in the house here with you. They can hide in a part of the house that he will not know they are here to where they can get to him without any trouble." Sherman said.

"That sounds good." Jasmine said.

"Do you have a handgun Jasmine?" Rita asks.

"Yes. I keep one here in the living room close to me all the time. You never know when you might need it." Jasmine said.

"That is good. That is what we were hoping Jasmine. We would like for you to shoot him when he tries to get you to dance for him at some point. When you shoot him Rita and Jason will take care of the rest. He will not get a chance to kill you before they will have him under arrest."

They explained it to her in detail what their plans were and exactly how they were going to carry them out. Jasmine agreed to all of it and said that she was scared out of her mind, but she still would go along with it.

She asked them would they all like something to drink. They all said they would. She went in the kitchen and got them a coke and brought Jason some Kool Aide that she had made.

Jason explained to her that he would know when the murder was going to happen and that he would let her know when they all needed to be prepared.

Sherman told them that when they finished drinking their drinks that they needed to go outside so that they would not be in the house in the way when things started to take place.

In a few minutes they left the house and went outside. Jason had given Will his car keys and told them to enjoy it while they had a chance. Will laughed at him and told him that they promised not to do any drag races in it.

The afternoon was about over. Sherman and Will had gone outside and found them a place to park in the neighborhood so that they could keep a close watch on the house. Will had given Jason one of his two-way radios so that he could call him on it if he needed to.

They were all ready to wait forever how long it took.

"

CHAPTER FORTY-ONE

Jasmine ask them did they want something to eat. They were hungry. The three of them went in the kitchen and they fixed a meal for them all. Jason called Sherman and told him and Will to come and get them something to eat. They came in the house and ate with them and when they had finished eating Sherman and Will went back to their posts.

Jason told Rita and Jasmine that he was sure that it was going to be tonight. He told them he felt it in his bones. It was just a strong feeling that he had this time. He told them that they would have to be careful. He explained that he would know before he came in the house. He always had a dream the night of the murder.

Jasmine told them that she was scared. Rita and Jason both walked over to her and put their arms around her and told her to not be scared that nothing was going to happen to her. They told her that they would have him before he got his hands on her. It made her feel a little better, but she was still scared.

They set in the living room watching a TV program and chit chatting. Jason told them that it was about time for things to start coming together.

In a few minutes Jason told them that they needed to get prepared that he was having a vision and that he was already in the neighborhood and that he would be in the house in a very short time. He told Jasmine that the murderer was going to ring her door bell.

He told her when the doorbell rang to let him in the house even with the sickle that he would have in his hand. He told her that he would not hurt her that he would want to have a long conversation with her before he killed her.

Jason told her to be sure to go back to her chair that she sat in and stay close to the table where the gun was so that she could get a hold of it. He explained to her that he and Rita had to take their respected spots so that they could keep a watch on what was going on so they could be there quick and stop him before he got to her. She had a small closet that someone could hide in in the living room next the kitchen. It was a good place to hide. Jason took the closet. Rita went in the bedroom and stood close to the bedroom door with it closed so that she could get out quick when she needed to.

They were all in their respected places when the doorbell rang.

Jasmine went to the door and opened it. When she saw the sickle in his hand it scared her, and she was not going to let him in the house. She started to close the door, but he put his food just inside the door and she could not close it. He pushed his way on in the house. She backed up and eased over close to her chair.

"Now that I am in here and I have the advantage I want you to do something for me." He told her. And he eased over to the couch that was across from where her chair was. He sat down on the couch holding the sickle in his hand and rubbing the blade with his fingers and licking his lips.

"And what is it you want me to do." She asked him.

"I want you to do some dances for me." He told her.

"She told him that she could not dance for him."

"You can dance for me or pay the price for not dancing." He told her.

Murder of Grace

"What is the price I will have to pay if I do not dance for you?" She asked him.

"I will have to hurt you bad." He told her.

"How bad will you hurt me if I don't dance?" She asks.

"I might just have to cut you to pieces. That would hurt I am sure." He told her.

"Why would you do something like that?" She asks him.

"I have been watching you for a long time. I ask you for a date one time and you would not go with me. You told me that you had other commitments." He told her.

"Well I was very busy. Everybody wanted to go with me. I did not have time for everybody. I did make prior arrangements." She told him.

"Well I decided that if I could not have you that nobody else deserved you and that I would just put a stop to it some way or the other." He told her.

"So you decided that killing us was the way to stop it all and keep us from having anyone else." She said to him.

"That is a good way to do it. That way nobody can have you then." He told her.

"So you are the one that killed all the other ballet dancers then." She said.

"Yes, I am the one." He told her.

Rita and Jason were hearing everything that was being said. They were both astounded that she was doing so well. They were very happy. There would be three witnesses that heard him say all this and she was saying and asking all the right things.

"Why don't you just leave me alone?" She said.

"Because I do not want anybody else to have you." And he got up off the couch and took a step towards her. He held the sickle up close to his mouth and licked the blade with his tongue and winked at her.

"I am not going to let you kill me. I will stop you one way or the other." She told him.

"Look at me. I am much bigger than you are. I have a weapon and you do not. You cannot stop me." He told her.

"You may be bigger than I am and you may have a weapon but I still can keep you from killing me." She told him. And stepped over closer to the table with the gun where she could get to it.

"I will have you tonight. You are mine from now on. You will never have anybody else after tonight." He held the sickle up again and rubbed the blade of it through his fingers and stroked the handle of it licking his lips with his tongue and slobbering while he was doing it.

"I will not die." She screamed and reached and grabbed the gun that he had not noticed. She fired it at him and hit him on the shoulder. He grabbed his shoulder and screamed from the pain dropping the blade to the floor. She fired her gun again and hit him in the leg. He screamed again and fell to the floor. She had kicked the blade away from him to where that he could not reach it.

By the time she fired the second shot Jason and Rita both were in the living room. He had gotten close to the front door. He opened the door and started out and a rookie cop was standing there with his gun pointed at him and told him to stop. He jerked the gun from his hand and started down the steps. He turned and fired it at the cop and hit him in the shoulder. He grabbed his shoulder and hit the floor.

Jason came out the door with his .44 magnum out and the FBI on the ground had their weapons out and ready to fire. Ray Bradford fired another shot toward Sherman and started to run. Jeffery Cochran told him to stop or that he would shoot him.

Murder of Grace

He started running and Jeffery shot him in the leg and he kept running. Jason screamed at him and told him if he did not stop that they would shot to kill if they had to. He would not stop running. Jason fired his .44 magnum and hit him dead center of the back. He fell face down on the ground.

They all converged on him and Sherman was over him and turned him over and felt for a pulse. He could not find anything. He was dead.

Rita had hovered down close to the cop that had been shot and was trying to make sure he was OK. She had called 911 for an ambulance. The ambulance got there, and they took the cop to the hospital for medical treatment.

Rita went over and hugged Jasmine real tight and held her for a little bit.

"Jasmine you did excellent. You did just exactly what needed to be done. We have three witnesses to what all was said here tonight. It is not just your word against his." Rita told her.

"He will never bother anyone else that is for sure." Jason told Jasmine.

"I was scared to death. I will just tell you the truth. I really did not want to do it, but I felt that I really needed to. I was so scared something would happen to me." She told them.

"You were so brave, and we are so proud of you. It would be nice to have somebody like you working for us." Jason said.

"I have been a ballet dancer for a long time. I hurt my ankles and I have not been able to dance for a while now. I would love to do something different." She told us.

Sherman and Will came in the house. Sherman went over and hugged Jasmine and told her how much he appreciated her being willing to help them catch him in the act.

Rita asked Sherman if she could have a few days off. He told her to take all the time that she needed and that he would see her when she got back to Quantico. He called the airport and booked him a flight to Dulles. He was ready to go home.

Will called the airport and booked him a flight to Birmingham.

They had their plans all made.

"I will take you to the airport and that he and Rita will head toward Sylacauga."

EPILOGUE

Jason and Rita went to Sylacauga. They spent a few days together. He did not have any more dreams while she was with him. She told him it was time for her to go back to work but that she really did not want to go. He told her that she needed to just stay with him and she would not have to go back to Virginia. She left and told him that she would be back again very soon.

Jason and Jake were standing on the side walk in front of their new business. Jason looked at Jake with a big grin and said that is one spectacular sign Jake. I like it. It is just what we need to make it look fabulous. They had named their new business Master Investigations. Calvin was standing there taking it all in and was so happy that they were keeping him. Calving asked Jason was he going to have his own office. Jason told him that he would have an office decked out with computers. Calvin was grinning from ear to ear. He was excited.

It had been a few days and Calvin had met a young lady that he liked a lot. She was eighteen years old. He asked her for a date. She accepted. They went to the movies. After the movies, they were sitting at the Dairy Queen eating a hamburger with French fries and drinking a coke.

He asks her why she always wore gloves. She told him she just liked something on her hands most of the time. She told him that she trusted him and liked touching him with her hands without the gloves on and that was why that she had pulled them off and put them in her purse.

She dropped a French fry on the floor. Calvin reach down to pick it up and he had to reach under the seat to get it. When he did, he found a knife hid up close to the side of the seat. He pulled it out to look at it and see what kind of knife it was.

Before she realized it, she had already touched it with her fingers. When she touched the knife, she shivered. Calvin ask her what was wrong. She told him that she had gotten a funny sensation after she touched the knife. She did not want to tell him the real reason that she had touched it. He laughed and said a funny sensation?

Yes, I did. Well Calvin when I touched the knife I saw that the knife had been used in a murder. The person that used the knife took the knife and they stabbed a homeless man ten times in the heart. That is what I saw when I touched the knife.

What are we going to do about it?

Calvin said that maybe we should tell Jason. Maybe he can help us with this. She told him that she did not want to tell anybody. Calvin told her he would understand about her being able to see things from touching something.

Calvin, that is why I wear the gloves, she told him. That way I do not touch something without having them on and then I do not see things. It is strange. But now you know the truth.

William Honeycutt

About the Author

I hope that you have enjoyed this book and the next one in the series will be released sometimes in November near the end of the Month or sometime in December. Check my website at www.williamhoneycutt.weebly.com . I till post there and let you know when it will be available. All my other books are listed on my website.

Made in the USA
Columbia, SC
26 August 2024